Cover art: Oleisha Proksa

Copyright © Alison Croggon and Daniel Keene 2018

Artwork Copyright © Oleisha Proksa 2018

Newport Street Books, Melbourne

ISBN: 978-0-6480676-6-5

First published by Newport Street Books, Melbourne, 2018

newportstreetbooks.com

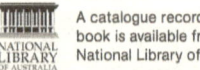
A catalogue record for this book is available from the National Library of Australia

FLESHERS

Book One: Newport City

Alison Croggon and Daniel Keene

Newport Street Books

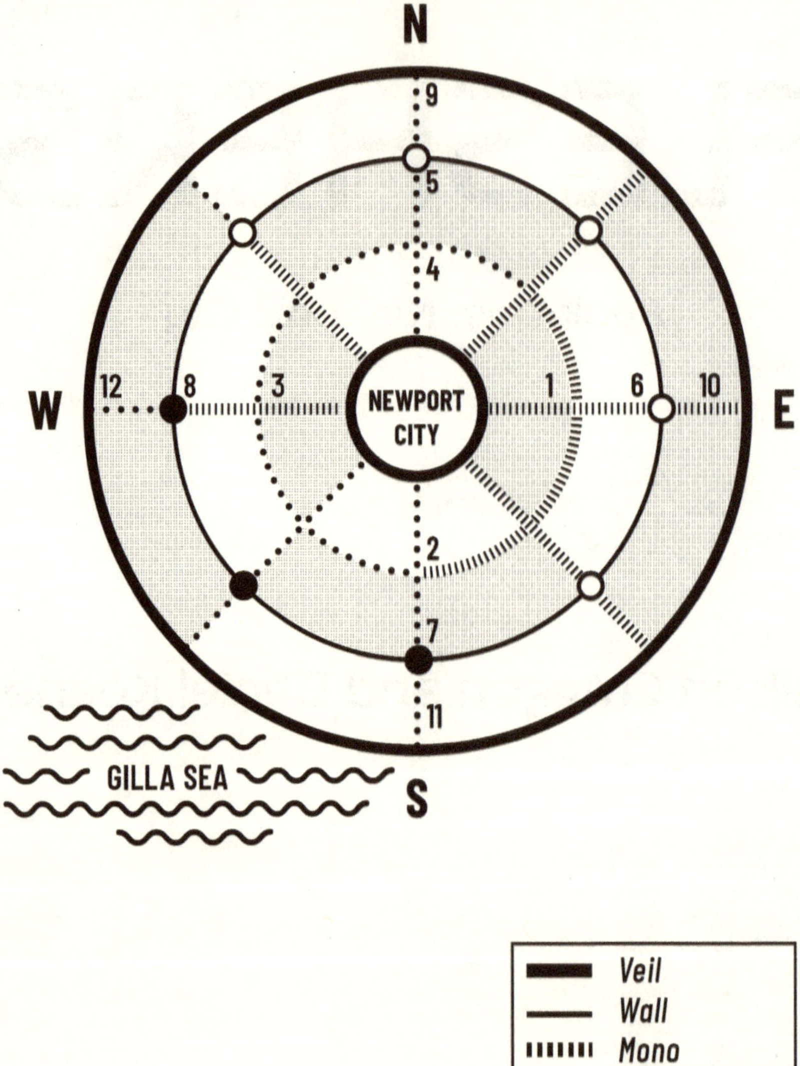

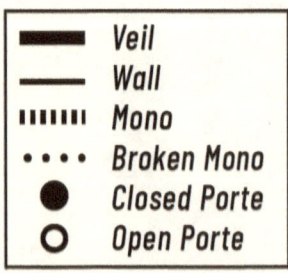

N

9

5

4

W 12 8 3 **NEWPORT CITY** 1 6 10 E

2

7

11

S

GILLA SEA

	Veil
	Wall
	Mono
	Broken Mono
●	Closed Porte
○	Open Porte

Schematic map, Newport City and surrounding banns
(Urban Affairs Department, Newport City Council)

GLOSSARY

Alchems	An informal band of dissenters against Newport City Council.
Ap	Local police in the banns. Short for "Anthropological Police".
Avants	Fleshers term for people who exist outside binary genders.
Banns	Outer suburbs of Newport, separated from Newport City by the Inner Veil.
Baju	Firewater made in the banns, usually from whatever is around. Varies enormously in quality.
Bogies	Miner slang for AI mine workers.
Credits	Newport City's official unit of electronic currency. Unless they are working in Newport City industries, fleshers use untraceable "black credits" that are stored in alternative databases.
Dasht	Anywhere outside Newport Outer Veil.
Disruptor	Tech that nullifies gene searches, used to get through a Veil.
Flesher	Derogatory term invented by Pinkers to refer to those born through natural reproduction. Appropriated by those who live in the banns.
Foodtowers	Towers where plant goods are grown, mostly for consumption in Newport City.
Gau	Animal evolved from a domestic dog.
Homebuild	Any home-made tech.
Homer	A vehicle for hire.
IMR	Short for *In Media Res*. Refers to the merging of virtual reality and physical surroundings.
Lenscam/chip	Camera/video chip inserted in lens.
Mokal	Sweet, sludgy drink, usually fruit flavoured.
Mono	Monorail in the banns, partly functional.
MPS	Magnetic Positioning System.
Neka	Animal evolved from a domestic cat.

OpSec	Operational Security. Originally applied to securing data, it now refers to all Newport City militia operations.
Pinker	Flesher name for clones of Newport City.
RTS	Rapid Transport System in the banns (now defunct).
Rues	Common name for streets.
Shijo	Marketplace.
Skinner	Flesher name for criminals who hunt flesher adolescents for the lucrative illegal hormone market in Newport City. Recognisable by the bandoliers that contain their extraction equipment.
Steadies	Close friends.
Suit	A suit is an electromagnetic personal shield that protects the wearer from a variety of environmental hazards, notably nanoviruses. A benign version of Veil technology, it keeps hostiles out rather than destroys them and usually includes temperature control. Worn as a belt.
Tubes	Generic term for visual media.
Veil	An electromagnetic shield that protects Newport from the environmental hazards in the dasht. Features a heightened gene filter designed to hunt down and destroy nanoviruses. The Inner Veil is tuned to exclude all genes not listed in the Newport City clone database and includes weather control.

Dez

The night everything went toxic began like any other winter evening. It had been storming for days, with a bad wind blowing in from the dasht. Even in the Second the rues were deserted, and anybody who was out was suited.

That afternoon the storm had finally cleared. Bo had gone out. He got cabin fever when the storms were up, and he'd been edgy all day, blowing up at Ma, picking fights with me. He wouldn't say where he was going, and we knew that meant he was heading somewhere dodgy. I figured it was the Tenth, one of the worst banns, because Flora and her mob had a gig on that had been doing the rounds on the tubes. I didn't tell Ma, because she would have hit the roof. I was pissed off because I wasn't invited. Flora and me had a falling out, and it escalated as these things do and now we weren't talking.

I'm two years younger than Bo, but I sometimes feel like I'm the big sister. Even though Bo and me had been shouting, I checked his suit and told him to be careful out there and to tell Flora to go screw herself. He flashed that grin and gave me a hug and left, and suddenly the house was peaceful. Ma met my eyes, smiling ruefully.

'That brother of yours,' she said. 'He'll be the death of me one day.'

'He's just bored,' I said.

I cooked dinner because Ma was looking worn out. We knew she was sick, although she refused to talk about it: she had good days and bad days. Today was one of the bad ones. Bo and me were saving up to get her a proper mediscan, although we didn't tell her that because she would have bitten our heads off. We ate, and then she said she was tired and went to her bedroom and shut the door. We didn't talk about Bo, but I knew she wanted me to stay up for him. I had planned to do some making, but it was cold in the cellar and I didn't feel like lugging the heater down there, so in the end I just curled up on the couch and watched the Newport City soaps on my lenscam.

I love those soaps. They're not supposed to be shown in the banns because they cause discontent, but we stream them through pirate consoles. I was watching *Days of Passion*, which I basically watch for the pinker clothes. Nobody in the banns dresses like that, nobody could afford it. In the soaps, the pinkers live in vast mansions and have endless parties where they're all feuding with each other. Newport City is another world. Pinker world.

Anyway. There I was, happily floating on Planet Lala, when somebody buzzed the door. When I didn't answer at once they leant on the buzzer, and then they started banging. I switched off the lenscam and went to the door, my heart going like a machine. My first thought was that something had happened to Bo. I opened the door and saw an Ap, with his AI sidekick just behind him.

He was one of the new pinker Aps, blond hair, grey eyes, bulky, his red coat glowing in the shadows. The AI floated behind him, blue lights flashing, a black, featureless torso with the red Ap logo branded on the front. It was a new model. I'd seen a few floating around the inner banns, but never close up.

One of the reasons Ma didn't want Bo to go out that night was because of all the new Aps around. They were making her anxious. So it was kind of ironic that the real danger was at home.

The Ap pushed past me into the house. Despite the cold, a little trickle of sweat ran down his temple. He was nervous. A bad sign. The AI drifted in after him, opening up its hardware like a cupboard full of knives. They don't bother to make the Ap AIs look like people. No skin, no hair, no face, voice deliberately metallic. They look the business, edges and weapon barrels. I know a lot of it is for show, but it doesn't make it any less scary.

'You can't just walk in like that,' I said, although I knew they could.

The Ap whipped around and stuck his taser in my face. 'Shut it or you'll get this,' he said.

I stood back, putting my hands out so he could see I didn't have a weapon. The AI floated there, humming. I didn't have to hack into it to know it had its scanner on. I thought of the hot bioware I had in my stash and went cold. I decided to be polite.

'How can I help you, officer?' I said.

'We've got traces from this address. You the homeowner?'

Homeowner, I thought. Such a pinker word. As we were talking I was transmitting to the AI, trying to find a way in, but these new ones had different crypto. I took a breath, trying to assess the Ap. I could tell he was young, a little scared, high on having the power to do what he wanted. The worst. My guess was this was his first solo raid.

'My mother's sick in bed,' I said, playing for time. 'I don't want to wake her.'

He shoved the taser at me again. 'You get her up.'

'I told you, she's sick. There's nothing here.'

I was almost into the AI. Ah, yes. There was that little click of satisfaction. I locked onto the scanner. To my chagrin, I found that there was a trace. Just tiny, but enough. I had been careless. I made the trace spike and then flicker.

'Range 121 meters, mobile,' said the AI. 'Correction, range 1 meter.'

'Sounds like there's something wrong with your AI,' I said helpfully.

'Shut it, meat.' That was pretty offensive, but I let it pass. Let him play the tough guy. He moved towards the kitchen and started throwing stuff around, kicking over the chairs, sweeping the unwashed dishes onto the floor. That seemed excessive.

'Hey, no need for that,' I said. 'I can show…'

'I said, shut it.' He turned around, and this time his face wasn't blank. He was enjoying this. He was going to turn into one of the bad ones.

'Correction, range 230 meters. Correction, range 31 millimetres. Correction, Officer Lann. Officer Lann, point zero is you.' The AI turned a full circle and turned its eyes onto the Ap, lifting a shooter arm. I chose its biggest calibre weapon, short of a rocket. 'Officer Lann, point zero is you.'

That was my little joke. Not so funny, as it turned out.

'Sounds like it's tracking *you*,' I said. 'You'd better check your AI, like I said.'

For a moment the Ap looked confused. I breathed out a silent sigh of relief. This guy was a dick, but I thought I could get him out of the house now.

And then Ma shot out of her room, pointing a gun. She was in her nightie but for some reason she had put her boots on, and her hair was standing up on end. She looked like a madwoman, but her expression was deadly. When she saw the Ap, she pulled up short. She told me afterwards that all the crashing in the front room had woken her up. She had thought some scumbag was robbing us.

Officer Lann whirled around and this time his taser was on kill. He was going to wipe my mother.

I didn't even think. There was no time to think. I switched the AI to combat mode, bypassing the friendly fire failsafe. It shot Officer Lann right in the back of his head.

He crashed into the wall with the force of the shot and then slid down into a crumpled heap on the floor. The whole front of his skull was blown out where the bullet had exited. I could smell the blood, hot and sweet and sickening. My god, I thought. My god. What a mess.

For a moment there was complete silence.

'Hostile neutralised,' said the AI. 'Report sent to base. Combat successfully completed.'

I jagged its circuits and the AI shut down. I didn't want it recording anything else. The combat report meant that there'd likely be Aps swarming around us any moment, it would have sent a target ID for sure. Aps shooting fleshers wasn't exactly a big event around the banns, but every time an Ap went down there was hell to pay. All of a sudden I felt exhausted, as if every bit of energy had been sucked out of me.

Ma stared at me, appalled.

'Oh Dez.' She stumbled towards the couch and sat down, staring at the dead man. 'Oh my darling. What have you done?'

I looked her straight in the eyes. 'I didn't do anything,' I said.

Bo

In the outer banns, you never go outside without a suit. You're too close to the Outer Veil, and sometimes rogue nanos get through. If they splice with your DNA, you're screwed.

You don't want to be anywhere near a person who's been hit by a nano-virus. You turn up your suit and you run. I've heard horror stories: a man's skin bubbling up and off him in less than a minute, his eyes turning to water and running right off his face. The worst I've seen was when we lived in the Ninth Bann, during one of the bad storms.

I was staring out of our window, bored because Ma wouldn't let us step outside, idly watching the people beginning to emerge from the tower-blocks as the storm died down. The worst was over and the black rain had passed. One man caught my eye because his suit was faulty. I could tell as he walked past beneath, there was a faint shimmer around him, a kind of static electric cloud, like the suit hadn't settled down after he'd switched it on. He was probably out of it on one thing or another and hadn't noticed. He paused under our window. I wondered why, and then I heard the siren warning that the veil had broken again, muffled through the double seal of the tower block. He turned around, as if he was wondering whether to go home, and that's when the nanovirus hit.

This one was quick. He staggered back, clutching his head, and then his skull kind of exploded, and out of it came this blue crystal that just grew and grew until it was bigger than his whole body. I couldn't hear anything except the faint wail of the siren, but I saw people running, and then someone must have sent a bolt into the crystal because the whole thing just shattered into a cloud of blue dust. The sweepers and vacs came through fast to filter the air before it spread, and there was a curfew for two days.

Dez told me it was a bad splice, maybe one of the worst. She said the day we have to worry is the day somebody survives a splice like that. She knows whereof she speaks. Dez got a nanovirus when she was ten. That's what happened to Dez, that's why she's the way she is.

The storms were why Ma moved us in closer to Newport City the moment she could afford it, about three years ago now. Outside the Wall there's only the Outer Veil to keep out nasties. The air is filthy, and it can get pretty rough. In winter it's ice blizzards, and summer brings the huge dust storms that blow in from the western dasht. They're bad enough on their own, but about half of them are toxic with nanos.

Ma found a house in the Second when I was fifteen. I think she got it through Brian Mac, it was a real bargain for what it was, but she never let on. It was the first time in my life that I wasn't living in a towerblock. The house was in one of the narrow, twisting rues near the foodtowers.

All the houses in these old districts are small, packed close together, lined up like peas in a pod. Every place has its own tiny front garden and a small patch of dirt out back. The house Ma found was a bit of a wreck, the pitched roof leaking, every single wall crooked, and she had to spend a lot of time getting it sealed. We had a bedroom each, and Ma let Dez use the cellar to do her making. Café Boite was across the road, and the shijo where Ma had her new stall was a five minute walk. It even had its own well in a corner of the back yard. We thought it was heaven.

When we lived in the Ninth, Ma kept a small stall in the shijo. She sold stuff she scavenged, steel pots, glass jars, bits of jewellery, even plastic, and ran a bit of illegal bioware and oldtech under the table to make a bit extra. The Aps looked the other way, she had some kind of arrangement. Dez and me knew she went scavenging in the dasht, pillaging the ruins for heavy metals, discarded tech and the like, but she never let us come with her if she went that far. Only that one time, and after that she never let us do it again.

She'd scanned an old locker and found some high-level oldtech that was worth a fortune on the black market. She needed us to help her carry it back. She told us later that she thought about it for days but she didn't trust anyone with what was in there, so in the end she took us. Dez wore an old suit that used to belong to Da, but that was faded as it turned out and didn't work so well. I remember the moment when I flicked the button on my belt and the suit glowed up around my skin, knowing we were going out into the dasht. I felt sick with excitement.

The dasht is dangerous. Nanos left over from before the megastorms float out there in the air, and over the centuries their code has glitched. Most are harmless, but some are dead infectious. Out there are mutant ferals, nekas and gaus, nightmare mechs, birds that can slice you just with their feathers, and worse things like the crystals. Some of the ferals can timeslip so you don't know they're there until their teeth are in your throat. Ma went out there maybe once a month. She was some tough mother.

I was around twelve then and I had wanted to go to the dasht since I could walk. It was the coolest trip you could take, totally toxic. Us kids skited about going out there, but of course we never did really, and when I finally did I didn't tell a soul.

I don't remember much about it except how cold I was. It was sleeting when we slid down into the old canal bed that took us past the Outer Veil. Ma had some kind of disruptor tech that meant the Veil didn't fry us, but it was rough getting through. By the time we made it out into the dasht it was snowing, thick grey snow that turned into sludge. Ma said that was good because it was easy to hide our signals and no tracks. By the time we reached the ruined building where the loot was I was crying with the cold, even with the suit. I thought my hands would break off.

Ma broke open the locker and that's when Dez fell down. I thought she must have tripped over but she didn't get back up. Then I saw that her suit had gone misty and through that I could just see her face. Sweat was pouring out of her.

We dropped everything and got her back home as fast as we could. I barely remember that trip. We had to hide her, because if anyone knew she had a nanovirus they would have finished us off. Everyone is terrified of splices. I was too young to be scared, it was my sister that was sick and I only had Ma and Dez. Ma had some pills that stopped the convulsions but then Dez just lay there all shrivelled up. That was one of the only times I saw Ma cry. She must have cried when Da disappeared, but I was only a baby and I don't remember.

We were both sure that Dez would die. The only way we could feed her was squeezing a cloth soaked with soup into in her mouth. We watched her moan and toss her head and sweat for a whole week. I'll never forget it. And then she sat up straight and said she was hungry and it was like there was nothing wrong with her except that she was just skin and bone and floppy as string after all that fever.

As soon as she was sure that Dez wasn't going to die, Ma went out to the dasht to get the stuff we'd had to leave behind. She had to go three times to get it all, but she refused point blank to take me. A week looking after Dez meant a week with no trade, and meds are expensive. We needed the credits. It took a few weeks before Dez could get out of bed. At first we thought she just got better and thought nothing of it. We counted ourselves lucky.

People think you can't survive a nanovirus. But we know better.

Dez

I'm telling Bo this is a backup in case everything goes wrong. At the back of my mind, I'm thinking that even if it all screws up, even if Bo and me and the others are disappeared, or our memories get scrubbed, or whatever, it's comforting to know there's something out there that says who we are. Maybe one day somebody might find it and remember us.

This smartpaper is oldtech. It's from before the Veils were set up, before the megastorms, before the magnetic flip switched the planet's poles. It's kind of magic to think and see sentences come out all blackblue on its smooth, creamy surface. Some of the words come out weird, but I can still read them. Ma made sure we learned letters when we were little. She had a story about a scavenger she knew who one day opened a container load of predator drones that lasered open his guts before he could blink, because he couldn't read the label on the top. You've got to know the signs, she said. And so we learned the signs.

Oldtech can bypass scans. It's why the Alchems use it, though I reckon it's mainly for cool. I have to admit there's something sexy about smart-paper. And best of all, once you freeze the surface that's it, the info can't be indexed or crunched through the databases, and you can lock it so no one can get in.

Not even OpSec. I worry about OpSec way more than I've ever worried about Aps.

Aps are just Aps. It's short for Anthropological Police, a hangover from when the pinkers decided that we were a different species to them. There's the bad ones, pinkers with filthy brains who get sent out here because they screwed up at HQ in Newport City. They hate us fleshers and they hate the banns. While they're here, they're just out for what they can get. It might be meatsex or secret credits or hot bioware they can't get behind the Inner Veil. And then there's Aps like Brian Mac, who are still arseholes because they can't help it, but not complete arseholes.

The skinners are something else. They hunt us for what we've got in our bodies and they're not particular about whether we feel any pain when they take our bodies away from us. The Aps are supposed to stop skinners, because up there in Newport City they're paranoid that someone will bring in some bad DNA that will taint their lovely clean genes.

But the skinners keep going because they've got buyers who pay high credits, and they get past the Aps by bribing them or, sometimes, killing them. They find it more difficult to get past OpSec, but they do. In Newport City the pinkers love to geek out on flesher hormones, and the real high quality comes from adolescents.

Obviously the skinners deal other shady stuff, drugs and implants mainly, but the hormone trade is the most profitable. Skinning is the only crime against us that OpSec take seriously, and that's only because it endangers Newport City. They don't give a toss for the kids who go missing in the banns and who turn up in the dumps days later with most of them missing.

The trick with Aps is to know which ones are in with the skinners, and then to make sure that you never cross their paths, never meet their eyes, never say one word to them, never be seen by them. The trick with skinners is never to get caught, ever. Which of course is easier said than done, though here in the Second Bann skinners are pretty rare.

Me, I've got some advantages. That nanovirus reconfigured me. My blood, my cells, my DNA. I'm a security nightmare. I don't even need to think about it, I can get into almost any frame and find out what I want. I can hear the infochatter of a skinner's suit from a klick away. I can *smell* them.

Only Ma and Bo know what I am, and even they don't know everything. But that doesn't mean that others don't begin to wonder. When you're selling illegal streamers that no one else can make or you get a name for retrofitting oldtech better than anyone else, it doesn't matter how low you keep your profile. Word gets out, one person says something to another person, and person three begins to put two and two together. I've known for a while that there are skinners looking out for me, sniffing around for my DNA. I'm *special*.

Let's be honest, I always knew that.

I like being me. I hardly remember who I was before the fever, it's like trying to remember what it was like when I was inside Ma. You know it happened, but you can't remember. But after, it was like I was born into this place of knowing things. There's a world out there shimmering with data, and I just plug right in.

Ma thought at first that I had lost it, that the virus had burned my brain and for the rest of my life I'd be like Isho, who got some bad fever as a baby and never totally recovered. He depended wholly on his mother. All the kids adored Isho's ma, she was bright and beautiful and strong, and she made these sweet mato balls that tasted glorious and gave them out to all the kids on the rue. She and Isho loved each other so much you could see it shining in their faces when they looked at each other.

But the second Isho's voice dropped the skinners got him. He must have been marked, some lowlife must have been watching and waiting for the pituitary to kick in. Isho was an easy mark because he never learned how to run, he trusted everybody. Somehow we thought that would protect him, but we should have known better.

It got pretty ugly in the bann after that, there was almost a revolt. The only reason it didn't spill over was because of Brian Mac. He did his job, and even though he's a mess, he's good at his job. He's not like those pinker tourists who come to the better banns like ours for a thrill, all suited up and horrified like they're walking through a sewer full of freaks.

I've got a bit of a soft spot for Brian Mac, weird though he is. Ma does too, there's history there, though I've never worked out what it was and it's not like Ma would ever tell me. He's been in the Second for twenty years. Not many Aps stay that long. I don't know why he stays. Living in the banns sucks, if I could live in the Newport City I'd go like a shot. But for us fleshers there's nowhere else.

The nano that got me must have been floating out there for centuries turning to glitch, splicing with random biomatter, becoming some other thing, and then I happened along and bang, it rams into my DNA and here I am. I worked out the probability once. It was point fifteen zeroes and recurring three. Seriously. There wouldn't be another person on this planet that this could happen to. That's not counting the chance of me being in the dasht with a faded suit at the just the right time. It's enough to make you believe in fate, though I don't believe in any of that shit.

When I was first sick all I did was lie on my bed and watch the pretty data flashing past. I did that for days. I couldn't parse it at first, it wasn't even images or numbers or code, it was just this flood of sparkle. Even after the fever passed, it took a while before I could mainline images or text out of the code. I didn't know how to control my receptors, or how to search. That kind of evolved all at once, and that's when I wasn't sick any more. Once everything became self-organising I discovered I could refine the processes just by wanting to. When I was still too weak to get out of bed, I watched every soap going in Newport City. I streamed the news channels. It was different from what they give us in the banns.

That was when I started realising how things are.

It's dangerous, knowing things. I know way more than I know I know, and sometimes it's a bit confusing. And sometimes I just want to be me. I'm a flesher through and through. I do all the flesher things: fall in love, cry, laugh, rage to the trance mobs. All the things that back in Newport City they envy us for, all the *authentic* things that they don't know how to do any more because their DNA is so clean and squeaky.

I've got all the feelings.

And feelings are trouble. I know that too.

Bo

The day the raid happened, I met Brian Mac out on the edge of the Tenth. Brian Mac isn't someone you can trust, nobody who's an Ap is someone you can trust. When he's off-duty he's pretty close to the edge, spiked up on juice or jerked on some temporary implant. One time I saw him when he was coming down from days of time bending, going forward and back through the same day. Don't ask me why. Eventually he ran into himself. The two of him had some kind of argument and it ended up in a fist fight. One of him got knocked out and woke up with skinned knuckles from punching himself in the head. I laughed about that for days.

I was coming home from Flora's gig, my ears ringing from the sounds her mob had pumped out. The gig had been in the terminus of what used to be the underground Rapid Transport System, which was closed down decades ago, after the tunnels began to collapse. Nothing gets repaired in the banns. The terminus was the deepest part of the network. We always had to pick places where nothing could be heard from the outside. Everything that hears our music comes looking for who's making it, to slice up, to thieve from or to feed on. Inside, it was all grinding steel with an in-your-stomach beat that purged your insides and made your outsides sting.

When I staggered out into the air I felt like I'd been peeled.

I was with two of my steadies, Beng and Fleet. They were heading for a party in the Fifth, low-key, a bit of dreamweed, a few beers. A lot of people sitting around not saying much. I wasn't that interested. 'I've had enough excitement tonight,' I told them.

'Suit yourself,' said Beng.

We parted company at the Wall. They headed through the porte into the Sixth and I kept on going straight. I didn't want to walk all the way home so I was planning to catch a mono back to the Second. I was already pretty whacked and it was a couple of klicks to the station, but I'd be home before midnight.

Once I was on my lonesome I kept to the darkest places, slinking like a rat. I'd almost reached the mono when I spotted the skinner. The skinners around the Tenth are the worst, the screw-ups and failures who grub a living at the bottom of their particular pile of merde. Everything is cheap around here and everyone is desperate. This one wasn't from the Tenth, he looked too clean. He was wearing a fancy bandolier with studs that winked in the dim light from the Veil, and his boots were expensive.

Luckily I saw him before he saw me. He was heading my way. I dived down a narrow side street, keeping close to the steel wall of what used to be some kind of warehouse. Like most buildings this far out in the banns it was a blank, an empty shape coated in the filth that makes it past the Outer Veil, doors welded shut, windows blacked out. I saw that there was a hole cut in the wall up ahead and I scurried through it into a small room.

A bent-over creep with a blotch for a face was sitting on a stool in the corner in the half circle of a lamp. He saw me but he didn't even blink. The place was a 25/10 joint that sold oldtech, filled with stacks of useless junk.

Someone was standing a few metres from me. Even in the dim light I recognized Brian Mac as soon as I saw him: thin as wire, two heads taller than me, his long red coat reaching to the ground, those weird military goggles he always wore that blanked out half of his face. Brian Mac was a fan of this stuff, splicing and grafting one bit of junk to another, trying to build who knows what.

When he saw me he grinned. 'Bo boy. You lost?

'Just cruising.'

'Been gigging?'

I didn't answer.

'Something wrong, Bo?' he said, stepping closer.

'A skinner,' I said. 'Heading this way.'

He stuck out his paw and gripped me by the shoulder, putting his face close to mine. I could smell his breath.

'Switch up your suit, bug.'

I switched to high and my skin buzzed for a moment. The feeling always made me feel a bit sick.

Brian Mac went outside. I stuffed myself behind a stack of gutted monitors close to the entrance. Footsteps approached outside, and I heard a thick, gravely voice. 'A word with you, Mac.'

The footsteps came closer and stopped.

Brian Mac said nothing

'You range a bit, don't you?' the voice said.

'I get around.'

'You touch a lot of shit, pick up the grime. You deal, you know who's on the rush, who's on the run.'

Brian Mac just grunted. I heard his boots shift on the ground.

'I'm looking for a particular flesher. A freak. Female, genius level. Maybe corrupted. Looks like a regular, but not so. Rare. Something like that gets talked about. I'm looking, listening, get nothing. A few of us are hunting. Share of the spoils and all that. Pretty sure she knows we're looking. Word's out, know what I mean?'

Brian Mac still didn't answer. He hates skinners and I could tell this guy was pressing him the wrong way. If it had been Brian Mac's turf, he would have wasted him.

'You got anything on that?'

'Got nothing on that, Dyer.'

'Would tell me if you did, right?'

'For a price. A big price.'

'If we net this one, there'll be plenty.'

There was a long silence. Maybe they were just standing there looking at each other, testing the strain. Dyer walked away but I stayed where I was until Brian Mac's goggled face bent down over me where I was hiding.

'You owe me one, Bo boy.'

I didn't answer, I just legged it.

I finally reached the mono. I didn't have to wait long for a train. I watched the city go by, thinking over what had just happened.

That skinner was talking about Dez. It had to be her. And the closer I got to home, the surer I was that she knew she was being hunted. She had to know. She can pick up skinners from klicks away, she's always on the alert for them. If there was word going around about some freak female, she'd know it was her they were talking about. She just hadn't told anyone, not even me.

I was so angry I could have spewed.

I knew there was trouble as soon as I heard the drone. It was the kind the Aps use when they want to frighten people. It screams, like a machine in some kind of agony, and it's armed. You don't hear them often in the Second. In the Tenth and beyond they're a daily event. Some real shit must have happened, because the drone was getting closer and lower every second. I couldn't see it yet, but sounded like it was right over my head.

There was a crowd outside our place, maybe twenty or thirty people, and up and down both sides both sides of the rue people were hanging out of their windows and doors, looking towards our house.

I pushed through the crowd to the front door, which was wide open. Nobody was going in, they were just standing there gawking into our front room. I could already smell something organic, and there was blast smoke drifting in the air.

As I stepped inside Ma leapt up from the couch and threw her arms around me, almost knocking me over. She was in her nightie, with an old overcoat thrown over it to keep out the freezing wind coming through the open door. I opened my mouth to ask what was going on, but nothing came out because I'd just spotted the body of the Ap lying on the floor a few steps from Dez, a thick, black pool of blood spreading out from what was left of his head.

The drone was screaming right above the house. It was coming down so low you could feel the heat of it. The noise was so loud that I felt like my whole body was being squeezed. Any minute my ears would burst and my brains would come spurting out of the sides of my head. Then the rue outside exploded in a blaze of light and everyone threw up their hands to shield their eyes and backed away.

Dez got up from the floor and kicked the button for the front door. The exact moment it slammed against the doorframe, the drone's screaming stopped. But it was still right above us, hovering, and we could hear the low, humming pulse of its stabilisers.

Ma put a finger to her lips. Who knows what kind of shit the Aps had already released into the room. They could probably hear our hearts beating. I went over to Dez and took hold of her arms. She was shaking worse than Ma, staring back at me like she didn't know me.

'What the hell happened?'

'The AI...'

I hadn't even noticed the AI on the floor, folded up like a giant dead spider. Dez opened our private line in my suit.

'I don't know what happened. Just don't panic or say anything careless.'

She snapped the line shut and I could hear the drone again, and the transport as it shuddered to a stop right outside. The door flew into the room, blasted off its frame. About a dozen Aps followed the door, weapons out, all their tech lit up. The whole room fizzed with a bad energy and every muscle in my body went rigid. I could hardly breathe. The Aps switched off our suits and pulled off our belts. They snapped a body brace on each of us and dragged us out of the door and into the rue.

There was an even bigger crowd of people watching, now they were sure that they weren't the ones in the shit, spread out around the edge of the light blazing from the drone. They were silent, just a wall of faces all turned our way. The Aps slid Ma into one of the pods in the back of the transport first, then Dez, then me, head first, like they were sliding corpses into a freezer. I heard the locks snap shut on my brace. The door closed with a soft, electric click. Darkness.

The ride to the Aps station was so smooth and silent it was like I wasn't moving at all. I don't know how long it took. The only thing that felt real was the pain. Locked rigid in the brace, my whole body began to cramp. My bones felt as if they were being twisted like wire.

When the transport door opened again I was blinded by yellow light. I squeezed my eyes shut as I was slid out and onto some kind of gurney. A blast of cold air washed over me. I couldn't look left or right, I could only see the ceiling high above me rushing past. I was moving in a straight line for a while, then left, then right, then into some kind of chamber where the ceiling was a different colour. I heard a door slide shut somewhere behind me. I was tipped upright and the brace was unlocked and pulled away from my body. I was standing on my feet, facing a shiny black wall. My legs felt like they were made of water and my head was spinning. I fell forward and hit the wall face first. I curled up into a ball and shut my eyes. A door shut, a buzzer sounded. Then everything was still and silent.

When I opened my eyes I was staring at myself. I sat up on my arse and pushed myself backwards. There were thousands of me, disappearing into infinity. The walls, the floor, the ceiling were all polished steel reflecting each other. When I looked at the floor I saw my face and behind my face the reflection of the back of my head looking down at my face. I looked like shit. My nose was bleeding.

At first it was impossible to tell how big this place was, where it began and ended. I felt around until I found a corner and pressed myself into it, dizzy and sick. I tried to calm myself down. I took some deep breaths, closed my eyes, waited until my heart stopped bashing away inside my chest. Then I opened my eyes again.

I was in a box about as big as an elevator. I couldn't see any sign of a door. It was filled with blinding light, but I couldn't tell where it came from. Looking around just made me feel worse, all those reflections of me spun around every time I moved my eyes. It was like I was hovering in some kind of shiny abyss. I stared at my feet.

I tried to think about what had just happened, to go back to the moment I came home, walked in the door, saw Ma and Dez and the dead Ap. I saw the people crowded outside the house. They were our neighbours. I knew them all. Kiko, who worked at the foodtowers, her boyfriend Trung, Tenzo and Clav who sold clothes at the shijo, Crush, Tak and Finley, Henna the tech head, Ginz with only one eye, Cho with their long braids. And Flora. She must have got back from the gig at about the same time as me. I glimpsed her as I was dragged out in the brace. She stared as I was loaded into the transport, her face stony, her lips pressed tight together.

I tried to pull myself together. I looked up and stared hard at my reflections in the steel wall in front of me. I had to stay calm, be strong. Then I heard a loud hiss and a foul stench filled my nostrils. I just had time to realise I was being gassed before everything went black.

Someone was whispering close to my ear. Was it whispering? Was it the wind blowing, was it water running? I was moving slowly. I couldn't tell if I was facing up or down. There was no up or down. Just this whispering and passing through space, as if I was floating. Maybe I was going somewhere. Maybe I was dead.

I was looking at a face. It wasn't my face this time. It was the face of a man, at least it was half a face. His eyes were hidden behind a black visor. I could see his lips, his teeth. His mouth was so close to mine I could taste his breath.

'What is your name?' the mouth said.

I didn't say anything.

'We know your name.'

He moved away and turned his back to me. He was tall and broad. His blood red jacket was tight across his shoulders. There was a keypad on the wall. He pressed some keys. The wall was white. Everything was white. I couldn't see a door. Maybe the door was behind me. I was sitting in a chair. I wasn't strapped in but I couldn't move. I could only move my eyes.

The face turned back to me.

'What is your name?'

You know my fucking name, you dick, I thought. But I didn't say anything. Dez had told me to stay calm, so I tried to stay calm. My guts were in a knot and I could feel the sweat running down my back.

'My name is Bo,' I managed to say. 'Bo Inaware.'

My voice sounded weird, hollow. My tongue felt swollen and dry. I was thirsty. I'd never been so thirsty.

The face smiled. He reached out and tilted my head back, put his fingers in my mouth and opened it. He sprayed something down my throat. Whatever it was, it was cold and it stung. My tongue went slack and my mouth just fell open like my jaw had been snapped loose. A flood of saliva ran down my chin.

The face backed away.

'A few moments. A few moments rest. Then we'll begin properly. You've had a busy day, lovely, haven't you?'

Dez

I knew they didn't have DNA scans at the banns precincts. One plus, against a lot of minuses.

It probably wouldn't occur to them to take a DNA sample. If they did, it would take less than an hour to get the results back from OpSec. That had to be avoided at all costs. Likely they would use memory scans, truth drugs, all that kind of shit. A lot of intimidation. Well, I wouldn't have to pretend to be scared. I was as frightened as I'd ever been.

Aside from the dead Ap – and that was a big aside – they didn't have anything on us but some illegal bioware. When they threw me into the mirror box, I shut my eyes and made an inventory. It could have been worse. I had sold a bunch of consoles the previous week, and had been gathering stuff to make a new batch. Most of my gear was locked safe in my stash, hidden under the floor of the cellar behind a deadwall and a passcode using a crypto none of these brainiacs had ever heard of. If they found my stash, we'd never get out.

I figured their chance of finding it was 0.001 per cent.

On my workbench there were a few basic tools, microtweezers, electron scope, that kind of thing. A couple of implants, dozers and a timeslip. The implants were probably what triggered the trace. I hadn't bothered to check them for signals, I'd bought them in the shijo that morning and just chucked them into the cellar to deal with later. It was lucky I hadn't got around to doing anything fancy with them.

If we ever got out of this Ma would kill me. She brought us up to be smart, to watch for the carelessness that made everything unravel. I thanked all the gods I didn't believe in that I had decided to watch soaps that night. If I had been working, they could have found me with everything spread out on the bench. *In flagrante delicto*, they used to say. In blazing offence. Though they used that for more organic crimes.

On the other hand, if I had been working, I would have had all the shields turned on, and there would have been no trace at all.

I couldn't work out if I was lucky or unlucky. I didn't feel lucky. I wasn't as unlucky as that Ap. I thought of the mess his brains made in our front room and then I tried not to think of it. It just made me shaky. Sure, he was a dick, but even a dick didn't deserve that. He wouldn't have been much older than Bo. I thought of what his mother might feel, and then I remembered that pinkers didn't have mothers, they were grown in labs and farmed out for adoption to approved families. But then, somebody would have loved him? Or did they? They did in the soaps.

I knew what Ma would say, that he didn't deserve one pulse of sympathy, that at least he died quick, unlike some others. By *some others*, she meant what had probably happened to Da. We never found out. But we could guess.

I was wasting time.

I did a brutal scan of my memory cells, tagging anything dubious I could find, anything to do with tech, the nanovirus, what had happened to the AI, anything at all. Then I filed it in the amygdala, the good old lizard brain, where (probably) the Aps wouldn't look. I forged a passcode, making it look like a random memory, and gave it the name Flora. When I saw Flora, which I would if we ever got out, it would unlock.

I had taken out so much it looked like I'd been comatose half my life. I thought a bit and filled up the gaps with soaps. I knew this was risky as hell; if they damaged me enough the passcode could corrupt. But I didn't have a choice. It was the only way past the truth drugs and the scans, and I was the dangerous thing here. Ma and Bo couldn't edit their brains, but maybe, just maybe, once the Aps saw how completely vacuous I was, they'd take whatever weird shit they found in Ma and Bo as some kind of VR fantasy that had rotted their minds. It happened.

I was counting on the pinkers thinking that fleshers are thick. Most of them give us credit for low cunning at best. It's pretty asinine of them not to allow fleshers into the Aps, frankly. It means that sometimes we can run under the radar, because they expect so little.

It wasn't a great plan, but it was the best I could do.

It took a bit of courage to lock off the master code. It was like diving into deep, black water. I didn't know if I would ever come out of it. I prayed for luck. And then I locked off.

My memories of what followed are pretty blurred. Which is good, because what I do remember is pretty unpleasant. My clearest recollection is Brian Mac yelling. There was a lot of swearing and gesticulating, and his face was bright red, which clashed with his coat. The soap opera part of me thought that was a very bad design idea.

He was jabbing his finger at a tablet. He asked them what they thought they were doing. He was saying, an AI shoots one of our own men, and you don't even notice? What's wrong with you? It's there in the combat report. Right there.

He jabbed the tablet again and then waved it in the air. Sabotage? Seriously? You want to charge them with sabotage? This kid barely knows she's alive. Look at the scan. Did you check the AI? Not yet? Do you even follow procedure with your own gear? OpSec's going to have a good laugh at this. Yeah, there'll be a lot of comedy in HQ when they get this report. You lot couldn't find your own arses if you had three hands.

I actually giggled, until one of them slapped me.

Next thing I remember, we're in the front office being signed out. Brian Mac was lecturing Ma on harbouring illegal tech, and we were sent home with a fine and a warning. I had never seen Brian Mac in official mode before, he was different, sharper, somehow bigger.

We got out of there with nothing but a slap on the wrist. That was all

Brian Mac. The other Aps didn't care if we were guilty or not. We might have just turned up dead in the cells, no questions asked.

After that I began to wonder again why Brian Mac looked out for Ma. They were old friends, I knew that, and Bo and me joked sometimes about him crushing on Ma. It was a bit creepy to be honest. But there had to be something else.

We had to walk home. It was a half hour to Rue Ballard but at that time of night, and with no suits, it seemed to take forever. Ma was still in her nightie and boots, with just her overcoat to keep out the cold. A thin wind laced with ice tore through our clothes and every single muscle hurt. I remember walking through the rues and the empty shijo, our footsteps echoing back from the walls. Every house in the Second was sealed shut, blank and light-less, the rows of pitched roofs like black saws against the soft yellow glow of the distant food towers. If anyone had decided to jump us we would have been easy pickings, but there was nobody about except a couple of mangy gaus which slunk off when they saw us.

There wasn't enough of me there to be afraid. I think I kept singing a jingle from an old ad. Ma took my hand and led me, because I had forgot-ten the way. She was crying, she thought the Aps had done something awful to me in there. Bo said nothing at all. He just walked very close to us, blood smeared on his face, grim and dark.

Luckily the first person I saw when we got home was Flora.

Flora and me. It's complicated. There's a reason why she was the first person I thought of, outside Bo and Ma, when I wanted to lock up all the most private bits of me. Even when we'd sworn we'd never speak to each other ever again, when we'd said the most hurtful things that we knew – and we knew all the most hurtful things, better than anyone – I trusted her with my life. I knew she'd be there, waiting. And she was.

She was sitting in the window of Café Boite, a smudge in the darkness. When she saw us coming up the rue she ran out and flung her arms around all of us. As soon as her face swum into my vision, I knew the code, and I was unlocked. I'd have to do some sorting, but it was all there. I was me again. I didn't know what the situation was, so I thought I'd better pretend for now that I was still the nobrain I'd been for the past few hours. I hugged Flora back and let Ma do the talking.

Our door was broken right off. It lay in the front room. We hesitated before we went in, afraid of what we would find.

One good thing, the body had been taken away. They'd used a vac to get rid of all the organic matter, so the only trace of Officer Lann's death was the hole in the wall. It wasn't out of concern for us. I knew the security forces didn't like leaving anything behind, in case it got used later.

The Aps had gone through everything. The couch was slashed, all its stuffing pulled out. The mattresses on the beds. Every cupboard had been emptied, every drawer, their contents strewn all over the floor. Our suits were thrown into a corner. Bo's was broken. They hadn't bothered to take the suits, because they looked like the cheapest models. Just as well: if they'd had a closer look, they would have found out that they were the best fitted-out suits in the banns, bar none.

There were a lot of broken things. Things that weren't of any value except to us: some of Ma's old scrawlings that she'd had framed for the walls, a glass bird that I'd loved since I was a kid, most of the crockery. All our clothes were dumped on the floor, and some of them had been slashed, including Bo's antique leather jacket that was his pride and joy. It was just malicious.

Flora stared at the wreckage, her eyes wide. 'I heard them smashing everything,' she said. 'I'm so sorry, guys.'

Ma patted her hand. She looked exhausted, ashen with shock. 'It doesn't matter,' she said. 'It's only things.'

'Yes, it does,' said Flora. 'It was so pretty in here.' Her face crumpled, but she didn't cry. She brushed back her hair. 'They shouldn't have done that.'

Bo spoke for the first time. 'They did something to Dez,' he said. 'Those fuckers.'

I winced. I didn't want him saying anything that might give us away while the spyware was operating. I trod on Bo's foot and he looked up in surprise, a sudden suspicion in his eyes, and to my eternal gratitude he shut up.

Flora was still talking, almost gabbling, her voice high with distress.

'I thought you weren't coming back, not after that. I couldn't sleep, so I thought I'd wait. Kojo said if you came back you could stay at ours. He said they'd trash the place.'

Kojo is Flora's father. It was a generous offer, because that would put them in the spotlight too.

'Tell Kojo that we're grateful, very very grateful,' Ma said. 'But we don't want to cause you any trouble.'

'But...'

'I'll fix the door for now, and we'll see what needs doing tomorrow. It looks worse than it is. You should go home, Flora.'

Flora saw that Bo and me agreed with Ma, and so she didn't argue. She nodded, and went back to Café Boite.

While they were talking, I did a deep scan for spyware. The Aps had stuck a few bugs around, low level tech, standard. Maybe these Aps were as incompetent as Brian Mac had said they were. I let them run for the moment.

The door was unfixable, so Ma propped it up and stuck the couch against it to keep out the wind. The heater was still working, so she turned that on. Then we put the stuffing back in Ma's mattress and found some blankets and lay down all together, like when we were little. It was the most comforting thing in the world.

I put the spyware sensors on a loop, so for the next few hours it would look like we were all sleeping. Then I nudged Ma, who was lying next to me, staring at the ceiling.

'I'm okay,' I whispered. 'Really okay. I just had to hide everything.'

She drew in her breath sharply, and then she grabbed me and held me tight. I could feel her body trembling. Bo just swore, and cuffed me gently.

Ma went to sleep almost at once after that, and then Bo. I listened to them breathing. I was so thankful they were there, that we were all still alive. For a while there I had thought I'd never see them again.

I waited for about half an hour, and then I got out of bed and went down to the cellar. The Aps had taken everything on my workbench and they'd done a scrub of the walls, but they hadn't found my stash. I thought they couldn't have, because they'd let us go, but all the same, the relief was dizzying.

Then I went back and woke Bo.

Brian Mac

Jul 25 09.32 hours

Rostered Day Off. Same old shit, only the shit is getting shitter. Went for a drink after my shift, thought about an implant, thought better of it, slept snug as cockroach, woke up with eyeballs rolled in sand, shot some painkiller, sixteen cups of coffee. Bad times, my boy, bad times. I can smell it coming.

Reckless to keep this, especially now. Reckless even when security is my call, when I'm the rat sniffing things out. You can't tell me that I don't have a tag on my file, no matter how many skinners I send to the injections.

You're just a romantic, Bel used to say, back in the day. Bel. She's a sickness I can't shake, like this diary is a sickness I can't shake. But maybe she's right. Maybe I just want to vomit all this up so I can find something pure that's left behind in there somewhere, some part of me I touched back in my twenties when it seemed possible to change everything.

I hate purity.

Maybe it's just that old habits die hard. It'll be the death of me. Maybe it's the death of me already.

You'd think I'd be past that. Self pity, I mean.

So yesterday this constable gets himself shot by his own AI during a routine raid. One of the new recruits, fresh and shiny, eyes out on stalks at being in the banns, prick all stiff with fear and excitement. Mediocre but ambitious, bad combo. Looks at me with pity and contempt. I know his sort. He's thinking how he won't end up like Brig Mackintosh, stuck in the outstations for twenty years, no hope of promotion to City duty, no better than a flesher. I've seen these men come and go over the years. Some of them settle down and learn something, some of them turn into the worst kind of cops. I promote those ones sideways into other precincts, I don't want to deal with that shit in my station. Some of them get nailed by skinners, who are smarter and hungrier and dirtier than they can even imagine.

I wasn't at the precinct when the trace came in, otherwise I'd have handled it myself, no harm done. I was out tailing a skinner called Dyer, who I ran into in the Tenth. He's been seen in the Second recently and I don't like that. I figured he must have had word on a particular flesher he was hunting. Not on my watch.

Dyer's one of the dense ones: if he was smart he'd know that I don't do deals with skinners. Maybe I'll wink at the small beer, oldtech and so on, in return for a word here and there. But the hormone trade is evil, and I don't say that about much. I get to hoover up what's left from the middens, I get to see the dismal remains of those kids. Even after all these years, all those bodies, I never get used to it.

I got rid of Dyer, which wasn't pleasant, and opened my comm to report job done only to find that everything was blazing. An Ap was down, his AI disabled, and they'd brought in the perps for interrogation. I streamed the details and went cold. It was Bel's address. Bel and her two kids. Bel's an old hand, she knows better than to do something like that, and that Bo is a shocker, wild and unruly like his dad. Maybe he might have shot the cop, but he couldn't have done the AI. Dez. Dez is something else. I've got my suspicions about Dez, just like the skinners have, and they're not comfortable.

I got back to the precinct to find the place swarming. The scrutineers had already done the interrogations, they said the perps were claiming that the AI did it. They didn't believe them, everyone knows that's impossible, and they were out for blood. I read the combat report the AI sent before it blew up, which nobody seemed to have read past the first line, and then I went to the mortuary and pulled out the corpse of Officer Lann, or at least, what was left of him. I asked what bullet had killed him. They hadn't even looked. They showed me the bullet. It was a Cyclops, hollow point, .205, AI-only issue. I did some more shouting until they looked at the AI.

At that point I saw my way through. I lost it. I asked them what had happened to their brains. Were they really wasting their time with these useless bums when an AI had gone feral? Had they checked the other AIs to see if they had any faults? They went quiet and did what I said, like they were kids back in Ap school who'd screwed up bigtime in front of the boss. I made sure I was there when they charged Bel with holding and watched them out of the door. I wanted to be certain.

Then I said I wanted the reports in the system by morning or there would be hell to pay and I slammed out. I'd been awake for 36 hours by then, so I went back to my room and did some thinking. Though I guess it was less thinking and more drinking.

I've got a bad feeling about this.

Bo

When Dez woke me up, it felt like I'd been asleep for ten seconds. She didn't say anything, just beckoned. I followed her down to the cellar, rubbing my eyes.

I don't come in here very often. It's Dez's private place, her lair. When she's working with her shields down it's like she's in a world all her own. There's no way to get her attention until she's finished, and even then it takes her a while to snap out of whatever zone she's gone into, her solo space with just her weird mind for company, all the stuff it comes up with and the things it can do. She's a bit scary sometimes.

Dez looked fragile, like she always does when she's stressed: her hair was messed up in a black tangle and her face looked hollowed out. Most of the time you forget how slight she is, but right now it was like you could snap her in two.

She gave me a damp cloth and told me to wipe the blood off my face. I hadn't looked at myself, so I had no idea what kind of sight I was. If I looked as bad as I felt I must have been a horror. The cloth felt good on my skin and I suddenly wanted a steamshower. I stank of the precinct and the Aps, of sweat and fear.

When I was done, Dez grinned tiredly at me. 'Some night, eh?' she said.

'Yeah. Really,' I said. 'Are you going to tell me what happened?'

She glanced at me and looked away, biting her lip. Suddenly I was boiling angry. For hours I thought the Aps had done something, that they'd screwed her mind in there and turned her into some witless drone. Don't get all coy with me, Dez, I thought. You wouldn't have woken me up if you didn't want to talk and you didn't know it was safe. Don't mess with me.

'You killed that Ap, didn't you? It was you.'

She sat there twiddling her thumbs, and then she said, 'I hacked the AI. I didn't mean to kill him. I just wanted to turn the AI on him and give him a fright. But then Ma came in shrieking and waving that damn gun of hers and he was going to shoot her. It all happened so fast.'

'But you wanted to kill him, didn't you?'

Dez just shrugged.

'And how come you didn't tell us that skinners are looking for you?'

Dez looked at me, her eyes wide. 'What?'

'You know they are. There's talk going around between the skinners, about a female flesher who sounds a hell of a lot like you. You must have heard that talk, you must have twigged it's you they're talking about. Right? But you thought you'd keep that to yourself, right? Not worth mentioning, was it?'

I don't think Dez had realised how angry I was. I couldn't help it. Sometimes she really gets under my skin. That big sister thing, even though she's not my big sister at all. For a moment I thought she'd yell at me. And then it was like she shrank and I saw how frightened she was under that spiky Dez shell.

'I didn't want to worry Ma,' she said, in a small voice. 'Or you.'

My anger died. We've seen some toxic things, but up to now a man with his brains all over our front room wasn't one of them. And we were both too tired and frazzled to fight.

'We're in deep shit now, aren't we?'

She nodded. 'They didn't get us for anything tonight, but you can bet they'll be keeping an eye on us. Brian Mac got us out, but he had to pull rank.'

I snorted. 'Who'd think that Brian Mac had a rank?'

'Whatever he is, we owe him.'

'There's worse people we could owe.'

'There's always someone worse.'

We didn't say anything else for a while. Dez got up and made us a herbal brew. Nothing had ever tasted as good as that tea.

'What are we going to do now?' I said.

'I know what I'm going to do.'

It would be like Dez not to tell me, but she leaned closer and lowered her voice as if there might be someone listening. 'If they take apart that AI, they're going to find interference, and I'm scared they'll work out it was me. My DNA will be all over this place, maybe they took samples and sent them to OpSec. I'm going to hack into their mainframe to find out if they know anything.'

'You can't be serious.'

'I am. Deadly.'

I didn't know what to say. I sipped my tea.

'You think I can't do it?' she said.

'I didn't say that. It's just so dangerous. And what if you do find out? So what? How's that going to help?'

Dez doesn't like being questioned. 'Don't be a dick, Bo.'

'I'm going to do something too.'

'Yeah? Like what?'

I don't think Dez expected me to have an answer. I'd thought about it all the way home from the precinct, feeling small and powerless, terrified that the Aps had screwed with Dez's brain, seeing the anger and worry on Ma's face. 'I'm going to talk to the Alchems,' I said.

Dez gave me the look I was expecting, scornful and slightly contemptuous. 'The Alchems are a joke, a bunch of tossers who think they're planning a revolution. What have they ever actually done? Zilch. They couldn't plan a trip to the shijo.'

'You don't know anything about them.'

'They're posers, deadbeats.'

'Flora doesn't think so.'

'What's Flora got to do with it? She wouldn't have anything to do with them. I'd know, anyway.'

'You reckon she doesn't keep secrets from you?'

I knew this was the wrong way to go, but it was too late now. I'd hit a sore spot. When Dez is hurting she's most dangerous, even for me. She stared at the floor while I waited for her to take me apart, but nothing happened. At last I reached out and took her hand. She didn't pull away.

'The Alchems want to change things,' I said. 'I don't know how they think they'll change them, but it's the wanting to that matters. And they're strong because they look after each other. They share what they know, they teach each other. They're building something.'

She looked up at me at last. 'I bet half of what you hear isn't true.'

'Even if only half of what you hear is true, then that's something, isn't it? Everyone says they've got hides, safe places. If things get bad, maybe they can help us.'

I hadn't worked out the details. Talking to the Alchems wouldn't be easy. I just knew the first step, and I knew Dez wasn't going to like it. I took a deep breath.

'I'm going to talk to Morro,' I said. It was an open secret that Morro was an Alchem leader. Dez's lips tightened but I ploughed on. 'Whatever you think of him, Morro's special. I've talked to him a few times. He's cool.'

'And where is Morro? He hasn't been seen for weeks. Maybe OpSec wasted him.'

'We'd know if they had. They'd be crowing about it, they'd let everyone know. You know that's what they'd do.'

'So how are you going to find him?'

I didn't want to argue with Dez about whether or not I could get in touch with Morro. There were ways. The Alchems are a network, not just one person. It wouldn't be easy, and it probably wouldn't be safe. 'I'll find him,' I said.

She went quiet, as if she was thinking it over and deciding not to say what she really thought, and then she looked me straight in the eye.

'Do what you have to do. I'll do the same.'

She looked so tired, so wrung dry.

'Let's get some sleep,' I said. 'We'll need it.'

We went back and lay down beside Ma. It would be light in an hour or so. Soon I could hear Dez breathing deep and steady. I hoped that she didn't have any bad dreams. I hoped that I didn't either.

Brian Mac

Bad morning after a night out in the Eighth. I think about slipping another day off into the system and then figure that right now I'd better keep my nose clean. I scroll the reports over my first coffees. Tech is 'concerned'. They're still testing out these new models. Option one, an unknown entity hacked in and both corrupted and disabled the AI. Option one, discarded, because the crypto is new and OpSec instructs it's impregnable. Option two is a bad circuit that got past quality control and lit up in combat. Still attempting to confirm but the circuitry is so scrambled it's impossible to be certain. Permission requested to refer upwards. Option three is they don't have an option three.

I send back instructions to keep investigating so we don't look like dicks when we do refer up. Spend a few minutes wondering how to keep a lid on this mess, how to stop it all going to OpSec. If I had half a brain I'd let it all go through and turn my back on Bel and her kids, forget about what happened with Flynn, forget the whole damn thing.

I don't like these new AIs. I had the old ones sussed, I could keep an eye on what info was flowing to OpSec. I'm pretty sure these models have a secret line that they don't let the Aps know about. *Quis custodiet ipsos custodes* and all that.

Mal's given me a few lectures about 'keeping in step'. Since when have I been in step? That's why I'm good, and he knows it. I've accounted for more skinners than any other cop in the banns. And nothing puts the wind up the City more than the skinners. They've promoted me up as far I'll go. I've known for years that I'm pushed against the ceiling so hard my face is flat. Would I go back to Newport City? I sometimes wonder. I don't even go there on vacation any more. It gives me the willies.

I don't think I could go back. This place gets under your skin.

Poor old Mal. I've watched his holo aging over the years, he doesn't bother with patches or implants. If he doesn't visit the biobooths soon they'll notice and pension him out and I'll have one of those new supers, baby faced, smooth as ice, heart of a fascist. I try not to think about that.

Since Osborne weaselled himself into the Mayorality and bumped Bremmer up to CEO of OpSec there have been changes. I saw the two of them once, just after Bremmer had taken over. It was some event for the cameras, a security announcement. OpSec, Aps, all clean and pressed, lined up like toy soldiers. I'd been ordered to go and couldn't get out of it.

Close up, Bremmer doesn't seem quite real. Like an overexposed holo. He has small eyes. They remind me of a pig's. Alert, like a pig's eyes, but there's nothing behind them. He's shorter than he looks on the tubes, and slightly overweight. He seems uncomfortable in his own skin, as if it doesn't quite fit. Osborne on the other hand is all confidence. He doesn't walk, he glides. Silky, smooth. They shared the podium but hardly looked at each other. They're specialists, bred for their jobs. What they share is underneath the veneer. It's fear.

Anyone with guts acts in spite of the fact that they're afraid. Not these two. They act *because* they're afraid. There's a big difference. Maybe only fleshers understand that. Bremmer and Osborne only believe in one thing: fear. It's what feeds them and what they feed others. It's a drug, and they're hooked.

One of those still winter days when the light comes late and when it arrives it dazzles silver over the banns. Your breath hangs in front of you, shining and crystalline. So cold it hurts to breathe in, but I still left off my suit. The cold cleared my head. And I wanted the air on my face, unfiltered sound, the smell of the ground, iron oxide coming off the walls, sharp and sour. Days like these, the Second is magic.

Face it, I love this place, these crooked old rues with their scrubby gardens and cafes and bars and shijos. I have a sudden hankering for pho. You don't get pho like this in Newport City, not with that real broth, wild mint and chilli grown in someone's plot, proper salt sauce fermented from snails in pots buried out the back. Organic, complex. No souped up molecular chef can match that, not even the sensory implants which they say can reproduce any sensation down to the smallest differential.

Yeah, maybe it's just sentimental. Maybe I'm just getting old. Tired, sure, but I've been tired for years.

I send in a report to cover my arse, that I'm following up yesterday's incident with the fleshers, no need to send someone, focus on the AI and get shit done. Maybe if I ride them hard enough they'll come up with something plausible and bury this crap. Then I wander down to Rue Ballard for some of Kojo's pho. Bel's standing in her front garden, hands on her hips, issuing instructions to an artisan. They'd blasted the door right out of its frame. We exchange nods, and I go into Café Boite and order the soup.

I slurp it slowly in the corner, watching Kojo and that daughter of his out of the corner of my eye. Black fleshers, they dislike Aps more than most. For good reason, I guess, black fleshers and avants tend to get the worst of it. There's no black pinkers in Newport City. They're dealing with the lunch crowd, heads down and busy, pretending that I'm not there, but I see the girl snatching glances. Pure, undiluted hatred. I don't hang around, I can see I'm bad for custom. Aps aren't popular in Rue Ballard today.

Then I go across to Bel's and we have a chat.

It's been a while. I try to stay out of her hair: better for me, better for her. I begin official, asking questions, checking the bugs. Bel plays along, asks me to sit down, makes a cup of tea. There's nothing suss on the bugs, I expect Dez saw to that, so I copy the record, call them in and disable them. Check in case I'd missed anything, give a warning, make as if to go. Turn off my comm.

I look at Bel properly. She looks tired, more tired than I feel. Grey at her temples, too thin. But still Bel. I kick away the old ache.

I'm sorry about last night, I say. I wasn't there when the trace came in.

For a moment her face hardens and I see the toll. Then she recovers herself. It's not your fault, she says.

Seems to me that Dez was careless, I say. You were lucky.

She glances at me quickly, and then looks away.

Bel, I tell her, I know Dez runs illegal tech. If you don't know that you're not as smart as I know you are, and I know you. You can't turn your face from that. If this hasn't been a warning, I don't know what is.

Bel isn't going to admit anything, even to me. She says nothing. I lick my lips. My mouth is dry, I don't know how I'm going to say the other thing. I'm not sure if Bel knows.

Dez, I say, she's different, isn't she.

There's that shy smile, half pride, half worry. She's a smart one, for sure, she says.

But more than that.

She gets defensive. What do you mean? Yeah, she's clever, too clever for her own good, like her dad. But she's just a kid. She meets my gaze, her eyes wide and clear and truthful, and I know then that she knows. She's lying through her teeth.

I'm just saying, maybe I can guess one or two things, I tell her. And not just me. There's a skinner alert out, she must have left some DNA lying about somewhere and some bright spark got suss and had it analysed. Maybe we could deal with that, skinners are just skinners. But after last night, I'm worried that OpSec might get involved.

Bel bites her lip, now she's not trying to hide.

It was her who did the AI, I say. I know that, you know that. I'm doing my best to keep a lid on it, but things are changing in the precincts, new admin, new protocol. I might not be able to. If it goes to shit, I'll let you know, but you'll have to be ready in case.

We just look at each other. And suddenly it's like twenty years ago and I have that sinking feeling in my gut, like everything's just run out of me and left me limp as a mollusc. I don't know why this woman does this to me. It isn't like she's beautiful. But she does, every time. And she knows it.

God damn it.

She takes my hand. I flinch. I'm mostly used to touching, but with Bel it's a whole other thing.

Brian, thank you, she says. That's kind of you.

I clear my throat. I tell her I'll send word if I can't stop it going up to OpSec. I squeeze her hand and let go. But you tell Dez, I say. No funny business now. She's got to be clean as a whistle. Cleaner. Until all this blows over. If it blows over, I think, but I don't say that.

We talk for a while, this and that, nothing important. It's the light in her face, I reckon. When she's thinking, and the thinking is in her eyes, and it's like that winter sunlight, cold and alive and dazzling. I've never seen it in anyone else. A little in Dez.

I don't want to go, but I leave soon after. It's too easy to go back there, and it's better not to. Better for me, better for her.

Bo

I went to see Flora at Café Boite and asked her if she could get in touch with Morro. I knew that she and Morro were friends: there was something between them, something solid. That was why Dez got so jealous.

'I can't get in touch with him,' she said. We were sitting down the back near the door to the kitchen. It was early afternoon and the place was half empty. 'But I know someone who might be able to.'

Flora never gives much away about anything. She likes to think of herself as enigmatic. To me it's just her being a pain in the balls.

'Tell him that I want to hook up, that it's important.'

'It might not happen.'

'It's not going to happen for sure if I don't even get to ask him.'

She didn't say anything to that. She pushed back her hair. It was always hanging down over her eyes in ringlets and sometimes it was hard to see where she was looking. She was looking at me right now.

'You were at the gig the other night.'

'Yeah. I was.'

'So?'

'So what?'

'We were doing a lot of new stuff, trying it out, new beats, a lot more impro.'

'It was brilliant. You know it was.'

She smiled, pleased and shy, and let her hair fall back over her face. It still surprises me, how different Flora off stage is from Flora on stage. You'd never guess that they were the same person, that such energy and joy, a kind of radiance, could burst out of her when she was performing with her mob.

I finished my mokal, spooning up the sweet sludge at the bottom of the glass. I stood to go, but Flora took hold of my sleeve. 'How's Dez?'

'She's okay.'

'Did they hurt her?'

'You know Dez. She wouldn't tell you if they did. She's shtum, like always.'

'Say hello to her from me.'

'Why don't you say it yourself?'

'You know why.'

'No, I don't really.'

Flora let go and picked up her drink. 'Sure. Whatever. See you, Bo.'

I left it at that. There was no working those two out. They'd have to do that themselves.

It was a couple of days before I heard anything from Morro. I was in the local steamer doing the weekly laundry when Kiko drifted in.

'Hey, Bo. I think you dropped this.'

'What?'

She held out her fist. I put my hand under it and she dropped something onto my palm. I looked down at what I was holding. It was a piece of yellowish bone, a knuckle maybe, from some feral. The letter 'M' was scratched on one side. I turned the bone over in my palm, feeling a sudden clutch in my gut. This must be it.

She leant close and whispered in my ear. 'S9.9W7.6.'

At first I didn't get it. 'What?'

She repeated the figures impatiently. 'Say it back,' she said. 'You've got to remember.'

I swallowed and did what she said.

'Two nights,' she said, and floated out without saying another word. I put the bone in my pocket, realising that my mouth was dry, and ran the numbers in my head to fix them.

Back home I brought up a map of the banns on Dez's portable, which I knew was secure. I tapped in the co-ordinates, clocked the location and then wiped the map.

It was going to be a long trip there and back.

Close to the Veil at the edge of the Twelfth, where it runs down to a narrow shoreline of black sand, there's what's left of a old power station. Nobody goes into that part of the Twelfth. It's sick with gaus and nekas and other ferals that roam in packs, seriously toxic.

I went downstairs to see Dez, who was finishing repairing my suit. She'd done more than just patch it up, she'd practically rebuilt it.

'You've really done a job on this,' I said as she handed me my belt.

'Switch on and you're invisible.'

'Really?'

'No, not really, you boofhead.'

I switched on. Normally I'd feel a little queasy for a few secs, but that didn't happen. I felt a kind of shock run up my spine and then it was like my skull opened up and filled with cool air. I felt light as a feather. Dez tried to hide how pleased she was when she saw the look on my face.

'It'll do,' I said.

The day I was to meet Morro I got up early, cleaned my room and took out the garbage. Then I kept a low profile. I had to be relaxed when I spun Ma the story about the gig I was going to. I don't like lying to Ma. Usually it's just about small stuff, like where a gig is happening. If it's in the Tenth, I'll tell her it's in the Eighth. That's as far as she thinks it's safe to go. But Ma can see right through me most of the time. It drives me bats.

She was lying in bed. She'd arranged for a pal of hers to open up her stall in the shijo. She said she was just tired, but it was more than that. She was like Dez when it came to keeping secrets. Her face was ashen, her breath short and sharp. Days like this came and went and she didn't want any fuss made. She'd get through, she'd always get through, she said, she just needed to be left alone. Sometimes Ma is too tough for her own good.

I brought her some cold water with mint leaves. 'You're very quiet today,' she said.

'I'm resting up. It's a big night tonight. A gig. Lots of dancing I reckon.'

'Call it dancing, do you?'

'Is there a better word?'

'Where's this happening?'

'Over in the Fifth. I'll catch the mono. I might be late.'

She sipped her water. She was thinking, which wasn't a good sign. 'The Fifth? Bit unusual.'

'Is it?'

'It's very quiet in the Fifth. The morgue's there.'

'I don't think anyone in the morgue is going to worry about a bit of noise.' Before she could say anything else, I made for the door. 'Anyway, no one will hear us, we'll be underground, in one of the old city reservoirs. They're huge, those things, and deep.'

'And dry, I hope.'

'They've been dry for a hundred years.'

Before I left I went down into the cellar to see Dez. She was bent over her workbench, busy with something, but I could feel that she didn't have her shields down.

'I'm going in a minute,' I said.

'Come here.'

I went over and stood next to her. She looked up at me. 'What do you think?'

My leather jacket was on the bench in front of her. Somehow she'd managed to repair the damage the Aps had done. I could still see where they'd slashed the leather, but now instead of gaping holes there were long, thick scars, like zippers of flesh. It looked brilliant.

'How'd you do it?'

'Trade secret, brother.'

I pulled on the jacket. It felt good.

'You got those co-ordinates straight in your head?'

'Yeah,' I said.

'Don't forget to use your map,' she said. 'I upgraded up the Magnetic Positioning System in our suits when I fixed them. It should be good within a centimetre now.'

Now Dez was just fussing. It's her way of expressing concern. We knew the danger that each of was facing. I'd be on the other side of the Wall and out of contact, Dez would be worming her way into OpSec. We'd both be on our own.

'I'll be fine,' I said. 'I should be back around midnight.'

'I'm not going anywhere. You want me to wait up for you? I'll tuck you up in bed.'

'Sure.'

'Be careful. I hope it's worth it.'

'You too.'

She stood up and adjusted the jacket on my shoulders. Then she stepped back and took a look at me. 'It looks really good on you. Really.'

'I know.'

She gave me a hug and then pushed me away. 'Don't do anything too ridiculous.'

'Would I?'

She sat back down and turned to her bench, already half absent, already focusing on some other project. She activated her shield.

'Dez...'

She didn't turn around, but the shield was suspended. 'What?'

'Flora says hello.'

Dez just nodded. The shield came down around her and she was gone.

It was getting dark when I climbed the stairs to the local mono station. The South-East line was one of the only two still functioning. Lines in the south and west had been shut down years ago and some sections in the Seventh and Eighth had been torn up for scrap. Things are mainly pretty good in the Second, but bits of it are falling to pieces, like they are everywhere. None of the lights on the platform worked. I couldn't remember when they last did.

There weren't many people on the platform. A couple and their three kids, a geezer in a motorized chair. On the platform opposite an Ap and an

AI out on patrol were just leaving, the little blue lights on the AI flashing slowly. A buzzer sounded as the mono slid into the station. It was an old driverless model, a yellow snub nose, covered in smears of rust, filth and graffiti. I took a seat by the window in an empty compartment. I'd travel as far as the edge of Tenth and go through the South-East porte into the Eleventh. I was pretty sure that I could catch a homer through most of the Eleventh. I'd probably hoof it through the Twelfth from there.

As the mono gained speed, I looked out of the grimy window at the city stretched out below me. Above the black horizon of the Wall, the Outer Veil shimmered faintly. Beyond it the sky was fading from blue to violet. A bank of clouds in the west shone like silver.

Lights were coming on in the rues and towerblocks and to the east I could see the flickering of hundreds of small fires. Parts of the Sixth had been blacked out for a few weeks and the rues were lit with torches and bonfires. My eyes rested on the Wall, the long band of darkness that separated the middle and outer banns. I'd be on the other side pretty soon, with nothing but the thin membrane of energy that was the Veil between me and the dasht. Whenever I was out there, it felt like walking along the edge of a cliff.

I checked the controls on my suit and moved around in my seat to hear the creak of my leather jacket. I touched the bone that Kiko had given me, still in my pocket. I felt good.

Dez

Me and Flora. Flora and me. It's been us ever since we moved to the Second. I remember the day we arrived, everything we owned in a beaten-up old transport. It was summer, clear pale blue through the Veil, cold sunshine. Kojo had put tables outside Café Boite, and Flora was sitting at one of them, her chin on her hands, watching us. It was novel enough having outside tables, in the Ninth no one would have dared. It was the first thing that told me things were different here, behind the Wall.

Our eyes met and she smiled and I felt dizzy. And basically that was it.

Once the transport left, Kojo did the neighbourly thing. He brought around a bottle of mokal and a plate of broken rice and introduced himself. Flora was really shy then, she hung around behind him, peeping out from behind her curly hair. Everything was still in containers except our beds and Ma had already suggested that we check out the café opposite for dinner. I saw Ma flush as she thanked him, as if she might burst into tears. Sometimes kindness does that.

Anyway, in less than a week Flora and me were inseparable. We did everything together. I even told her about me. She's the only person who knows, aside from Bo and Ma. And then, after a gig a few months ago when she was there singing, her hair all staticed up around her head in a halo so she looked like a goddess, one thing led to another and we were more than friends. That's when all the trouble started. I told you feelings are trouble.

That's when I began to want her all for my own, which I hadn't really felt before. I'd get toxic when she saw other people.

Flora doesn't take well to that, she says that I don't trust her. She says that just because I love her, it doesn't mean that I own her. Of course she's right, but that's not the point. I didn't really care until she started talking about Morro and I heard that hero worship in her voice. Well, who wouldn't think that Morro is a hero? Enigmatic, handsome, charisma of a rock star. Only he's not a rock star and Flora actually is. I think he's just an arrogant prick who wants to steal my girlfriend.

And then Flora disappeared overnight after a gig, snapping closed our private line. I knew she wasn't in trouble, her suit was still registering as live and undistressed, and as far as I was concerned there was only one reason to lock me out. Morro had been at that gig doing the full glamour, eyeliner tattoos, silver glitter sweeping up those chiselled cheekbones, hair sharp as a knife. Usually the Alchems get around in cast-off military gear, all kinds of anonymous grunge, but when they party they go all out. Tight silver jacket, crimson cravat, velvet pants, silver codpiece. No one has the right to look cool in gear like that. He was staring at her all through the gig like he was hypnotised.

When Flora turned up again I went for her like a feral, all teeth and viciousness, and said every ugly thing I could think of, whether I believed it was true or not. She wouldn't tell me what she had been doing. She told me I was a freak, that she didn't know what she'd seen in me, that I could take my mutant freak wired body and fuck right off out of her life.

That was more than a month ago and things have been bad between us ever since.

It's taken every bit of willpower I have not to put a trace on her, so I know what she's doing every second of the day. That's too creepy even for me, and if she ever found out I'd done anything like that, it would be the end. So I haven't. I know she wonders sometimes if I have. All my not trusting her has made her not trust me.

But despite all that shit, I knew she would be there when we came home from the precinct. And she was. It should have been all right then, but some-how it wasn't. We'd had such a bad fight, we'd said unforgiveable things. I still didn't know if she'd forgive me, and when I saw her in the rue, I was sure she hadn't. She'd lift her chin and flick away her eyes, and then my pride would kick in. It was like a standoff, who was going to say sorry first. I was sure as hell that it wasn't going to me.

I missed her so badly. It was like a toothache, it was there all the time, and I had nothing to keep my mind off it. Ma didn't ask me about Flora, but she knew. She was just extra kind. Sometimes she'd grab me and hug me for no reason. But I knew there was something else. Ma told me that Brian Mac warned her about me, that he had guessed about my abilities. If Brian Mac was speculating it was bad news. He wouldn't be the first. And whatever the skinners knew was probably more specific than I realised.

So I was keeping a low profile. I talked to my dealer and said no dice until everything calmed down. She knew about the raid so she asked no questions. After I fixed our suits and Bo's jacket and the broken security, I put all my special gear away in my stash. I had a few jobs, fixing comms and seals and that kind of thing, but that was just routine stuff I didn't have to think about. I was bored out of my skull and I had nothing to do except worry.

I spent most of my time wondering how to get into OpSec. Over the past few years I'd plugged into most of the Newport City networks, but up to now I had left anything to do with OpSec alone. The crypto bristled with danger, bells and alarms everywhere. I knew I could get in, I just didn't know how to do it without anyone noticing. Secretly I hoped that I wouldn't have to break in at all. But then I'd think about what Brian Mac told Ma, about protocols changing under the new admin, and the new AIs. I was pretty sure that there'd be plenty that a lowly precinct Brig didn't know about, and it was nagging at me. All those new Aps meant something.

The person I would normally talk to when I was worried was Flora, but that wasn't on. For days my thoughts went around and around, like a rat in a cage that didn't have any door.

After Bo left to meet Morro, I tried to go on working, to stop me worry-ing about what I was going to do after Ma went to bed, but I couldn't. One more thing to worry about. The Twelfth was one of the worst banns and Bo was going out of my range, behind the Wall, so I wouldn't know if anything happened to him except if he didn't come back.

It wasn't just skinners. There were animals living in the ruins, some of them as dangerous as anything you might meet in the dasht, and hot zones that were still poisoned even after all these years. Bo's suit would take care of most of it, but if a feral gau went for him and broke something, he'd be screwed. I tried not to think about what might happen and the more I tried not to, the more all the worst scenarios played out in my head. I went upstairs and talked to Ma, but she saw I was jumpy and started questioning me about where Bo had gone. He'd spun her some story about a gig, so I backed it up, but she was still suss.

I kept looking out of the front room to Café Boite. They'd just closed for the night. Flora was wiping down tables, chatting to Kojo. Even from this distance I could tell that she knew I was watching her. She was pretending that she didn't notice.

'Why don't you go over,' said Ma suddenly. She was sitting at the table drawing a portrait of Bo. She often drew pictures of us, especially when she was anxious, she said it calmed her down. 'Just say hello.'

I didn't answer for a while. 'What if she won't talk to me?' I said. The way I was feeling, I didn't think I could bear it.

'You wouldn't be any worse off than you are now,' said Ma. She gave me one of her direct looks. 'Go on. I can't stand you glumping around the house. You're miserable. Do something about it.'

I hunched my shoulders. 'She should say sorry first,' I said. Even as I said it, I knew I sounded five years old.

'You're being ridiculous,' said Ma. 'You're both sorry. You both know it.'

She turned back to her scrawling, and I thought about it. Ma was right, she usually was on things like this. Maybe I should just do it. If I thought about it any longer I knew I wouldn't, so I stood up, kissed Ma on the cheek and went out.

I could see Flora watching me as I crossed the street. I almost changed direction, pretended I was heading somewhere else, but I didn't. I walked up to the door and knocked. Kojo answered. There was a twinkle in his eye which I ignored, the last thing I needed was anyone laughing at me. Flora was sorting cutlery, her face turned away from me. I walked straight up her and held out my hand. Kojo went out the back, being tactful I guess, and we were alone. I took a deep breath.

'I'm sorry,' I said. 'I'm really sorry. I miss you so bad.'

She looked at me through her hair, her mouth set in a straight, stubborn line. My heart dropped. This wasn't going to go well. I waited for her to tell me to go to hell and never come back.

'You hurt me, Dez,' she said. 'I never want you to hurt me like that ever again.'

I opened my mouth to tell her how much she had hurt me, and then I remembered what Ma said and thought better of it.

'I don't want to hurt you,' I said. 'I never wanted to hurt you.'

I went to pull back my hand, because I felt silly standing there like that with her ignoring it, but she grabbed it and pulled it to her cheek. I saw that there were tears brimming in her eyes.

'I miss you too, Dez.'

It was like a light turned on in my chest. I thought that I'd burst with happiness.

Bo

As the mono approached the south-east porte I looked up at the Wall, a massive, blank nothingness as tall as a towerblock, black with age, unreal looking. The Wall was the next layer of protection from whatever mean shit might get through the Outer Veil. Halfway between the Outer and Inner Veils it circled the city, dividing the banns. There were only half a dozen portes.

The thing that always struck me about the Wall was how silent it was. It was ridiculous really, I mean how could a wall not be silent? But this thing seemed to throb with silence. If you yelled at it there was no echo. If you threw something at it, it made no sound. It seemed to absorb everything and give nothing back. It was just a solid block of emptiness.

Now that I was on the other side I'd have to be vigilant. It could get filthy out here.

As soon as I stepped into the rue outside the mono station I felt a presence. I turned up my suit. My skin cooled slightly, my awareness heightened. I felt naked, exposed, which was weird because actually I was the opposite. The suit didn't pick up any threat, but the feeling still nagged me. Maybe I was just imagining things. This side of the Wall, there was no way that Dez could reach me. Maybe I just felt vulnerable. I was on my own.

It was dark by now and hardly anyone was out on the rues. They felt hollowed out. A new water drilling site had started operating just a block from the mono station and houses around the site's perimeter had been emptied. Hundreds of people had been tossed out of their homes. There had been protests and a lot of raids and opposition to the drilling had been crushed. Now people were hunkered down, staying out of sight, out of trouble. I could see the site in the distance, floodlit, surrounded by a steel fence, guarded by militia. I kept well away.

I turned on my MPS. The Eleventh was pretty much a blank to me. I'd been to plenty of gigs in the Tenth because that was where the first wave of the music I loved had started its life, in those backblocks. But the further you went into the Eleventh the less people there were. I'd never ventured very far into that territory. By the Twelfth I'd be in a wasteland.

I needed to find a homer. If I couldn't I had a very long walk ahead of me. It was more than twelve klicks across the Eleventh, most of it in darkness.

I started walking. I made myself think about music, the mobs I'd seen play in abandoned buildings, in the shells of the factories and the dried-out city reservoirs. That was where the music happened, where the young guns made their noise, where I'd made my steadies and first felt how music could tell you things you'd never heard before and let you know that what you felt didn't make you a freak, that you weren't alone. I remembered the music, I let it play in my head.

It didn't help. Something kept bothering me and I couldn't shake it.

Three blocks into the bann and there weren't any working lights. I could only see my way because of the glow of the Outer Veil above me. It was a weird, dead kind of light that flattened everything out, made shadows black.

I heard the homer before I saw it, the click of the ignition, the rattle and throb of the engine. The yellow beam of its headlight washed over me as it came out of a narrow street on my left, moving at walking pace. As it came closer I made out the driver. He was in red leather, black shades, a long white beard to his waist.

'Need a ride?' he said.

I nodded and hopped into the side car.

'The Twelfth.'

The driver grunted, revved the engine. 'We'll see about that,' he said.

The engine struggled to get much over thirty klicks an hour. We went down rues lined with dozens of boarded-up factories, abandoned or fire-gutted towerblocks standing like sentinels against the pale glimmer of the Veil, wide, empty patches of ground. Here and there I saw a light in a window or the glow of a small bonfire in the distance. Two mangy gaus leapt across the road in front of us, barking. We passed under the dead mono rails of the South Line.

The driver didn't talk, just stared straight ahead. I wondered how he could see anything from behind those black shades. His long beard blew back over his shoulder like a ragged flag. He took me as far as the demolitions and stopped, the engine idling.

'Ride's over, buddy,' he said.

I paid and got out and he went back the way we'd come. I watched until he was well out of sight and started walking. I'd heard about this place, but I'd never seen it.

Whole blocks of the Eleventh had been torn down thirty years ago. Back then there had been a plan to raze the whole of the Eleventh and Twelfth to make them a no-go area. Like so many things, the work was started but never finished. Now there was this wide scar, a dead, wind-blown place, like a dasht in the middle of the city. I could have gone straight across, but feeling the way I did I decided to skirt around it. It would take me a while, but I wasn't going to put myself out there in the open with nowhere to hide.

I headed down a narrow rue between two decayed tower blocks. I hadn't gone far when I felt my suit fade. I looked at my hands and they were blurred, opaque. I hit the booster switch Dez had installed. She'd told me to only use it in emergencies because it was a power drain, but I decided to risk it. I felt a surge of energy through the suit and my hands cleared. I kept moving.

I hadn't gone more than a klick when I heard her voice.

'Vous êtes seul, tout seul?'

She was somewhere close. But her voice was more inside my head than outside so I couldn't tell what direction it was coming from. I froze.

'J'arrive tout de suite.'

They speak this lingo in the Tenth, mostly in the Rift, a mess of home-builds and oldtech wire-ups that run along the edge of a deep concrete gash filled almost to the top with garbage, black with rubbish and pollution. I'd been there a couple of times because I'd heard that there was a new kind of sound coming out of the shanties, mobs playing home-mades and squawking shit no one had ever heard before. It didn't appeal. It was like having your head sliced open.

I drew my taser from inside my jacket. It wasn't much of a weapon normally, the kind of thing that you might use to scare off ferals or blast rats. But Dez had done a job on it, like she did jobs on everything we had. Now it could blow a person's head off.

I held the taser against my chest, my finger on the trigger, and slowly turned 360 degrees. Nothing. Just the walls of the tower blocks, the broken windows, the doorless holes into the blackness inside.

By the time I'd turned back to where I'd started, she was standing in front of me, no more than two metres away.

She had no face.

Her black coat reached to the ground and she wore a blue bandolier that carried her hormone extraction gear. She was wearing blue gloves. Where her face should have been there was just a blur, some function of her suit that erased her features, moving like a patch of head-shaped sky filled with clouds.

She was holding something in her right hand that looked like a thin strip of steel. As I watched it grew long and thin, tapering to a fine point, catching what little light there was. She held it upright. It was a stinger. I'd heard about them but had never seen one. It wasn't much more than a needle, but it was a metre long. Flexible yellow steel. A skinner weapon.

Her head tilted. 'What's that you've got there, sweetheart? You want to blast me?'

I clutched the taser hard against my chest. I didn't want her to see that my hand was shaking.

She took a small step forward and lifted her stinger. 'This doesn't have to take long.'

I threw out my arm and pointed my taser at her head. If she had had a face I think I would have seen her smile.

'Très drole, mon ange.'

I pulled the trigger. The blast threw me backwards and onto my arse. The air cracked and the whole rue lit up. My arm cramped and was sticking straight out in front of me, the taser still shrouded in green vapour.

I heard her stepping towards me. 'This will hurt, sweetie. Be brave.'

She lifted her stinger and pointed it straight at my eyes. I clamped them shut. They'd finally got me.

Fuck this, I thought, fuck it.

And then nothing. My heart was bashing away so hard inside my chest that I could hear it. That's all I could hear. I don't know how long I was on the ground like that. Time had stopped.

'Having a little nap, are we?' I opened my eyes to see Morro's face hovering over me.

He pulled me to my feet. I was shaking so much I could hardly stand up. Morro took the taser from my hand and I managed to lower my arm. He slipped the weapon back inside my jacket. It was still warm. The skinner was on her back a few metres away, her head a little ball of blue flame.

I turned to Morro. 'How did you...what did you . . .?'

'Sonics,' he said. 'Beyond hearing. Like boring a hole.'

He went over to the skinner, wrenched the stinger free from her hand and stood there admiring it.

'But how did you get here?' I said. 'Were you here all the time? How the hell did you do that?'

He turned to me. I couldn't read the look on his face, but it was something between a grimace and a smile.

'I'm not here, Bo. I doubled. See you at the meeting place.'

In a blink he wasn't standing there any more.

Dez

The way I figured it, the secret was speed.

If I was fast enough, maybe OpSec wouldn't pick up an invasion. I've perfected a lot of techniques over the years trawling through Newport City data, inversing quantum entanglements to nullify my presence, that sort of thing, and I'm always fast. But OpSec is something else, and their new crypto even more so. I knew what I had been doing so far wasn't good enough.

Maybe OpSec had picked up that data was being copied from the city media frames before I figured out how to cover my tracks, back when the splice first happened, and they got alarmed. Or maybe they just figured they had to keep ahead. Whatever the reason, over the past year they'd kicked up the security.

The new OpSec system uses tachyon computing, which means they can move the data faster than light. I know to manipulate tachyons. OpSec uses a highly refined version of the tech used for timeslip implants, which are nominally illegal because they make all sorts of causality trouble even when the slips are stabilised and the subject doesn't explode in a puff of exotic matter. Mainly the street implants fake it with VR and IMR, *in media res*, so the timeslip is illusion more than anything, but you still have to have at least a bit of the real thing to get the buzz. Brian Mac uses the hardcore implants, I know that for sure because I know his supplier, and I know his supplier because she gets the implants from me.

It's hard to describe in words what I do when I'm streaming data. No, it's impossible to describe. Words are too slow, they're flesher things, mouth, palate, tongue, breath. When Flora called me a mutant freak wired body, she was right. That's why it hurt so bad. I *am* a freak. I can go through an exabyte of data in the time it takes to say 'boo'. It's not just my brain, it's everything. Every single one of my 37.2 trillion cells is a little bioquantum computer.

This doesn't make me smarter than your average smart person. I'm smart, sure, but holding a lot of data isn't the same as understanding it. There's other dimensions to knowledge. Which is why I like slow things, words, music, sex, why I'm a flesher first and last, why I won't permit myself to become a data ghost. I could become like that, I know I could, and sometimes it's tempting to lose myself in those shimmering webs, but I won't let that happen. I'm me and I always will be, no matter what. Even when I die. Especially when I die.

I've thought about all this a lot.

If someone's analysed my DNA, I'm in real trouble. I'm pretty careful about DNA hygiene, I vaporise all my hair and nail clippings and so on, but basically I've relied on me being impossible and therefore not something other people would even think of looking for. But skinners are always tracking biomatter and maybe someone caught a trace of me. If a skinner's scanned my DNA, it won't be long before the Aps or OpSec get hold of that information. Because I'm the missing link, the actual bond between AI and biosentience. They've hunted that for centuries, never quite getting there, leaving a trail of broken minds in their wake. In the end everyone basically agreed to let AIs do what AIs do, and let the biosentience get on with what it does. The Ap-AI model. It works pretty well.

But me, I'm it. I know it. And if they look at my DNA, they'll know it too. And then hormones will be the least of my troubles.

The only way I'll know my status for sure is if I can get into the classified files. And here I am, back at the beginning. How do I do it without getting caught, without them even knowing I was there?

Speed. I have to be faster than the speed of light, and then faster than that.

That's impossible. But then, so am I.

Or maybe...

Maybe I could go in slow. So slow they couldn't see me.

Bo

As I entered the Twelfth, I could see the power station in the distance, a tall dark shape against the glow of the Outer Veil. Before I reached it I had to pass through a wild. There are a lot of them scattered through the outer banns. At one time they might have been parks or market gardens or maybe just open spaces. There isn't anything like that now.

I know something about plants. Ma's good at growing things, we've got our own garden, and she's taught me what she knows. Us fleshers grow our own food in little gardens all over the banns, and Dez and I have both worked in the foodtowers. Some pinkers like their delicacies hand-picked, stuff like their winter flowers, their purple greens and their ice berries. It gives them a buzz, that feeling they call authenticity, although they make sure it's not too authentic. When you work as a picker you have to wear a biosuit, two-skin gloves and a breather. We don't actually touch any plants. We don't even breathe on them.

In the wilds, anything that survives the winds that blow in from the dasht has changed. The insects are bigger, midges like mini drones, fat, black flies buzzing in swarms. The plants reminded me of things I'd seen growing in the foodtowers, but everything looked a little distorted, thicker, greener and heavier. Everything smelt stronger. Some smells made you gag, or stung the back of your throat.

It took me about half an hour to pass through the wild. When I got to the other side, the power station rose up in front of me, seven stories high and just as wide, a bleak-looking, black steel square. From here, I could hear the wind blowing out over the Gilla Sea. I wondered how I was going to find Morro in such an enormous place, but after what had happened with the skinner, I figured that Morro would find me.

The huge doors were open. I walked into darkness. I couldn't even see my hand in front of my face. I tried to turn on the lights in my suit, but there was nothing doing. I turned around and looked back outside. The faint glow of the Veil had vanished, as if a wall had slammed down behind me, but I could still feel the air moving on my face.

I called out for Morro, but I could hardly hear myself, it was like I was shouting under water. I kept moving forward, one step at a time, thinking that I'd come to something, a wall maybe or some stairs, anything. But I was so cold and the darkness felt so thick around me, as if it was somehow clinging to my body, that I could hardly move at all.

I shouted Morro's name again, as loudly as I could. I could feel my voice tearing my throat, but now I couldn't hear myself at all. I gave up. I just stood there waiting. But maybe there was nothing to wait for. Maybe this was another skinner's trap.

A hand dropped onto my shoulder and I nearly jumped out of my skin. 'Don't wear yourself out, Bo.'

It was Morro. I wanted to punch him in the face.

'Did you have to scare the shit out of me?' I said. My skin tingled with sudden warmth and the light from outside slowly flooded over me.

'It takes a while for the lightlock to disengage,' said Morro. 'Sorry about that.' He turned and walked up the iron stairs which were right there next to us. I followed him, trying to regain my cool. As if I had any left.

At the top of the building we walked along a narrow corridor whose broken windows looked out over the Gilla Sea. Up there the wind howled. I could see Duiwel Island prison floating far out in the darkness, its domed Veil glowing. It looked unreal, almost beautiful.

I caught up with Morro. 'So what's this doubling thing?'

'It's complicated,' he said. 'I can't hold it for long, not if I want to actually be there.'

I could tell he wasn't going to explain any more. He opened a steel door at the end of the corridor and we entered his inner sanctum. 'You can switch off your suit. This place is sealed.'

I stared, trying not to look too impressed. The room was filled to the ceiling with stacks of oldtech. There were two long work benches crowded with who-knew-what kind of instruments and glassware. I saw the stinger Morro had taken from the skinner leaning up against one of the benches. Plants in huge pots stood in each corner—the dreamweed they chew in the Outer Banns—and there was a large table in the centre of the room covered with rolls of yellowed paper and shiny transparencies. And piles of books.

'Where'd you get those?' I said, pointing at the books.

'They're the Newport Annals,' he said. 'From back when people still made those kinds of things. Even when they were first printed they were a throwback, a symptom of nostalgia. Of course, it was a nostalgia for something that they never actually experienced. But it was real all the same.'

I hoped that Morro wasn't going to launch into one of his lectures. He knew the whole history of Newport, but it seemed to take as much time to tell it as it did for it to happen. I'd sat through a couple of his raves in the past. I hadn't managed to stay awake through either of them.

Morro grinned. Maybe he'd plugged in and could read me.

'Thanks,' I said. 'Thanks for seeing me.'

'You make it sound like a medical appointment. What do you want?'

I decided to get straight to the point. 'We could be in trouble. Me, Dez and Ma.'

'I know. Bad news travels fast.'

'What do you know?'

'More than you, probably.'

Morro can get kind of annoying. It's that superior Alchem pose. I took a deep breath. 'I'm asking for help,' I said. 'I mean, if we need help. I want to know if you can do anything.'

'Like what?'

'The Alchems can disappear people.'

'That's what OpSec does.'

'I don't mean like that.'

He looked down at the floor. 'It's possible to hide people. Sometimes. It can be done if it has to be. But it's hard for everyone involved. We can only hide individuals.' He looked up at me again. 'If you're hidden, you'll be on your own.'

'But we'll be alive.'

'Yeah. You'll be alive. But even that isn't always possible. We have to find places and times that are outside of the usual. We have to find…exceptions to the rules, cracks in the wall.'

He beckoned me over to the table and spread out one of the rolls of yellowed paper. It was a map of some kind, covered in markings that I didn't recognize and lines that snaked over the page in weird circular patterns. 'You can touch it if you like,' he said.

He must have been reading me. I wanted to touch the paper as soon as I saw it. I brushed it with my finger tips. It was as smooth as water. I imagined that I could feel the age of it flowing into my fingers. It was like it was alive.

'It isn't exactly a map,' said Morro.

'What is it?'

'It's a frequency of possibilities chart.'

'What's that?'

'I use it all the time. I guess the easiest way to explain it is that it notates the singular possibilities of change in an unchanging repetition of events. If it was a sheet of music it would be notating the notes between the notes, the ones you don't hear.'

'I hear those all the time.'

Morro smiled. 'I thought you might.'

I don't know how long we spent talking. I went through everything that had happened. I could tell that Morro was holding back, keeping up his guard. I did the same. When he started asking questions about Dez, I was especially careful. He knew that Dez was a genius with tech, he knew that there was something about her that made her different, but he didn't really know what it was.

I said that I didn't either. 'I just know that she's brilliant,' I said.

'What really happened to the Ap?'

'The AI killed him.'

'Sure, but why? How?'

'I don't know. I wasn't there.'

Morro didn't push it any further. He glanced at me, and then looked away. For a moment he almost seemed shy. 'Dez doesn't think much of the Alchems, does she?'

I shrugged. I wasn't going to tell him the things Dez says.

'That's what Flora told me,' he said.

'What else did Flora tell you?'

'This and that. Her and Dez are pretty close, aren't they?'

'Not just now they aren't. Anyway, that's their business.'

'Does Dez know you're here?'

'Yeah, she does.'

'I'd like to have a proper conversation with Dez one of these days. I think if she knew more about the Alchems she might not dismiss us so easily. We could really use someone with her capabilities.' He grinned at me. 'Whatever they are…'

I tried to imagine Dez and Morro having a conversation. They'd spoken to each other a few times, but it wasn't much more than two gaus giving each other a sniff. I didn't know what would happen if they actually had to talk.

Morro rolled up the map. 'You should go,' he said.

I felt like I was being dismissed. 'If the worst happens, if OpSec come after us…'

'We'll do what we can. It'll be complicated, and dangerous.' He grinned. 'Which is just how I like it.'

This time we took a different set of stairs, darker and steeper than those we climbed earlier. I clung to the railing the whole way, trying to keep up with Morro, who flew down as if they were brightly lit. At the bottom we came to a small chamber. Morro opened a steel trapdoor in the centre of the floor.

I looked down and all I could see was a black hole with no bottom, a ladder disappearing into the darkness.

'This is part of the old sewerage system. It runs to the Eighth. It's crawling with rodents and other things, but you won't run into any skinners.' He reached into his pocket and took out a small transparent sphere. 'You'll need this.'

He held it out to me and it lit up, filling the chamber with a soft, yellowish light.

'No need,' I said. My turn to show off. I switched on my hands. They began to glow softly, pulsing for a second or two before growing brighter and brighter, filling the chamber with intense, white light. I held my hands up and opened and closed them. Morro was impressed. The sphere he was holding went out and he slipped it back into his pocket.

'Dez rejigged my suit,' I said. 'They didn't work in that lightlock of yours, though.'

'Tell Dez. That'll ruffle her feathers.'

I laughed. I knew that it would.

'It'll take you about an hour or so to get to the Eighth. It comes up by Rue Maxim.'

I switched on my MPS and climbed into the hole. I looked up at Morro.

'Good luck,' he said. 'I'll be in touch.'

'Thanks,' I said.

When I got home, Dez was waiting.

Dez

Bo came in over the back wall, which he only did when he was especially paranoid. That meant he'd had a bad night. He sent a signal as soon as he was in range, which was unusually thoughtful of him, though as it was getting late I might have started pinging him every five minutes. I did that sometimes when I knew he was with a girl, it pissed him off bigtime. Even though I knew he was on the way home, I felt a whoosh of relief when I heard him fumbling at the door. I'd been curled up in my chair in the front room, waiting, terrified that he might stumble into something bad on the last leg of his trip.

Bo looked like shit, as if he'd lost about three kilos in the past few hours. There were black shadows under his eyes and his lips were pressed tight. Even so, the moment he saw me he knew something was up. Bo can pick up on my moods like no one else, not even Ma. It's annoying.

He slung his belt on the table and sat down heavily, studying my face.

'So what's wrong?'

I met his eyes. I was so tired I couldn't dissemble, but at first I didn't know how to answer.

'You haven't put OpSec onto us?'

I shook my head. 'No,' I said. 'I don't think so. No, I'm pretty sure they haven't tracked me. But Bo. It's awful.'

'What?'

Instead of answering, I put my head down on my knees and started crying. It just came out of me, I didn't expect it. I never cry. I felt Bo's surprise, and then he stood up and came around the table and hugged me.

'Hey Dezzie,' he said, like when we were kids. 'Hey Dezzie. It's okay.'

Finally I was able to stop. I gulped and wiped my face.

'It's not okay, Bo,' I said. 'There's going to be another cull.'

'A *what*?'

'A big cull.' I stared down at the table. I couldn't even imagine. Millions of people, massacred. 'They're saying there are too many of us. There's going to be a cull.'

I'd gone in like I planned, fast and slow. I oscillated between superluminal speeds and vibrations that were sometimes as long as a hundredth of a second. My theory was that it would make the security impossible to gain any purchase on me, but it was hard to hold. It seemed to work, and I didn't set off any alarms that I could sense. The crypto was a problem, because the new ones evolve organically, switching through an algorithmic process that builds unpredictability into the coding. But OpSec have to be able to read their own files, so once I was past the main firewall, they were back to basic coded data.

Then it was just a matter of stealing the data without anybody knowing I was there. Difficult, but I've done it thousands of times.

I searched our IDs, copying anything I could find so I could study it once I was out of there. There wasn't much. It seemed that Brian Mac had managed to stop anything about the dead Ap going further than the precinct, at least for now. Our names weren't even mentioned on the incident report.

Then I did a general search for anything about skinner informants, rogue DNA, that kind of thing. That's when I hit another firewall, much the same as the one I'd broken through to get into the system, but with two levels of coding. Super classified, restricted only to top level eyes. Something about it gave me the willies. Even most of OpSec wouldn't know that it existed.

I knew I'd regret it if I didn't look. So I did. I got in there, copied everything I could find, and got myself out as quickly as I could, inversing as I went, making double sure that everything went back to a state where I had never happened. On my way out I saw another firewall, even stronger than the second one. I wondered if I should get behind that too, but I was already pushing my luck. Any longer, a bot would notice. I got out of there.

The whole adventure took a few seconds, if that.

Back in my cellar, crunched through the data. Ours first.

Routine surveillance, nothing surprising. Ma was tagged, but we knew that; it was why she couldn't get work in the foodtowers or the low-tech factories in the banns. A hangover, she told us, from her wild youth, a part of her life that she never talked about. Bo and I respected her reticence, because it was tangled up with grief. We knew that Flynn, our dad, had been the love of her life, and that he and Ma had been up to all sorts of shady stuff before he was disappeared. We had both assumed it was about illegal scavenging and trading, but for the first time I started to wonder if it was something else.

Anyway, since Flynn had gone, Ma had kept her nose clean. There was nothing in her file, just a note on where we lived, and that she had two kids. 'Fleshbred' was the official term. Even through that dry OpSec officialese, you could hear the disgust.

Pinkers aren't born. They're made, grown in the baby farms and handed out through the family ministry once they pass the quality control. No mess of childbirth for them: no pain, no blood. Sex is all virtual, and for all their moralising about meatsex – which is what the rest of us call ordinary sex – they get pretty perverse with VR and IMR. That's why there's such a flourishing trade in flesher porn, and in the hormones that they flush through their systems to make them feel real. I'd read somewhere that the 'authentic' hormones aren't any different from the synthetics, but that doesn't stop them wanting them. And killing us to get them.

Fleshers are what they call us, though we use the name as a kind of perverse badge of pride. *Fleshers, breeders, meat*. They have all kinds of names for us. We call them pinkers, because of their skin, I guess, so smooth, so unmarked. They don't call themselves that. Pinkers don't call themselves anything. They don't have to, they are the measure of what is human.

Beyond our address, nothing much on us either. The dates Bo and I worked at the foodtowers, assessment reports. Standard stuff. Nobody had picked up on my dealing, not that high up, anyway. Good.

But my search had turned up a file on a suspected flesher splice who might have bonded with a rogue nano. A skinner informant, Habit Dyer, recently reported terminated. Dyer had noticed an odd aura around a DNA trace left on a timeslip implant and had it scanned. Well, that was handy to know. I was careful about DNA traces, like I said, but maybe living in the Second I had become complacent. I made a mental note to check my steriliser. Luckily Dyer had no access to the Newport City scanners, so he used a homebuild, and the results were predictably dodgy. But it interested OpSec enough for them to pay for the information and mark it 'for further investigation'.

They hadn't matched it with me. Yet.

There was no mention of our arrest and interrogation. Officer Lann was reported terminated, workplace accident, but there were no details on how. An ominous note, 'report forthcoming', but it was all pretty low level.

I made myself a brew and had a think. The only explanation was that Brian Mac was covering up the AI malfunction. The longer he kept the investigation local, the better our chances the whole thing would slip beneath the radar. I didn't know how he was doing it, but the raid was three days ago now. There should have been something in the files. Maybe Brian Mac had his own means of controlling intel. It made me feel slightly hopeful. For whatever reason, Brian Mac was protecting us.

Then I turned to the secret files. I zipped through this much more quickly. The first few files were harmless enough. Complaints that the previous administration had been slack, that there hadn't been a census of the banns for more than a decade. A few weird studies on flesher social habits, which were like something out of some sick pinker porno and resembled nothing I had ever witnessed in the banns. There were confidential reports on subversive activities from the Alchems (I read these with interest, I hadn't realised they were causing so much trouble, and felt a reluctant flicker of respect). A review of the resources of Newport: water, tech minerals, food production. Conclusion: resources were limited, and diminishing. The most serious problem was clean water.

I knew that already. That was what all the drilling in the banns was about, looking for new sources of water. It was all over the infonews. Some huge project, drilling in two sites in the Eighth and the Tenth. There'd been a bit of trouble when fleshers were thrown out of their homes.

Then I came to Plan One. Eliminate excess populace.

It hit me in the gut, like a physical blow. I felt sick.

I forced myself to read it.

Comments and further thoughts were invited.

I read those too.

According to the population estimates, there were more than five million people living in the banns. In Plan One, they figured that Newport City only needed one million fleshers, if that, to keep the foodtowers and low tech factories operational. (They don't trust fleshers with high tech, that all happens behind the Inner Veil).

There was a paragraph where they considered getting rid of all the fleshers, then concern expressed that total eradication might cause unrest and dissent in Newport City itself, quite aside from the labour shortage. I snorted. There were pinkers who worried about what happened to fleshers? Sure.

Well, I guess Brian Mac did. Up to what point, though?

There was a lot about politics, about getting the plan past the Newport City council. There were still people there from the old admin, who were in favour of letting the banns run themselves, limited rights for fleshers and so on.

I knew that the last really big cull was forty or fifty years ago. They stopped altogether when Ma was young, after some big rebellion made the pinkers sit up and take notice. That was when they totally banned fleshers from Newport City, but they also made concessions that allowed many of us to build some kind of decent life.

But even back in the bad old days the culls hadn't been on the same scale. They were talking about sterilising eight districts, everything but the Inner Banns.

Sterilising. What a word.

I read on. There were suggestions of biowarfare, some kind of plague, but those was discarded as too hard to control. The first plan was to send out AIs and drones and raze everything in sight, create a dead zone. Concern one: executing a cleansing on that scale without destroying the Veils. It would require munitions that would be difficult to contain safely, especially if there was resistance. Concern two: riots among the fleshers in the Inner Banns. Concern three: potential protests in Newport City. Concern four: getting rid of biomatter.

All those corpses. Millions of corpses. Research and development on dealing with that was well advanced. I felt the hair on my neck rise up with horror. I couldn't find any details on the research, and started wondering what was behind that third firewall.

The final document I read was signed off by Bremmer, CEO of Newport City OpSec, authorising preliminary plans to go ahead. The idea was to soften any resistance with a series of aggressive manoeuvres. At worst it would inspire a flesher revolt. If that happened, it would be politically safe to go ahead and cleanse everything, subject to safety requirements.

Safety requirements. I felt sick.

A reminder that Plan One had to remain strictly confidential. A suggestion that with the proper preparation, operations could begin as early as spring. It was still winter, spring was three months away. It was now Jul 29. Jul, Ag, Sep. A cull could begin mid-Octo, if approved by the proper authorities.

I looked to see if there was any approval. Couldn't find any.

One hundred and thirty eight days, maybe, until they murdered four million people.

I couldn't read any more. I put all the intel where I couldn't see it, safely walled off in the lizard brain.

Suddenly, fiercely, I wanted to be with Flora. I wanted her arms around me, her breath on my skin. I wanted the taste of her, the smell of her hair.

Before I did the OpSec attack, Flora and me had talked for a long time. After, she'd gone out. It was like a test. I didn't ask, and she didn't say. I didn't tell her what I was planning to do, either.

I could have pinged her. She would have come over straight away, she knew when I needed her. But I didn't know how to tell her what I knew, and I didn't know how not to tell her. And things between us were still delicate.

I sat in the dark, waiting for Bo to come home.

Bo

I'd slept so deeply that waking up was like dragging myself through a long, thin tube. Images from my dreams were melting into each other inside my head; the clumps of writhing black rats in the sewer, the long yellow stinger pointed straight at my eye, Morro's weird map swelling up into 3D and turning into water. My head throbbed. Then I heard the sirens start up. I got out of bed and pulled the blind open a crack. It was still dark out and there was a frost over everything. Nothing moved. I quickly got dressed, snapped on my belt, pulled on my leather jacket, grabbed my taser.

Dez was in the front room. She was standing by the door, her suit switched on max. She looked at me.

'Drones,' she said, pointing up.

I couldn't hear them, but I knew Dez could. All I could hear were the sirens, the pulse pitched so high that it made your teeth hurt. I switched on my suit, turned it up.

Ma came in. She was already dressed and suited as well, and she seemed calm. She went to the front window and looked out into the rue just as it went up in a blaze of light. I could hear the drones now, louder than the sirens. I stepped up beside her. The rue was empty, all the doors closed fast, the windows shuttered.

The sirens stopped. The drones' engines switched down to a low, pulsing hum. There hadn't been a big raid like this for a long time, but they always happened the same way. First the blast of sound and the light. Then nothing, a pause, everyone behind their doors, the whole rue holding its breath.

Dez's head went up, as if she'd heard something. She spun away from the door and moved fast out of the front room. Ma grabbed my arm but I brushed her off. I followed Dez.

She was pressed hard against the door of her bedroom, listening. She looked at me and pressed a finger to her lips. I lifted my taser and aimed. She beckoned me to stand close behind her, and opened the door.

Morro was slumped on the floor against the foot of the bed, his head hanging. Dez and I froze. He didn't move. His eyes were open, but they were blank, they weren't seeing anything. I got down beside him and put my hand on his chest. He was breathing, but only just. There was a trickle of blood coming from his ear. Dez helped me pull him up onto the bed.

His skin was cold. Dez quickly scanned his body. She looked puzzled. She pulled back one of his eyelids and scanned him again. Suddenly he threw back his head, his mouth open wide like he was screaming, but with no sound. He collapsed onto the bed and rolled onto his side. A long, thin stream of vomit flowed out of his mouth.

Ma came into the room. She looked down at Morro, her face blank, then turned to me.

'Transports,' she said.

I could hear them. They were close and getting closer.

Dez and I grabbed Morro under the arms and dragged him off the bed. Ma headed for the cellar door. We carried Morro down the stairs. He was coming around. His eyes focused, he looked up at me and grinned. His teeth were coated with blood. We laid him on the floor. Dez pulled me around to face her and glared at me.

'What are we going to do with this dick?'

'We're going to put him in your stash,' said Ma.

'You're kidding me, right?'

Ma was already kneeling down over Morro and had grabbed hold of his hand. She looked up at Dez. 'Come on, girl, move.'

I looked Morro in the eyes. 'Can you talk?'

He shook his head.

'Can you move, can you stand up?'

He nodded and lifted his head. Ma and I got him to his knees, but no further. Dez opened her stash. We guided him into the dark gap behind the wall. We could already hear the voices of the Aps. Ma ran out of the cellar, slamming the door shut behind her.

I folded Morro into a corner. Dez shut the stash, locked the deadwall, switched off her shield.

We were heading up the stairs when the door flew open and we saw two Aps coming in, their weapons drawn, an AI hovering above them, its steel arms opened out and twitching.

It was what the Aps call a percussion raid, something to scare the life out of the banns. If it had been a capture or kill they would have been loading bodies into the transports like so much meat.

Dez shut herself down while we were being questioned, but I could feel her boiling inside, shaking with anger. It was just the regular Aps so Ma played the frightened woman. Eager to please, wouldn't stop nattering. I had to stop myself smiling when she offered the Aps a cup of herbal tea.

'It must be a terribly long day for you boys,' she said. 'What with all the miscreants out there causing bother.'

The Aps scanned the house, knocked a few things over, stood too close for comfort, asked us about illegal tech, ran a credit check, wanted to know about our movements, where did we go, who did we associate with? It was the usual bullshit, just more aggressive, more threatening. The same thing would be happening all along the rue.

After the Aps left, Dez came back up to speed, seething. Before she said anything she scanned the house and debugged it, scraped the air clean, looped the listeners. Ma looked wasted. She flopped down on the couch, leant her head back and shut her eyes.

'You were great, Ma.'

'I didn't overdo it, did I?'

'You bored them to death.'

'You'd better look at that boy in the stash. Morro, isn't it?'

'You know him?'

'I've seen him around. And you've mentioned him... once or twice.'

Ma was being kind. I'd mentioned Morro a lot. She knew that I looked up to him, that maybe I had some sort of crush on him. But it was Dez that I had to hide it from. If she thought I had any strong feelings about Morro she'd do her best to wipe them out.

I went back down to the cellar. Dez was cleaning up her workbench. The Aps had trashed it but there wasn't any serious damage. She'd calmed down a little, but I could sense her anger still flickering. I tried to be cheerful, which was probably a mistake.

'That wasn't so bad, eh?'

She didn't even turn her head to look at me.

'We've still got to clean up that shit in the stash. And I'm not doing it.'

'Listen...Dez.'

She spun around, her eyes blazing. 'What does he think he's doing, coming here? Why did he come here? Did you invite him or something? What's wrong with you? You know what kind of hole this could drop us in...'

Before she could throw anything at me, the stash opened and Morro stepped out, looking like he'd just woken up from his beauty sleep. He glanced from me to Dez then back to me.

'I'd love a cup of tea,' he said.

I thought that Dez might explode right there on the spot. She was staring at her open stash.

'How the hell did you do that?'

'I'm sure that getting out is easier than getting in.'

Dez shoved Morro aside and shut the deadwall.

'I can tell you how I did it, if you like,' he said.

Dez was already heading for the stairs. 'Don't bother,' she said as she left, leaving the door open behind her.

Morro turned to me. He really did look as fresh as a daisy. 'How about that tea?'

'How about you explaining what's going on?'

'That sounds like a fair exchange.'

We climbed out of the cellar and I boiled the water. Dez was nowhere to be seen.

Brian Mac

Jul 31, 23.13 hours

So the command comes through at 04.00 hours, percussion raids on selected banns before daylight, Second, Third, Seventh. Militia reinforcements from the city. I look through the intel and see there are some high-level targeted hits going on in the Outer Banns and guess these raids are supposed to be a distraction.

No warning, no consultation, no fucking reason. I hit the roof, open a line to Mal, shout for a while. He nods tiredly until I stop.

Brian, I'm sorry, it's high up, he says, when he has a chance to say anything. Nothing to do with me.

It's my bann, I tell him. It's my fucking beat. He tells me to calm down, that it's just a percussion raid. I say, don't pretend they're not just using us as cover for their dirty work elsewhere. And meanwhile they're fucking over my bann.

If anyone's going to fuck over the Second, I think, it's going to be *me*.

Mal, unusually for a cop, is a courteous man. I can see him wincing every time I curse. He tells me again to calm down.

Since when does someone arrange a major raid without consulting the local Brig? Since when?

Since forever, says Mal. There's an edge in his voice now, he's losing patience. It's not your bann, Brian, he tells me. It never has been. It's under the jurisdiction of Newport City OpSec. Stop talking like you're some kind of Mayor. You're not. You're a Brig Level 11 and I'm your superior officer Level 15 and you do what I say.

When Mal starts talking like that, I know I've pushed him too far. I back down. Okay, but why? I'm the one who has to clean up the mess after. In a bann like the Second you could have riots.

He just looks at me. Well, Brian, that's the problem, see? There shouldn't be any riots anywhere.

That must be some kind of new directive. It chills me to the bone.

I sign off quickly and stare at the wall. I don't like this. I don't like it at all.

Jul 31, 25.33 hours

You just sit your nerves jangling from the noise and the light and the shouting and even now I can feel the thud of percussion in my chest like its changed the rhythm of my blood, it's still echoing in there, back and forth across the cavity where my heart is supposed to be. Long, boring, punishing day. Can't sleep, too tired to go out, and if I did I might get jumped by some angry flesher and who could blame them.

I know how to run a raid and maybe as a sop to my pathetic outraged authority Mal puts me in charge so at least I'm not answering to some Newport City fop. I speak to Harrison in the First, he's not happy, he has a militia clone in there getting in his face. Small mercies.

Those fucking clones.

Well let's face it, Brigadier Mackintosh, Brian, Level 11, is a clone. I'm one of the experimental variety, when they decided that autonomous thinking and empathic traits were the way to go. That didn't last long, they stopped making us twenty years ago. Me and Harrison in the First are the only ones left in the banns. They still have to program some human into them, or they all have breakdowns once they're let out of Newport City and suddenly there's people touching each other everywhere in meatspace. Even with the desensitisation programs it's culture shock to the max. They can't handle it.

Now the Aps they send me are trained-up killers, obedience coded into every chromosome. There are too many of them, and they don't stay long enough to get any sort of feel for the banns. The ones tonight were there just for assignment, seconded from the mining convoys, militia grade. Why this now? It's not as if anything's suddenly changed out here. I keep a weather eye on Alchem activity and those other groups that spring up now and again, and it's no worse than it's ever been, aside from the riots about the drilling. If anything, it's better.

The tubes have been pushing the issue of security threats for a couple of years now. You can't tell me that's not Osborne, back when he was head of media. Suddenly there's all these ultraviolent soaps about terrorist fleshers and ads warning about subversives undermining our way of life. I take notice of that stuff, nanos in the wind, that kind of thing. And then Osborne stood for Mayor and won, and since then everything is turning to shit.

This Bremmer is bad news, but everyone knew that when he was appointed. The real bad news is Osborne. Smooth as silk, glamorous hair, trust-me smile, avuncular voice, mind like an empty metal box. *I'm here to take care.* Like hell he is.

They've cracked down on some of the City intellectuals, nothing too heavy, but enough to notice. There's hardly any of the old gang left in the City now.

The City loves Osborne. Of course they do, what do they know.

As a wise flesher said to me once, when they start taking notice, you're in real trouble. For a long time everybody ignored the banns, they let them just get on with their business. As long as they supplied everything they were supposed to supply, everybody was happy.

They've started taking notice again. I don't like it.

Bo

That night Ma had a bad turn.

Morro and Dez had spent the day avoiding each other. In a house as small as ours, that isn't easy. Dez went out the back of the house into the patch of earth that Ma turned into a vegetable garden. She said she was going to dig a new row, that we should plant some more tates. The weather had been so cold lately that the earth was practically frozen, even under the greenhouse domes. She laboured away under a heavy, colourless sky, and kept at it even when she had to turn on the floodlights and it started to rain.

Morro watched her from the window of my room. 'Does she ever stop,' he asked me. 'I mean just...stop?'

'Dez doesn't like being idle.'

I studied Morro's face. I could hardly believe how he had recovered from whatever he'd put himself through to get to our house. 'So...why are you here, Morro?'

He shrugged. 'I couldn't think where else to go,' he said. 'The raid you had here was nothing compared with what went down in the Outer Banns.' He started pacing the room. 'It wasn't Aps, it was militia, hundreds of them. They moved through the Tenth and Eleventh like a tidal wave. Then I got word that some of our chapters were taken out.'

'Chapters?'

'It's what we call a small group that works together. Never more than three or four people. Stigg and Clemence in the Tenth, brothers, into info-tech in a big way. Queenie, Ella and Church in the Ninth, makers, they can build anything.'

It wasn't like Morro to be so forthcoming, but maybe it was some kind of trade-off for the danger he put us in. I decided to push it. 'What happened to them?'

Morro didn't answer for a while, didn't look at me. I realised he was still shaken. 'I've got a hide in the Tenth,' he said. 'I went there first. The Aps had scorched it. I couldn't even get close. I went into the Seventh to contact the chapter we've got working out of the shanty below the towerblocks, the ones that have been condemned.'

'On Castell Place? Where all those scavengers and remakers are?'

'It's all gone. The whole place was torn up by striker drones. There's hardly anything left standing.' He slumped down on the edge of my bed. He suddenly looked whacked. 'I could have gone to Flora's, but she keeps any connection to me under wraps, especially from her old man. He's cool, but if anyone put Flora in any danger, he'd wipe them.'

'Did you do...that doubling thing?'

'No. I had to get both of me here,' he said, and grinned. 'Do you know anything about those failed matter transfer experiments that were abandoned forty, fifty years ago?'

I shook my head.

'Some of that crap still exists, fragments of it. You can get your hands on it if you know the right people...hoarders, amateur scientists, remakers. I had a prototype I was fiddling with. First time I used it. I thought I was going to die.'

I was going to ask more, but Ma started calling for Dez from her room. I didn't like how she sounded.

She was on her bed, soaked in sweat, breathing fast, her clothes stuck to her skin. Her lips were so dry that they'd started to crack and bleed. She'd been fine a couple of hours before. She'd said that she was feeling tired and was going to have a rest.

Morro had followed me. He took hold of Ma's wrist, checking her pulse, and stared into her eyes. Ma didn't recognize him. She looked frightened. He turned to me. 'What meds have you got?'

'The stuff she takes now and then, painkillers, sleep tabs.'

'Give her the painkillers. I'll be back.'

I found the painkillers on the shelf above Ma's bed. I gave her two shots. Then I went out the back to get Dez. She went straight to Ma's room. Morro was in the middle of the herb garden, scrambling about.

'Have you got any sage?'

I was taken aback. 'Sage? I don't think so.'

'Feverfew, milk thistle, ringdrops, anything like that.'

'I don't know everything that's out here. Ma did all the planting. There's mint, parsley, kepweed...'

'Milk thistle's a weed, where are the weeds?'

'There's weeds by the back wall.'

I left Morro to his gardening and went back to Ma. Her breathing was sharper, sucking in air in short gasps. I was really worried now. Her lips were a weird blue colour. I could see that Dez was suppressing panic. 'She needs proper treatment.'

'Like we can afford that.'

'Don't you have any credits?'

'Not enough. She's been bad before and she's come out of it okay.'

Dez didn't take her eyes from Ma's face. 'Not this bad. And she's bad more often than she was.'

'She's getting older.'

'She's not old.'

Morro appeared in the doorway, his hands covered in earth. 'Bo, have you got any ice?'

'In the freezer.'

'Get it and wrap it in something, a cloth, and use it to start cooling her down. Put ice on her lips.'

Dez bristled. 'This has got nothing to do with you.'

'Yes it has,' Morro said. 'I can help.'

'You're not doing anything to her.'

Morro held out his hands. He was holding two bunches of small twigs and leaves, a long white tuber. 'I can make this into a poultice,' he said. 'It'll draw the fever, maybe act as an antispasmodic. It might calm her as well. It won't hurt her.'

'How do we know that?'

'You eat this stuff, you make tea with some of it.'

'Please, Dez,' I said. 'Let him do it.'

All we could hear was Ma's shallow breathing. Dez's shoulders dropped and her eyes filled with tears. She looked at Morro.

'Okay,' she said. 'Do it.'

It didn't take Morro long to make the poultice. He ground everything up in a bowl and mixed it with clay, making a paste. It smelt like the earth when you dig deep. He smeared it across the top of Ma's chest. Dez and I were already cooling her body with ice, wetting her lips with it, wiping it across her forehead, but it melted in the heat that was coming off Ma's skin.

It was late and the rue was quiet. We were shut up in our own prisons, just the way the Aps wanted us to be.

Dez was getting some rest. I was dozing in a chair in a corner of Ma's room, hardly able to keep my eyes open, when Morro went over to Ma. He felt her forehead with the back of his hand and beckoned me over. I could see that Ma's fever had eased. She was breathing easier and her skin was almost cool.

'I like your Ma,' Morro said. 'She's a good one.'

I felt too miserable to speak, so I just nodded. I like her too.

'I don't know how long the poultice will work,' he said. 'She needs someone who can go deeper. I know someone. I think we should get them here tonight.'

'Who?'

'Jenna. She's a dowser, the best there is. She's lying low at the moment in the Seventh, shacked up with a bunch of needle freaks and implant addicts.'

'Will she come here?'

'If she knows I'm asking. Will you go and get her?'

'Couldn't you just…'

'No tech. Our private lines might be compromised. We have to do this the old fashioned way. I'd go, but I think I should keep an eye on Bel. I've got a couple more tricks up my sleeve.'

I woke Dez and told her that Ma was looking better.

'Maybe she would have pulled out of it anyway,' she said.

'You reckon?'

'No, I don't reckon.' She paused and looked up at me. 'Doesn't give Morro a free pass, though.'

'No one's forcing you.' Like anyone could force Dez to do anything.

'Where is he?'

'In with Ma. He's worn out. You should say something to him, like thanks. I'm going to leave you to it.'

'Where are you going at this time of night?'

'Morro thinks she could turn bad again He knows someone who might help, but I've got to go and get her.'

'You shouldn't be going anywhere, not after all the crap that's happened today. We don't know what the Aps are going to do next.'

'Morro thinks it's best not to wait. I'll be back in a couple of hours.'

I turned and left, glad that I had an excuse to get out of the way. Dez and Morro would have to talk to each other on their own.

Dez

The moment I heard the drones I put a shield up around the whole house so the heat sensors wouldn't see me in the cellar. The last thing I wanted was any attention paid to that part of the house. I threw the valuable stuff in my stash, and left a few cheap tools and a couple of malfunctioning seals around, artistically arranged to look as if I were in the middle of some basic repairs.

And then Morro turned up, and I couldn't bring the shield down in case a sensor picked up that there was one body too many in the house. I could have killed him. Once we got him behind the deadwall I had to lower the shield slowly, if it had snapped off suddenly somebody would have noticed for sure. By the time the drones arrived in our street it was down completely, but it was a close thing.

And then he opens up my deadwall and steps out as cool as a cucumber, flashing that handsome smile, and I have to put the shield back up again toot sweet, cursing because who the hell knows who's watching the energy levels for any suspicious activity going on in Rue Ballard. Behind that deadwall Morro wouldn't even know if there were Aps in the house.

How dare he put us in danger like that, especially knowing we'd just been arrested. How dare he.

Typical Alchem douche-canoe arrogance.

It's bothered me for a long time, Bo's fascination with the Alchems. It's the kind of thing that can get you into trouble, and we've got enough things to get us in trouble already. Me, for a start. Ma and whatever she did to get her file tagged. Bo began to get obsessed when we lived in the Ninth, he'd slip off to a gig and come back all excited, full of stories about whatever the Alchems were doing now. A lot of the music he liked used Alchem codes in their beats, a way of being edgy.

Rumour surrounded Morro like a glamour. I'd sometimes see him at gigs, always surrounded by girls, eyes pinpointed from some upper he'd taken, those sharp black cheekbones glimmering with silver. I thought he was all show, and I didn't take much notice. And then Flora got gooey-eyed over him, and all that shit blew up between us, and it got a bit personal.

After Bo left I looked at Ma, sleeping pale and drawn under the blanket. She didn't look good, but she was a thousand per cent better than she'd been before. I had really thought she was going to die. Now she just looked sick.

Then I thought about what Bo had said. I kissed Ma's cheek and told her that I'd be back soon, even though I knew she couldn't hear me, and went into the front room.

Morro was sitting in my chair, staring at nothing. He looked up when I entered but he didn't say anything. I didn't mention that he was in my spot, although I'm very territorial. He looked tired, his face slightly puffy, his hair dull and frizzy.

'Thanks,' I said. I found it difficult to say, like I was admitting defeat, and my lips felt stiff and formal. 'I'm grateful for whatever it was you did in there.'

'The least I could do,' he said, giving me the ghost of a smile. 'I know you wanted to throw me out.'

'Yeah, I did.' I met his eyes, and looked away.

'Sit down, Dez. We should talk.'

'Why?' I could feel my chin jutting out.

He sighed. 'Why not?'

'Lots of why nots. Maybe because you stole my girlfriend why not.'

For a moment he looked taken aback. 'Your girlfriend?'

'Flora.' She didn't even mention me, the bitch. I felt all the ugly things stirring inside me and bit them back. Once I began I wouldn't stop. 'You didn't know? She never thought it was worth mentioning?'

He combed through his hair with his fingers and leant back in my chair, giving me a long, slow look. I didn't like it.

'I'm too tired for this. Really, we should talk.'

This time I sat down, in Ma's chair. I met his gaze, to show he wasn't going to intimidate me or charm me.

'First thing. I knew you and Flora are friends, of course she talked about you, though not much. I didn't realise you were that close.'

I opened my mouth but he waved his hand. 'No, listen Dez. Flora and me, there's no question… I mean, I don't know what she said to you, but she's not my kind of girl, I mean, there's never been anything.'

'I've seen you looking at her.'

I saw anger spark in his eyes. 'She's amazing. An amazing musician. An amazing person. Of course I think she's great. Doesn't mean I'm going to try to get into her pants.'

Like hell, I thought, but I didn't say anything. I couldn't read him, he had some kind of protection up, who knew if he was telling the truth.

'I swear it. You should trust her. If you ask me, she's a woman worth trusting.'

I flinched and went quiet, because I knew he was right. Either I trusted Flora or I didn't. It was hard letting that vicious stab of jealousy go, I'd got so used to it by now, like a loose tooth that you enjoy fiddling with. Maybe the idea that I could trust Flora was more scary than the fear that she had betrayed me. The thought flickered into my head, and I let it sit there. Like I said, just because I know stuff doesn't mean I'm smart.

For some reason, I believed him. I had no reason to, I couldn't see into his head, but something inside me settled and made sense.

I didn't like being lectured by Morro, especially if he was right, so I changed the subject.

'So who's this person Bo's gone to get?'

'A dowser. Jenna. I can't deal with what's wrong with your mother, but maybe she can. You'll see when she gets here.'

'It's dangerous for him to go out.'

'Bo's smart,' said Morro. 'He'll be all right.' He gave me another of those slow looks. 'You should trust him, too.'

An awkward silence fell between us. I broke it by standing up and asking Morro if he wanted something to drink. 'I've got some beer,' I said. 'Or I could make a brew.'

'A beer would be champion,' said Morro, flashing me that smile. I knew he knew that I'd forgiven him and I briefly hated him for it. Smug bastard. 'Thank you.'

As I got the beer I realised I felt better than I had in weeks, as if suddenly I had some perspective on myself. Believing Morro when I didn't believe Flora, that was poor. No wonder she was angry with me. All that pain and rage, over nothing. And it was my fault, nobody else's. I wanted to open a line straight away, just to tell her I love her, that I'm humble now and I know it was my fault. I resisted, I didn't think it would go down well. I'd said all those things already, but I hadn't really meant them. I just wanted her back.

I'm an arsehole sometimes.

Morro took the beer and had a long swig. When he put the bottle down, it was half empty.

'That,' he said, wiping his mouth, 'is the best beer I've ever tasted.'

'It's one of Kojo's brews,' I said.

'A master brewer, obviously.' He sat back, toying with his belt, studying me. 'Okay, Dez. Like I said, we have to talk. Not about Flora, I hope that's all done now.'

I felt a vague alarm. 'About what?'

'About your…abilities.'

I tensed. What had Bo said to this man? 'What abilities?'

He smiled. 'For a start, I can't read you. I can read almost anyone. But not you.' He took another sip. 'You can't read me, right? You know you can't get in. There's not a lot of people out there like us.'

'I thought you had some protection up.'

'I do. It's me. I don't need any other protection.'

'And you undid my deadwall,' I said slowly. I had thought that was some kind of tech too.

'I can do stuff. I think you can, too.' He held my gaze, and there was a challenge in it. 'Did you think you were the only one?'

'Yes, I did,' I said. 'I worked out the odds once.'

'You would have worked out the odds for the kind of splice that happened to you,' he said. 'There's all kinds of splices. Some radical, some less radical, some fatal. It's more common than people realise.' He smiled again. 'As you know, there are good reasons to keep it secret, so it's easy to feel like it's only you.'

'So you got spliced?'

'No, not me. One of my forebears. I don't know which one.'

I stared at him, and then I finished my beer.

I don't know what I felt. I was almost dizzy with the surprise of it, as if I'd looked up and there was this new world hanging right above my head, populous and brimming with life, that I had never suspected was there. I don't know why it had never occurred to me to wonder if there were other splices. I guess I'd worked out the odds and figured there couldn't be. So, I'm not as special as I think. But on the other hand, I'm not just some edge-level freak, there are other people out there like me.

I felt happy. A strange kind of happy.

I held up my bottle. 'Want another one?'

So we talked. Morro told me what he can do. He has a self-healing ability, he must have some kind of medibot in his genes. And this other thing that he calls 'doubling'. He has some weird theory about what it is, he says he sends out his soul. If you ask me it's some kind of quantum ability that ought to be totally impossible, for a whole person anyway, but whatever. Morro says one of him is real and one isn't, whatever that means. He's not just sending out a holo, he can pick up objects, fight if he has to. But whatever he projects is a fake Morro, and the authentic Morro is the one who projects.

When I said that both of him sounded like they were equally real he looked kind of hurt, so I left it. I didn't feel like having some kind of existential argument, but I'm chary of anyone who talks about being *authentic*, it's too much like pinker talk. The Alchems are full of romantic shit, like this obsession with oldtech. Some of their knowledge goes back centuries. I think whatever Morro did to help Ma is that old. Mind you, a lot of it is plain doolally. He pulled up a holo of this damn map that he called a 'frequency of possibilities chart'. I couldn't make head or tail of it, it made no sense at all. 'I use it all the time,' he said, looking earnest.

I wanted to laugh. But I guess, if it works for him…

Then he asked me what I could do. When I told him, his eyebrows went up into his hair and he whistled.

'Seriously? I never heard of anyone who could do that. I mean, I can do a bit of remote, but nothing like that. It must have been a perfect splice.'

So, I *am* special, after all.

I guess it was inevitable that I'd tell him about how I'd gone into OpSec, and what I'd found out. He didn't look shocked, or even surprised.

'We've suspected that this was coming,' he said. 'A couple of the chapters have picked up rumours. Redborg has a contact in the Aps who warned them something big was going down. But there's been nothing solid.'

Redborg was an Alchem? I knew them slightly through Flora, they often did gigs together. I guess I shouldn't have been surprised, but I was.

'OpSec have been ramping things up the past few months,' said Morro. 'All those new Aps, new investigations. They got onto my tail, which is why I had to disappear.' He scratched his chin. He hadn't shaved for a couple of days and had a shadow beard. Like everything, it suited him. 'But this. This is worse than we thought.'

He shot me a speculative look, and then spent the next half hour trying to persuade me to join the Alchems. I told him joining isn't my thing.

'Well,' he said, when he saw that I was getting stubborn. 'Even if you won't join us, we're the ones to stop this cull. Do you want to help?'

Of course I want to help. 'What chance do we have? Really?' I didn't say that I thought a bunch of deluded tossers like the Alchems had exactly zero possibility of preventing Newport City OpSec from doing anything it liked, but he knew I was thinking it.

'Don't underestimate us, Dez. I know you don't think much of us, but we do a lot of missions nobody knows about. Not even OpSec. There's a lot of us, here and there. We've got friends.' He paused. 'And enemies, of course. Someone has been informing on us. This raid, they took out three of our chapters, they torched five of our hides. I think they know about my lair in the Twelfth, I had to lightlock it and I can't go back. That's deep insider intel.'

For a moment he looked entirely bleak, as if he might cry, but he brushed his hands impatiently over his eyes. 'We all know that we have to kill ourselves before we're interrogated, but that doesn't mean that we're always able to. I don't know who's arrested, who's dead. Who knows what they've got?'

I knew what was coming, and braced myself to say no.

'Dez, do you think you could go in there again, do a sweep for anything they have on the Alchems? Maybe find out who the informer is?'

'I can't,' I said flatly. 'Once was bad enough. I'm still not sure that they didn't notice something when I got through the firewall. If I do the same thing twice, it's literally a thousand times the risk. They use an intelligent algorithm, and that's just the beginning of it.'

'Couldn't you get in another way?' He stared at me like a gau begging for dinner, eyes as big as hope. He had no idea what he was asking.

'If I go in again, I might as well just paint a target on my forehead and knock on the front door of OpSec. Once was it, and that was a terrible risk.'

'But Dez, they want to murder millions of people. Isn't it worth it? Just once more?' He was pleading now.

'If they catch me, the Alchems will be in worse trouble than they are now. Think of what I know about you already.' And I wasn't going to put my family in any more shit.

He knew there was no point in arguing further, but he looked so desolate that I felt like a total arse.

'I'm sorry,' I said, as gently as I could. 'I just can't do it.'

Bo

It didn't take me too long to get to the Seventh. Morro told me to take the knuckle bone as a token. 'Jenna will probably be jumpy,' he said. 'She'll want some reassurance.' I knew I was jumpy. I had my suit turned all the way up, all the sensors primed, but I couldn't pick up any threat. It only made me more nervous.

The towerblock where I'd find Jenna was in the Seventh, not far from where the old mono line divided it from the Second. This part of the mono network had been blown up three decades ago, during the protests and riots after the last big cull. It had never been repaired. The rails were twisted and snapped, rolled up into weird knots and clusters. It was once the highest mono that had ever been built. Now its crippled shapes loomed over everything, like shadows scrawled across the glow of the Outer Veil.

The towerblock stood on a desolate corner next to a row of low tech factories, most of which had long gone out of business. I'd been this way before. There were plenty of abandoned buildings that could be used for gigs, once you broke in, did a bit of tampering, and milked some juice from the local grid.

There were a few windows lit, scattered far apart, high up. Jenna was on the fifteenth floor. The lower floors of the building had been gutted by scavengers and the squatters and freaks who lived in the block still fought a constant battle with them to hang on to what remained. There was no elevator, so I'd have to use the stairs.

Climbing through the first few floors I thought of our towerblock in the Ninth. As bleak as it was, it had been in better shape than this dump, but it was still the same kind of place, the same grime, the same damp chill, the constant noise soaking through thin walls, the smell of other peoples' cooking, other peoples' shit. Ma was so happy when she managed to get us out of there. We were all happy.

I've got no problem with needle and implant freaks. I mean, they don't scare me. The only people they're a danger to are themselves. They might try to skin you for credits if they're desperate, but you can usually see them off with a kick in the curls. Some of these freaks are pinkers, or had been. I don't know what they turn into. They're failures, deadbeats, crims maybe, from behind the Inner Veil. They crawl into the banns looking for some kind of life. Pinkers have less resistance to the kind of stuff that fleshers live with all the time. A sickness that will knock a flesher flat for a day or two will kill a pinker stone dead. It's the same with needles. A flesher can deal with the damage, with the morphs and the bonebends and the bleeding, but a pinker, once they're on the jag and can't turn back, will just calcify and crumble. They fall apart quick, and it isn't pretty. Their faces fall apart first.

The stairwell was pitch black so I gave myself some light. I got as far as the tenth floor before I ran into anybody. It was some creep coming out of a bodyswap, half man, half neka, crouched in the stairwell, its tail thrashing, its human mouth open in a soundless howl, hind legs twisted together, feet coming out of paws. I skirted around, my back pressed against the wall. Next floor up I saw a punk about ten years old squatting in the corridor taking a shit. He looked at me as I passed and hissed at me between his black teeth. I heard someone screaming behind a door. I had to step over a pool of blood on the next landing. I climbed up through the next two floors with my taser drawn. I didn't see anyone else, but I could feel the lives all around me, down the corridors, behind the doors, all of them screwed up and in pain.

When I reached the fifteenth floor I was sweating and short of breath.

There was some light up here, just enough to see by, a flat, dead kind of light that didn't make any shadows. There weren't any numbers on the doors. Morro had told me that Jenna's was the third one along, on the left. He'd said to knock twice, wait, then knock twice again, then wait. I got to the door and knocked. I didn't hear any sounds coming from inside. I waited. I tried to slow down my breathing. My sweat stung under my suit.

The door finally opened, but there was no one standing behind it. I took a couple of cautious steps inside. It was just a single room with nothing in it except a mattress and a blanket. Light came from a glowtube in the corner.

'Morro sent me,' I said, feeling foolish talking to the empty air.

Nothing.

I said it again. 'Morro sent me.'

'Okay, okay, I heard you the first time,' said a voice. A deadwall opened right beside me and Jenna stepped out. She looked me up and down. 'Who are you?'

'I'm Bo. A friend of Morro's.' I held out the knuckle bone. She took it, but she barely glanced at it.

'He has friends?'

'You're a friend of his, aren't you?'

'Did he say that?'

'Not exactly.'

'What does he want?'

'He wants your help with someone who's sick.'

'Another friend of his?'

'It's my mother.'

Jenna held my gaze. Her eyes were a mismatch. Her left eye was a dark, watery green, her right was blue, almost black, and a little larger. Her bleached hair was cropped short and I could see that underneath the bristles she had some kind of tattoo that covered the whole side of her skull. She was about my age, maybe a year or two older. When Morro said that she was a dowser I had thought that she'd be ancient. I'd seen dowsers a few times, water searching when wells dried or when there wasn't any rain for a long time, and they were all twice Ma's age.

Looking at Jenna, I felt kind of breathless. She was beautiful.

She handed the bone back to me. 'So what's wrong with your Ma?'

'She's been sick off and on for a long time. But right now she's really bad. Morro made a poultice that seemed to help, but he's worried.'

'What did you say your name was?'

'It's Bo.' I paused. 'Will you help us?' I heard the catch of need in my voice.

Jenna looked at me, as if she were weighing me up. 'I'd go just about anywhere to get out of this hell hole. And I haven't seen Morro for a while. And yeah, maybe I can help with your Ma.' She sealed the dead wall. 'So let's go.'

'Don't you have to bring anything?'

'Like what?'

'Meds? Tech?'

'No. I just have to bring me.'

Going down the stairs I realized how tired I was. It was all I could do to keep up with Jenna. My hands were lit up, but fading. I'd have to turn my suit down if it was going to last all the way home.

We didn't run into anyone on the way down. The body swap mess was gone, but the place where it had been stank of neka. It was a relief to get back out on the rue. I caught up with Jenna and we walked side by side.

'Where are we going?'

'The Second,' I said.

'You know a quick way?'

'I know all the short cuts.'

For a while we didn't talk. As we walked through the Seventh, I remembered that we were passing through one of the banns that OpSec wanted to cull. Right now the rues were deserted, the buildings dark, but come daylight there'd be people going to work, or taking little punks out in their prams, neighbours talking, homers buzzing up and down, stallholders calling out their wares, people buying or just gawking at the local shijo. I found it hard to comprehend that so much life could simply be erased.

We were in the Second when Jenna asked me about Ma. She wanted to know what symptoms she had, and how long had she been sick.

'She's always been a little poorly,' I said. 'But she's tough.'

'Has there been any sickness in her family? Even from way back?'

'She's never talked about her family, not really.'

It felt strange saying that, but it was true. I had no idea who Ma's family were, not even if she had brothers or sisters. I couldn't imagine that one day Dez might never even mention my name, that I might forget about her, put her out of my life. But how did I know what Ma thought? If she had siblings maybe she did think about them. Maybe something happened to them that she didn't want to remember.

Jenna threw me a look. 'You don't say much, do you? Are you usually this quiet?

'I thought that you were quiet. That's why I wasn't...you know...talking.'

'I haven't had many people to talk to lately,' she said. 'Maybe I've forgotten how.'

'I couldn't see that towerblock providing great conversationalists.'

'But it's a great hide. The Aps avoid it, usually.'

'They were at our place this morning.'

'What happened?'

I told her what had happened. By the time we reached home I'd been gone for close on two hours. It would be daylight pretty soon.

When we walked in, Dez and Morro were standing in the kitchen alcove, making tea. There wasn't a trace of the tension that had been hanging in the air all day. Jenna nodded a greeting at Morro and asked me where Ma's room was. She went straight in. We all followed her.

Ma was still asleep, but the fever was coming back. She was restless, rolling from side to side, beads of sweat running down her face. Jenna knelt beside the bed and stretched out her hands, holding them just above Ma's chest. She closed her eyes and began to take deep, long breaths. She seemed to be working herself into some kind of trance. After a while, Ma grew calmer and then went completely still.

Morro moved to the other side of the bed, speaking quietly. 'Jenna, Jenna...can you hear me, Jenna?'

Jenna looked pale, and her hair was damp with sweat. She didn't answer at first. 'Yes,' she said at last. It sounded as if she were talking from a long way away.

'Do you know what it is?'

'I think it's a leech. It's been there a long time.'

I looked at Morro. 'What's a leech?'

'It's a kind of bot, I guess. An early kind. It embeds into the body like a tumour,' said Morro. 'They called them infectious deterrents. They used them to put trouble makers out of action, or for tracking. But they were unstable, there were a lot of duds. This is one of the duds.'

Jenna opened her eyes and looked up at Morro. 'I think I can draw it.'

Dez spoke sharply. 'What does that mean?'

'I think that I can draw it out.'

'How?'

Jenna didn't answer. Dez swung round to me, her face hard. 'She's not doing anything to Ma if she doesn't even know what she's doing.'

'She can save your mother,' said Morro.

'I'll leave you to decide,' Jenna said. She stood up and walked towards the door. 'But don't take too long. I have to do it soon or it'll be too late. I'd say it's been dormant for a long time, but it's growing fast.'

'Please, Dez,' I said.

'Shut it, Bo.'

Dez's voice was icy, her jaw set. When she talks to me like that, I know that there's nothing I can say that will change her mind. I could see how afraid she was for Ma. But I trusted Jenna, even if I didn't know why, and I wanted her to try whatever it was she said she could do.

I followed Jenna out of the room, closing the door on Dez and Morro. Morro looked determined, but I knew he'd have a fight on his hands to convince Dez.

Jenna sat on the couch in the front room. She already looked tired. I brought some water and sat down beside her.

'Is Ma dying?'

'Maybe. Or something worse.'

She said it so matter of factly that for a minute I didn't know what to say. I didn't want to imagine what she meant.

'And you can stop that happening?' I said.

'I think so.'

'What do you have to do?'

Jenna looked at her glass of water and held it up. 'I can sometimes draw water to the surface. I can feel where it is and make it rise. I can draw up other things as well, I can draw splinters out of fingers, stones out of mud, I used to do that when I was a kid, it was a game.'

She put her hand over her glass of water. The water rose up to the rim of the glass, swirling and spilling over the sides, until the glass was empty.

Morro came into the room. 'All good, Jenna,' he said. 'Dez is cool with it.'

I didn't know how Morro had managed to get Dez to change her mind, and so quickly. Whatever he'd said to her must have hit the spot pretty hard. It would have hurt her to back down.

Jenna took a deep breath, handed me the glass and followed Morro back into Ma's room. I held back for a minute, not knowing if I wanted to go in or not. But I had to, I had to be there for Ma.

Jenna was sitting on the bed close to Ma. She was putting herself back into a trance, breathing deeply, locked inside her head. I went over to Dez who was standing in a corner of the room. She grabbed my arm and held it tight.

Morro knelt down beside Ma and slipped one hand gently under her head, lifting it away from the pillow. With his other hand he opened her mouth and kept hold of her jaw.

Jenna put both her hands, one on top of the other, over Ma's open mouth. She pressed down. For the longest time, nothing happened. The only sound was Jenna's breathing, getting deeper and faster.

After a few minutes, Ma's head jerked back and her body arched. Morro tightened his grip. Ma's eyes opened wide, but they were sightless, glazed with some kind of opaque, watery film. She began to moan, the sound muffled by Jenna's hands. It looked like Ma was being suffocated. Dez rushed to the bed, as if she was going to stop what was happening. I grabbed her and held her tight.

Ma began struggling and thrashing around. It was all Morro could do to keep hold of her head, to keep it steady. Jenna pressed her hands harder against Ma's mouth, gasping now, her head bowed, sweat dripping off her nose. It seemed to go on forever, but maybe it was only a minute or so. And then Ma's back straightened and she sank back onto the bed. She lay very still, but I could see the tiny movement of her chest rising and falling under the blanket. She was still alive.

Jenna slowly lifted her top hand away. She let the other stay there for a while, then lifted that hand away as well. She was shaking uncontrollably. Clinging to her palm was a shining, pulsing clump of matter that looked like a mollusc. Jenna turned her hand palm up. The clump started to writhe and shudder, slowly twisting itself into a perfectly smooth ball, and then the shine on its surface began to dull so it seemed as if a light inside it was slowly dying. It lost shape until it looked like a withered, black flower.

Morro moved quickly around the bed and caught Jenna just as she collapsed, unconscious.

Brian Mac

Itching for an implant. What I wouldn't give to get away from myself right now. Inadvisable, like I might say to one of those over-eager new recruits. Inadvisable, dickhead. Did you hide your brain in your arsehole?

Back in the old days, a year or so ago, I had good days. A good day meant wiping a skinner hero-style, followed by a dazzling implant, a good pho, a few hours in a cathouse with a jigged-up dolly, IMR hair whipping around the room, astonishing breasts. A bad day? Any day I'm stuck in the precinct or have to talk to OpSec. At the moment it's all bad days.

Spent all of today doing data entry on the arrests from the raids. A bunch of frightened fleshers, most of them kids, up on bullshit charges. Resisting arrest (meaning trying to run away), illegal tech (meaning a hotted up shield or fake implant). I know almost all of them. Any real criminal knows how to deal with Aps. Recruits have no idea what they're dealing with. They believe that fleshers can't think, that at best they have some low-level rat cunning. Fleshers like Bel run rings around them.

I check that Bel and the kids weren't among the arrests, read them all warnings, send them snivelling home.

Bel and the kids. I'm sitting on that AI report. Buried it in a file under 'other items' with a bunch of erroneous orders for office supplies and it's just lying there like a low-level migraine waiting to explode. Maybe with all this new activity I can just wait a while and then quietly delete it by mistake. Someone in Tech got a little too smart and figured that the only way the officer got shot was if someone broke the unbreakable crypto. They're suggesting that there's some kind of new interference tech around that we should be looking out for. I told IT that's impossible and that they should get out of fantasyland back to the real world. If I send that report upcity the Second will suddenly be in the middle of the map all lights flashing and that's just what I don't want, especially now.

Too many things getting tense. There's OpSec militia floating about the precinct muttering into their buzzers about trawling the banns, special sweeps for god knows what. Stamping all over my authority is what they're doing. Another pointless OpSec exercise, some new higher up getting off on his power. My officers like OpSec as much I do, the militia look down their noses at the regulars, and there's a bit of pushing and shoving in the precinct because of the crowding. Had to discipline Sheen and Foster, two of my best, after a brawl in the canteen this morning. I don't like it, they don't like it. Some hard-faced militia Super standing behind me in his shiny suit, mouth like a trap, practically sweating contempt.

Another 36 hours straight. Can't keep taking the nosleep pills, hitting maxed out as it is. Left before I should because I want to punch that Super just for the pleasure of seeing the astonishment on his smarmy pinker face. Aps like me aren't supposed to be able to do that. Delegate the data entries, go for a walk along Rue de Pisan to clear my head. The old quarters, prettier than they have any right to be, with their patched up single fronts and scabby gardens shining in the starlight. The sleet has lifted, wind like knives. Rues totally deserted after the raids, all I can see is a scuttle out of the corner of my eye as some alarmed citizen vanishes down an alley at the sight of me. Turn up my suit, saunter about like it's summertime, buy a bottle of the raw stuff from Freemart. Come back here.

The me that everybody thinks they know. Doesn't add up to much of a life.

A room with a bed. The stink of yesterday's dinner. A couch that ought to be condemned. Dead plant in the window from some time I thought I should get serious about home decorating. I was probably going through a hopeful phase.

Privacy. That's worth something, maybe the only thing I've got that is. Nothing, and I mean nothing, can get in here that I don't know about. I've still got skills, and I'm even more paranoid than OpSec. Too paranoid to have someone to come home to.

Might have been possible once. Back then, I don't know what I thought I'd be doing now, but it sure wasn't this.

You're full of surprises, Mal said a few years ago, when I broke a skinner gang that was getting past everything that OpSec threw at it. I laughed. If only he knew. Maybe the most surprising thing is that I'm still alive. I should have been dead a long time ago.

Bo

When Jenna came to she was as weak as a baby. I don't think she really knew where she was, but she recognized Morro. Dez helped us to carry Jenna into her room, where we put her to bed. Dez washed her face and got her to sip some water. Morro and I left Dez sitting by Jenna's side. Then I used Dez's steriliser to dispose of the dead leech. The sun was just rising.

We checked on Ma. She was sleeping peacefully and the colour had come back into her face.

'She looks ten years younger,' I said to Morro. 'You, on the other hand, look ten years older.'

He grimaced. 'Does it suit me?'

'Maybe in ten years it will.'

'I've spread myself a bit thin over the last couple of days. Do you mind if I crash on your bed?'

He was asleep in five minutes.

I was past being tired. I made myself something to eat and sat in the front room. The house was quiet. Outside it had begun to sleet again. There was hardly any wind, so the white rain fell straight down, spreading an icy sheen on the rue.

After I'd eaten I went to check on Dez and Jenna. Dez was fast asleep but Jenna was sitting up, rubbing her face.

'How's Bel?' she said.

'She's good. Asleep. How are you?'

'Starving.'

I made her a lemon balm tea and cooked some tates and greens, which she wolfed down pretty quick.

'Can we go outside?' she said when she'd finished.

'It's freezing.'

'I just need to get some air.'

She borrowed Dez's long coat and I pulled on my leather jacket. We went out the back and sat on the bench Ma had built at the side of the herb garden, under the greenhouse domes. The sleet had eased to a soft drizzle of rain.

'Ma likes to sit out here when the weather's good,' I said 'She likes the sun on her face.'

'She's a real maker, I can tell. Dez is too, isn't she?'

'She can make all kinds of tech. She's brilliant.'

'And what about you?'

'Come on, I'll show you something.'

Without thinking, I took hold of her hand as we stood up. 'Sorry,' I said and let go.

'You're blushing.'

'Am I?'

She put her arm through mine. I felt dizzy with the pleasure of it. 'What are you going to show me?'

I took her to the container that stood in the back corner of the yard. It was a steel cube that Ma had found abandoned at the edge of the Seventh, where a transport terminal had once stood. She had it brought home by a carrier and we now we used it as a shed.

'I cut open half the roof, put in a few sheets of perspex and a light,' I said. 'It's not big, but there's enough room for the plants Ma's put in here, and for what I'm doing.'

I opened the door and we went in. Ma had built a few shelves along the back wall, where the plants best caught the light as it slanted down through the skylight. The other half of the space was taken up by my mess.

'I'm building a homer,' I said.

Jenna looked at my narrow workbench crowded with motor tech in various states of assembly, dead consoles and loops of wires and home made tools. I'd made the body of the homer from an old quad. I'd found it in a rusting pile of junk out in the Tenth a year or so ago. It took me and a couple of steadies an entire day to drag it home.

'It's a quad,' I said. 'The miners use them in the dasht. Four-wheel drive, independent suspension. This model's meant for just one rider, but I've put on a side-car.' I slung my leg over it and sat on the metal frame of what eventually would be a seat. 'You'd sit there.'

I pointed to the arrangement I'd fixed to the side of the quad, an old fuel pod from a heavy transport. I'd hacked off the top so it looked like half an egg shell. Jenna crouched down inside.

'I'll put a seat in, of course.'

'Does this thing actually...go?'

'It doesn't have wheels yet, but, yeah, it goes.' I set the gyro, opened the fuel valve, flicked the ignition and pressed the throttle, praying that the engine would start. 'It runs on a synthetic methane derivative. There's still a bit in the tank.'

The engine whined and shook for a couple of seconds, then finally fired. It purred like a giant neka.

We sat there for a while with the engine running. I imagined that we were heading through the Third and Fourth, riding circles around the food-towers. Maybe we'd stop and listen to the bees working inside them, that low, sleepy hum. I don't know what Jenna was imagining, she sat there smiling, going somewhere in her mind. When I switched off the engine I helped her out of the pod and we ended up standing close together, face to face.

I felt myself blushing again and tried to think of something to say. 'What you did for Ma was amazing.'

Jenna lowered her eyes. 'It'll take her a while to get over what she's been through. And she might be changed.'

'Changed?'

She looked up. 'I drew the leech, so it won't be poisoning her any more. But I can't tell what it might have left behind. Whatever it is, I don't think it can hurt her. But...'

'But what?'

'We'll see.'

She must have seen my worry, because she lifted her hand and touched my cheek. 'You look tired, Bo. You need some sleep.'

'Yeah. I guess I do.'

'Thanks for taking care of me. I'm okay now. I'm fine.'

We walked back into the house and Jenna went to check how Ma was doing. I got a blanket from the cupboard and curled up under it on the couch in the front room. Falling asleep, I could still feel the touch of Jenna's hand on the side of my face.

Dez

I scooped most of the contents of Newport City Library a few years ago, but I never got around to reading much of it. When I woke up, I spent a while in bed reading up on culls. Catching that Alchem virus, I guess. They're hot on history. I'm beginning to see why.

The last big cull was called 'population control', same deal about running out of resources, criminal infection and so on. It was a real screw-up, they killed maybe two hundred thousand people in the outer banns by dropping incendiaries, and what do you know, they broke the Outer Veil and all but put paid to their precious Inner Veil. Disposing of the bodies was another screw-up, they hadn't thought ahead on that, and all the decomposing flesh temporarily poisoned their water sources. Hahahaha. But not really. There's nothing funny about treating us like we're a plague of vermin.

It explained some of the things that had puzzled me in the OpSec reports, why the pinkers might be a bit leery of doing a big cull again.

Culls on a smaller scale continued until about twenty years ago, but fleshers kept fighting back. There were riots, protests, all sorts of unrest. Eventually a bunch of fleshers, Alchems probably (the histories don't say), broke into Newport City and burned down OpSec HQ.

I didn't know that. I felt a rush of pride and astonishment that they'd managed to do something so incredible. OpSec killed most of them but the pinkers finally decided it would be better to negotiate. They made concessions, a deal between the banns and the City, and ushered in a period of accord.

This is what me and Bo grew up in, this time of accord. Some of us could begin to build some kind of a life, like Ma did for Bo and me. Only some of us, of course. Most of the banns are still versions of hell, one way and another. And now they want to change it back, because now it's long enough ago that they think the old times were better. Better for who? Not us, that's for sure. But there are no flesher historians writing down what it's like for us. Not in Newport City Library, anyway.

Whether pinkers thought the accord was good or bad seemed to depend on what book I was reading. Some said it led to uncontrolled population increase, smuggling, increased rates of crime, a bigger threat to Newport City. On the plus side, people talked about a new prosperity, because resources were reallocated from OpSec to things like meditech and media and fleshers started making their own economies.

That's when skinners began to be a problem. I guess pinkers had enough time to start feeling anxious about their quality of life. They began to worry that they weren't quite real, that their feelings weren't real feelings. What the hell does that mean? If you have a feeling it's a feeling. End of. If you hurt, you hurt. If you love, you love. It's what you do about it that counts.

Anyway, none of that was very cheery reading, so I put it away.

Flora pinged that she was up, so I went across the road and had breakfast at Café Boite.

You know when you know everything is going to shit and you're so happy and you feel like you haven't any right? That's how I feel, light as petals, light like I'm glowing. In the middle of everything, there's Flora. There's always been Flora, there will always be Flora. It means flower, and that's what she is, a beautiful flower turning her face to me, that half smile, mischievous and so sexy, the dimple in her cheek, her smell, musky heaven. I want every cell of her. I can't believe that she wants me. How lucky am I? Very lucky. Way luckier than I deserve to be.

After the raids, so quiet in the bann. Streets almost empty, most people crouched at home like rats hearing the exterminator walking above their nests, wondering what's going to happen next. Even the shijo is closed. Nobody knows what I know, but even so everyone's scared. At Café Boite I heard people wondering in hushed voices if there'd be another…you know. They mean another cull. Bad memories die hard. Nobody wants to say it out loud in case that makes it come true.

I turned my back on that sick feeling of dread and looked at Flora. Kojo was behind the bar giving me suss looks. He's so proud of his daughter, overly protective, and his first thought is whether she'll be happy and safe. I think a lot of flesher parents are like that, coming out of such bad times. I don't know what happened to Flora's mother, I'm not sure Flora knows, and even now I've never dared ask.

At first Kojo wouldn't let Flora play gigs, and they had some terrible arguments. But Flora, she's a warrior. Kojo taught her every way of fighting there is, unarmed combat, how to use a gun, a knife, a taser. I saw her deal with a gang that jumped us once, six of them. In around thirty seconds flat they were on the ground groaning, and Flora was standing there, the taser in her hand, the wind blowing the hair back from her face. Maybe that's when I first fell in love with her.

Behind that shyness, she's fierce. I think I've lost every fight I've had with her. And in the end Kojo gave in, though he still pings her constantly when she's back late from a gig. The night she disappeared he was almost as feral as I was. Almost.

I mostly get on fine with Kojo, but he can get dark if he thinks I'm any sort of threat. I think he was happier when Flora and I weren't talking. But he loves her enough to know how unhappy he'd make her if he didn't let her have her head, be the person that she wants to be. That she is.

Sitting there, twiddling her ringlets, looking at me. I wanted to kiss the tiny blue bird tattooed high on her right cheek.

'Stop smiling so much, Dez,' she said. 'I'm not used to it.'

I pressed my lips together but the smile kept breaking through. 'I can't help it,' I said. 'I'm just so happy to see you.'

'What have you done with the real Dez? No really, where is she?'

'Here,' I said seriously. 'Right here.'

'Let's go to my room,' she said. 'I want to get out of here.'

We finished breakfast and went upstairs. And everything, just everything, was roses.

Bo

Ma was still weak and a little dazed, but she could sit up in bed. She didn't remember much about what happened the day before, which I thought was for the best. Dez made her some soup and fed it to her.

The skies cleared during the morning. Jenna and I went out to the garden again, because it was the only place we could be private. We chatted about this and that, unimportant everyday things. I showed her my back route into the house, over the wall, which made her giggle. We talked about gigs we enjoyed and places we liked, things like that.

A silence fell between us, a comfortable silence. I thought about all the things I wanted to tell her, the things you don't say to somebody you've only just met. Finally I blurted out, 'I wish things weren't so difficult right now.'

'We could pretend that they aren't.'

'How would we do that?'

'If things weren't so difficult, what would we do?'

That was easy. 'We'd go Café Boite for a drink and some of those delicious pastries that Kojo makes. Then walk over to the Sixth. There's a swapmeet today, all kinds of geeks getting together to exchange stuff, mostly old tech, but instruments as well. A lot of musicians turn up. Maybe a snack at a bar afterwards. There's some nice joints around there.'

Jenna smiled. 'You've got it all worked out, eh?'

'I didn't know that I had, but, yeah, that's what I'd like.'

'Then we will. Only not now.'

I didn't want her to go. It was more than just liking her, though I really liked her. It was stronger than that, something that I couldn't explain. It was like part of myself was going to walk out the door. I wanted to say that to her, but I couldn't. I could already feel the ache of being away from her.

Dez threw out a floating shield from the front door. It was narrow, a corridor running for about a hundred metres. It wouldn't last long, but it would get Jenna and Morro to the end of the rue. After that they were on their own.

They switched on their suits and I opened the door. To my surprise, Morro gave me and Dez a hug. 'Thanks, both of you.'

Jenna paused in the doorway and turned back. She flicked off her suit and kissed me.

And they were gone.

Dez followed me around the house for the next hour nagging me about Jenna, asking me stuff I didn't know or didn't want to answer. She wouldn't let it go. 'We're friends,' I said, which annoyed her no end.

'Since when?'

'Since yesterday.'

'She kissed you. On the lips.'

'I noticed.'

'Was that the first time?'

I love Dez, but she can be a complete pain. She really enjoys getting under my skin. Finally I'd had enough.

'I'm going out,' I said.

'Where?'

'A swapmeet.'

'You should stay home. We still have to be careful.'

'I will be careful.'

I threw on my belt, checking that my suit was fully charged, and grabbed my old keyboard from under the bed. I didn't need it any more, I had a new one that Dez had jazzed up for me. It made my playing sound better than it should, given how little I practice. The old one still worked okay and had a great sound. Some music tragic like me, dreaming of playing in a cool crew, would snap it up.

'Don't ping me,' I said. 'I won't be long.'

'I'll ping you if I want.'

'Fine.'

'Where's this swapmeet?'

'The Sixth.'

'Get me something.'

I was halfway out the door. 'Pardon?'

'Get me something.'

'What?'

'I don't know. Anything. As a token of your esteem.'

As I walked to the Sixth, I tried not to think about Jenna. I wished she was with me, going to the swapmeet like I'd said earlier that day. I didn't want the thought of seeing her again to bore into in my head, making me feel like every minute was a minute spent waiting. We both had our own lives. We'd only just met. I didn't really know what her life was. And how much did she know about me? What was there to know?

Of course, the more I tried not to think about her, the more I did.

I'd just swung into Rue Paradis when I saw Giro up ahead of me. I guessed he was heading to the meet as well. He was pushing a handcart loaded with all kinds of musical junk. He built instruments and did repairs for musicians in the local banns. He was the best. He was a big guy, about fifty and overweight, with long greying hair down his back and two enormous silver earrings. I ran and caught up with him.

'Bo, old bug!' he said. 'Nice to see you. You might be interested in some of this, I've got a heap of cast offs to unload. I'm looking for parts I can use in a new beats phaser I'm building, fusion of old and new tech, a beast.'

The meet was just around the corner in Mishkin Square, where the local well used to be. The well had dried up long ago but the square was still used for various gatherings, like an artists' shijo once a month. There were a few tables set out around the edges where you could lay out whatever you'd brought, and maybe twenty or so people wandering about. I recognized a few faces.

'Not much of a turnout,' said Giro. 'Doesn't look very promising.'

I was helping him unload his merchandise when I heard the noise. It wasn't like anything I'd heard before: a high pitched whine with a deep under-sound that hit you right in the chest. I thought that it was some kind of drone, but there was nothing in the sky above us. I was still looking up when Giro tapped me on the shoulder and pointed down Rue Mishkin.

Something was approaching us. It looked like a kind of silver cloud, blurred with static, fizzing.

'And behind,' said Giro.

I swung around and saw the same thing coming into the square from the opposite direction. There was no way out. My whole body went cold and heavy with dread.

Both clouds stopped moving and hovered where they were, pulsing, heavy with energy. Everyone started moving towards the centre of the square, around the old well, as far away as we could get.

A voice boomed from one of the clouds, its echo bouncing off the surrounding buildings. 'Stay where you are.'

Nobody moved.

I pinged Dez, sending a distress signal. At least she'd know where I was. Or where I had been. Almost as soon as I'd pinged, my suit went dead.

Then it was like the clouds came into focus, as if the blurring that encased them had dissolved. They were transports, but not any kind I'd seen before. The red Newport City logo was right there on the side. A circle within a circle.

The front of the first transport opened and a line of heavily armed militia filed out. They headed straight for us, all in step, until they were only a few metres away, when every second one branched off to either side. They were grey from head to foot and when they moved their shapes blurred. It was difficult to tell where they were going, or how fast they were moving. When they had us surrounded they stood there, motionless. It was completely silent.

Giro took a few steps forward, slowly lifting his hands. 'Nobody here is causing any trouble,' he said.

I didn't see where the shot came from, but one of the militia blasted him. He flew backwards, landing just where he'd been standing a moment ago. There was nothing left of his face.

Dez

Ma got out of bed when Jenna and Morro left and didn't go back, even though I kept telling her that she ought to rest. Aside from saying that she felt fine, she acted like she didn't hear me. We had an argument about who was going to cook lunch, which I won by pushing her onto the couch and starting it myself. She just laughed at me and stayed there, chatting with me in between checking out the tubes to see what was going down in the banns.

I covertly inspected her as I fried up some tofu and beans. She really did look ten years younger, though it was hard to say how. Her life was in her face, she was a flesher woman who had raised two kids on her own, making a future for us against all the odds. But a greyness in her being, a heaviness, had now lifted. I thought of the black thing that Jenna had hauled out of her. She'd been fighting that all these years. I felt a sudden overwhelming rush of love for her, as if I'd never really understood before who she really was.

I scraped the meal out of the pan onto the two plates we had left after the first raid and Ma came to the table and began to eat. 'You should leave Bo alone,' she said.

'You didn't see how he was looking at Jenna.'

'That's his business,' said Ma. 'Stop being jealous. It doesn't become you.'

'I wasn't jealous. I was only teasing.'

She gave me a narrow Ma look that said, *I know you, don't think I don't.* 'Yes, you are,' she said. 'Sometimes teasing is fine. And sometimes you should just leave be.'

'It's okay, Ma,' I said.

'Just stop getting at him, girl,' she said.

This was one of Ma's serious talks. She never did it much. I knew she was annoyed with me for driving Bo out of the house, so I didn't argue any more.

I was putting the dishes in the steamer when Bo's ping came through. I'd programmed trouble codes into our suits, red for skinners, blue for cops, double for urgent, in case there wasn't time to send details. The location was where he said he'd be, Mishkin Square in the Sixth. This was blue and urgent.

Ma's head jerked up. 'What was that?'

I was trying to open a line to find out more, so I didn't answer. Bo's suit was dead. I felt a huge chasm open in my chest. My god, not Bo, please, not Bo, please let him not be dead…

I met Ma's eyes. I didn't have to say anything.

'Where?' she said.

I felt like my lips were frozen. 'Mishkin Square. That's where the swap-meet was.'

Ma started searching the tubes to see if anyone had posted alerts.

'Nothing…nothing…no, wait. Transports heading up Rue Mishkin.' I saw her shoulders slump and then she kind of braced herself. 'Weird ones. Not the usual Aps transports.' Then she went silent for a while. I watched her, feeling numb. I could have looked myself, and quicker, but all I could feel was overwhelming dread. Bo.

'There's a snap from someone who lives over the square.' She twirled the screen around and expanded it so I could see. It was blurry, taken from out of a window maybe four floors up, and there was no sound. The camera couldn't pick up the transports until they stopped, it looked like they were coming out of nowhere. Dozens of militia stepped out. The camera zoomed in on the people in the square, all of them moving into the middle as they were surrounded. I couldn't see Bo at first. Giro was near the front, easy to pick out because of his hair. I watched as he stepped forward, his hands out in front of him, and then he was blown backwards, blood blooming out of his skull. People around him recoiled in horror and I saw a glimpse of Bo, his mouth open, before the snap stopped abruptly.

Giro. Damn them all to hell. The most harmless person in the banns. Everyone knew him, everyone liked him.

I started scrolling the tubes myself, blinking tears out of my eyes, trying to find out what was happening. Messages were beginning to circulate, shocked, angry, frightened, rippling out from Mishkin Square. As far as I could tell nobody else was shot, but several posts said everyone in the square had been arrested. Nobody had seen anything like those transports before, they were already being called clouds. I switched into a more secure protocol, hunting through the dark tubes. An anon called Achilles had loaded up the Mishkin Square snap, someone else had collated a bunch of tube posts. There wasn't much at all.

I looked up. While I was searching, Ma had opened a private line and was talking to someone. She named a time and snapped it shut. I tested it. It was a *very* private line, one even I didn't know about.

'So, what can you find?'

'Not much,' I said. I felt my voice trembling, so I swallowed, trying to match Ma. She seemed calm, even cold. 'It's only just happened.'

'We need to find out more. Did you search the dark tubes?'

I nodded, feeling amazed. I didn't think Ma knew about the dark tubes.

She met my eyes. For a moment I thought she was going to break and cry, but she didn't.

'We're going to get Bo back,' she said. She said it with an absolute certainty that made the hair rise on the back of my neck. We didn't have a chance of getting him back. It was absurd even to think it.

'How?' I said. 'We don't even know who took him. We don't know where he's gone.'

'He's my son,' she said. Suddenly her eyes were blazing with fury, it beat out of her, radiant, fierce. 'He's your brother. We're going to get him back.'

It was maybe five minutes since Bo had pinged me.

Brian Mac

RDO. Not official as such, a little fiddle with the roster to bring some hours forward. I'm pissed off, exhausted, sick of being around militia clones, the way they smell, like some kind of floral antiseptic, sick of everything. Lie in bed a couple of hours staring at the ceiling, trying to be bothered to get up, maybe go out, find something to eat. Don't want to go out, don't want to go anywhere.

Wondering if maybe I should get another job. I mean, I think this every day, but some days I think it more…pungently. I could set up a little business in Newport City, maybe some kind of hole-in-the-wall offering authentic bann cuisine, the little dumplings you get in the shijos, home-grown berry pastries, that sort of the thing. It's quite fashionable among the cognoscenti these days.

Only problem is, I can't cook. The only thing I'm good at is frying skinners.

I get out of the steamshower and drag on some clothes and Bel opens up a line. I set it up when she lived in the Ninth, so long ago now I forgot it even existed. It has its own channel, one of the deep lines I use for informants and such. She's never used it, not once, not even when that damn Ap got shot in her damn house, when I might have been some use to her. When I see what the signal is, I break out in a sweat, like a physical shock.

She tells me that son of hers just got scooped up in some kind of OpSec roundup. She wants to know where they're taking him. I say I don't know, it's my day off. She says we need to talk. I tell her to come here at 17.00 hours, I need time to find out what happened, though really it's more I need time to think. She takes a sharp breath, I hear it over the line, and then repeats the time and closes the line.

Something in her voice, like something's leapt back alive, an edge I haven't heard for years. Cool, crisp, decided, like she's planning some op. I had a sudden flash of memory, Bel in that black suit she used to wear, she knew she looked good in it, belt low on her hips, hair scraped back in a tight black plait, those cheekbones, dark eyes. She affected a silver lens chip back then, a flash of lightning in her iris. My god. She was magnificent.

She'll be wanting him back. I didn't tell her there was no way to get him back, that I'm not militia, they have nothing to do with Aps. She's knows that already.

She's going to ask something impossible from me. Maybe she has the right. Maybe I owe her something impossible. Let's face it, some debts hang heavy. Some get heavier over the years.

Still in a sweat. Calm down, Brig Brian Mackinstosh. Sweating because she's coming here. Nobody comes here, to my house. Fear. I can smell fear in me. Not of Bel, I don't think it's Bel, she always scared the shit out of me, but not in that way. Fear of what she's going to make me do.

Do I care? Seriously, Brig Brian Mackintosh, Level 11. Do you care about your miserable wormshit life? Could it get any worse?

Of course it can get worse.

Jul 33 13.43

These militia raids are giving me the willies. No curfew announced but they're conducting sweeps on public gatherings, subjects to be taken to

Black Site 34b. The operational orders tell me almost nothing. They are looking for 'samples', precise numbers from different banns, and they're not
using Aps. Bel says they picked Bo up from a swapmeet in Mishkin Square.
There was an op in the Sixth, but that's all I can find out. No IDs, not even
a record of how many they took, which is kind of weird, given the instructions.

OpSec is big on data. They like to have everything in the records, nice
and tidy, so they know what they have to hide. It's not like they don't send
us constant memos about bad book keeping.

Find out more from scanning the flesher tubes. A few snaps showing
these new transports. I've heard of them, never seen them, they said they
were developing them for operations in the dasht because the camouflage
confuses predators. Sounding more like black ops to me. They don't need
them for the banns. Well, up to now they didn't. Do the pinkers really think
they won't use this tech on them?

In any case, none of this is adding up to routine.

I get itchy when OpSec decides to get all creative, it's always bad news.
If it was my bann I could send some of my men in to mess with them and
maybe haul Bo out of there. The Brig in the Sixth is Kellway, one of the scum
I promoted sideways out of the Second. He owes me, and he hates the militia as much as I do, but that doesn't mean shit. I open a line and tell Kellway
that the militia have scooped up some of my flesher informants and that I
want them back. He hems and haws and says he might be able to do something to screw OpSec up. He doesn't say what he's thinking and he's not the
kind of man you can push, so I'm crossing my fingers and hoping for the
best, which is never a good bet in this part of town. Kellway's not one of the
smartest spinos in the bunch.

Finally decided to use Mal's passcode, which could get both of us into
trouble, so hopefully if he notices some unauthorised usage he might keep
shtum. It gets me past the first wall, which is something, but then I run into
another raft of classified intel. I don't know why, but they're sending the
fleshers to a secure medical facility in Newport City Western Hospital. A
medical facility? What the hells?

Bo

I'd never seen this kind of tech before.

The OpSec transports appearing like shapeless clouds was one thing, the militia's uniforms having some kind of distorting capability was another. There was just a grey blank where their faces should have been, some kind of visor that seemed to float and ripple, as if it was made of water. Even their weapons were surrounded by an aura that made them difficult to see, as if they might not really be there. But what one of them did to Giro was proof enough that they existed.

They bound our wrists behind our backs with some kind of flexible material that began to harden as soon as it touched our skin and herded us into one of the transports. We were pushed into a long, narrow chamber that ran along one side of the transport's interior. A door slid shut and we were left pressed shoulder to shoulder in total darkness. We couldn't feel any movement, or hear any sound.

I was soaked in sweat. I tried to move my fingers, but there was no feeling in my hands at all. It was getting hot. The wall in front on me was so close that I could feel my breath on my face. My whole body started to hurt, my back, my legs, my neck, my arms. It was impossible to move, to do anything to ease the pain. I thought I was going to scream. But I didn't scream. I passed out.

I came to on the floor of a large, brightly lit room. It was completely empty apart from a small camera in each corner. My wrists had been unshackled and I was lying on my back. I rolled over and threw up, a long thread of bile that burned my throat and the inside of my mouth. The room was freezing. I was still soaking wet from sweating so much in the transport, and my skin felt as if it was covered in a thin sheet of ice.

I looked for the faces that I recognized when I first arrived in the square. Rioka was here, and Ziyin and Mish. Arjun was curled up in a corner, sobbing. I didn't know any of these people well, they weren't steadies of mine, but I'd seen them at other swapmeets and gigs. We were all young, into music and making stuff. Harmless. But, yeah, enemies of the state, obviously. Ten men, eight women.

We started to talk, trying to piece together what was going on. Everybody's tech was dead. Giro's death was the one thing we all remembered. None of us would forget that.

Nobody had seen any Aps. This was a militia operation. You knew what to expect with Aps. Even the new ones who been put out into the banns lately were more or less predictable, even if they were more brutal. But this was something else.

This place was probably a black site. We'd all heard dark rumours about them. We'd been swept up and hidden away. Disappeared.

Dez

You can't live in the banns without running into one kind of trouble or another. If it isn't the Aps, it's skinners. If it isn't them, there's a shijo turf war or some lowlife trying to muscle in on anything you're making. And if it's not that, well, there are the nanostorms, or a snap freeze turning your blood to ice if you're caught in it, or not having enough to eat (though it's been a few years since that had been an issue for us). I mean, you get used to risk, living in the banns, and you get used to living with the knowledge that every time you go out, you might not come back. You rub your lucky charm and you get on with what you have to do and most of the time you're all right.

But now the rules are changing. Whatever Bo's got himself into, I don't think it's the kind of trouble that a few credits here or there can fix up. The usual laws don't apply.

When Ma said she was off to see Brian Mac I told her she wasn't thinking straight. First of all, for going out, when who knows what was going down in the banns, and second of all, for thinking that Brian Mac would be able to do anything about it. Ma nodded, but she still went.

Maybe Ma knows something about Brian Mac that I don't. Well, I'd say that's a certainty. I've started wondering the past few days what went down with those two. All I know is that they've got history. It's no use asking Ma straight out, she'll just purse her lips and say nothing, or scold me for something else that she's saved up so she doesn't have to answer questions she doesn't want to answer.

Anyway, she told me to contact Morro, and when I said I didn't know how to do that she just looked at me until I worked it out. I'd seen that look before, kind of certain and hard, but somehow it was more focused, like having a laser bore into your soul.

It took my mind off thinking about Bo. I didn't have a contact with Morro, but I knew they'd gone back to Jenna's squat in the Eighth. I did a scan of the dark tubes, thinking maybe I'd luck out and find something that way. No dice. Then I remembered that Flora had put Bo in contact with Morro, and that I hadn't spoken to her since Bo had been arrested. I opened our private line and told her what had happened. She had no idea there had been arrests, her dad had told her to work in the kitchen all day and wouldn't let her step outside.

'Oh Dez,' she said. 'Oh, Dez. Not again. Not Bo.'

'It's some kind of militia raid,' I said gruffly, so I wouldn't cry. 'Not Aps. So we can't get him out like Brian Mac did with us. Ma says we need to contact Morro.'

There was a slight pause. Morro was still a sore spot. 'I can do that,' she said. 'I'll get back to you.'

Five minutes later she was on the line. I realised that she must have some private line to Morro. All that mysterious faffing around with Bo was just more Alchem gameplaying, then. More lies.

'He'll send,' she said. I had no idea what that meant. 'Jenna's on her way already. She's very upset.'

'Bo and her only just met,' I said. I couldn't help myself.

Again there was a pause. 'Sometimes it's like that, Dez,' she said softly. 'You know that.'

Something inside me clutched tight. 'What, with Morro, you mean? You just look at him and instantly fall in love?'

'Dez, will you just stop it? What's wrong with you?'

'What's the deal with you and Morro, anyway? Why won't you tell me?'

'Because I swore not to,' Flora said.

'And it's okay to keep secrets from me?'

'Not everything is your business. Some things are just my business.'

'Like what?'

There was a pause. A long pause. 'I'm an Alchem, Dez. Nobody knows. Except Morro. And you. Now get off my back.'

She snapped the line closed without giving me time to answer.

I sat there staring at the wall. Flora was an Alchem? I felt that fury rising inside me again, but now it was mixed with fear. What was Flora getting up to? God knows what shit Morro had her doing. I knew she could look after herself, but I didn't want to lose her too.

And now she was angry with me again. I'd said I wouldn't hurt her, and here I was. I took a deep breath and went into the front room.

Ma was making bread, pounding the dough like it was one of the militia. She looked up, frowning.

'Morro's sending, whatever that means. Jenna's already on her way over.'

'You'd better set up some kind of field,' she said. 'I don't think we can risk the shield again.'

'A field?'

'It's a bit oldtech,' she said. 'But done right it fuzzes the energy surveillance. I'm sure you can make it cover two extra bodies. Flynn and me used fields all the time before you were born.'

I blinked. This new Ma was taking a bit of getting used to. I mean, I always knew Ma was tough and smart, that's how she managed to survive when Bo and me were little. But since Jenna got that thing out of her there was this other side to her, which I had glimpsed but never quite seen. And she almost never talked about our dad.

'All right,' I said. 'I'll find out what that is, and try to set one up.'

'It will need some finessing,' she said. 'But I'm pretty sure they never quite tracked how it worked, and then people stopped using them anyway because shields were more efficient.' She wiped her hand on her brow, leaving a white streak of flour.

I got some basic tech details from Ma because I couldn't find anything in my files, and then tinkered for the next hour. It took my mind off everything: the awful fear that Bo was already dead that lay underneath; the rage that possessed me whenever I thought about Flora and Morro. Maybe the anger was a way of not thinking about Bo. Even in the middle of it I knew it was ridiculous, but that didn't stop me feeling it. Feelings. I'm not very good at them.

When I set the field up Ma examined what I'd done, and then she put her arm around me and kissed the top of my head.

'That's fantastic,' she said. 'Way better than anything we did.'

'What else did you do?'

'I'll tell you about it one day.'

'How about now?'

'When we get Bo back and all this is over.'

The little leap of pleasure I had felt at doing my job well died into ash. I didn't know if we would get Bo back. And maybe this would never be over.

'My clever girl,' she said. 'I knew you could do it.'

And then I started crying, for the first time that day. Ma didn't cry. She just held me, saying nothing.

Brian Mac

Well, that was difficult. More difficult than I expected. The way Bel looks at me. Maybe she knows more than I think she does, though I wouldn't put it past her to have guessed.

Maybe it's time you made a choice, Brian, she says. You've never really chosen. In any case, I can't make it for you.

Then that pause, she's carefully not meeting my eye, carefully giving me space.

I trust you enough to think that you won't spill us to your superiors, she says, as I search for ways to respond. I don't know if I can trust you more than that.

I tell her that I don't know either, trying to be honest. She gives me an odd look, kind of contemptuous but also...kind. That's the only word I can think. Like I'm some flesher kid she's caught trying to thieve something from her, and she's decided isn't worth punishing.

I clear my throat. Things are changing in Newport City, I say. I'm not sure what I can do.

I know, says Bel. All the same, you have resources. We need all the resources we can get.

What about all the other kids they picked up? I ask her

She goes silent.

I want Bo back, she says.

And so does every other mother out there, I tell her. Why should you be so special?

For a moment I see the hurt in her eyes, before she hides it under that cool look. That was always the best way to hurt Bel, to show her that you saw her selfishness. God forgive me, in that moment I want to hurt her.

She asks if we can get the others out, and I tell her that getting one body out from under the nose of OpSec is stretching it, and getting all of them out is pretty much the definition of impossible.

Then we get as many as we can, says Bel. Typical Bel.

Maybe we can get one out and fuzz the records, I say. But I don't know where they are being kept.

She looks at me, weighing my words. Yes, you do, she says

I'm not even surprised. She could always read me.

It's some new secure facility, I say.

Okay then, she says. You can give me the intel you have and leave it there. Your hands will still be clean. Or just mildly filthy, at least.

I tell her she wouldn't have a chance without me covering her tracks.

Maybe, she says, maybe not. She says something about how she has other resources and for some reason I know that she's thinking about Dez and a shiver trickles down my spine. I suddenly find myself wondering what Dez can actually do. I know she has abilities beyond the average flesher, some kind of DNA splice that should have been eradicated, but I'm beginning to wonder if she's a bit more radical than I thought, that maybe for once rumour isn't exaggerating.

In the end I say that I'll give her what I know, but it's not much.

She shrugs as if it doesn't matter. And then?

I don't know, I say.

I'm hoping to get a team together tonight to talk over ideas, she says. I could let you know.

Her tone is super casual, but I hear the decision under her voice. She's serious about this, god help us all, things always went toxic when Bel was serious.

Now it's my turn to shrug as if it doesn't matter. The choice. There it is, its teeth shining sweetly in the dim light. No matter what I do, yes or no, it's a trap, it's going to slam shut on me. I know that already.

Up in the labs they like to think they can program us pinkers. DNA as destiny, that kind of thing. Although of course they explain that this is nuanced, that ancient argument about nature versus nurture which nobody has finished after all this time. They say they can predict our behaviours in any given circumstances pretty much ninety nine point nine per cent accurate. I had a close look at my clone program once, when I was interested in these things, and maybe there's a truth in it. I was programmed to be autonomous, to dislike authority (up to a point), to choose risk (up to a point). I never worked out where that point was, though I know obedience is ultimately programmed in. I feel it in how I bow to the militia supers, no matter how much I want to smash in their faces. In the final moment I bow before the hierarchy, I let it go. In the final moment, I need the system just as much the system needs me.

Maybe I need it more. The system doesn't need me at all. It's evolved, moved on. It's smarter than me and bigger than me and better armed, and it can predict to ninety nine point nine per cent accuracy what I will do in any given situation.

Or it thinks it can. How much do I get to choose, if I do have a choice?

Let me know, I say.

Bo

We'd been in the room for maybe six or seven hours. It was hard to tell. It must have been late into the night when the door slid open and a line of gurneys was rolled in, each of them pushed by an AI. Four armed militia stood watch at the open door, blurred bodies with masks of grey water.

The AIs unloaded a body from each gurney as we watched. Nobody said anything, nobody moved. It was as if we were seeing a replay of what had happened to us. Twelve young men and eight young women this time. The AIs wheeled the empty gurneys out and the door closed behind them. It had only taken a few moments.

We did what we could to help the people on the floor. They were all as dazed and afraid as we were. They had been in the Sixth, preparing the rue outside the towerblock where most of them lived for an event that night. For the past few years the local homer drivers had been running an annual race through the rues around the bann. It was a lot of fun: almost everyone in the neighbourhood turned out to watch and cheer the drivers. There had been talk of cancelling the race because of the raids but they decided to go ahead, partly to spite the Aps, partly to show OpSec that there were some things that they couldn't control.

The militia turned up. The only difference between our experience and theirs was that no one had been killed.

I ended up sitting with Rioka and Mish. Rioka was a stallholder in the Fifth, selling scavenged oldtech with a sideline in implants and home brewed booze, the raw stuff. Mish was a musician. He was into trance beats, brain music. I'd seen him play a couple of times, he was good. We weren't steadies, but we knew each other and went to a lot of the same gigs. None of us had any idea why we had been hauled in by OpSec.

'We haven't been scanned for ID,' said Rioka. 'They don't care who we are.'

She was right, though I thought that maybe they scanned us when we were unconscious. We'd just been collected and dumped.

'I haven't seen this kind of militia before,' I said. 'The tech is new, those weird transports. Maybe this is some kind of trial run for something else…'

'Whatever it is,' said Rioka. 'I think that we're in seriously deep merde.'

Before we could say anything else, half a dozen militia entered the room, followed by someone of higher rank. He was a head taller than the rest, with some kind of black insignia on his sleeves, and we could see his face. His name was on the flap of his breast pocket. Slocum. He looked about sixty years old, but with pinkers it's hard to tell. He could have been eighty or ninety, or even older. He had that smooth, gleaming skin, jet-black hair, eyes like green ice. On his signal, the militia began hauling us to our feet. We were pushed up against a wall and formed into a line. Slocum gestured for us to be taken out of the room.

We were marched down a long, featureless corridor. I sensed that we were now deep under the ground. Mish turned to say something to me and one of the militia clouted him across the side of his head. He stumbled and fell, clutching his face, and I stopped to help him up. We were shoved back into line.

Finally we were herded into a narrow room. Slocum stood in front us, his hands folded behind his back, and slowly surveyed us. You could tell that to him we were little more than animals. Having to deal with us was a task he probably felt was beneath him.

As he opened his mouth to speak, a door to our right slid open and a squad of Aps appeared, led by a Brig that I'd seen around in the banns, Kellway. I'd encountered him before. He fancied himself a hard man, but he was just cruel and callous. Before he'd been promoted to Brig he was under Brian Mac, and we'd all had our run-ins with him in the Second.

Slocum stared at Kellway, his face turning a darker shade of pink. For a moment neither of them said anything.

'What are you doing here?' he barked.

'We're here to make our contribution,' said Kellway.

'Your what?'

Kellway waved his squad forward. They ushered in about twenty frightened fleshers, some of whom had been roughed up badly, and shoved them towards us. We made room for them as best we could. The groups merged, pressing tightly together.

What followed was one hell of a barney. Slocum pulled Kellway as far away from us as he could, but there was really nowhere for them to go except into a corner, standing close, face to face. They started yelling over each other, Slocum telling Kellway that he had no right to be where he was and Kellway insisting that his orders came from the highest authority and that his detainees were assigned to Slocum's operation.

'You have no authority in this operation,' said Slocum.

'Whatever happens in the banns is within my jurisdiction, and as such my authority is assumed,' said Kellway.

'I don't care what you assume. Your assumptions are incorrect.'

'I have had orders that contradict that position.'

Despite myself, I had to admire Kellway. He was giving as good as he got. He totally ignored the fact that an Ap, no matter what his rank, has no authority over any member of the militia.

'You will take your men and you will leave. Now,' Slocum said finally. 'Your detainees will remain here and I will deal with them. You can tell whoever gave you your orders that you have carried them out.'

Kellway left, looking smug. Once he and his squad had gone, Slocum yelled at the guards.

'Forty, give me forty! Take the rest to processing in section three. Be quick about it.'

The group was quickly divided into two. None of us had any idea what this meant, or what section three was. Slocum led one group and half the guards out of the door in front of us. The rest of us were herded through a door to our left, into another long corridor. It ran straight for a long time and began to slope downwards. We were going deeper. The light was softer here, no more than a bluish glow, but I could feel the pressure growing in my head, as if the whole weight of the ground above was pressing down. We were being buried alive.

Section three was a black room. They pushed us in and shut the door. It was like being inside Morro's lightlock.

Up until now, no one had spoken. We had seen what happened to Mish. Now, standing in complete darkness, we felt free to talk. People whispered each other's names and began moving in the darkness. Mish was somewhere nearby and when I said his name he felt his way towards me. Rioka heard us and reached for me with her hands, finding my face. I took hold of her and drew her close.

The conversations around us sounded like the wind blowing through the leaves in the foodtowers. Underneath the whispering someone started crying. It sounded like a young man. Someone must have embraced him because his sobs became muffled, as if he was being pressed close to another body.

So far we'd held our nerve. We were fleshers after all. We were used to being pushed and shoved, treated like beasts, our lives disrupted, hauled off by the Aps for reasons we didn't understand. We'd learnt how to live with it.

We all knew this time was different.

How many other people had been swept up by the militia? Had the same thing happened to Dez, to Ma, to Flora? Where was Jenna? She was hiding out in that towerblock, among all those broken, desperate, ugly people at the bottom of the heap, among all the pain ignored or feared by everyone else. She had to be so strong to do that. That didn't mean she wasn't vulnerable. She could be scooped up like we had been, like fleas being scraped off a gau's back, and tossed into some OpSec pit.

If I could speak to Jenna now, what would I say? Would I tell her how helpless I felt? I hardly knew her. I wouldn't even tell Dez how afraid I was, and I love Dez and I know that she loves me. What would I say to Jenna? How alive I felt when I was near her? I wanted to believe that I'd get back to her somehow, that I'd see her again, that I'd kiss her. I wanted her to kiss me again. That's all I would say if I could talk to her, if I could find the guts to say it straight out. Kiss me, I'd say. Kiss me.

A loud buzzer sounded and above us a red light began to flash, giving us brief glimpses of each other huddled in tight little groups, blasted by what looked like pulses of fire.

An entire wall of the room slowly started to lift and light flooded in. In front of us a long platform ran inside a steel ribbed tunnel, with a train standing alongside. It was an single carriage flat-nosed mono, driverless, squat and square-sectioned. There were two small windows at the front and long narrow windows along the side. It was coated with rust and scarred with darker patches of flaking corrosion along its sides that looked like blast marks. All the windows were blacked out.

A line of militia stood along the platform. Four peeled off and pointed their weapons at us. For the first time, I heard one of them speak. 'Board the train,' he said. His voice was amplified and flat, without any modulation. 'First door.'

Inside, it was very cold and brightly lit. The low-ceilinged carriage had been gutted, leaving just a metal shell. We stared at each other, blinking as our eyes adjusted. The carriage doors closed and we heard the locks snap shut. The engine whined as it engaged and the train shuddered forward and began to gather speed, rolling a little from side to side. As there was nothing to hang on to, it was impossible to keep your balance standing up. I sat on the floor, next to Mish and Rioka. Across the carriage was a woman with thick, red hair falling to her waist. I knew her. Her name was Rouge and she worked in the shijo making soups and hot snacks for the stallholders. A young boy, perhaps about twelve, was leaning on her shoulder. Perhaps he was the one we had heard sobbing in the darkness.

Rioka shivered and Mish pulled her close and put his arm around her shoulder. I put my arm around him. Soon we were a little warmer. The bruise on the side of Mish's face was already starting to show.

'Any theories about where we're going?' he said.

'Duiwel Island?' Rioka said.

'Maybe we're still heading for section three,' I said. 'Maybe that last place was just a transit point.'

'Perhaps that's all section three is,' said Mish. 'And now we're heading somewhere else.'

'Maybe they're letting us go,' I said. 'We'll come up at the mono station around the corner from my place. You're both invited back. I'll make us some tea.'

'I'd kill for a cup of tea,' said Mish.

I don't remember falling asleep, but I woke up when the train stopped. All around us people stirred. A woman pressed her ear against the door, listening, as everyone watched. Eventually she turned to us and shook her head.

Nothing happened for a long time. Then the door slid open and a group of maybe a dozen men were literally thrown into the carriage, falling to the floor in a struggling mass. They were bound together at the wrists by a thick length of carbon cord. They were a ragged, painfully thin bunch, barefooted with shaven heads, but you could tell that they were pinkers. Under the grime there was that pale flesh, those strangely smooth faces. Behind them stood a phalanx of grim-faced Aps, almost as ragged and filthy as their prisoners.

'So long boys,' one of them said. 'See you in hell.'

The doors shut and locked. The train jerked forward and we were on our way again, quickly gathering speed.

The pinkers dragged themselves across the floor to a corner of the carriage, like a weird tangled beast. They didn't even look at us. We moved out of their way, getting as far away from them as we could.

They closed in on themselves, folded together as if they were a strange plant closing its leaves.

'Duiwel,' Rioka whispered.

Mish nodded and turned to me, his face pale.

'We're going to the mines,' he said.

Dez

By the time everyone arrived, it was well into night. Flora came over just after I set up the field. I hadn't asked her to come, and Ma wasn't too pleased when she saw her, but I was glad.

She looked at me and saw I was sorry. She didn't say anything, she just kissed me.

'I'm sorry.' I said it out loud, just to be sure.

'I know,' she said. 'You're such a pain in the arse, Dez. Almost as bad as my dad. It took me ages to talk Kojo into letting me cross the road. He's paranoid about letting me out of the house.'

'Maybe with reason,' said Ma. 'I wish I hadn't let Bo out. I don't think you should stay. We'll be talking business.'

'I want to help. I can help.'

'I think you should stay out of trouble. The more you have to do with us, the more trouble there'll be.'

'I bet you wouldn't say that to Dez if we were in trouble,' she said. 'I bet you'd send Dez over to see what she could do.'

'I'm not so sure I would.'

'I bet you couldn't stop her.'

My eyes met Flora's and, despite everything, I couldn't help laughing.

She looked so mischievous. And then, to my surprise, Ma smiled. 'Your call, then,' she said. 'But don't get angry with Kojo for wanting to keep you safe.'

So Flora stayed. Jenna pinged me when she was about a klick from our house, and then quickly opened a line to check it was okay to meet. She came over the back fence and banged on the back door, and for a heart-stopping second I thought it was Bo, that he'd escaped and come home by himself.

'I'm so sorry,' said Jenna, when we let her in. 'I heard about the arrests, but I didn't realise Bo was taken.' Then, to my astonishment, she burst into tears.

'It's not like you'd even met him a week ago,' I said.

'Dez!' For a moment I thought Ma was going to slap me. She gave me her laser look of deadly force, and I shut up. Yeah, okay, maybe I *was* jealous. He was my brother, after all. Is my brother. *Is.*

'Are you hungry? I've made a mash,' said Ma. 'We might as well eat while we're waiting for the others.'

'There's only Morro to come,' I said.

Ma gave me another look, and I shrugged. 'Anyway, I'm not hungry.'

Ma dished out her mash, which was one of my favourite things when we were little. It was a stew made from whatever was left over, with miso and green onions and loman, a kind of mushroom we all grow in the banns. She served it with fresh flatbread and my mouth started watering, so I asked for a small serve. Then, when I started eating, I had that strange thing of food turning to ashes in my mouth, becoming difficult to chew and absolutely tasteless. I always thought that was some kind of exaggeration. I pushed the bowl away and left the table and curled up in my chair.

Ma and Flora and Jenna glanced at me, and then went back to chatting as if nothing was the matter. I knew that all of us felt Bo's absence, and also that they knew it was best to leave me alone, but to me it felt heartless.

Bo. Like I said, often it was as if I was the big sister, but now I was remembering him as my big brother. Sometimes we fought like nekas, and we got under each other's skin all the time, but when it came down to the knuckle Bo was always there for me. One of the only things I remember about being sick was Bo sitting beside me, stroking my hair. When that bouncer Igor tried to wipe me off the street back when we lived in the Ninth, Bo knocked him down, even though he was a head taller. And he had stayed down, too. Bo looked out for me. We talked every day, even if we weren't home we were always chatting through our suits. And now he wasn't there, and I didn't know how to deal with the silence. I wished I was as strong as Ma. Maybe she had felt like this after Flynn was disappeared. How did she cope?

Morro strolled in shortly afterwards, as if he'd just been hanging out in Bo's bedroom. He obviously didn't need doors to get into a place. For reasons best known to himself, he was wearing his silver jacket. There was an unreal sense about him, it wasn't like you could see through him, but I had a strange feeling that he wasn't really there. Ma didn't start proceedings. She didn't say why, but we knew she was waiting for someone else.

Brian Mac arrived about ten minutes later. When Ma let him in, I almost didn't recognise him. He was wearing a shabby old jacket with narrow lapels, of a kind that went out of fashion so long ago they were now coming back in. I had only seen him without his goggles that time at the precinct, and I had never seen him without his long red coat. They were so much part of him that he seemed to be a different person.

'Bel. Dez.' He nodded. He looked a bit nervous. I was picking up a strange buzz around his suit, and realised with a small shock that it was similar to the field I had put around the house. He had some tech in that jacket to stop him being followed.

'You hungry?' said Ma.

'Nah. I ate earlier.' He sniffed the air. 'Smells good, whatever you made.'

'It was,' said Jenna. She was studying Brian Mac curiously, waiting to be introduced.

'Brian, meet Jenna and Morro. Jenna, Morro, this is Brian,' said Ma. 'He's Brig of the Second Bann.'

Morro didn't react at all. Jenna went white to her lips. 'What?'

'What I said. I've known him for more than twenty years, Jenna, and I have reason to trust him.'

'But he's an *Ap*!' Her voice was high with shock. 'A *pinker*? What are you thinking?'

'Like I said, I have reason to trust this man. And he can help us, if he chooses to.'

'What if he chooses to, you know, just report us all to OpSec? Or arrest us? What then?'

'I won't.' Brian Mac was still hovering by the door as if he was expecting to be sent out of the house any minute.

'You just take his word on that? You know someone's informing on us, right?'

Brian Mac just looked at her, the ghost of a grin on his face. 'Not to me, they're not,' he said.

There was an awkward silence, and then Jenna stood up.

'I'm not staying here,' she said.

'Jenna, I understand…' Ma began, but Brian Mac interrupted her.

'I don't know what you kids know these days, but maybe the name Culcullan means something to you?'

It didn't mean anything to me, but Jenna halted halfway to the door.

'Culcullan? They never knew…'

'No, they never found out who it was. For what it's worth, that was me.'

There was another long silence, and then Jenna went back to her chair and sat down. 'How do I know you're not just saying that?'

'Because I knew who he was too,' said Ma. She turned to Brian Mac, a sudden gentleness in her voice. 'You didn't have to say that.'

'I think I did.'

'I wouldn't have.'

Flora and I were just watching, not knowing what the hell was going on. An inscrutable glance passed between Brian Mac and Ma, and I shifted uncomfortably in my chair. So this was some of that history that Ma never talked about? I started running through my files, trying to find a reference. Surely there'd be something in the Newport City Library…

'Culcullan was an Ap?' Jenna seemed dazed. 'An *Ap*?'

'How do you think he got inside the security?' said Ma. 'Of course he was.'

'So is anyone going to tell us what this means?' Flora said.

'If you don't know, then let's keep it that way,' said Ma, infuriatingly. 'It's dangerous enough that you know even this much.'

By now I'd scanned all possible spellings of Culcullan. There wasn't anything in the files I'd downloaded. That was also infuriating. Pinker histories, worse than useless. I opened my mouth to argue, but Morro spoke first.

'Well, well, well,' he said. 'So the real Culcullan has finally been identified? That's a turn up for the books.' He leaned back, putting his hands behind his head. 'Didn't stop you arresting my friends, did it?'

Brian Mac kind of shook himself, and finally sat down near me, away from the others. 'You might have noticed that the Second precinct never was involved in Alchem arrests,' he said. 'My speciality is skinners.'

'You might be the legendary Culcullan,' said Morro. 'But you're still a cop.'

There was a silence, and then Ma stood up, her hands on her hips, and looked around the room. 'We're all here,' she said. 'And maybe, instead of wasting time squabbling, we can talk about what we're here for.'

'I can't stay for long,' said Morro. 'We'd better get down to business. I'm in read-only mode.'

'You're what?' said Flora.

'Read-only. I can't do anything much except talk and listen. Means I can be here longer, but an hour is about tops.'

For some reason I looked at Brian Mac. He didn't seem surprised at all by Morro. He must have known something about him already.

Morro leaned forward. 'So, the plan is that we walk in under the noses of the Newport City militia and rescue Bo?'

'That's the idea,' said Ma.

'Excellent. We don't know where he is. He could be on Duiwel Island. He could be in some black site anywhere in the banns. He could even be in Newport City. And even if we did know, we'd have to get past militia clones and AIs and walls of nanotight security without anyone noticing, and get ourselves out with Bo, again with nobody noticing. It's impossible.'

Ma nodded. 'We're going to do it anyway.'

Bo

We were all sinking, drowning in half sleep. I began to imagine that there was no destination, that this train would simply keep travelling until all of us were dead. Maybe we were just travelling in circles under Newport, around and around under the banns in an endless loop. This was section three, this going around in circles forever. And there were other trains, in front of us and behind us, dozens of them, hundreds, travelling in the same circle. All of them filled with people like us who were growing weaker, falling into this thirsty sleep and then into unconsciousness. Trains filled with corpses, with bones and dust.

I shook myself awake. The pinkers were still folded up in their corner. They seemed to be breathing in sync, the slow rise and fall of their bodies like a pulse. I felt the pressure in the carriage slowly begin to lift. I could tell that we were climbing, coming out from under the ground. My ears popped. We must have been coming up on the far side of the Gilla Sea. How many klicks was that? I had no idea. Now we were travelling overground, out into the dasht.

Despite everything, I was dying of curiosity, but I couldn't see anything through the blackened windows. I'd only been in the dasht that one time, when Dez got the nanovirus. All the things I had ever heard about it crowded into my head.

Out in the dasht are the remains of cities that were abandoned during the megastorms. Some of them are buried by shifting sands or rockslides, or fell into the earth when chasms opened up like wounds in the skin of the planet. Some still stand above ground in tumbled ruins. The miners scavenge these old cities for heavy metals, optic fibre, plastics, or any kind of old tech that can be recycled. When the miners' convoys move on, there's nothing of value left. The names of these cities are forgotten now, except maybe by Morro. He knows more about history than anyone else.

The work is dangerous. Hundreds of miners die every year, nobody knows exactly how many. But it's a job that pays well for the most skilled workers. If they survive, they return rich, but many come back sick or broken.

Inmates of Duiwel are often sent out to the mines to do the low-skilled work when there's a shortage of labour. They don't last long. Their bodies are thrown out into the dasht. Outbreaks of nanovirus are common, and all kinds of splices. The worst affected victims are simply put down. Others are sent back to Newport City in sealed pods for analysis. Experiments. Vivisections.

At least that's how the stories go. Not many stories come back from the mines. Or from Duiwel Island.

I had begun to drift back to sleep, my head filling with confusing dreams, when the train jerked to a halt and startled me awake. Before I knew what was happening I'd been hauled to my feet, dragged out of the carriage and man-handled into a kind of cage, tall enough for me to stand up in but only as wide as my shoulders. I was wedged inside and the cage shut.

We were in some kind of huge, brightly lit storage shed. I didn't recognize the uniforms of the goons doing the hauling and the shoving. They weren't militia, they weren't Aps. It was hard to tell if they were special edition mining clones or AIs. They wore black coveralls and goggles and there were dozens of them. Some people tried to resist as they were pulled out of the carriage. They were tasered and shoved unconscious into the cages. I caught a glimpse of Mish being pushed into a cage, and then of Rioka being dragged unconscious from the carriage. The only ones to escape this kind of treatment were the inmates from Duiwel. They were goaded into a line with short, black prods and led off separately, stumbling as they went.

The cages began to move. We were on a conveyor belt that travelled along the platform and through a narrow opening that led into a smaller, dimly lit space. It was difficult to see anything: I was so confined that I could only turn my head a little from side to side. After a while, the conveyor belt made a ninety degree turn and our cages rattled and banged together. We went through another door that slid shut behind us.

I could see the sky.

The cage doors swung open automatically. We stumbled out onto the floor of a large room. There was a row of folding beds along one wall and canisters of water. At least there was water.

In the crush of thirsty people, I found Rioka and Mish. 'Are you okay?' I said.

'I've been better,' said Rioka.

'Look,' said Mish, pointing up.

'I know,' I said. 'I know.'

The ceiling was very high, sloping at a steep angle. It was made of thick glass that was coated in grime, but you could still see through it.

The sky was yellow, streaked with bands of black cloud that slowly turned around themselves, like gigantic strands of twisting rope. That jaundiced light and roiling black clouds were signs that a bad storm was on its way.

Sometimes these clouds just passed overhead. But if the storm hit here, there wouldn't be anything to protect us except those sheets of glass. No Veil. No nothing. I saw anxious glances flickering between the groups of fleshers. We all felt it: we were abandoned, vulnerable. And there was nothing any of us could do about it.

Like everyone else, I kept checking nervously while at the same time trying not to look up. This time the clouds passed over us and the sky cleared. I could feel the tension subside in the room as people settled, finding their places and people, trying to create normality in a situation that was anything but normal.

Rioka, Mish and I stayed together. When this whole thing started we hardly knew each other. Now there was no way that we'd let ourselves be parted. Looking around, you could see all kinds of similar alliances.

We're fleshers. We've never lived a day of the shining, perfect lives of the pinkers, the kinds of lives that Dez watches on the soaps, where everyone is sure of what belongs to them and what they have a right to expect. We make do with the simple warmth of each other, making fun of what's hard or unfair. Small pleasures are large in our world, suffering is ordinary.

The sky darkened quickly as night closed in. People fell asleep holding someone they hardly knew, resting in the closeness of another body. Just knowing that someone as cold and hungry and as frightened as you was breathing beside you was enough. It had to be enough.

Dez

I'll never forget that night. The field I'd put around the house had a weird effect on the light, making it seem kind of shimmery, like you couldn't tell where it was coming from. There was Morro, his dark face watchful and sober, his smile flashing out when something excited him. Jenna next to him, her skin and hair so pale she seemed bleached of all colour, her eyes big and sad. Flora and me, and then Ma at the head of table. And strangest of all, Brian Mac, sitting opposite her at the other end.

I knew he wasn't a typical pinker, he didn't have that smoothness that the other Aps did, the shiny, pink skin that looked as if it didn't have any pores. You could see the age in his face, around his eyes and mouth, and there was a scar on his cheek that he'd never bothered to get scrubbed. His eyes were pinpoints, so I figured he was on some kind of upper or implant, but he didn't seem blurry or intoxicated in any way.

I realised I'd never looked at him properly before. Why would I? He had always been a weirdo Ap to me. Maybe one of the better Aps, but an Ap all the same. The byword in the banns was, never trust an Ap. And yet there he was. I saw Jenna and Flora making covert glances too, still uncertain about his presence, but Morro seemed completely unfussed.

Ma took charge, as if she did this kind of thing every day of the week.

'First thing,' she said. 'We have to find out where Bo is.'

'We do know,' said Brian Mac. 'He and the rest of the detainees have been taken to a secure medical facility in Newport City Western Hospital.'

Even Morro looked surprised at that. 'A medical facility? What the hell for?'

'How do you know?' said Jenna.

Brian Mac cleared his throat, and put his hands on the table, looking down as if he were going to read from them. As we waited for him to speak, I suddenly realised that he felt exposed. Maybe he was shy. I wasn't very comfortable with realising these things about Brian Mac.

'There's something going down in Newport City,' he said. 'These raids, the precincts haven't been consulted about them. We weren't even warned. That's very unusual. There's some scare, or some plan, and I can't find out what it is.'

Morro looked at me. 'I think we know,' he said.

'Shut up, Morro,' said Ma. 'You can speak after Brian.' Morro glanced at her in surprise and for a moment I thought that he'd argue, but instead he nodded.

'Carry on, then. But remember I'm in read-only mode, I can't stay long.'

Brian Mac squinted at Morro and clearly decided to ignore him. He went on. 'Some of you will know that there's been a recent change of admin in Newport City, and there's a whole bunch of new policies being pushed in. The new Aps in the banns are a part of that, a different kind of clone. I haven't been able to look at their programming, which is unusual. I demanded access, and was denied. That's also unprecedented, the Brig needs to know what his staff can do. So they've been sending in these recruits since last summer, not in a big way, but enough to make the old Brigs a bit unhappy. We're sniffing the wind, shall we say. Something's changing.'

Flora shifted impatiently in her chair. 'What's this got to do with where Bo is?'

'I'm getting there.' He smiled for the first time since he'd arrived. 'That'll do for the background briefing. I don't know how up you are all are on City politics.'

Flora looked baffled because she never watched the Newport City infonews, but everyone else nodded. I thought of the new boss Osborne with his smooth smile twinkling at the cameras, all the soaps about evil fleshers, what I knew about the cull.

'Anyway, the orders for these arrests today, they're nothing to do with Aps. The percussion raids yesterday, they weren't either. The raid on the Alchems, that was all OpSec, from top to bottom. Suddenly the City is interested in the banns, after years of not giving a fuck unless their precious biosecurity was threatened. And none of us know why. So I used my super's passcode and checked the operational instructions. He's still too low-level for me to find out what it's all about, but OpSec is rounding up fleshers from every bann to send to this secure hospital unit. They don't care which fleshers. They just want samples. They ordered precise numbers.'

Samples. I didn't like the sound of that. It sounded a lot like something a skinner might say. I stole a glance at Ma. Her face was hard, expressionless.

'The good news is that the Newport City Western Hospital is near the border of the Second Bann,' said Brain Mac. 'That makes a rescue a little more feasible. We just have to get through security in the City. It's been tightened but they don't do DNA checks on the way in, they rely on the veil to screen out any nasties. Technically speaking, no unauthorised DNA should be able to get through.'

I frowned, because unauthorised DNA gets through all the time. The skinners showed that: if they couldn't sell what they took from our bodies, they wouldn't bother to hunt us.

'So how do skinners get through?' I asked. 'And why doesn't the City do anything about it?'

'There are always ways and means,' said Brian Mac. 'It's a real tech war out there. The skinners get through, OpSec catches on eventually, kills the trading ring, patches the breach. The skinners find another way. It's why I've still got a job, they know I'm good at stopping skinners. The best, in fact.' He said this without pride, just as a fact. 'Fortunately for us, I am the first line of defence against City corruption by rogue DNA.'

He paused. Everyone was paying attention now. I think he was enjoying it.

'And it's not just skinners who get through.' He paused. 'There's the meat trade.'

Ma looked up sharply. 'No way are any of these kids going in that way,' she said.

Brian Mac leaned back, folding his arms. 'You got a better suggestion?'

Ma said nothing. I knew a little about the meat trade, but not much. There were brothels in Newport City where pinkers could go to have meat-sex with real fleshers. Very specialist, apparently, a real fetish. Every now and then there was a raid that made the infonews, but the authorities kept it under wraps because of the scandal. I wondered again about pinkers. They were very weird.

Morro was frowning. 'You sure that Bo and the rest have been taken into the City?' he said. 'Maybe we should double check.' Here he turned to me.

I didn't want Morro talking about what I can do in front of Brian Mac. 'It might be an idea,' I said, throwing him a dirty look. 'But why would Brian Mac be wrong?'

'Does he have a positive ID?' said Morro. 'We're talking a very high-risk operation. You'd want to be sure of what you're doing.'

'They didn't take any IDs,' said Brian Mac. 'Which is also unusual. But they're very precise about where to send the detainees.'

'Do you know what they want to do with them?'

'No,' he said. 'That was in a locked file.'

Morro looked at me speakingly. I knew he wanted to me to go into OpSec again, and I gave him a warning stare. Everyone else was silent.

'We do know, from our sources, what the new policy is,' said Morro. 'OpSec want to do another cull, the worst ever. They want to sterilise the Middle and Outer Banns, kill everyone and everything. They're saying this coming Octo. So I guess all these raids are the first part of the plan.'

Jenna was the only person who didn't look shocked. Morro must have told her already. Everyone else gasped. I hadn't told Ma or Flora. Somehow I couldn't bring myself to when I first found out, I'd have had to tell Ma that I'd gone into OpSec and she would have killed me.

'Your sources?' said Brian Mac.

Morro managed not to look at me. 'I'm not sure I can reveal them here,' he said. 'But this is top level info. Make sense?'

Brian Mac nodded slowly, like a bunch of things were slotting into place. 'Yes,' he said. 'I'm afraid it does.'

'So I know Bel here just wants to get her son back. Yeah, we all want Bo back. But there's more at stake here. You see what I'm saying? There will be millions of Bos if we don't stop this.'

'So what are you saying?' Ma said sharply.

'I'm saying that we don't have many resources, and that we should be focusing on the real problem.'

There was a silence. Then Ma spoke. 'The real problem is that they've taken Bo, and we have to get him back.'

'One thing, they'd notice for sure if there was a prisoner missing. It'd set up alerts.'

'I can alter records,' said Brian Mac.

'Even at that level?'

'I have my methods.'

'I don't see why we should help,' said Morro. Jenna stared at him, a protest on her lips, but he avoided her eyes. 'I know it sounds harsh, but the Alchems are already under pressure. We've lost a lot of our crew. There's a bigger picture here.'

In that moment, I hated Morro. Really hated him.

'Then why should we help you?' I said.

He looked at me. 'What do you mean?'

'You want something from me. So maybe if you help us, I'll help you.'

Morro tried to hide it, but I could see a flash of satisfaction in his face. Maybe this was why he came, he figured that he could make me go back into OpSec. He really had no idea how risky it was. Or maybe he didn't care. If they figured out what I was doing and OpSec traced it to me, it would cause way more trouble than a failed mission to rescue Bo ever could. Hiding in the lizard brain wouldn't be enough, they'd be into every single cell of me as soon as they got a sniff of my DNA.

Morro pursed his lips, as if he was thinking. 'Maybe we could do a deal,' he said. 'We all need intel.'

Ma was looking between us with a puzzled frown, but I could see that she was beginning to put two and two together. Brian Mac wasn't far behind her.

'Yeah,' I said. 'I hacked into OpSec, and that's how we know about the cull.'

I saw the amazement in Brian Mac's face. Obviously he suspected that I had abilities, but he hadn't had a clue what I could actually do. Ma just looked shocked, and then incredibly sad.

Flora took my hand. 'Dez, no,' she whispered. 'How could you take that chance?'

'I did it after the AI shot the Ap,' I said. It was weird how long ago that felt, it seemed to have happened months back. 'I wanted to know if OpSec had got hold of my DNA.'

'And did they?' That was Ma. I think she wanted to slap me and hug me, and didn't know which she wanted to do more.

'No,' I said. 'Not yet. Brian Mac sure did a good cover up. I thought there'd be alarm bells going off everywhere.' Brian Mac blushed slightly at that, which amused me.

'So, if we help, you'll go into OpSec again?' said Morro.

'Maybe we don't need the Alchems' help,' I said.

'Depends what help they're prepared to give,' said Brian Mac. I could tell that Morro was getting up his nose too.

Morro shrugged. 'As if I'd tell an Ap, just to have you use that intel against us later,' he said.

Brian Mac turned towards Morro with exaggerated politeness. 'I can see this team functioning with extreme efficiency.'

'Team. Huh.' Flora was angry too. 'Morro, you don't give a stuff about Bo. So why are you here?'

Morro opened his mouth to argue, but Ma stood up. She's not very tall, my Ma, but when she's angry you don't notice. Now she was furious, and she seemed to tower over us.

'Shut up, the lot of you,' she said. She didn't shout, but even Morro subsided. 'We don't have time for arguments. My first priority is to get Bo back. Then we can talk about the cull.' She turned to Brian Mac. 'So, am I right in thinking you already have an idea?'

Brian Mac nodded. 'I spent a bit of time looking up architectural and security plans this afternoon,' he said. 'We could get in. We could get out. I can fudge the records so if we do it without raising an alarm, nobody will notice that someone is missing. I don't dare do it for more than one person, though. You can't get any heroic ideas about this. We'd have to go in for Bo, and Bo alone.'

For the first time I properly understood how selfish we were being. How many people had been arrested in those raids? Twenty? A hundred? If they scooped up that whole swapmeet, it would be mostly younger people too. People like Bo.

'It won't be easy.' Brian Mac looked at Morro. 'It would help if we had someone with, er, special abilities. Of the kind you have, Morro.'

Morro blinked. 'What kind is that, copper?'

'I know you can be in two places at once. You're not as discreet as you think, kid.'

There was an awkward pause, and then Jenna stirred and spoke for the first time.

'Don't be a dick, Morro,' she said. 'You owe these people, remember? I'm in.'

'I don't think you should risk it,' said Morro. 'We need you.'

'You can't stop me,' said Jenna.

Morro knew it, too. I saw it in his face.

'Okay,' he said. 'The Alchems will help. It's against my better judgment, but if you're determined to do this, I guess we do it as well as we can. But only if Dez goes into OpSec again and finds out what they've got on us. And who our informer is.'

He turned and looked at me. Everybody was looking. I felt my cheeks growing hot with mingled self-consciousness and anger. It seemed unfair that now it was all on me. I'd have to figure out a completely different way of getting past the OpSec firewalls, and I had no idea where to begin. But maybe something would turn up later. Now, we were desperate.

'I'll do it,' I said. 'When I see Bo back home, safe and well.'

Ma drew in a sharp breath, but she didn't object. Morro flashed his irrepressible grin.

'Good girl!' he said. 'We have a deal!'

I wanted to kill him.

Bo

I was dreaming about Dez, when she was ill with the virus. Ma was beside her bed, exhausted after watching over her all night. Dez was as bright as a spark, sitting up in her bed, as young as she was when she was sick, but fierce and strong like she was now.

'Where's Bo?' she kept asking Ma. 'Where's Bo?' Ma shook her head and said that she didn't know and fell asleep, slumped in the chair beside Dez. Ma dreamed of Flynn, and then Flynn was in the room, our Da, right there. I couldn't see what he looked like, but I knew it was him. Da was asking Dez, 'Where's Bo?' and Dez was shaking her head. And then Ma woke up and Flynn was gone and Dez was dead, lying in her bed still and cold, her skin as waxy and pale as a pinker's.

I woke up thinking that I was at home in my own bed. Mish was still asleep in the bunk beside mine, the bruise on the side of his face blacker than it had been the day before. I turned over and saw Rioka in the bunk on the other side. She was propped up on her elbow, watching me.

'You were talking in your sleep,' she said.

'I was dreaming about Dez.'

'Who's Dez?'

'My sister. I think she's trying to find me.'

I was hurting all over. I swung my legs over the edge of the bunk and stood up. My head started spinning and I sat down again. I looked up through the glass roof at the sky, a grey blank, a sheet of nothing.

'What happens now?' I said.

Rioka didn't answer. A squad of goons was already coming into the room, carrying tasers and prods. They began pulling us from the bunks, chivvying us in a line against the wall. Didn't they ever speak? One of them walked down the line, checking us off. All present and correct.

In the next room another lot of goons waited for us, belts slung across their arms. They fitted us with them one by one and switched the belts on remotely with something that looked like a taser. A shock went through my body, a cold sting that took my breath away. It took a few seconds to fade, but it remained faintly, as if it were under my skin. I looked down at the belt. There was no way to turn the suit off.

Then we were taken to another room, a kind of canteen, where something that resembled food was laid out on metal trays. Our bellies were empty, so we ate. I don't know what it was, yellow cubes that tasted like a curd of some kind. It had a dry aftertaste that made my mouth feel as if it was full of dust.

Eating it made me feel as if my veins were being flooded with static electricity. My heart began to race and all my aches and pains dissolved. From the looks on people's faces, I could tell that the same thing was happening to all of us. The initial buzz lasted a few minutes at most. When it passed I felt as if my tiredness had been swept away and replaced by a feeling of elation, not emotional, but physical. It was as if I had a new body.

After we'd eaten, a militia officer walked into the room. He was a pinker, middle-aged, tall. He stood at the head of the table and gave us a long look. Obviously these pinker officers specialised in these looks. I was already getting tired of them.

'I don't know who you worms are, or what I'm supposed to do with you,' he said. 'I assume that you're criminals of some kind. That's how you'll be treated. So you will work.'

His voice was cold and very clear, very clipped. He was used to this kind of thing, telling people exactly what the facts were. 'You've been issued suits. They'll protect you from everything but the worst you'll encounter out here. From the worst, there's no protection.'

He gave us another of those looks.

'You'll be working outside. You'll be supervised by a miner team. They will supply you with the equipment you'll need. Listen to them. Do what they say.' He paused before continuing. 'We're here in B75C for another month. Maybe by then someone will have told me why you've been sent here and what I'm supposed to do with you. Now piss off.'

He watched in silence as we were rounded up by the goons and marched out.

This time we were taken to a locker room. Here there were dozens of yellow coveralls hanging on the walls, with boots, hardhats and breather units. The goons directed us with gestures and hand signals to equip ourselves. They still hadn't said a word. I was beginning to think that they couldn't speak.

From there they took us to a chamber, about as big as the steel cube in the garden at home. It was a tight squeeze. The goons shut the door on us, a light above the door began to flash red and the cube started moving. We travelled for maybe fifteen minutes, until it stopped with a jolt and everyone was thrown sideways. Something heavy crashed against the door outside and the light flashed blue.

The door opened and we stepped out onto a long steel ramp. We were in B75C. It stretched out in front of us under a bright blue-green sky.

A city.

Brian Mac

So I'm going to help them get Bo out, I'm going to help Bel and this bunch of punks get Bo out from under the nose of OpSec. Yeah, and I'm going to make it rain credits as well, I'm going to free the slaves, I'm going to kill the King. Long live King Brian Mac.

The anguish of disobedience. It's almost not there, just a low level ache. I need to get a grip. Think straight. Be practical. Get out the old gear, the old skills. The old Culcullan. They could never work out how he did it, how he got past all their walls. They figured it had to be an inside job, they even suspected me at one point. But they just never got their finger on that sweet spot.

Why did I have to mention Culcullan? Because I figured that those young Alchems would know who Culcullan was? Bel and Flynn were the only people who ever knew it was me. All these years I've kept that quiet, and one word, it's out. My own vanity astounds me. Hating myself I can live with, I've grown used to it, I know how to feed it, how to starve it. But admiring myself makes me want to slit my own throat.

That Jenna, she's something. It's too easy to dislike Morro. He reminds me too much of myself. My previous self, I mean. Who knows what I am now? I don't.

It's not Bel. It has never been Bel. It's what she does to me. It's what she makes me do to myself. She wakes something up, something I thought was dead, that I hoped was dead. I look at her and I feel it. I feel who I was when I first looked at her, when I first knew I loved her, when I knew she would never love me back, not the way I wanted her to. She wakes up that man.

I was young then. I taught myself to be reckless. I took all the hunger and anger and I turned it into Culcullan. The man no one could touch, the man no one really knew, the man who hardly knew himself. Who didn't want to know.

For a while it worked. I fed on danger, I ate it up. The more my life was at risk, the more alive I felt. I was the Ap, rising through the ranks, a little unconventional, brilliant at his job, and I was the subversive, destroying the work of the Ap, unpicking his threads, fucking him up, winning. I was both of them, sincerely. And they sincerely hated each other.

There was never only one Brian Mac, there were two, and they were both me, a two-headed monster at war with himself because it was the only way he knew how to be at peace. I could be obedient and a rebel. I could be the law and the crime. It was beautiful. It was hell.

When I see Bel I'm looking through those eyes. She makes me remember, she makes me want to be Culcullan again.

Maybe that's enough mirror gazing. There's nothing in the mirror but me.

Dez

The next day I entered Newport City for the first time in my life. I hadn't had much sleep. I'd been up most of the night preparing our suits.

Despite everything, I couldn't help feeling excited that at last I would see Newport City for myself. I expected something different from what I saw. Something like that fabulous world I had seen in the soaps, I guess, all shiny windows and weirdly perfect people. Or, at the very least, something like what I'd seen in the infonews, which was slightly less sparkly, but glamorous all the same.

It wasn't like that at all. You don't see this part of Newport City on the infonews. As we walked through the alleys and shuttered shops, rues of down-at-heel houses and early cafes turning on their lights for their first customers, I felt a nagging disappointment. There was less rubbish around and yes, there were streetlights, which were a novelty in the banns, but it didn't look much different from the Second. People here looked poor, maybe a bit messed up. They were all the same colour, but otherwise pinkers looked pretty much the same as fleshers.

Getting through the Inner Veil was easier than I expected. It seemed that Brian Mac paid for his implants and other vices with a bit of petty corruption, and he had contacts in the meat trade who owed him a few favours. Ma wasn't very happy about this. We all knew why. You could make a lot of money in the meat trade, at least by our standards, but it was dangerous for fleshers: if you got caught by the authorities, it was an instant death sentence, no questions.

Pinkers are paranoid about fleshers, they think our bodies are some kind of infection that has to be sterilised pronto, in case it sullies their purity. There are practical reasons for that, we all know what happens when rogue nanos get wild with your DNA. But then again, look at me. It's not all bad.

When he briefed us, Brian Mac had told us that fleshers and pinkers weren't all that different. We all looked sideways at each other when he said that. The one big difference, he said, is that pinkers are raised not to touch each other. Most pinkers think that actual touch is disgusting. It's all enhanced reality, VR and IMR.

'It makes it easier to control people,' Brian Mac said. But, he said, there's always a few who want something else than what's officially on offer in Pinker City. 'They've tried over the years to weed out the genes that cause people to go rogue. But you can't. You end up with too many cases of psychosis. And there's always people who think that something is missing. That's how you end up with the skinners. And the meat trade.'

And, I thought, how you end up with Brian Mac.

We all knew Brian Mac's attitude to skinners, but he didn't seem to have a problem with the meat trade. Ma had a big argument about it with him, before she agreed to let us go ahead with our plan. She almost didn't let me and Flora go at all. I knew why, she was afraid she'd lose both me and Bo, but in the end she saw that we needed my abilities if we were going to succeed. Saying goodbye to Ma that morning was one of the hardest things I've ever done: not because she made a fuss, Ma never made a fuss, but because she didn't. Flora didn't tell Kojo what she was doing, he would have hit the roof. She just said she was spending the night with me.

It was me, Flora and Jenna. Jenna was going to stay close to the Inner Veil, relaying info if we needed her to, because the range of our suits was limited. Flora and me were going in to the hospital. There was a bit of an argument about that, but I wanted her as my sidekick. I didn't know Jenna well enough, and I needed someone who didn't need things explained.

One thing, when Brian Mac got going on something, he was efficient. He had spoken to his meat trade contacts the previous afternoon. We were being smuggled in as workers. At 07.00 hours that morning we met Brian Mac at Rue Soyinka, near the foodtowers. He was back in his usual uniform, goggles, long red coat, but this time he had some kind of field device working on his suit. It was kind of a relief to see him looking like a normal Ap again. Well, as normal as he got, anyway.

He led us to a blank-looking warehouse in Rue Ban Gu, a tiny side street that had only about three buildings in it. There was a heavy at the door who scanned us for weapons. He didn't pick up the minitasers Flora and I had hidden in our pants. I'd worked hard to make them untraceable, but I held my breath until he waved us through.

We went down some dingy corridors and then through a couple of locked doors with more heavies into a room that was full of stacked crates of vegetables from the banns: mint, spinos, tates and other roots. It wasn't what they grew in the foodtowers. I realised that flesher DNA wasn't the only thing smuggled into Newport City. The more I thought about it all, the more toxic it became. The pinkers had so much more than we did – clean water on tap, all the food they wanted – and yet they wanted our stuff too. Even what we had in our bodies.

At the end of the room was a big, black, smart desk, which looked totally out of place. Behind it was a woman who was even shorter than Ma. Even at that time of day she was dressed with style, like a pinker. High heeled shoes, which I had only seen on the soaps, liner sweeping up from the corners of her eyes, hair that looked like it was sprayed on. She was studying something on a screen when we came in.

'Morning, Ava,' said Brian Mac.

Ava looked up, waved her hand at the screen so it disappeared and swivelled around to face us. 'Hi Brian.' I could feel her eyes travelling over us, assessing us as if we were some kind of unsatisfactory merchandise. 'These the kids you want in?'

'The very ones.'

'I won't ask why.' She studied us further, trying to read us. We were all blocking her, but she didn't seem worried. 'The blonde could make quite a bit of money if she wanted to join our outfit. Interested?'

Jenna met her eyes. 'I don't want,' she said.

'Don't knock it until you try it, girl,' said Ava. 'Most pinkers don't even know what sex is. You'd spend your time washing their hair or holding their hands while they sob brokenly.'

'Thanks for the offer,' said Jenna. 'But it doesn't appeal.'

Ava shrugged. 'Whatever. Keep us in mind, if you're short a few credits. You others, you'd be flesher exotica. Just I'm full up on that market at present.'

Brian Mac seemed amused. 'They're not here to be your employees, Ava,' he said. 'They're mine. A sting in Newport City. I need you to tell your staff to look after them.'

'All done already,' said Ava. She looked at Jenna regretfully. 'Shame, though. You should think about it.'

She reached into a drawer and came around the desk holding three red wrist bands. I could sense them from where I was standing. I had expected we'd be using disruptors to get through the shield, but these were a kind I didn't know. The problem with disruptors was that they could interfere with what I'd done to our suits. I hadn't seen ones like these before, they were good work, smart, not so much powerful as clever. I downloaded the configurations, so I could work out what to do if they did nuke our suits.

'Put these on,' she said. 'Don't mess with them, they're not active yet. I don't think we need to worry about a costume, they'll fix you up on the other side. You've all checked your suits? Any malfunctions and you'll fry.'

We nodded and snapped the bands around our wrists. Even though they were turned off, I felt a chill in my skin: getting through the Inner Veil was going to be rough. But now Ava was talking to Brian Mac.

'I'll take this consignment personally,' she said. 'I've got business in-city. If there's trouble I'll let you know.'

'I'll be at the precinct,' he said. 'If there's trouble, I should know already.' He turned to us. 'You lot, you know what you have to do. We'll speak later. All being well.'

All being well. I didn't want to think about what might happen if it wasn't. We nodded back, and he turned on his heel and left. I watched him go, feeling abandoned. Now it was just us.

'Follow me,' said Ava.

She opened a door behind her desk and led us down another corridor. I walked behind her, admiring how she was balancing on those heels. It was astonishing. I figured she must have had reinforcements put into her ankle tendons, but if she had, I couldn't see any trace of them.

The warehouse seemed to be mostly empty, the skeleton of a concern that had once been thriving. There were a lot of buildings like that in the banns. There were doors open on either side of us, and through them we could see dark, empty rooms. I thought about Brian Mac's dealings with the meat trade. Ma had recoiled in revulsion at the whole idea, but he didn't seem to find anything wrong with it. And yet we all knew that he was totally immoveable on skinners, nobody could bribe him. He was a weird one. The only light was from dim solar bulbs that let out a yellow, directionless light. You could see dust spinning in the air. We went down a flight of steps, along another corridor, another flight of steps, another corridor, a stairwell that went down four floors. Here a door barred our way, and Ava unlocked it with a gene key. By now we were well underground and we couldn't have got back to the surface if we wanted to. If I didn't have my MPS on, I would have totally lost my sense of direction.

At last we reached a blank brick wall. At least, that's what it looked like. Ava turned around, her face hard, and spoke to us for the first time in what seemed like hours. 'Mackintosh vouched for you three,' she said. For a moment I didn't know who she meant. Oh. Brian Mac. 'But if word gets out about this operation, I'll know who to blame. And make no mistake, I will find you. And I will kill you.'

A chill that had nothing to do with the surrounding temperature went down my spine. I totally believed her.

'We've got no reason to tell anyone anything,' said Flora. 'We've got our own secrets.'

Ava nodded. 'Good. Just so we're clear.'

She did something rapid with her hands that my eyes didn't quite catch, and the bricks disappeared. In their place was some kind of elevator. Inside it was pitch black. Ava stepped in, switching on a light on her suit, and we followed her. She pressed a couple of buttons, and the floor shuddered. Something creaked alarmingly, metal on metal. And then, so fast my stomach was left behind, we plunged down into the earth.

Bo

We stumbled down the ramp to find eight miners waiting for us, three of them fleshers. They were gruff and impatient, but at least they talked to us.

'Come on, come on, don't fart about. We've got work to do.'

They quickly divided into us two groups. I stayed close to Mish and Rioka and we ended up in a team with two flesher miners. Their names were scrawled on the back of their coveralls. Pace and Steady. I guessed that it was some kind of joke. The other two miners were pinkers. We never found out their names.

As they led us off, two nekas started trailing us, about twenty metres away. Now and then their stink wafted towards us. It's scary enough when you come across one of the feral nekas in the outer banns, but these were twice as big, covered in thick, matted hair, their long yellow teeth curving down from their jaws. Steady took hardly any notice of them, but he knew they were there.

'They won't come any closer,' he said. 'There's too many of us. Make sure you all stay together.'

'Some of them can timeslip,' added Pace, with relish. 'You won't see them coming. They'll be at your throat before you know it. If you fall behind, you'll be mincemeat.'

There was no one guarding us. Out here, walking through these blasted, crumbling rues, under the wide open sky, there was no need for a prison.

These streets had once been rues, just like at home. Here were houses, there were towerblocks, that was a place where a shijo could have been, a shop that might have been like Cafe Boite. Now nothing lived here except things that wanted to eat us.

'You're in luck,' said Pace, striding ahead of the group. 'Today's a good day. Clear sky, not much wind. You'll be all right.'

We headed for a tall building the end of the rue. It stood ten stories higher than anything around it. One side of it was blackened from the ground to the top floor, as if it had been burnt. Not far from the entrance was a nest of cutsnakes, a black, writhing heap, their razor frills catching the light. We all flinched, but Pace picked up a lump of broken pavement and heaved it at them and they slithered away, hissing.

'It's the glass we're after,' said Steady. 'Special glass, energy conductive. Not much left of it. Just get it out, it'll be picked up later.'

We entered the building through a gaping hole where the doors had once been. We began climbing the stairs. The windows on the lower floors had already been removed. Our equipment was already laid out on the fifth floor. Steady handed it out, power saws and magnetic grips.

'Three to a window,' he said. 'One to cut, two to hold. The glass is heavy. We'll show you.'

Steady and one of the pinkers attached the grips. Pace picked up the power saw.

'Just get the glass out,' he said. 'If it breaks, salvage what you can. It's all to be ground up in any case.' He began to cut around the window.

They worked urgently, as if there was no time to waste. Once the cutting was finished, Steady and the pinker lifted the glass from its frame and laid it on the floor.

'Come on, get to it,' said Pace.

We worked like that for several hours, finishing the fifth floor and moving on to the sixth. There were only a few windows left intact there and we soon moved to the seventh. Mish, Rioka and I worked together, taking turns with the power saw. It was easy work, but tiring after a few hours. Finally Steady called a break and we put down our tools.

I stared out of the empty window. From up here we could see how big the city was. To the east was a cluster of towerblocks, one of which had partly collapsed and leaned against the one next to it. There were tall, skeletal structures to the South that looked like the remains of foodtowers. Around the foodtowers there was a grid of narrow rues and small houses. I suppose they would have been what we call the banns. Several of the rues were just blackened heaps of rubble. Beyond that, the dasht had started to bury the city under its pelt of sand and stones.

Below us to the east I saw another team of miners, their yellow coveralls bright in the ruins. There were about a dozen of them, moving slowly along the bottom of what might have once been a canal: a wide, black scar running between low buildings which looked like they might have been factories. A flock of ripperbirds circled in the distance. They were rare inside the Veil, and smaller. These looked huge. They dipped and rose in the air, their silver wings spread wide, catching the light, each feather as sharp as a razor.

Pace and Steady handed around water and some more of those yellow blocks of food. There was that same static buzz in my veins as I ate, and my tiredness vanished.

The two pinkers ate in silence, sitting apart from the rest of us. They also worked alone, taking turns with the power saw, the other holding both magnetic grips. They were strong and fast. I couldn't stop snatching glances at them. They weren't exactly identical, but even if I knew their names I'd be hard put to tell one from the other. They were the first to start work again.

By the end of the day we'd reached the ninth floor. As we put down our tools, I felt the sting under my skin grow more intense. It had been there all day, just under the surface, like an itch. I looked at Rioka.

'The suits are telling us it's time to come back,' she said.

We walked back to the cube through the fading light. We went a different way through smaller rues, which Pace said was quicker. Sand and stones had blown in from the dasht and lay across the rues in drifts, like a frozen sea. Now and then I saw things that I half recognized, ordinary, broken things worn by the years and the weather into smooth strange shapes. Something that might have been a bowl, half buried, an upturned cup, a chair leg. Or was it a bone?

The cycles of the weather continued, the landscape changed, was worn down, the sands shifted: but human time stopped the day the megastorms hit.

When we got back the other group was already on the ramp, covered from head to foot in white dust. They looked like ghosts.

'Where've you been?' I asked one of them, a young woman.

'We've been cutting stone all day,' she said. 'White stone. I don't know what the place was. It was huge.'

She looked exhausted. I thought we'd had the easier work.

In the locker room we stripped off the coveralls and put everything away. There were steamers to clean ourselves up a bit. Everybody looked tired, glad the day was over. It was as if we'd just come home from a normal shift.

At dinner the cubes were blue, although they still tasted of nothing much. The effect was different this time: they made you sleepy. By the end of the meal I was yawning.

Back in our dormitory, I looked up. The sky was black. I flopped down on my bed, completely wrecked. Rioka was speaking to Rouge and her boy, who had been in the group cutting stone. The boy kept very close to her, never letting go of her hand.

'Have you seen anyone else?' Mish asked from the bed next me.

I opened my eyes. 'What do you mean?'

'I caught a glimpse of that group of miners in the canal. But I haven't seen anyone else. You'd think there would be hundreds of workers on a site like this.'

'Sure,' I said. 'I guess so.'

'Those prisoners who were on the train with us…where are they?'

'No idea.'

'We're being kept away from everyone else. I think that no one much cares about us. We've sort of been put to one side. That guy, that Ap who spoke to us last night, he said as much.'

He was going to continue but I put my finger to my lips.

'They can't hear us,' he said

'How do you know?'

'Rioka's making sure.'

I looked across the room at Rioka, still chatting to Rouge. They seemed to be getting along.

'She's not doing anything,' I said.

'She's...removed us from surveillance. I asked her to. They can listen to everyone else, but they can't hear us.'

'How does she do it?'

'She can produce...I don't know what they are, but she calls them folds. She can fold information. She says she just has to think of it...and it's done.'

It sounded like Dez. 'So she's...'

'A splice, yeah. She works for me at gigs as my sound engineer. She edits out my mistakes, all my bum notes. She knows my music inside out.' He grinned. 'If any other musicians knew what I was doing, they'd murder me.'

I looked over at Rioka, wondering why Mish was telling me this. I could be anyone. Or did he guess something about me? 'Does anyone else know?'

'Her family know, of course. There's only her three brothers left, and they think of it as a curse. They won't even let her talk about it. Well, you know, splices...'

I thought of Dez, about how we protected her. Ma and I were proud of her, amazed by what she could do. 'How does Rioka deal with them?' I said.

Mish grimaced. 'She ignores them.'

Rioka swung her head around to Mish and raised her eyebrows, shaking her head very slightly. Mish cursed under his breath. 'That's it,' he said. 'We're back on air.'

If there was something else he wanted to say, it would have to be another time. I was too tired to be curious. I closed my eyes and fell asleep as quickly as a stone falls through water.

Dez

I don't know how far we were beneath the surface, but it was a long way down. We stepped out of the elevator into a tunnel. Thinking about it now, it must have been some kind of mine-shaft. It was too regular to be natural, a hole hacked out of stone.

'Turn on your suits,' said Ava. 'We're never sure what's down here.'

The air was dead and stale, there couldn't have been any ventilation. Ava was in a hurry now, pushing us on although we were beginning to gasp even through the suit filter. We didn't have to go far before we reached the Inner Veil. I hadn't realised it went underground, but now I thought about it, I supposed that made sense. I felt it intensify as we got closer, toxic and fierce, like an acid fire in front of my face. I could feel how it hated me, down to every non-pinker chromosome. About three metres away from its edge, Ava put up her hand and we all halted.

'Switch on your wristbands now,' she said.

We fumbled at our wrists. I was expecting a sting and braced myself, but it was still a shock. Flora cried out in pain. Even Ava gasped. That disruptor had a nasty bite, and it didn't die down, it just went on howling through your nerves like a saw.

'It'd feel worse without it,' said Ava. She sounded as if she were speaking through clenched teeth. 'You'd all be fried. Now. Run. Fast.'

We sprinted forward, trying not to fall over. The veil was probably about two metres thick, and its aura was fierce for around three metres either side. It was only a short distance, but those moments felt like forever, as if we were passing through several hells. I could feel the hunter tags in the Veil mobilising, alerting to our presence, and then the nauseating sense of the disruptor waves knocking them onto different trajectories. The problem was that it was doing that to us, too. It was the shittest feeling ever, it did things to your nerves and your brain. I felt Flora stumble beside me and grabbed her hand and pulled her along.

On the other side, Ava signalled us to turn off our disruptors. The relief was incredible. We all slumped to the floor, gasping, and Jenna and Flora threw up. Every single bit of me seemed to be screaming, like I had the worst case of pins and needles in the world.

'No time,' said Ava, pulling Jenna to her feet. 'Get up. Get up. Not far now.'

We staggered along, trying to breathe, trying not to vomit again. At last we reached another elevator and Ava pushed us inside. After another stomach-turning ride we emerged, our ears popping, and this time she let us rest for a few minutes. The pins and needles were beginning to subside but I still felt terrible. All I could think was that we'd have to do that all over again if we wanted to get back.

We reached the surface through a maze of tunnels and basements, stepping out into a dead-end alley. I looked up at the sky. There were heavy rainclouds overhead with lightning running through them, the kind that meant torrents in the banns, but no rain was falling here. I remembered that Newport City has its own weather system. There was that song, *It never rains in Newport City...*

That must be weird. No rain, no sleet, no fog, no snow. All part of the purity, I guess. Our weather is filtered, but they don't bother to control it, so we're stuck with all the bad bits. We're just a buffer zone.

Ava was hiding us from surveillance tech with a portable shield, but I couldn't sense any close by. That felt weird as well. It doesn't matter where you go in the banns, there's some kind of tech surveillance. It's just part of the environment and we all have ways of subverting it. I build a few of them into my suits. So being in a place without any surveillance, not even tame nanobots, was a bit disorientating. It meant that pinkers put a lot of faith in the efficiency of the Veil. In a funny way we all did, fleshers as well as pinkers; even though at some level we all knew things got through, we all thought of the Inner Veil as impregnable. I was beginning to realise that the world was much more permeable than I had thought, that there are gaps and spaces where things wriggle through. That was kind of exciting. It was also a bit scary, because some of the things that might wriggle through are pretty deadly. Viruses. Crystals. Black rain.

Us. We'd wriggled through too.

As I followed Ava past down-at-heel take-aways and bio booths, I let myself enjoy that. It was only the first step, but we'd done it.

It was hard not to rubberneck. I remembered how those tourist pinkers looked in the banns, gawking at everything like we were all monsters, and I tried to copy Jenna. She looked super casual, as if she walked along these streets every day of her life. Some little kid snivelling on a step looked up as we passed, his face smeared with dirt and tears. Why was he alone? Why was he crying? On the soaps all the kids lived in clean houses with two parents, one man and one woman. They designed their perfect babies like they designed their perfect houses. Nobody cried.

We turned two corners and reached our first destination. There wasn't any sign, it looked like another boarded-up factory or warehouse. Ava unlocked a small door and swung us inside smartly. We crossed a covered yard and entered an empty room. Crossed that, went down a corridor, up a flight of stairs, through another door. Each door needed a different key, and the final door was gene locked.

Ava swept us through it and into another world.

I blinked. Everything was pink. The walls, the furniture, even the plasma pictures on the ceiling. So much pink, bathed in a warm pink light.

It took me a few seconds to notice the receptionist, who was sitting behind a pink security console, filing very pink nails. I'd never seen hair like that in real life, a tower of golden pink curls. I couldn't help it. I just stared. I kept noticing new things, like the tiny pink light-globes attached to the end of each eyelash, or the little moving faces painted on each fingernail. They were on a loop, smiling and blowing bubbles.

'Darling Ava!' said this wonderful creature, wiggling fingers at us. 'Darling newbies! You're late!'

'Don't you darling me, darling,' said Ava. 'I feel like shit. I want a cup of tea. And I bet these kids do too.' She turned to us. 'These are a special lot, not for us, a favour. They need costumes. Flora, Dez and Jenna. This is Gloria.'

'How very peculiar of you, Ava,' said Gloria, pouting. 'I never knew you to do a favour for anyone.'

Ava glared at her, and Gloria laughed.

'Okay, okay, I'll make the tea. You'd better come through.'

Bo

The storm hit just before dawn.

First the wind, growing steadily louder, howling and groaning around the building, shaking the walls. It woke everyone up. The sky filled with massive clouds that seemed to be on fire, rolling and boiling, collapsing and suddenly expanding. And then the rain, black rain, sheets of it. It ran down the glass ceiling in thick ripples.

Somewhere inside the building a siren began to wail, but the wind had grown so loud now that you could barely hear it. The lights in the room came on, flickered for a moment, then went out. The black rain grew heavier, pounding on the ceiling. It was thicker now, rolling slowly down the glass, pierced by shafts of red light from the burning clouds.

The door flew open and a dozen goons rushed in, carrying lights, prods and tasers. Outside the storm was growing in intensity. It sounded as if any minute the whole structure would be torn out of the ground.

All I could feel was naked fear. Black rain. No Veil. We were all going to die.

The goons herded us out, pushing us through rooms and corridors until we reached a narrow flight of steps. At the bottom was a steel door, opening onto a dark tunnel. Inside it was pitch black. I'd lost sight of Mish and

Rioka. I tried to look around for them, but in the crush at the bottom of the stairs I could hardly move. Nobody wanted to enter the tunnel, but the goons switched on their tasers, so we went through the door, one at a time. It was so low that we had to stoop almost double to get inside. Then they slammed the door shut behind us, leaving us in total darkness.

They only thing we could do was move on. There was no way back. We shuffled in single file, feeling our way in the darkness. The person in front of me tripped and fell, and I fell over the top of him. Someone fell on top of me. We clawed our way out of the tangle and kept moving.

After a few minutes, someone at the front started yelling. 'Stop, stop!' Her voice boomed inside the confined space. We all halted, wondering what was happening. After a while, there was a hollow pounding. A door? Yes, the whisper came back along the line. There was a door. A way out.

The pounding stopped. No response. It started up again. We waited, crammed together, our chests heaving, not speaking, just waiting. And then a click, the squeak of hinges. Light.

For a moment, none of us moved.

'Come in you lot, stop mucking about.' It was Steady.

We tumbled out onto the floor, gasping, a few of us laughing, some-one sobbing. It was some kind of safety pod. There were breather units on shelves, bunks set into the walls, a long metal table and stools, canisters of water. Pace was beside Steady, looking down at us, hands on his hips.

'We just got here ourselves,' he said.

There were half a dozen other miners there already, all fleshers, who must have come in through a steel door on the other side of the room. They shifted to make room as we got ourselves off the floor. The space was designed for maybe twenty people, now there were almost twice that many.

'What happens now?' said Rouge.

'We wait,' said Pace. 'It looks like a big one, so it might be a while.'

One of the miners went to a luminous panel on the wall and passed his hand over a small scanner beneath it. The room filled with the howl of the storm. All us fleshers flinched, but the miners didn't respond at all. They just looked bored.

'Turn that off, please,' said someone. The wail cut off abruptly.

'We'll be right in here,' said Pace. 'There's food and drink.'

'What if...what if everything above us is destroyed?' asked Mish.

'You lot never seen a storm like that up close, eh?' I couldn't tell if Steady was being friendly, or just mocking us. 'You'll get used to it. We all do.'

'What were those clouds?' I said.

'Rogues. Nanospawn. Hedge there knows more about them.' He pointed to a stocky, dark haired man sitting on a bunk on the other side of the room. He was about the same age as Steady. He looked fierce, with a long, deep scar running down one side of his face and a tattoo of a knife on the other. He took a while to say anything, and then he licked his lips as if they were dry, and I realised with surprise that he was shy.

'There's a particular rogue that splits when it's exposed to certain kinds of energy, fire for instance,' he said at last. He stared at the floor, taking care not to meet anybody's eye. 'The trauma of the exposure will cause the nano to split and split again, like cells reproducing. And each time it splits it creates more energy, a kind of chain reaction.'

I couldn't stop staring at his hands, which were resting on his knees. On the right hand, his middle finger was missing. The left hand was a claw, with only his thumb and index finger left. They were huge, out of proportion to the rest of him.

'That's what those clouds are, nanos reproducing themselves, millions of them every second, and all of them on fire. From moment to moment they're not the same clouds. They're a self-generating crisis. Millions burn out, of course. As they make themselves, they're also dying. That's what causes the rain. Dead nanos. The storm stops when there's more dead nanos than live ones.'

'So there you have it, from Professor Hedge,' Steady said. 'Is anyone hungry?'

There were ration packs in cupboards around the walls. Steady and Pace broke them out and passed them around.

'You'll have to share, one between two,' said Pace.

The food in the packs was better than the meals we'd been given before. It tasted like actual food, even though most of it was dried and chewy, or in some form of gel. And it didn't have any effect, except for filling your belly.

An hour or so passed before we listened to the storm again. It sounded different this time, with a deeper sound under the high pitched howling of the wind that sounded like some gigantic creature in pain. A few of the miners nodded their heads. I asked Steady what it meant.

'It's playing out its last,' he said. 'It won't be long now.'

'The rain will come now,' said Hedge. 'The real rain. At least, as real as it gets out here.'

All we could do was wait. The miners mostly ignored us. Two were playing a game with three multi-faced dice and counters, sending the counters back and forth across the table. Mish asked them how to play and the miners invited him into the game. The rest of us just sat around talking, passing the time.

After another hour the miners grew restless, moving around quietly, getting ready to leave. My mood lifted. We all felt as if the worst was over.

I was sitting with Rioka, a little apart from the others. 'Is anyone listening to us in here?' I said.

She looked me straight in the eye. 'Mish told you?'

I nodded. She glanced at Mish, who was losing badly at the game of dice and counters, and shrugged. 'He must have thought it was important. It's all right with me. I mean, does it matter out here?'

Mish had lost all his counters. He threw his hands up in defeat and grinned across at us. Rioka seemed to relax.

'No,' she said. 'No one's listening.'

'So what kind of stuff are you picking up?'

'Some things from Newport City, but it's scrambled. There's so much interference out here that nothing much gets through clean.'

I was about to ask her what she'd heard when lights above both tunnel doors began to flash.

'It's all passed,' said Steady. 'You can go back. It must be morning by now. There'll be word about today's shift. It might be a day off.'

Nobody wanted to go back into the tunnel, but Steady stood by the door to encourage us through. 'You'll be right,' he said. 'Those bogies will be waiting for you at the other end, I expect.'

'Bogies?' I said.

'That's what we call 'em. Cheap AIs they make for the mines.'

'What-fuckin-ever,' said Pace, dismissing them with a wave of his hand. 'They're more trouble than they're worth. One of them got his cleaning and cooking circuits scrambled last week, and fried my boots.'

We climbed into the tunnel.

Ava was right, tea made you feel much better. We sat in the cosy back office of the FeelGood Salon in Newport City, feeling the jangle of passing through the Inner Veil gradually die down.

Dez

The office was much less pink, a comfortable, businesslike space crowded with worn couches and cushions. Ava gestured towards the couches. 'It's downtime now,' she said. 'Nobody's here. Make yourselves at home.'

In the middle of the room was a big, low table on which were scattered some data screens and unwashed cups. A little solar stove in one corner where Gloria boiled water for the tea, a portable heater, cold store well stocked with snacks and drinks, a huge rack of clothes all along one wall. I eyed the clothes rack uneasily. From what I could see, there wasn't a single costume that wouldn't make people turn and stare in the streets.

We had around ninety minutes before Flora and me had to move. From now on we had to watch the time very closely. Brian Mac was going to do some of his own hacking back in the precinct, and Morro was on standby.

I watched Gloria make the tea, the skirts of their shimmering dress floating up around us with some kind of anti-gravity trick that made it look as if they were moving underwater. I was trying to work out if Gloria was a flesher. For all their exotic costuming and smooth skin, there was something about their manner that wasn't pinker. Flora asked straight-out.

'No, sweetheart,' said Gloria. 'I'm one of those gene "accidents" that apparently never happen here, and nobody noticed until I was ten and it was too late to flush me into the sewers.'

We must have all looked confused, because Gloria explained for us. 'Look, I know you fleshers don't have problems with avants.' We all nodded; avants, neither male nor female, or maybe both, were common in the banns. One of my favourite singers, Redborg, was an avant. Nobody thought anything of it. 'They do in Newport City. Here you're supposed to be a man or a woman, and that's it. People like me aren't supposed to happen. It's a huge embarrassment.'

'That's weird,' said Flora, frowning. 'Why?'

Gloria smiled a little bitterly. 'People in Newport City are all sorts of screwed up,' they said.

'Is it true that nobody touches each other?' I asked shyly. I didn't want to pry, but I was dying of curiosity.

'Nobody actually touched me intimately until I was twenty,' said Gloria. 'I mean, even hugged me. I still find it a bit difficult.'

We all fell silent for a few moments.

'I couldn't imagine that,' said Flora, sounding awed. 'How lonely you'd be in your skin. Do you get punished if you touch someone?'

'It's not that simple. We're conditioned to find it disgusting. They still haven't worked out how to stop people…finding out how to touch each other. And people like me. We don't do so well, if anyone finds out.' Gloria was beginning to look a bit distressed, so when Flora opened her mouth to ask another question I gave her a warning glance and asked what kind of tea we were drinking, to change the subject.

Ava, who had been idly scrolling through some files, frowning, then got businesslike. We were to be disguised as orderlies, low-level med staff. This was the part of the plan that made me most nervous. Even with IMR gizmos, could we really pass as pinkers?

'First,' she said. 'Costumes.'

Jenna studied the array of garments critically. 'I like the feathers,' she said. 'Discreet. Nobody will notice you in that.'

'Or the neka suit,' said Flora. 'That'd suit Dez.'

Ignoring us, Ava hunted through the rail of clothes and turned around triumphantly with two grey uniforms with the Newport City logo on their front pocket. 'Luckily we have clients with med fetishes.'

I didn't want to ask what she meant.

Flora and I put on the uniforms over our belts. They were decidedly unglamorous, and a little too big. Ava studied us, her head to one side, and adjusted something on a remote she was holding. The uniforms shrank until they fitted us. Smartwear. This was expensive tech, almost no one had smartwear in the banns. I touched the material nervously.

'Now, the rest of you. We don't need to do much.' She rummaged in a drawer and took out three tiny IMR transformers that looked like lapel pins. 'These should do it. Wear them on the inside of your uniform, if anyone notices you're using this tech they'll start asking questions.'

We attached the pins. I studied them curiously. They were about as big as my fingernail. It was another kind of tech I wasn't used to, although of course I knew about it. We don't use IMR transformers much in the banns, low-tech gear like glitter and make up is thought much cooler. And, of course, it's cheap.

Ava called up a screen and activated the IMR, her fingers flickering over the dials like an artist. I watched as she changed Flora into a pinker. Suddenly her skin was pale, almost white, with that strange smooth surface that pinker skins have. Ava narrowed her nose and jaw and thinned her lips.

I didn't like it. She wasn't Flora any more. Flora must have seen it in my face, because she took my hand and squeezed it. 'How do I look?'

'Toxic,' said Jenna.

Flora grinned at me. 'Your turn.'

When Ava had finished her IMR magic on me, Flora seemed a little spooked. 'Wow, that's weird,' she said. 'I prefer the old you. Like, way more.'

I blew her a kiss. 'I'll be back,' I said. 'Once we get the job done.'

'Final thing,' said Ava.

She handed me the third transformer, which we would be using on Bo, and showed me how to use it without the screen. I zipped it into my pocket. It was slightly more powerful than the ones we were wearing. We couldn't carry a spare uniform in there with us, so this was the only way we had to hide him. Then she gave me a gene key to use on the way back. She didn't want us using the same entrance. This one opened a building a block away.

I spent the next half hour checking and rechecking our equipment. The suits had suffered a little from the disruptors, but not as badly as I had feared. It was nothing I couldn't fix. The ID chips Brian Mac had given us seemed to be unaffected. I was surprised that they only used chips, you'd have thought a hospital would have a gene lock at least, but Brian Mac told us that, except for places like OpSec, Newport City security was very standard. 'They put all their paranoia into the Inner Veil,' he said. 'You should be fine.'

I wondered about the secure unit and prayed he was right.

After that there wasn't much to do except wait. Jenna pinged Morro and Ma to let them know we'd reached first base. Ma would send a ping on to Brian Mac so he knew we were on track. Once we got into Newport City Western Hospital, we'd only be able to open a line to Jenna, and even that would be risky. Brian Mac said there was no guarantee that security wouldn't notice any strange comms coming out of there, especially when the system was down.

We had maps and the hospital plans uploaded into our suits and I ran through them over and over to make sure we knew where we were going. The secure unit was in the basement, and the fleshers had been brought there overnight. After that we didn't know what had happened to them, but Brian Mac reckoned that they'd probably be kept there for the day at least. I wondered how they got so many fleshers through the Veil without burning them to ash: they must have had a way of turning it off for special consignments.

10.45 hours. Time to go. We would enter the hospital at 10.55. It would take fifteen minutes to get to the basement, another four minutes to walk to the secure unit where the fleshers were held. Brian Mac would be blasting the energy supply for the hospital at 11.23 precisely, turning off comms and security, and by that time we had to be at the door. After that we had to move quickly.

I could feel my heart jumping. Now this was real. The FeelGood Salon was our last friendly place. Once we were out of there, we were in enemy territory.

I nodded at Jenna. She'd be monitoring the comms while we were in there. Jenna was our back up plan, if anything went really wrong. Brian Mac had given her an official scanner and a fake ID, which she could use to send false sightings.

'We'll ping when we're on our way back,' I said. 'Hopefully you won't hear from us before then.'

'Good luck,' she said, and smiled. 'I'll be waiting.'

I took a deep breath and crossed myself for good luck. We stepped out into the streets. Everything so far had gone without a hitch. It made me nervous.

Getting into the hospital was easy. We just flicked the wrist-chips over the scanner and walked through. Nobody took any notice of us, although when I looked around I realised our uniforms were slightly different from other orderlies, more stylish and certainly better fitted. I swung us into some toilets and made some adjustments, toning down the colour so it matched better, making the tunic more bag-like, and then called up the hospital map to recheck our route. Down some stairs, more corridors, a service elevator.

'All okay?' said Flora. Her voice wobbled slightly.

'Yeah,' I said. I could feel the seconds ticking by. Tick tick tick. 'Let's go. Look busy.'

We had almost reached the service elevator when a medic who was walking past us stopped and turned around, frowning.

'What are you doing?' he said. He was a typical pinker, maybe about fifty, smooth pink cheeks, slim, artistically swept hair with grey tips. I could smell the money in his jacket. He had an ID tag: Surgeon Whitney. 'Orderlies aren't permitted here.'

Even through the IMR I could see the panic in Flora's face. I swallowed, hoping that he didn't notice. 'We're on our way to the ICR unit, sir,' I said,

'I don't remember your types,' he said. 'Haven't seen 831s in the hospital before.' His eyes swept over Flora. 'Not 724s either.'

He was talking about clone types. We hadn't checked what clones they used as orderlies. It hadn't even occurred to us. I silently cursed Brian Mac and started an emergency search of hospital files. This man was a Level 9 medic. He probably didn't have much to do with emergency admissions.

'We're new here. We usually work in emergency, sir.'

'Who sent you?'

I was running through hospital files as he spoke. 'Doctor Stephens, Ward 601, sir,' I said. 'It's an urgent case. We're in a hurry.' Tick tick tick.

He looked doubtful, but mentioning Doctor Stephens seemed to work. I had chosen a senior name, one of the heads of bioengineering, Level 15. Doctor Witney waved us on. 'Make sure you don't dawdle. This is a restricted zone.'

'Yes sir.'

We put our heads down and walked past him fast, feeling his gaze on the back of our necks. Now we had to head to the ICR, which was not the direction we needed, until Doctor Whitney was gone. It was 11.16. We only had seven minutes.

We turned a corner. I checked the security cams. The corridor we needed to be in was empty. I put the cams on a two-minute loop and pulled Flora after me down towards the service elevator. It didn't need an ID.

We went down three floors and came out into another corridor. Not a pinker in sight. I breathed out with relief, and put the cams on a loop again. We hurried towards the door of the secure unit, left, right, left again. Third door. It was easy to miss, it looked like any other door, except there was a gene lock.

11.22. We'd only just made it.

Now Brian Mac had to do his thing, or we were stuffed. I swear that minute waiting was the longest of my life. We'd chosen this time because it was between shifts, and there would be minimum movement through this part of the hospital. According to Brian Mac, no one was rostered in the secure unit until 12.00 hours. It should be empty.

I watched the security cams, praying that he was right. People didn't always follow routine. If they didn't, we were in trouble. We'd have to disable anyone we encountered, there was no other choice. I had a taser, super quiet and efficient, that would knock the stuffing out of a feral gau. I mapped a million scenarios as we waited, hearing Flora's breathing harsh beside me. I'd never deliberately damaged another person in my life. Could I do it?

11.23. The lights flickered and then went out.

'Phew,' Flora whispered. 'He did it.'

All the security cams were down. I took out the electronic lockpick and fiddled with the door, trying to stop my hands shaking. Brian Mac hadn't been sure the lockpick would work, even with the power down. He said he was ninety per cent certain. Right now, ninety per cent didn't seem good enough.

It seemed an age before I heard the gene lock on the door sigh open, although it was less than a minute. I took Flora's hand and squeezed it. I could feel the relief flowing through her.

We went in.

Bo

They didn't feed us the next day. Our suits had been turned off, but the belts were locked on. People lay on their beds and dozed, or talked. The swap-meet in Rue Mishkin seemed like a hundred years ago. We were beginning to know each other: Tilly and Rosa, who were tailors; Maxim, Ziyin and Tomas, who were neighbours in the Sixth; Cherian, who painted houses; Mara and her younger brother, Will; Arjun, who made drums. All the weariness and fear at the bottom of all our hearts rose up like water bubbling through the earth when a dowser did her magic.

I thought a lot about Jenna. I wanted to feel her hand on the side of my face again and the touch of her lips on mine. That was like finding water, like something rising through your body and being released into the free air.

Towards evening Mish came to my bunk and stretched out beside me.

'Rioka says no one's listening,' he said quietly. 'They're too busy. It's going to take a while to get the whole operation going again. Apparently that storm did a lot of damage.'

'We're probably lucky to be alive.'

'Yeah, I feel really lucky.'

'You know what I mean.'

He didn't say anything. We lay there together, side by side, staring up at the sky. Then Mish turned and put his mouth close to my ear.

'There's a way out,' he said.

Later that night while everyone else slept, Rioka, Mish and I huddled together on my bunk and talked for a long time. I didn't know that much about Mish. I knew that he was a good musician, and that Rioka made him seem better than he was, but there was more to their friendship than that.

'My mother was a water reader,' he said. 'She could feel the water, like a grower reads plants or a birther can tell when a baby's coming. She could feel its...it's hard to describe...she could feel the water...My Da could do it to, but he wasn't as good as she was. He ended up fixing people's taps and wells, that sort of thing.' He took a breath. 'And I can do it too.'

He leaned in close to me. The bruise on the side of his face was red around the edges now, almost blue in the centre.

'I can read the water,' he said. 'And the water's calling us.'

So Mish read the water.

He stretched out on his bunk, his arms crossed over his chest, and closed his eyes. I watched him curiously, unsure whether this was some strange delusion. Nothing happened for a while, and I glanced at Rioka. Her eyes were dark and serious, fixed on Mish.

After a while he began speaking, in a slow, measured voice. 'The canal we saw was the main water artery of the city,' he said. 'It began to dry up before the megastorms. They poisoned the water, and it drew back its gift.'

He grimaced as if he were in pain and Rioka touched his forehead with the back of her hand.

'The fever's starting,' she said.

'Fever?'

'It's what happens. It means that he's reading right, the water's coming to him.'

Beads of sweat broke out on Mish's face, rolling in tiny rivulets down his neck. He didn't speak or move. His eyes fluttered open. Now they were globes of clear liquid, their surfaces trembling. They darkened, grew bright again, clouded over and then cleared. His clothes were drenched. Rioka and I watched over him as if he was a sick child.

Nobody took any notice of us except Rouge and her boy, who came over to our bunk, standing a little way off. 'Is he sick?' asked Rogue.

'No, not exactly. He's...listening to something,' Rioka said.

Rioka had told me that the boy was Rouge's cousin, Didi. A year or so ago his parents had disappeared. They'd been workers at the foodtowers and had become been involved with a small band of tillers and pickers who were asking for better conditions. The Aps rounded them all up one day while they were at work. That was the last time anyone had seen them.

Didi was staring at Mish, his eyes dark and huge. 'What's he listening to?'

'To the water,' I said

Rouge looked confused but Didi nodded, as if that was enough of an explanation, and pulled Rouge away.

Rioka felt Mish's forehead again and covered him with a blanket. 'He's cooling down. It won't be long now.'

Mish's eyes fluttered again and closed. In a few minutes he came to, and sat up on his bunk, pulling the blanket tight around his shoulders. He was shivering.

'The water's very cold,' he said.

His face was lit with the first pale hint of dawn, and I realised that we had sat with Mish all through the night. It didn't seem that long. I didn't feel tired at all.

'The water comes from very deep underground,' Mish said. 'It's been asleep for a long time.'

I looked at Rioka, lifting my eyebrows. She shrugged.

'It's a way out of here,' said Mish. 'I felt it the moment we arrived.'

I didn't know what he was talking about. Mish must have seen it in my face.

'What's the matter, Bo?'

'Nothing,' I said. 'I just don't...'

'Do you want to stay here, take up a career in mining? Or let OpSec do whatever it is they intend to do with you?'

I shook my head.

Rioka touched Mish's hand. 'How is the water the way out?'

'The water's still there, under the city,' he said. 'It's waking up.'

He had stopped shivering now and some colour was returning to his face, which had been ghostly pale when he had first come out of his fever.

'The water forgot. It went to sleep, long, long ago. But it calling us. It's waking.' He looked at us both in turn, the trace of a smile on his lips. 'And it runs to the Gilla Sea.'

There was no work again that day. About mid-morning some goons brought us trays of food, only the blue stuff this time.

'Is anyone going to tell us what's happening?' asked Tomas, as they left. One shook his head, so at least we knew they could hear us.

Rioka and I ate in a corner away from everyone else. We leaned back and looked up at the sky. Today it was cloudless, the palest of greens. I glanced over at Mish where he lay snoring on his bunk.

'Is he mad?' I said.

'Not completely.'

'Has he said anything else to you? I mean, is he planning anything?'

'I wouldn't call it planning.'

'Has he talked to anyone else?'

Rioka looked around the room at our companions, this random bunch of fleshers, thrown together for reasons we didn't understand.

'Who would you talk to?' she said.

I didn't answer, though I knew the answer at once. Maybe I was wrong to think that there was something to Mish's ramblings, maybe it was just snatching at hope, but somehow I believed him. Rioka and Mish felt like kin somehow. I'd latched on to them out of instinct. Nothing needed to be said, nothing explained.

I knew that if there was a chance of getting home, and if that chance only included me and Rioka and Mish, then I'd take it. There wasn't a single person in the room who would blame me for it. They'd all do the same thing. Every flesher knows that their neighbours' lives are as hard as their own, that we all face the same choices every day. That doesn't make us hard or unfeeling or the choices we have to make any easier, it makes us realists. And there's a generosity in that common knowledge, a kind of forgiveness.

Rioka was watching me, still waiting for an answer.

'I don't know,' I said. 'Anyway, what would I say? I don't know what Mish is thinking.'

'Neither do I,' she said.

We ate in silence for a while. I looked over at Mish again. I thought of Jenna and her power over water, how she made it rise out of the glass.

'Is it some kind of splice?'

'I don't know,' Rioka said, and smiled. 'I call it a gift.'

Dez

Now we had to find Bo, and we had to find him fast. We had ten minutes at most, probably less: Brian Mac figured that it would take the system nerds at least three minutes to identify where the breakdowns had been, maybe a few more to figure out why the back-up generators weren't working. Our hope was that there would be so much chaos in the hospital, nobody would worry about what was going on in the basement. We could count on five minutes before the lights came back on. If we were lucky, more.

We lit up our suits and went in. According to the hospital plans, the fleshers were being kept in box units at the far end of the secure unit. Bodies in low animation, stacked like vegetables in a shop. We didn't know what state Bo would be in. We had an adrenaline pen to shock him awake if he wasn't conscious.

Flora's job was to guard us. She had her taser up in case we hit any trouble, but we were in luck. The first lab was empty. Flora swept her light around and whistled. They had everything here, equipment I would kill for. So clean, everything shining.

The files in the secure unit were kept on a separate system to the rest of the hospital, which was suss to begin with. And in any case, the system was down. I had to find a monitor, plug in a micro power source to turn it on and hack in directly, but it only took a moment to decode the key. Thanks, brain. Once I'd broken in I didn't have to stay with the monitor, I could download remotely. I covered my tracks as I went, hoping I hadn't set off any alarms.

There were sixty fleshers. Sixty. Fuck. None of them were ID'd by name, or even by credit ID, which was the usual system. Instead they were all classified by some kind of genotype tag. Our plans depended on me being able to identify Bo really fast and this was going to make it much harder.

I flicked up and down through the files, beginning to panic. How could I tell which of these people was Bo? Would we actually have to pull out each unit and look? How long would it take to search through sixty people? Maybe we were stuffed already.

Flora was following the floor plan on her lenscam, counting under her breath. One door. Two doors. A corner. Along this wall. First door.

'Here,' she whispered in my ear. 'This is the room.' She clicked a door shut behind us.

We were two minutes in. At worst we had another ninety seconds before lights started coming back on, at best another eight and a half minutes. I prayed that the chaos was total, we needed time. I played the light over the room. One whole wall was lined with steel drawers. Inside them were people. Sixty people. And one of those people was Bo.

Unfortunately two pinkers were also in the room, staring at us. A woman and a man. Flora hid her taser behind her back.

'Do you know what happened?' said the woman, her face white in the shadows. She sounded frightened.

'No,' I said. 'No idea.'

In my anxiety I forgot to put on the pinker accent, which is more clipped than how we speak in the banns. I saw the woman frown and turn to the man, who stepped towards us. 'You're not authorised staff,' he said, his face sharp with suspicion. 'Who are you? What are you doing here?'

'Doctor Stephen sent us,' said Flora. She sounded way calmer than I felt.

'Stephen? Why the hell would he do that?'

I shrugged. 'I don't know. We've brought some stuff that Doctor Helios wanted.' Helios was the head of the secure unit. 'Had to be personal delivery.'

We didn't want to taser them if we could avoid it. The idea was to get in and out through all the confusion without anyone noticing. Unconscious bodies would be hard to cover up.

'Maybe you should check with him,' I said. 'Open a line.'

'Lines aren't working,' said the woman. She turned to the man, about to say something.

Too many questions. I felt Flora decide to act. She tasered them both, full stun, and they fell soundlessly to the floor.

'We got to move quick. Where's Bo?'

'It's going to be difficult.'

I'd finished downloading all the files. I'd worked out they'd been classified by skin shade. Dark one end, light the other. Bo would be in one of the drawers on the right, medium melanin. I ran and pulled open the first drawer, praying that it wasn't locked. They didn't need locks. Nobody in those drawers was going to get out.

The drawer rolled out with a smooth sound, light as a feather. It wasn't Bo. I shone my torch on a sad face, a kid of about fifteen I guessed. Eyes dull, unseeing, traces of tears on his cheeks. I pushed the drawer shut and opened the next, and then the next. Some were empty. After a moment, Flora started opening drawers too, nearer the middle of the room.

'This end,' I said. 'They're not using IDs. It's all skin colour.'

Flora tried another couple of drawers to be sure and then joined me closer to the right.

One face. Another face. Frantically opening and shutting these damn drawers. Not one of them was Bo.

Tick tick tick.

Our time was running out.

No Bo. No Bo. No Bo.

These faces were breaking my heart. I knew I would dream about this for the rest of my life. Oh my god. Jules. I had seen her only the other day.

No Bo. No Bo. The lights were still out. Now we were in the lighter skin colours. Maybe they'd filed him differently. Bo had intense blue eyes. Maybe that put him with the blonds. DNA classification isn't one of my strong points. It's a pinker thing.

As we flung open the drawers, I zipped through the files, hunting through their logs. They'd checked all the bodies in, but no analysis was planned until later that afternoon, after some 'preliminary investigations'. They hadn't hauled out any of this batch. They called all these people a 'batch'. Bo had to be there.

No Bo. No Bo. Simpa, who sometimes worked for Ma at the shijo. No Bo. Serim. Gaunt. No Bo. Ifant. No Bo.

In the end we opened every damn drawer, even the empty ones. Bo wasn't in any of them. He wasn't there.

Five minutes up now. I frantically started opening the drawers on the right again. Maybe I'd missed him somehow, maybe there was one I hadn't opened.

'He's not here, Dez.'

Flora took my hand. I shook my head. I was trying not to sob. I wanted to collapse on the floor and bawl my eyes out.

'We've got to get out now. Now.'

'All this, for nothing?' I bit my lip. 'We should take someone with us. We can take one. Brian Mac said. Just one.'

'Who?' I could see Flora was shaking with anger and fear. 'Who do you choose to save, Dez? Serim? Gaunt? Little Nino?'

I closed my eyes for a moment. 'Jules. There's no one else for her kids.'

Flora glared at me, but she didn't argue. I was already pulling open the drawer. Jules was in the third. She had no restraints on, she was just kind of frozen, staring straight ahead. There was a bruise on the side of her mouth. And she was naked. Fuck.

We lifted her off the tray, and Jules crumpled onto the floor. I jabbed her with the adrenalin. She gasped and opened her eyes, crying out in panic.

'Jules, it's Dez,' I said. 'Stand up. There's no time. We have to run.'

She was shivering so badly she could barely stand. Flora looked around the room frantically and then ran to the woman we had tasered and tore off her lab coat. She wrapped it around Jules, zipping it up. Then I put the IMR pin on the costume and turned her into a pinker. It didn't look very convincing, if you looked too closely.

'We've got ninety seconds at most,' said Flora. Now she sounded oddly calm again. 'We've got to get out of here.'

We ran, supporting Jules between us. She was heavy, her feet dragging on the floor. We got through one room. The next. Just this corridor. I was sweating now, panicking. We were reckless to bring someone, but I couldn't do all this for nothing. And even what we'd done was not nearly enough. I could see those faces as if they had all been printed inside my eyelids. I knew what was going to happen to them now. And I couldn't save them.

We'd just reached the door when the lights flickered back on.

Bo

Our suits were turned back on early the next morning. The shock woke me up. That meant that there would be work today.

We went through the same routine as the first day. Walking through the city the storm damage was obvious. There were pools of black rain hardening in the daylight and fresh scorch marks on some buildings. Sand and stone had been swept up into high undulating ridges along some rues, while others had been swept clean by the wind. At one point we stepped over a sheet of bright orange ice. The damage looked random. I realised that what had seemed like one massive event had actually been a cluster of smaller storms of different intensities.

Back in the building where we were mining the glass, we discovered that some windows had melted. Flows of hardened glass ran down the walls.

A panel on Steady's hardhat crackled to life. He touched it and listened, frowning.

'Boney, we only just got to Sector K,' he said. 'You could have said earlier.'

There was more crackling.

'That's a few klicks. I'm not walking there. You'll have to send transport.'

There was some kind of argument about power shortages, recharge time, priority. In the end Steady got his way. He pointed at me, Tomas, and Kat, a young woman I hadn't yet spoken to. She was tall with short black hair, and had a bird tattooed on the back of her neck.

'Come on,' he said, hurrying us towards the stairs. 'All got your breathers? You'll need them where we're going.'

We waited on the side of the rue and Steady passed around a canister of water. He lifted his face and sniffed the air.

'There's a breeze today. Do you feel it?'

'Is that good or bad?' I said.

'Could be either. After a storm like that there's often a breeze. Sort of clears the air a bit...or brings some other shit.'

Our vehicle arrived before long in a transport that just dropped it in front of us and drove off. I couldn't believe what I was seeing. It was a quad, a later model and bigger than the one I had at home. It had all-terrain tracks, a hydrogen conversion backup, seating racks on both sides. I stepped back and admired it. It made the one I had at home look like a toy.

'Never seen one of these before, eh?' Steady said.

'Not this powerful. I'm converting a smaller model to a homer.'

'Yeah? Never seen that done.'

'I'm doing it, all the same.'

'Not now, you're not. Come on, load up, we're wasting time.'

Steady gunned the engine and we took off. We flew along the rues, over humps and piles of debris, passing between rows of towerblocks, ten and twenty stories high. We went through a part of the city that seemed to be a grid of public spaces, with large squares connected by wide boulevards, places that might once have been gardens but were now just blasted fields of stone. As we crossed the canal, I looked down into the filth at the bottom, smears of black rain, rubble, the burnt out shells of transports, long drifts of sand.

After about twenty minutes we reached our destination. Below us, the city flowed down into a shallow valley. The sand and stones of the dasht had blown in over the centuries, like a slowly encroaching sea drowning everything. In the distance we could see the tops of some taller buildings poking above the ground. In the vast open space before us stood a circular building more than five stories high, its smooth walls made of some kind of red stone. It was topped by a gigantic dome of green glass that was cracked in places, and smeared here and there with residues of black rain.

Its two massive doors stood open and we drove straight inside. The cavernous interior was filled with a mottled, greenish light. We climbed off the quad, staring at a huge, egg-like structure in the middle of the space. It was at least four stories high and its seamless metal surface was oxidized, a dull red. For a moment all of us were struck speechless.

'What is this thing?' asked Kat.

'We don't know yet,' said Steady. 'Another team was just about to investigate when the storm hit and they had to pull out. You'll find detectors already inside, the tools, everything you need. We're after heavy metals. Cadmium, chromium, nickel, lead, zinc, strontium. Your detectors will indicate the position and strength of any you come across. Use the tools. Get it out as quick as you can.'

He paused a moment and looked at each of us in turn, suddenly serious.

'We know there's nanos in here. The sweepers and the vacs have been through the first area, but not beyond. And they can't cover everything. I've got an alert, which'll hopefully pick up any problems. And remember that some rogues can mask, they can hide themselves behind a false signature trace. There's nothing to do about them except hope there's none around.'

We all nodded. I could see my own fear reflected in the others' faces, but none of us said anything.

'I'm going to turn your suits to high. This won't be comfortable, but it won't last long.' He took a small black cylinder from his jacket pocket and flicked a switch.

The initial shock was intense, reaching into the centre of my bones, and it lasted much longer than a few seconds. Kat staggered and almost fell, but Tomas managed to catch her. The sting afterwards was deep, leaving lingering pain under my skin, and there was a soft buzzing in my ears, a kind of static.

Steady waited until we'd had recovered.

'Put your breathers on,' he said.

He led us towards the egg. There was a hole with scorched edges cut into its smooth surface.

'It took us three days to cut her open,' Steady said. 'We couldn't find any kind of door at all. Nothing showed up on our scans either.'

Inside lights were already set up. Steady switched them on and we blinked, momentarily dazzled. As our eyes adjusted we saw that we were in a large empty space. It was massive, stretching high over our heads. For a moment all of us were struck speechless.

Nearby a ladder was bolted to a wall, leading all the way up to a small hatch in the ceiling. 'Up you go,' said Steady. 'I'll follow. When you get to the top, wait there.'

We were going up there? I swallowed hard.

Kat went first, then Tomas. I hesitated at the bottom of the ladder, and Steady grinned at me.

'Scared of heights?' he said.

'No,' I said. 'Not a bit.'

He knew I was lying, but he didn't say anything else. I put my foot on the first rung.

The important thing was to keep going and definitely not to look down. Or up. I kept my eyes on the rungs, moving one hand, then one foot. If I stopped I'd never get moving again. I realised that I was holding my breath so I sucked in some air and blew it out. I probably wasn't even half way to the top but I could already feel my legs trembling under my weight. I didn't know how far I had climbed and I didn't dare check. I kept going.

Finally I emerged into a large room. Kat was holding up a work lamp, passing it over the walls, which were lined with three tiers of shelving behind glass doors. The shelves were divided into body-length sections, and all of them were empty. In the centre was a narrow steel table with a gutter around its edge.

Steady came through the hatch, puffing slightly.

'What is this place?' asked Kat.

'The morgue, as far as we can tell.'

'There's space for...how many people?'

'About a hundred, maybe more,' said Steady. 'We don't know if it was used.'

I looked around at the glass walls, imagining them lined with bodies.

Our equipment was laid out on the floor in a corridor leading off the morgue. Lamps for our hard hats, tools, gloves, heavy metal detectors.

'This is as far as they got before they had to leave. We don't know what's beyond here. Stay together. Our comms don't work inside this thing, no signal gets out, so I can't call for help if we need it. We're on our own.'

We picked up our gear and attached the lamps to our hard hats. Steady led the way. Now we really did seem like miners, moving along the corridor in single file, our lights bouncing off the low ceiling. We continued for a short way and then turned left and stopped. I craned my neck to see around the others. Steady was feeling around the edges of a door, looking for some kind of mechanism, a switch, anything.

'There's a panel over here,' said Kat.

Taking a small, sharp tool from his kit, Steady prised the panel loose. It flipped open like a little door. He put his hand inside and felt around. 'Maybe there's some kind of –' Before he finished speaking the lights in the corridor switched on with a low hum, and the door slid open. Steady looked as surprised as everyone else.

'Still working?' said Kat.

'Why not?' said Steady. 'There's a lot we don't know about these cities.'

From then on the going was easier. There were panels like the one Kat had found in every room and corridor, but Kat discovered that if you just touched them lightly in the bottom right hand corner, they sprang open. There were several switches inside. Some of them seemed to do nothing at all.

We'd been inside the egg for maybe an hour and our detectors hadn't picked up any of the heavy metals that we were looking for. The rooms we passed through were all empty. It began to feel spooky.

'There's got to be something,' said Steady, as we entered yet another empty room. 'It can't all be gone. I mean, the lights are running, there's live tech somewhere.'

What happened next is hard to remember, because it happened so fast. And because I don't want to remember.

The temperature suddenly spiked. It hit us like a blow, a wave of heat that seemed to suck all the air out of the room. Kat slumped to the floor.

Steady gasped, staggered forward and fell against the wall, as if he'd been struck from behind.

He clambered upright, blood running from his nose, and pulled a small red disk from inside his coveralls and pressed it between his palms.

An icy, bright blast crashed us against the walls. All the lights, including our hard hat lamps, went out. For a few moments we were in complete darkness.

The lights came on again, flickering. Then I saw Tomas.

He was standing bolt upright in the middle of the room and he was on fire. He was naked, and you could see into his body, where flames twisted under his transparent skin. They gave no light or heat. I could see his heart beating, his lungs expanding and collapsing. And then his mouth opened as if he were screaming, but it kept opening, wider and wider, until his entire face was an open mouth. I thought I'd throw up with the horror of it: it seemed as if he was swallowing his own head, his mouth folding back over his skull. As we watched, the fire began to die. A thick, cold wave of shadow passed over us.

Nobody moved. Steady pulled off the mask of his breather, which was filling with blood from his nose. He was still holding the red disk in his trembling hand. He held it up to his face and squinted at a read out.

'It cleared the room,' he said flatly. Then he looked at Tomas. 'But not quick enough.'

Tomas wasn't naked any more, and he had a face. He was frozen in the first moment of shock as the nano hit him, his eyes wide, his teeth bared, his mouth twisted in pain. But he was grey, completely grey. The air around his body was dark, as if it had been stained.

Kat shakily pulled herself to her feet and went to him. As she approached the dark air around his body seemed to dissolve.

'Kat...don't,' I said.

'It's okay,' said Steady. 'it's okay now, it's over.'

Kat gently touched Tomas' cheek. She pulled her hand away and started to tremble. I walked over and put my arm around her shoulder.

'Touch him,' she whispered.

I stroked his face with the tips of my fingers. He was freezing cold, hard, as if he had turned to stone.

'We can't just leave him here,' I said. My voice rasped my throat.

'If we take him back the bogies will throw him out into the dasht,' said Steady.

We carried him to the morgue. When we lifted him up, we discovered that he weighed almost nothing. He was hollow and fragile, like pumice. We laid Tomas on one of the shelves and turned him onto his side, his terrified face to the wall.

Whatever had killed Tomas had hurt Steady as well. His nose was still bleeding and his skin had turned a greyish colour. He pulled a small phial from the breast pocket of his coveralls, swallowed the contents and said he'd be all right, he'd be looked after when we got back. 'We'll get out of here after we find the power source,' he said. 'It can't be far.'

More empty corridors, more empty rooms. I was beginning to feel that we'd be stuck in this place forever, hunting for something that didn't exist.

'It's just a tomb,' said Kat.

'It is now,' I said.

Not long after we found what we were looking for, a room containing a black, circular unit about as tall as a man. We saw ourselves reflected on its shiny surface.

Steady switched on his detector. Strontium, lead, chromium and silver. 'At fucking last.'

'This is what powers the doors, the lights, yeah?' said Kat. 'If we take it, we'll never get out of here.'

We all stood staring at our reflections.

Dez

We got out of that basement as fast as we could, dragging Jules along the corridors to the service elevator. I was looping the cams as we went. We could hear alarms going off all round the hospital. If Morro had done his work, there should have been a trolley waiting for us as we exited the elevator at 11.35 hours. The idea was to wheel Bo out, covered in a sheet, after disabling the smart sensor on the trolley. We'd figured that he'd probably not be able to walk. After putting the trolley there, Morro was supposed to create a distraction so no one would take any notice of two orderlies hurrying a body out to the biodisposal unit.

There was no trolley. I rechecked the time. It was 11.36. We could hear announcements booming over the PA system saying that the power outage had been rectified and now would everyone return to their duties. Okay. Maybe they didn't think it was a security breach.

Deep breath. On to plan two. This plan had a few holes, I mean, more holes than plan one. We had known there was a chance that Morro couldn't double through the Inner Veil. He hadn't done it before, but he was 99 per cent sure he could, because it wasn't as if he had to pass through the Veil as such. I accepted that, if doubling was anything like quantum, but I should have been more sceptical. I wanted to weep with anger. Someone might have already put two and two together and figured they were under some kind of attack. And if anyone went into the basement and found those stunned medics, the whole place would go into lockdown.

I should never have made that deal with Morro. I wasn't thinking straight. Well, now I had a reason not to follow through.

I looked up the corridor. A group of people was clustered together arguing. Nobody was looking at us.

'Stand up,' I hissed to Jules. 'Otherwise we're all dead.'

She shook her head. 'I can't.' Her words were slurry, like her tongue wasn't working properly.

'Or we *die*, Jules,' said Flora. 'We don't get out of here. Do you want to see your kids again?'

Jules slumped and then, with a superhuman effort, lifted her head and stood up. 'Okay,' she whispered. She took one step, and nearly fell on her face.

'God damn it.' Flora caught her up. 'This way. We don't want anyone seeing us near the service elevator.'

Pinkers never touched each other. Holding Jules up like we were forced to would look weird to any pinker. We turned a corner, out of sight of the first group of people, and nearly ran into a medic who was shouting at an orderly. A real orderly, not one like us. He didn't look at us, but the orderly did. Her eyes widened. She knew at once that we didn't look right.

She tried to interrupt the medic to point us out, but he took no notice and kept on shouting at her. Something that had gone wrong was her fault. Someone had died, their machine had failed, they couldn't bring them back. He was furious.

That was probably us jamming the power. Even though it was a pinker who had died, I felt bad. The medic was treating that pinker like he thought she was a flesher, a lower being. He wouldn't even look around to where she was pointing, he just kept shouting.

We edged past the shouting medic, praying he wouldn't turn and see us. We rounded the first corner we could find. Jules's eyes were closed, I could hear her breathing, harsh and loud. She was barely conscious.

'Those IMR things,' said Flora. 'Could we use them to make us invisible?'

I didn't answer. There was a storage room just ahead. I swung us into it and slammed the door shut. Jules collapsed on the floor as soon as we let her go. She had broken out into an cold sweat and her face was the colour of ash. Maybe it was the adrenaline on top of whatever they'd pumped into her in that laboratory. I didn't like it.

'I don't know,' I said.

I was running through the hospital plans and checking out the security cams at the same time. Maybe there was a better way out than through the kitchen, which looked fine while we were planning but too far away now we were on the ground. Ventilation shafts? Too small and difficult to navigate, especially for Jules. The kitchen was still the best way, but we had to reach it. Hopefully no one would take any notice of that orderly who had seen us. I crossed myself for luck. Weird how I do that. Underneath it all, despite everything, I'm still a superstitious kid.

The cams told me there was an empty trolley about a hundred metres away. We had to get past a monitor station. We needed to avoid those, the reception AI would check our IDs and ours were only good as catering staff. There weren't any other empty trolleys close by. I cursed Morro again.

Maybe I could make us invisible, or at least difficult to see. Our body heat would still show up, but I didn't know how to nix that. We just had to make sure that nobody raised an alarm.

I had a quick look through the IMR pins. They were powerful, but not powerful enough to take in all the visual information of the environments we passed through, which would be a way of effectively camouflaging us, if no one looked too closely. Maybe if I thinned the data out? I tried it on Jules. She just looked pixillated, even more noticeable than before.

Flora was twisting her hands. 'Hurry, Dez,' she said.

I nodded. 11.41. Maybe if I just worked on making Jules invisible. That was better. It wasn't perfect, I couldn't get the three dimensionality quite right, so sometimes, depending where you looked from, Jules would look like a glitch.

'Lift her up,' I said to Flora. She pulled Jules to her feet. I switched the new pattern on.

Even this close, Jules seemed to vanish. Flora was just standing oddly, as if she was holding up air. She moved slightly, and the illusion became less convincing, you could momentarily see the outlines of Jules's body.

Flora breathed out. 'You're good, Dez. So good.'

'Let's just hope that nobody actually looks at us. We're going to have to carry her to the kitchens. Keep your head down.'

Just like going through bad rues in the banns. Keep your head down. Don't walk too fast. Don't walk too slow. Don't meet anybody's eyes. Keep to the shadows.

Except there weren't any shadows in Newport City Western Hospital.

'All right then,' I said, squaring my shoulders. 11.46. 'Let's go.'

The kitchens were on the ground floor, at the end of a wide central corridor that ran through the whole building. We hit the corridor in about the middle of the building about a hundred metres from the kitchens. It was crowded and loud: orderlies, medics, AI reception staff and medibots, ordinary pinkers who were just visiting, a real thoroughfare. The crowd made me feel safer, though it was now impossible for me to fiddle the security cams.

We'd just turned towards the kitchen when, to my dismay, the cams showed half a dozen men in OpSec uniforms marching through the big double doors at the hospital entrance. Behind them floated an AI like the one that had come into our house with the Ap. Even the hospital staff didn't like seeing OpSec there, people were turning around to look, asking questions. Newport City OpSec look evil, tight black uniforms, ensign on the shoulder, blank helmets that cover their eyes with heat scanners in their visors. Heat scanners. Shit. IMR wouldn't work if they switched those on, they'd see we were carrying Jules.

'Deep breath,' said Flora. 'Keep going.'

We kept going. I was monitoring every cam I could and trying to hack into the AI and the OpSec scanners, which meant that it was hard to concentrate on where I was walking. I relied on Flora to guide us. I bumped into somebody who swore at me. I scarcely saw them. Just fifty metres to go, then right, then through some double doors, through the ID station and kitchens, out past the biodisposal, out into the street.

The OpSec uniforms turned their blank faces towards us. Something must be registering as wrong. I still couldn't get into the scanners, or the AI. I was stretched too far. There were maybe three dozen bodies between us and the OpSec men.

'Shit,' said Flora. She quickened our pace. 'Dez, do something.'

'I'm trying,' I hissed.

'Try harder.'

'Keep us behind people,' I said. 'I don't think they've worked out which bodies we are yet.'

I got into one heat scanner and disabled it. Getting into the others took less than a microsecond. I checked the cams again. Now the OpSec guys had stopped, looking confused. One of them took out a taser and all the pinkers nearby recoiled, creating a space around him.

Twenty metres to go. We pressed on. Jules was really heavy now, dead weight. I could hear the police shouting at people to stand against the walls, so they could be properly ID'd. If we kept moving they would see us. If we stopped they'd work out who we were pretty quick. All the pinkers were beginning to line up against the wall, and now a couple of them were looking at us suspiciously. Things were happening too fast now, it was all about to spiral out of control. Flora caught my eye. She was beginning to panic.

And then Morro strolled through the front doors, straight through the ID station, which set off an ear-splitting alarm. Everyone froze and turned around to look. I knew at once it was Morro, even at that distance I recognised his silver jacket and boots, but basically nobody else has that swagger. He was tossing a big stinger up and down like it was a baton, doing tricks. Three turns and he'd catch it, handle side up, every time.

Morro is like a magnet for attention, you can't help looking at him. Charisma, I guess. He was turning it on full wattage. His smile was deadly, radiant. He seemed twice as tall as everyone else, and you had this frightening sense that you couldn't guess what he was going to do next. All the pinkers scattered except for one blonde woman, who was staring at him in fascination.

The AI malfunctioned. It was spinning around in circles making weird noises, like its speech patterns were running backwards. That wasn't me,

I hadn't been able to get into it. The OpSec guys stopped fiddling with their helmets. Their mouths, the only part of their faces that you could see, dropped open. They all pulled out weapons, heavy duty guns. People started to scream and run. Suddenly that hallway was chaos.

I usually want to kill Morro every time I see him. But this time I wanted to kiss him.

Like everyone else, we got the hell out of there.

Bo

Steady was growing weaker. We decided that I'd drive the quad back to the rest of the group. We put him on the seating rack next to Kat, who kept tight hold of him. I started the quad. I could feel the power of the engine: someone had really done a job on it. I hoped that I remembered the way back. It wasn't far.

Once I found the bridge over the canal I felt more certain about the direction I was heading. Steady was beginning to drift in and out of consciousness, and his breathing was laboured. Kat was struggling to keep him upright.

We were less than a klick from the building when I saw the smoke. Kat leant towards me, her face close to mine, pointing. 'That's our building, isn't it?'

I hoped not. 'I think it is,' I said.

I gunned the engine. As we drew nearer, I saw figures outside the entrance. One of them started running towards us. I pulled up and cut the engine as he reached us. It was Mish, his face smudged with soot. He stood there struggling for breath.

I jumped off the quad. 'What's happened?' I said.

'We got...to the eleventh floor...there's something...on the eleventh floor...'

I looked up. I could see the flickering of bright red flames inside the windows.

Kat was running towards the building. I called her back, but she kept running.

'Pace is dead. And the two pinkers,' Mish said.

'How? What happened?'

Mish just covered his face with his hands.

'Stay here,' I said to Mish, and ran after Kat. When I reached her she was kneeling beside Maxim, who was lying on the ground clutching his shoulder. Cherian was holding Tilly in her arms a little way off. There wasn't anyone else. I looked at Kat. 'Where's Rioka? Have you seen Rioka?'

'No. She must be still up there.'

I ran into the building and began climbing the stairs. I saw Ziyin stumbling down a flight above me. We crossed on the first landing.

'Don't go up,' said Ziyin. She stank of smoke. One side of her face was red, already blistering. The arms of her jacket were singed.

'What happened?'

'Don't go up.'

Smoke was beginning to drift into the stairwell and I put on my breather. By the time I reached the eleventh floor I could hardly see.

It was one large open space, a vast room. The fire was burning along the wall to my right, but flames were spreading out, moving slowly across the floor. Smoke was hanging in a thick cloud and inside it I could see brightly burning patches, the same as in the storm. Where the patches were most intense, black rain fell onto the floor.

I could hear Rioka screaming my name. I searched through the haze and saw her crouched on the floor against the wall. Mara and Will were beside her, holding each other. Beside them was a body. It was Rosa. I ran towards them, skirting the fire. As I got near, Rioka pointed at the ceiling. I looked up.

The two pinkers were floating above me, suspended in the cloud, runnels of flame crawling across their bodies. Behind me I felt a rasping gust of hot air. I turned to look at the fire.

Pace was walking slowly towards me. He wasn't dead. I don't know what he was. He had grown larger, much larger, and he was naked, his body covered with a thousand pinpoints of light. Black rain dripped from his hands. His eyes were open wide, bloodshot, cold. I could see nothing in them, no emotion, no thought.

The flames coursed around him, running up the sides of his body and down again. It seemed that he couldn't move faster than the fire. I backed away towards Rioka and she reached up with one hand and grabbed my leg. I looked down at Rosa's body. She seemed untouched, unhurt, except that in her half-open mouth trembled a small tongue of flame. Mara knelt in a spreading pool of blood, her legs crumpled oddly beneath her.

Pace was getting closer to the stairwell. I helped Will pull Mara upright, but she couldn't stand without support. Rioka scrambled to her feet. I saw that her left hand was badly scorched and hung limp at her side.

'Now,' I said. 'We have to go now.'

Will and I lifted Mara between us and wrapped her arms around our necks. Locked together, we stumbled to the stairwell. The flames were so close that we could feel their heat on our backs. Rioka ran ahead and paused, looking back up the stairs behind us.

'He's there,' she said.

I didn't look back. We reached the landing, turned, went down the second flight, across another landing, another. We fell over on the sixth landing. Mara was losing consciousness, the grip of her arms was slipping. I looked back over my shoulder. Pace was willing the fire on, walking in its wake as the flames cascaded over the stairs.

'He's coming,' I said.

I don't remember feeling tired, I must have been totally spaced out on adrenaline. We scrambled down two more floors before I made Will stop. We laid Mara on the landing. I felt her neck. There was no pulse. Nothing.

'She's gone,' I said.

Will looked at me as if he didn't understand what I'd said.

'She's gone. She's gone.'

Will leant down over her, shaking her by the shoulders, trying to get her to sit up. He pulled her towards him. She fell lifeless against his chest. Rioka called up from below. 'Please, please...we have to keep going.'

I pulled Will away from Mara and pushed him towards Rioka. He crashed into her blindly, but somehow she kept him upright. He was screaming Mara's name.

From then on, I only looked back once. I saw the flames beginning to crawl over Mara's body and behind them Pace, his thousand-pointed body, dripping black rain.

When we reached the first floor I left Rioka to take Will the rest of the way. I sprinted down the stairs three at a time and headed out of the building. Mish had driven the quad up to the entrance. He asked me what was happening but I ignored him and reached into Steady's coveralls to find the red disk. I didn't know if it would work more than once, but it was our only chance. When I ran back into the building. Rioka and Will had just reached the bottom of the stairs.

'Hurry,' I said. 'Get out, now.'

I leapt up the stairs. One flight above, Pace was just stepping off the landing, fire twisting at his feet. The heat coming off his body was fierce, sucking up the air. Black rain dripped down the stairs in front of him.

I knelt down on a step, curled up as tight as I could and pressed the disk between my palms.

I came to at the bottom of the stairs. 'That was some blast,' Mish said.

He dragged me outside. I couldn't get my eyes to focus properly, everything was a fiery blur. Then I passed out again.

The next thing I remember is voices arguing. I'd been lifted onto the quad. Mish was arguing with Kat, who was holding Steady's unconscious body.

'We leave him,' said Mish.

'We can't leave him,' said Kat. 'He saved our lives.'

'He's sick. He's probably dying'

'He's not dying.'

'The goons can look after him,' said Mish.

'They'll just let him die.'

'I thought you said he wasn't dying?'

'I'm not letting him go and I'm not getting off the quad.'

Rioka suddenly stiffened.

'Shhhh! Listen...listen!' she hissed.

Mish and Kat fell silent. Then we all heard the drones. They were still some way off, coming towards us out of the glare of the setting sun.

'They won't be long,' said Mish. He climbed onto the quad and started the engine. 'We're going.'

I tried to ask him what he was doing, but my head was still spinning from the blast. I saw Tilly, Cherian, Will, Ziyin, and Maxim, their faces turned towards us. 'We can't leave them behind,' I said. I don't think anyone heard me.

Mish revved the engine.

'There they are,' said Rioka.

I looked up. Two drones were buzzing towards us like malignant ripper-birds, black against the orange sky. Mish twisted the throttle.

We took off too quickly for me to read the expressions on the faces of those we left behind.

Dez

I pinged Jenna the okay code the moment we got out of the hospital and turned on our suits. She acknowledged, but we didn't open any lines, too risky. Our escape worked according to plan. We made it in time to the back gates, slipping out under the cover of the 12.00 biodisposal unit. The air was already thick with nanobots swarming into the hospital district, but I'd been refining the field tech that Ma told me about. It effectively wiped us from view.

Jules had come to, but she was shivering so violently she could barely walk. We hotjacked a scooter we found in the rue to save time. Nobody was around. Up a lane that ran alongside number 21 Finnegan Street, my arms screaming from holding up Jules. Down a dark flight of stairs. We rode the scooter straight to the door. Pressed Ava's key into the lock. The door opened. Inside. I followed the directions back to FeelGood automatically. We were under cover now, nothing was watching us. We had got away with it.

But we didn't have Bo.

I tried not to think about Bo. I knew as soon as I did I would never stop howling.

When we got back, I had to tell Jenna, and it was like saying it out loud made it real. Bo wasn't there. He must be dead. My brother. Dead. I couldn't believe it, I didn't believe it. I gave the details I'd found on Jules to Jenna for her to pass on to Brian Mac, so he could wipe her from the files.

After that, I only have snatches. Jenna, standing up, her mouth an O of shock as she took in our news. Ava hustling us into the back room, tut tutting and patting our hands like we were five years old. That surprised me, I hadn't figured her as a motherly type. Gloria fluttering with distress, all their pink turning blue, the little faces on their fingernails crying. All I remember about Flora is the smell of her, her warmth, her arm across my shoulders, holding me close. I didn't shed a tear. I didn't say a word.

Bo.

We went back through the Inner Veil an hour later. Ava said she had done her business and she wanted us out of there before the FeelGood opened at 15.00 hours. We had to leave Jules, she wasn't in any shape to make it through that day. By the time we left, she didn't look nearly as deathly as she had when we arrived: she had stopped shivering and she was less grey. She sat by the solar heater wrapped in a fluffy yellow blanket, her eyes haunted. As we left, she looked up and whispered 'Thank you'.

I flinched. I couldn't help it. We didn't deserve thanks. If Bo had been there, she would have been left with the rest of them. And we might have chosen someone else. It wasn't like anyone else in those boxes didn't have a right to their lives. I bit my lip and nodded, and we left.

I tried not to think of the people we'd left behind. I tried not to think about Bo. Now I had to go home and tell Ma that we hadn't found him, that all this had been for nothing, that we'd never see Bo again. I didn't open a line. I didn't even ping her. I had to tell her face to face, so we could hold each other, so we could feel each other's tears in our skin.

Kojo saw us coming up the rue to our place. Before we'd even had time to say hello he came barrelling in our front door, beside himself with fury. What the hell did Flora think she was doing? Not one ping until an hour ago. What was she thinking?

Ma told me later he was calling her all morning. He didn't buy Flora's cover story, somehow he knew something was up. Ma had told him that

Flora and I had gone to some gig, that we knew how to take care of ourselves, that she was as worried as Kojo, that yes, kids should know better, but they grew up and there was nothing you could do, nothing you could do at all. Finally, she confessed what we were doing. It was a mistake.

Kojo was wild when he was angry, but I'd never seen him completely lose it before. It was frightening. All the veins stood out on his neck and forehead and the spittle flew. In the end he grabbed Flora's arm and tried to drag her out. Flora ripped herself away and slapped him across his face, her eyes blazing. For the first time I realised that Flora was as tall as he was. I mean, I always knew she was a warrior, but this time I really knew it.

'Don't you touch me like that ever again,' she said. 'Don't you fucking dare.'

We were all shocked. We knew that Flora adored her Da, even though they fought so much, but now she was looking at him like she hated him. Kojo seemed to deflate before our eyes.

'I'll come home when I want to, Kojo. I'm safe, all right? It's my life, all right? *My* life.'

He stood very still. He wasn't looking at Ma and me.

'Okay?'

Kojo just turned on his heel and left.

Flora glanced at me and then turned her back on us and walked to the galley. 'I'll make a brew,' she said.

Ma already knew, the moment she saw us walking up the rue without Bo. I think she had hoped we'd had to leave him somewhere, but underneath she knew.

She sat down, twisting her hands in her lap.

'Well then,' she said. 'Well then.'

'They must have shot him, Ma,' I said. 'Brian Mac said that all the detainees had been sent there. But Bo wasn't there.'

And then we did cry and hold each other, but it didn't make anything any better. Flora went into my bedroom and shut the door behind her. She didn't want to go home, but she didn't want to get in the way, either. There isn't a lot of space for grieving in our house.

Morro pinged me about an hour later. I pinged back and turned on the field, and he was coming up the steps from the cellar in less than a minute. He flopped down on the couch and grinned at me and Flora and Ma. We were pretending to eat a meal at the table.

'Good operation, Dez.'

'You almost screwed us,' I said. 'We needed that trolley.'

'Sorry.' He rubbed his chin. 'I had a little trouble getting through. But you have to admit that my distraction was genius.' He was buzzed, triumphant, and it grated.

'We didn't get Bo.'

'You what? I saw you. You had him with you.'

'It wasn't Bo. He wasn't in the secure unit.'

'Who was it, then?'

'Jules Webber. From the Fifth.'

'There were sixty of them in there,' said Flora. 'Sixty. We could only rescue one person. So we took Jules.'

Morro shook his head. 'It could have been a disaster. What difference does it make?'

'It makes a hell of a difference to her kids,' said Ma sharply.

'I still kept my end of the bargain,' said Morro.

'The deal was Bo home, safe and well.'

'I'm sorry, Dez. I'm really sorry it didn't work out. But there'll be lots more Bos if we don't do something.'

'Maybe there's nothing we can do,' I said. 'Nothing that'll make any difference.'

'That's not true. That just means we're defeated because we don't even try.'

There was a long silence. Morro's mouth was set in a straight line. I could sense how angry he was from where I was sitting, but he didn't want to say anything, because he was sorry about Bo. A huge wave of exhaustion broke over me, sour, cold, and then withdrew. It left anger behind it. A hot, burning, deep anger. I remembered the faces I had seen in the drawers, faces of people I knew, faces I'd seen around the banns.

I wasn't going to fight with Morro.

'Listen,' I said. 'I downloaded everything I could find in there. Those people were taken as part of a new program. They've sussed that some fleshers are spliced and have ended up with weird abilities. They're taking random samples to see how widely spread it is through the population. They want to know how they can harvest the genes and use them in their own cloning programs. It's top secret because Newport City would freak if they thought they were surrounded by some kind of super mutants, and they'd freak even more if anyone was cloning pinkers with flesher genes.'

'Super mutants?' The edges of Morro's mouth quirked up. 'That sounds pretty toxic.'

'They're calling it the Chimera program. It sounds ridiculous to me.'

'Pretty ironic, huh,' said Flora, who'd been listening intently. 'To think they've spent the past few hundred years thinking we're not even human. And now they're terrified that we can do things they can't even imagine.'

'Yeah.' Morro was frowning. 'Maybe it's linked to the cull?'

'I don't know,' I said. 'I just scooped up the data I could get. It's a locked off bank, not even connected to OpSec. But it's definitely under OpSec authority.'

Ma stirred. 'Morro, do you know how many people have abilities?'

Morro shook his head. 'I think it's quite rare,' he said. 'But how many people know about Dez? Nobody talks about this. You know what happens to people if anyone thinks they've spliced with nanos.' He drew his finger across his neck. 'You were lucky, Dez. When my parents found out I was doing weird things they pretended it wasn't happening, and when they couldn't ignore it any more, they kicked me out.'

I couldn't tell what Morro was feeling, his face was totally expressionless, hard. 'At least they didn't kill me,' he added. 'Anyway, it was a long time ago.'

I thought about how Morro had said his abilities came from some ancestor. 'How do you know it's not from a splice, then?'

'Because I had an uncle who was the same. Uncle Zack. He got me into the Alchems. A lot of the Alchems are like us. He told me, after they threw me out. But that's enough about my sad story. The bad news is that the pinkers have found out.'

He sat up and looked straight into my eyes. For once he was being totally sincere.

'You're going to have to go into OpSec now, Dez. We have to know what they're planning. The cull. These experiments. The whole deal.'

Ma flinched, but she didn't say anything.

'I know,' I said.

Bo

We hit the canal a few minutes after leaving the others behind. We knew that the mines would be tracking us: from the moment we stepped out that morning, they'd have known our every location. But maybe the fire had confused things, and whatever signals the goons picked up were a mess.

Steady had told me that out here, anyone who escaped was considered dead. No one survived the dasht. Why would they bother chasing a few fleshers, anyway?

Mish wasn't taking any chances. As soon as we were out of sight, he disabled the tracking device on the quad by bashing the shit out of it with a spanner from the toolbox. He'd asked Rioka to do her thing for as long as she could. If she was able to hide our position for a while, we could make some distance before anyone knew where we were. And if he'd read the water right, we could be away and free. Whatever that meant.

The light was fading now, the sky turning from pink to grey. Mish tracked along the edge of the canal, looking for a spot where we could safely get down the steep sides to the bottom. He found a place where the canal opened out, widening into a great concrete dish that must have been some kind of ornamental lake. We dived down into the muck and debris at the bottom.

We passed under two, maybe three bridges. We could hear drones above us, but we couldn't see them. Mish drove like a demon along the bottom of the canal. Eventually the canal ran into an enormous pipe, passing under a small cluster of crumbling towerblocks. Mish drove straight in. The floor of the pipe was a deep, undulating layer of bone-dry silt. He flipped on the headlight and we continued into darkness for a while before he stopped. We listened. We couldn't hear anything above us.

Mish went to the back of the quad and checked the battery while the rest of us stripped off our yellow coveralls.

'Maybe a day's worth of juice,' he said. He stripped off his own coverall and threw it on the ground with ours. 'Should be enough.'

I wondered how we'd get home in a day, but I didn't say anything. Mish opened a pannier and grabbed lightsticks, a first aid kit, two ration packs, a canister of water.

'Supplies!' he said. 'Might as well stop for a while. We could do with a rest.'

Kat had been holding Steady so tightly that her arms had locked up and were cramping. We practically had to prise the two of them apart. We laid Steady on the ground. He was still breathing, but that was the only sign of life. Kat tried to rouse him, to get him to drink. He blinked awake, his eyes rolling in his head. We propped him up and wet his lips with some water and laid him down on the bare ground. He muttered something and Kat leant over him to catch what it was, but she couldn't make it out before he slid back into unconsciousness.

Mish took out gel, a roll of bandage, sterile water and painkiller from the first aid kit. It was basic stuff, but a lot better than nothing. He shot the painkiller straight into Rioka's arm, and then he gently washed and dried her injured hand.

My head was throbbing, plus I must have landed on my shoulder when I was thrown from the blast. It hurt like hell. I propped myself against the quad and watched the other two for a while. They looked as bad as I felt.

'What happened back there?' I asked.

Mish was tying up the bandage. I saw him flinch at my question, and for a moment I was sorry I'd spoken.

He answered me in an emotionless monotone. 'I felt it as soon as we reached the eleventh floor,' he said. 'Something didn't feel right, there was an odd energy in the room.'

'I saw it first,' said Rioka. She inspected the bandage and smiled at Mish, cradling her arm. 'It was like...like a tiny cloud, not much bigger than a hand. It floated up from the floor in front of Pace, and it caught the light, the way you can see specks of dust in sunlight. It was opaque, it had no colour, it didn't seem...alive. Then it kind of ignited and wrapped itself around Pace's head. It all happened in a moment. We just stood there and watched. It was too...unbelievable to be real.'

'That's when Pace caught fire,' said Mish. 'The floor under him caught fire, the ceiling, this...column of fire. Pace's skin bubbled up and began to split, there were...little holes all over him. He killed the two pinkers first, just picked them up and tossed them into the air. And then they stayed there.' He stood up and moved away a few steps, letting out a long breath.

'Mara picked up one of the power saws,' Rioka continued. 'She rushed at Pace. I don't know what she thought she was doing...he just tore the power saw from her hands and slashed at her legs. She just dropped and fell in a heap in the flames around Pace. Ziyin and I pulled her away, that's when we were burnt.'

They both fell silent. I didn't push. I could tell that as they spoke, they were seeing all these things again.

'It was hard to make out anything through the smoke,' said Mish at last. 'I saw Pace reach for Rosa...he just touched her...and flames shot out of her mouth. She fell down, just fell down and she was dead. After that...after that I don't know...I was on the stairs...Maxim fell in front of me, I picked him up...I thought Rioka was behind me...we got out....'

He met my gaze. His eyes were swollen and bloodshot, the bruise on the side of his face black and purple.

'Then you arrived.'

It must have been well into night by now. After a short argument with Kat, who said it was too dangerous, Mish walked back the way we came to see if anything was following us. He took a lightstick with him, turned down low.

I watched the blueish light dwindling into the darkness.

Kat fell asleep beside Steady. I realised how small the miner was. Lying asleep, he looked like an overgrown child, stocky, solid, worn down. I picked up his wrist. His skin was dry and hot and his pulse was racing. Some kind of battle was raging inside him.

I offered Rioka something to eat from the ration pack but she said that she wasn't hungry. She looked completely exhausted. Somewhere inside her head she was hiding us, folding us into the chaos, the drones talking, the suit signals, whatever else was out there. Were they searching for the missing miners? Maybe they'd already found the pinkers, floating in that cloud of smoke.

'It's quiet now,' she said. 'I'm not picking up anything, it's all shut down.' She lay on her side and in a moment she was asleep.

I was tired to my bones, but I thought that I should wait for Mish. I kept dropping off, my head nodding, chin hitting my chest, waking up with a start, falling back to sleep. My eyes felt as if they were full of sand.

Mish came back about half an hour later.

'There's nothing,' he said. 'The sky's clear. No drones. Nothing.'

He looked at the others.

'Sleep, yeah?' he said. He lay down next to me, tucked his hands under his head and closed his eyes. 'And then we find the water.'

Brian Mac

So, all that for nothing. Get the intel from Dez on the temporary line we agreed, erase the line, stare. They hadn't got Bo, they'd taken some woman instead, Dez doesn't say who. OpSec used no names or credit IDs, they just had DNA codes and mug shots. Dez has already wiped the record in the hospital, I just have to change some figures in the arrest codes. Use Mal's ID to log in again, cover my tracks, and then wipe it.

Not standard procedure, not at all. Nothing going on here is standard.

Think of opening a line to Mal just for a chat, but he knows me too well, he'd know I was fishing. Wouldn't be any use, anyway. He probably knows less than I do. Check the incident reports. There's almost nothing about what's gone down. Reports about a power failure, a possible terrorist incident at the Newport City Western Hospital. Nothing else.

OpSec has buried any info about the roundups so deep that it's beginning to feel like it never happened. There are just traces, hairline cracks in a wall of silence. Bo disappears into a militia transport, gets swallowed up. Not in the hospital. Where did he get spat out?

Asking Kellway to stuff things up was a mistake. Talking through his arse, as usual. He knew nothing. He was so pleased with himself I could have puked. He screwed them good he said, he got one over on them. Flooded them with bodies they didn't want. I could hear the snigger in his voice.

So they had too many detainees. I guess that's what happened. The figures they ordered were precise. So what did they do with the extra bodies? Kellway doesn't have a clue. Nothing in the records. Some fleshers disappear. How many? Who cares? Who were they? Again, who cares? They've been ground up in a machine. The machine just keeps on running. There's been a blip, a minor malfunction. Move along. Nothing to see here.

OpSec is cruel. No surprise there. It's also incompetent. No surprise there either. The two go hand in hand.

But I still don't believe that Bo is dead. There is nothing, absolutely no reason for me to think he's still alive. So why do I think he is? Me, who always thinks that the worst outcome is the most likely, that bad news is always true.

Fuck it. I want a drink.

So I do the hard thing and go to see Bel. Cover is an official checkup, they're still on a watch list. Being watched by me. I think of taking something, anything, before I go around there, something to make me numb. But in the end I go there just as I am, all my nerves exposed. With Bel, there's no hiding.

She flicks the field on the moment I'm in the door so we can talk, but we don't say anything at all. She just stares at me, her eyes empty. I can't tell her that I think Bo is still alive. I've got nothing to prove it, nothing to go on. It's just a feeling. It would be pouring salt into her wounds. I just stand there and let the grief hit me.

Dez comes into the room and I meet her eyes. They're blank. No blame. No questions. I barely exist. I'm just a shadow. And then she turns around and leaves.

I don't stay long.

Come home, drag myself through the door, guts in a knot. Just want to sleep. Sleep would wipe it all away.

Take a pill to keep myself awake.

Bo

I was as old as Brian Mac, but even more washed up. A deadbeat stalking through the banns, haunting the rues, hands in the pockets of my scarred leather jacket, hunched, alone, angry, frightening the little punks out playing, making babies cry in their prams. It felt great and sad and lonely, just the way it should feel. I kicked through puddles, bit my lips, cursed under my breath at nothing and everything.

I was a freaking legend, the nobody that everybody knew. Ma was dead, Dez was dead. There was just me. I hadn't been home for years.

I turned into our rue.

The house was gone.

I sat bolt upright to find Mish sitting beside me. 'A nightmare?' he said.

I shook the dream from my head, rubbed my face.

'Do you feel it?'

'Do I feel what?' I said.

'Your suit.'

'My suit? No, I...'

'They've been turned off. It happened a couple of hours ago. It woke me up.'

It was true. The sting was gone. The relief was indescribable, like when a bad itch goes away.

I fiddled with my belt. The locks must have been centrally controlled: I could take mine off at last. I let it drop to the ground.

'That means we're screwed if we run into anything toxic,' said Mish. 'Let alone anything as bad as what hit Pace.'

I thought about that. I honestly didn't know if that was worse.

Steady came around a little. He didn't seem to recognize anyone and anything he said was mostly incoherent. The one thing he understood was that his suit had been turned off. He kept fiddling with the switch on his belt. After a while, he became angry and started shouting gibberish. Kat tried to calm him down but he lashed out at her, striking her across the face.

'Just leave him be,' said Mish. 'There's nothing you can do.'

We all had something to eat and drink. There was a little water left, but that was the last of the ration packs.

'We have to get moving,' said Mish.

'Where to?' said Kat.

'When we reach the source of the water that used to flow through this canal we'll find a way to the Gilla Sea.'

'The Gilla Sea?' said Kat. 'This is a joke, right?'

'We follow the water,' said Mish.

Kat looked around us. 'What water?'

'We'll find it. I can feel it,' said Mish. He spoke with complete certainty.

'Hell's bells,' said Kat, shaking her head. 'We really are screwed, then.'

Rioka wasn't listening. She was tuned in, listening for signals, comms, any kind of activity. 'There's nothing going on out there,' she said. 'Just the usual routines. Another work day. Like nothing's happened.'

'They've written us off,' I said.

'I thought they would,' said Mish. He shifted slightly. 'Now. We have to decide about Steady,' he said.

'What is there to decide?' said Kat.

'We leave him.'

'Like we left the others?' I said, looking Mish straight in the eye.

'You were quick enough to go.'

'Doesn't mean I wanted to.'

'Just shut up,' said Rioka, her voice high. 'People are dead, people have been left behind. Are we going to sit here and argue the toss about whether any of it's right or not? None of it's right.'

There was a small silence.

Kat opened her mouth to say something else when we heard Steady howl. She was the first to get to him. The sickness raging inside his body was reaching a crisis. He scrambled to his feet, tore open his coveralls, threw his head back and bared his teeth. We all saw the tattoo on his chest. It was a map of Duiwel Island. The name looked as if it had been cut into his flesh and below it, in thick, black scrawl, *Hell's Gate*.

There was nothing any of us could do. It was terrifying. He dug his fingernails into his flesh, bit his lip until blood ran down his chin, thrashed his head from side to side. For a few infinitely long, painful moments, he was possessed with an incredible energy. Then, with a horrible suddenness, he collapsed.

He lay on the ground. A dead, half-naked flesher, his body scarred with his history.

We crossed his arms over his chest, and left him on the silt.

The pipe curved gently in long arcs one way, then another. In less than an hour we saw a glow ahead of us, growing brighter as we approached. It was like some strange sunrise.

Mish stopped the quad about a hundred metres before the end of the pipe. I went with him to check out what was outside. Ahead of us the canal ran on under a clear sky. The walls on either side were high and steep and we couldn't see over them. Up ahead there were steps cut into the wall. At the top, standing on the edge of the canal, we could see a small structure that looked like some kind of guard box.

'A monitoring station, I guess,' said Mish. 'Let's have a look.'

There was no debris in this part of the canal. The silt felt different under our feet, solid rock, baked hard by the sun, I guess. It was difficult to imagine it filled with water. It would have been so deep, so wide. I tapped Mish on the shoulder. He stopped and turned to me.

'How do you know that we're going in the right direction?' I asked.

'Look around.'

I looked around. 'At what?'

'The patterns in the silt. It's almost like a picture of the water. It's the shadow the water left. You can see the way it ran.'

He was right. I could see where the silt was pushed up against the canal walls, where it dipped and flowed.

'It would have been travelling fast here, into the mouth of the pipe,' said Mish. 'You can see how the canal runs slightly downwards. The water would have flowed up against the sides and crashed down, made waves, white caps. It would have been amazing.'

His eyes were shining. Mish was on some jag, like Morro when he starts blathering about history. We reached the steps and Mish went up first. It was more like a ladder, the steps not much more than foot holds.

'My guess is that there's a sluice gate,' he said as he climbed up the steps. 'Or something like that, not far from here, something like a weir maybe.'

I didn't know what he was talking about. 'Sure,' I said.

We reached the top and Mish flung out his arms. 'Look at this, eh?' he said.

All around us, on both sides of the canal, was flat, open ground, marked by a grid of widely spaced paths. About a klick away there was a featureless grey tower, rising about three storeys. Probably a dead climate machine. Beyond that, just visible, a ring of low buildings, and beyond them, more towerblocks.

'This must have been a farm,' Mish said.

'Like...a what?'

'Before there were foodtowers there were farms.' He shook his head and laughed. 'A farm, right in the middle of the city. It's amazing.'

There was nothing now, just a pale crust of cracked dirt. It crumbled when we stepped on it. We walked over to the structure we'd seen from below. It was a square, squat building, not much bigger than a single room. There was a large window on one side, facing the open ground. Mish pushed the door and it swung open. We looked at the remains of control panels set around the walls.

'It's a pumping station,' said Mish. 'It would have controlled the water brought from the canal to irrigate the fields.' He moved to the window and looked out. 'Imagine all of this space filled with corn, vines, vegetables, stands of wheat. Trees, maybe.'

All I could see was a wasteland, dead soil, emptiness. What was the point of imagining how it was? It would never be like that again.

I didn't want to see any more. I wanted to get where we were going. Under the ground, Mish had said, deep under the ground. That would suit me. I wanted to get out of this bleak daylight, this poisoned place of broken buildings, empty rues, dead earth. We climbed down the steps and headed back to the mouth of the pipe.

Dez

I knew I shouldn't, I knew there was no time. I knew that what Morro said was right, that if we didn't do something there would be lots more Bos. But I couldn't help it. I just shut down.

Grief. Such a cold country. Colder than a winter night when all the heating has broken down. A sky that sucks the light out of everything. Nobody can speak to you there, the words freeze into meaninglessness. If you try to speak the sounds die on the air, they make no connection.

I couldn't hear Flora. Not even Ma. They spoke to me, out of their grief, and I answered, but I couldn't hear them, I couldn't hear myself.

Bo.

Two days passed. Three days, four days.

Things kept happening, as things do. More arrests. A riot in the Sixth. I watched the tubes, I watched the infonews, the pictures and sounds went into my brain and through without touching the side. I didn't care. Everything was over, everything had already been lost.

On the eighth day, Morro appeared in my bedroom. Literally zapped out of nowhere on the red rug that covered the concrete floor. He was dressed in his Alchem camos, leaning forward on one knee as if he was about to start a race. And he was angry. He didn't even say, hi, or ask me how I was.

'You know what day it is, Dez?'

I was on my bed, knees up to my chin, watching the infonews on my lenscam. I stared at him through the scrolling feed without bothering to flick it off or minimise the images. Something was on fire. People were running. He looked like a ghost behind an apocalypse.

'It's Ag the second, Dez. The first day of spring was yesterday.'

I shrugged. I didn't care.

He switched off my lenscam.

I blinked with shock. Nobody should be able to do that. Nobody should be able to get into my gear.

'Dez, we need to know about what's happening with the cull. We need to know what the hell they're doing in Newport City. We need those secret files. Why don't you wake the hell up and do something useful?'

'I can't,' I said. 'I just can't.'

He stood up and moved towards me, sticking his face in front of mine so aggressively that I flinched. I noticed there was a smear of blood on his jacket, another on his forehead.

'You fucking coward. I guess you know you're safe here in the Second, not like those poor shits in the outer banns.'

That stung. I slapped his face. My hand went right through him.

'People are already dying, Dez. You could help. Flora's out there. Do you know what Bel's doing? I wish you were half the woman your mother is.'

What was Ma doing? I thought she was just there, grieving like me, making dinner.

I felt tears running down my face. They didn't have anything to do with me.

'Everybody's lost someone, Dez. Bel's lost her son. I've lost people. Lots of people. It happens to us, all the time. We're fleshers, we don't matter, everybody loses something. Eventually we lose ourselves. Why are you acting like you're the only one this has ever happened to? Why are you being so fucking selfish?'

'I'm not,' I said. 'It hurts…'

'Yeah, it hurts. Pain is authentic, yeah? Pain is what makes us fleshers, yeah?'

Morro was so angry I'm not sure he even knew what he was saying. I could see white spittle on his lips.

'Why are you so angry?'

'They almost got Jenna today. She's hurt. She only just escaped. Do you even care?'

'Jenna?'

'Yes, Jenna. Jenna who saved your mother's life. Who put her neck on the line to help you, even though I told her not to. Do you even care?'

'Is she all right?'

'No, but she will be. Maybe I'm next. Someone's informing and we need to know who it is. I don't know who I can trust any more, it could be anyone. People disappear and I don't know if it's because they're traitors or because they're just dead. Redborg? Jenna? Maybe it's you. How the fuck would I know?'

I could feel the panic under his rage now, pulsing, raw. I sat up, trying to think of something to say.

'You're the only person who can help on this,' he said. 'So wake up. Just fucking wake up and do something.'

He blinked out. I stared at the spot where he had been. It was just empty, like me.

I got out of bed and had a steamshower for the first time in a week. And then I went and asked Ma what was going on.

Bo

Ominous clouds streaked with red lightning filled the sky when we finally reached the end of the canal. We passed under a pumping station that had been gutted by the miners, leaving only a rusting steel shell cupping the mouth of a huge outlet pipe. Everything was bone dry.

Mish turned on the headlight and we drove in.

After less than half a klick, the pipe ended in a cave. The floor was iron-hard bedrock that sloped gently down for about twenty metres before levelling off. We travelled for about a quarter of an hour before the cave narrowed abruptly. It was too small for us to get through. Mish stopped and turned off the engine. For a moment none of us dared to speak. We couldn't go forward. But how could we contemplate going back?

We decided to remove the seating racks from either side of the quad. Mish backed the quad up a spot where we had a little more room and he and I got to work with a couple of spanners we found in the panniers. Once the racks were off, Kat sat behind Mish, Rioka squeezed on behind her, and I clung to Rioka, straddling the engine cover.

We got going again, the quad's tracks scraping on the rock. We ground our way through, our hearts in our mouths. The rumbling of the motor in such a confined space was near deafening. We couldn't have been very far below the surface, but it felt as if we were travelling through the centre of the planet.

And then the floor of the cave sloped down steeply and the walls either side of us seemed to disappear. Mish stopped the quad and held a lightstick up high.

We were in an enormous cavern, its high, arched roof patterned with bands of different colours, like a sky of stone streaked with clouds. We drove through to the far end. There were three ways out. Straight ahead of us was a fissure about as wide as the one we'd just passed through. The other two were wider caves, veering off to the left and right.

Kat groaned. 'What the hell do we do now?'

'We follow the water,' said Mish.

'What fucking water?'

'Don't worry. Water will find water.'

'Yeah. And then we drown.' She bit back whatever she was going to say next and took a deep breath. For a moment I saw the panic in her face.

'I know what I'm doing,' said Mish calmly. He grabbed a water canister and knelt down in front of the middle cave.

I wished I had Mish's certainty. Most likely we were already lost and would die deep underground of thirst and hunger and cold.

Mish poured a little water out onto the ground. It pooled and didn't run. He did the same in front of the entrance to the cave on our right, with the same result. But when he poured some water out in front of the third cave, it trickled along the rock and into the darkness.

'This way,' said Mish.

We climbed back onto the quad and headed into the left cave. It was almost perfectly round, its walls smooth, with more than enough room for the quad. I was losing track of time. I don't know how long it was before the cave ran downwards into a kind of shallow basin. Here it forked again. Mish repeated his little water ceremony and this time we went right. We began to travel downwards in long, sweeping curves.

The temperature began to drop. It had been cold since we first went underground, but now it was freezing. My face and hands began to hurt. Mish twisted the throttle and we picked up speed.

Rioka was getting bumped around and it was clearly hurting her. 'Slow down,' she said, through gritted teeth. Mish ignored her and pushed the accelerator. After that, we all just concentrated on hanging on. We raced through the cave, sweeping through the curves, deeper and deeper underground. If it wasn't so terrifying it might have been enjoyable.

When we hit the ice we were travelling too fast. Mish slammed on the brakes, but we were already skidding. We spun and crashed into the side of the cave rear first, facing sideways. I was thrown off and came down hard on my back.

Mish switched off the engine, plunging us into darkness. For a few moments all we could hear was each other, panting.

'Is everybody all right?' said Mish.

'No, you dickhead,' said Kat. 'You almost killed us.'

There was a tense silence. Then Kat found a lightstick and turned it on.

'All present and correct,' she said, surveying us. 'Well, not correct exactly.'

Rioka giggled. It was infectious: soon we were all laughing helplessly. I couldn't stop, although my ribs were killing me. After we'd calmed down, we pulled the quad around to face the right direction. When Mish made for the steerer, Kat gently pushed him aside.

'I think I'll drive for a while,' she said.

'She's right,' said Rioka. 'You're a menace.'

Mish didn't protest. Kat started the engine and slowly moved the quad forward. As the tracks gripped, she eased out the throttle and we were on our way again. As we went further, the ice climbed up the walls until we were driving through a glistening tunnel. The beam of our headlight glanced on the walls, breaking into flashes of greens and violets and bright reds that burst all around us like exploding stars. It was like some strange, exhausting, endless dream.

We were still travelling downwards when the cave narrowed again. The floor levelled and we rolled out onto a broad sheet of smooth ice.

'It's the water,' said Mish. 'We're here.'

Dez

I never realised before how brave Ma is. At some level I knew she was keeping everything normal so I could cope. She cooked me meals that I barely ate and kept her stall at the shijo although almost no one was buying. She was busy, much busier than usual, sitting on the dark tubes, frowning. We had a field up around the house all the time now.

Every night, very late, she came to my bed and stroked my face. I pretended I was asleep so I wouldn't have to see her grief. And all the time she was coping with the same thing, the same howling absence where Bo should be. It was just as bad for her. I knew that, and I hadn't helped her at all.

She never said a word of reproach. Not one. I was so ashamed of myself. When I tried to say sorry, she just hugged me and said not to worry about it.

There was no way she wouldn't have heard what Morro said to me. When I came into the front room that morning, all cleaned up, she looked at me uncertainly, and then she smiled and kissed me. She made something to eat, and we ate it together, as if it were just another ordinary day.

And then I asked her what was going on.

Things had got much worse. Much, much worse. OpSec wasn't even pretending any more. Everyone in the banns believed there would be a cull.

Nobody needed to break into OpSec to find that out: all the signs were there. They just didn't know where or when. Ma told me they'd been doing the same things as they did before the last cull: ramping up security, putting roadblocks and checkpoints between banns, shutting down the monos. The infonews was wall-to-wall propaganda. They had even shut down the tubes, although so much of the network was feral, hosted on homebuilds and so on, it was hard for the authorities to stamp it out completely. So far they hadn't had any success with the dark tubes.

Ma told me that public gatherings of any kind were now forbidden. The day before there had been a protest in the Ninth, and the OpSec clouds just floated in and opened fire, killing dozens of people. People tried to pick up the dead and injured afterwards, and they shot them too. Now the bodies were just left there, in the street, the dead and dying together.

'Was that when Jenna was hurt?' I asked.

'No, that's something else,' she said. 'I don't know the full story on that yet.'

'Morro said she was hurt bad.'

Ma was silent for a time, her lips pressed hard together. She looked exhausted, but there was a strength and determination in her face I hadn't seen before.

'Dez,' she said. 'Listen to me. When I had you and Bo, when Flynn… disappeared, I swore that I would do everything I could to make sure that my kids would never have to face the things that we had to. I wanted you to have a life that we couldn't have when we were kids. I wanted you to be safe, I wanted there to be enough food, I wanted you to have a future.'

Ma had never spoken like this to me before, and I could hear in her voice that she was finding it hard to say. I just nodded.

'For a long time it seemed that all those struggles had got us a little foothold where we would be left alone. That's what we fought for, to be left alone to live our lives, to build something, to not be afraid all the time of the next arrest, the next disappearance, the next cull. That terror. And no, it wasn't good, it could always be better. Most fleshers are still poor, and then there were the skinners scooping up our kids, and the Aps were always a problem. But mostly, it was okay. I got us this house, and I thought…'

Her voice broke, and she turned away from me, hiding her face. I reached out and took her hand. She wiped her eyes and turned back.

'I really thought you and Bo had some kind of future. And now, suddenly, you don't. None of us do. It's as bad as it was when I was a kid, and maybe they want to get rid of us altogether. And I'm so, so, so sorry we didn't keep fighting. I'm so sorry that we failed.'

I swallowed hard. 'It's not your fault, Ma.'

'Maybe it is. We thought, this is enough. We should have tried harder, when things were a little easier, instead of thinking that was enough. We were all so tired. But what I'm saying, Dez, is that I still want to protect you. I don't want you risking your life.'

I understood now why she had left me alone, why I had been allowed to indulge my grief while everything had been going to shit.

'Ma,' I said, as gently as I could. 'You can't. You know you can't.'

'That's why I understand why Kojo's acting the way he is,' she said. 'I think he's wrong, I think he's destroying his relationship with Flora, but I understand it. He remembers how it was before.'

Another stab of guilt. I had barely thought about Flora the past few days. 'Where is Flora?'

'She's out.' Ma wasn't going to tell me, I could tell. That was Flora's business. 'She hasn't been home since you got back. She's been sleeping in Bo's room.'

Flora had been here all the time, and I hadn't even known. From what Ma said, she probably hadn't even spoken to her father. Her heart must be breaking, and I hadn't been there for her at all. I felt even more ashamed of myself. Where had I been?

Feelings. They're the best things in the world, and the worst things. Maybe I should just put them aside, become pure AI, a cloud of sparkling logic that never has to deal with pain at all. I could do that. But then I wouldn't be me. Maybe that's why I don't know how to control what I feel, because I'm so afraid I'll lose the ability to feel altogether. I don't know how to solve that one.

I could tell that Ma knew what I was thinking. She changed the subject abruptly.

'I don't think you should break into OpSec again,' she said. 'I don't believe it will make any difference. We already know what they're going to do. Brian Mac has already looked.'

'But he can't get into the files that I can, Ma. You know that as well as I do. We have to do everything we can. And that includes me. I've done less than anyone.'

'But is it worth the risk?' For the first time I saw the fear in Ma's eyes, the terror that she might lose me as well as Bo, that she might have no one left. There was no argument against that. I could only say the truth.

'It's a risk. It's a big risk. And I won't know until I go in whether it's worth it.'

She knew that I had already made my decision. She nodded.

We didn't talk for a while. I picked up the dishes, put them in the steamer, streamed some music. Ma just sat there watching me, her face full of unspeakable sadness.

'So are you going to tell me what you've been doing?' I said at last. 'Whatever Morro was talking about?'

She shook her head. 'It's better if you don't know,' she said.

'No, it's not.'

'I'm not going to argue with you.'

'Good. That means you'll have to tell me what you've been doing.'

I could be just as stubborn as Ma, and she knew it. She gave me her I've-had-it-with-you-kids look. And then she told me.

So I went into OpSec.

I spent the morning trying to figure out a new method of getting through. It was more dangerous the second time because covering my tracks left a negative trace. After I'd been through, the particles retained a kind of ghost memory of my presence. If I went in again, I'd be waking that memory up. I'd be making the same kind of disturbance on quantum particles that had already been rearranged in that particular way. It was kind of like the particles were scarred and my appearance made the scars open and bleed.

My negative trace would amplify by several orders: I wouldn't just be twice as visible as the first time: it might be a few thousand times more.

That's still tiny in the larger scheme of things, but it could well make the difference between no one noticing and a bot sending an alarm up the pipes to a surveillance AI. And if that happened, I'd be in trouble. I might not even be able to get out. They have ways of shutting things down.

If I could find a new method of getting past the firewalls, the risk would go back down to very low. But the slow-fast thing was the only vulnerability I could think of.

My only hope was to go in through a different portal. On my first visit, I had mapped a couple of dozen portals, but mostly they were all quite close to each other. I needed one from another end of the system. Not that it has 'ends', mind you, distance and time are different things in dataspace. But in submolecular terms, it needed to be as far away as possible from where I'd entered before.

Wow, it's hard to talk about this stuff in slow flesher language. None of it's quite right.

I could maybe lock the door behind me after I went in. Metaphorically speaking, of course. It might buy me some time. And by 'time' I mean a whole second, maybe more.

A girl can do a lot in a second. If she's a girl like me.

Dataspace. How do you describe it? It's not pictures, it's not words, it's not touch or smell. It's not thought, either. Sometimes it looks like it is, but it isn't. It becomes those things as the wet brain negotiates its codes. Dataspace sparkles, it's in constant motion. You can lose yourself in those endlessly intricate patterns, the flows and currents. It's logic, cold and beautiful and crystalline.

I can't describe it, not in any way that makes sense. You need senses for things to make sense. But it's part of me, part of who I am, as much as being a flesher is part of me. I don't feel these things are in conflict, somehow they meet and together make me, but sometimes I'm aware that they might split, and sometimes I can feel one way of being stepping over the other. If either of them ever took dominance, I wouldn't be me any more.

I wondered if Morro felt the same way, because he had abilities that aren't so far from mine. But he was still impressed by what I could do. Maybe he doesn't know what it's like, not like I do.

I cracked the firewall quicker than before, although I could feel it evolving faster and faster, trying to evade me. I got in, and started vacuuming up as much data as I could. I was in a hurry, the bots were beginning to track me, sniffing changes before I could negate them. I got faster still. I made it through the second firewall. I found the third firewall, and cracked that.

I could hear the bots crunching behind me. Well, not 'hear' as such. They were stretching out their algorithms, beginning the alarm patterns that would alert an AI. I threw out a muffle code. No hope, once I'd done that, of covering my tracks. I copied all the files. I finished copying just as the bots broke the muffle code and reached a critical consensus to send an alarm up to an AI.

I got out of there microseconds before the AI woke up. Like a gau yapping at my heels before the gate slammed shut. But not at all like that, of course.

I left a databomb behind me, the most vicious I knew how to code. I seeded it with some pinker signatures, so with any luck they'll figure that the attack came from inside Newport City and not the banns. The databomb would screw them up, ripping all their files to bits. It was a desperate thing to do, because now every alarm in Newport City would be screaming. And who knew what would happen next?

My invasion was, in short, not entirely successful. But I had the data that Morro wanted. I was pretty sure that they wouldn't know exactly where I had been. They probably wouldn't realise I'd broken the third firewall, because I hadn't been there before, and the scarring would be low. They'd be panicking enough that I had breached the first wall. And it was the data behind the third firewall that we needed most of all.

Morro was in the house less than a second after I got back. He'd cleaned himself up a bit after his visit that morning, the blood was gone, and he was just wearing black fatigues, a beaten-up old leather jacket like the one Bo used to wear. My heart hurt when I saw it.

'You went in.'

I nodded. I was almost too exhausted to speak, trembling as the shock of the risk I'd taken hit home. I almost hadn't made it out. I didn't know how he knew I'd done it. Maybe he'd picked up an alert.

'Did you get everything?'

'I've copied as much as I could get,' I said. 'I almost didn't make it out.'

I could feel Morro's impatience, he was humming with it, but he didn't nag me. 'Should I make you a brew while you get your breath back?' he said.

'Yes, please,' I said. Why not be nice.

By the time he returned with a steaming cup, I wasn't quite so shaky. He'd made one for himself as well, and sat down next to me on my bed, like he was one of my best friends. I resented it.

'So,' he said. 'Have you had a chance to assess what you've found?'

I'd had a look at the data while he made the tea and I wasn't sure I wanted to speak to him.

'Seriously, Dez. We're in trouble. We need to know what kind of trouble. And what we can expect now.'

'Trouble, for sure,' I said.

He scratched his chin, frowning. He had the beginnings of a beard, and I had an irrational desire to reach out and stroke the stubble. Like when a little punk gets his head shaved and you want to run your hands over the bristle, for the pleasure of it under your fingers. I shook my head. I was losing it again.

'I know who your informer is,' I said.

His head jerked up. 'You do? For sure?'

'Yes,' I said. 'It's you.'

Bo

The roof of the cavern was at least twenty metres above, a massive canopy of undulating rock. Beneath it, stretching right and left as far as we could see, was Mish's water, a broad river of ice. There was nothing to tell us which direction to take.

Mish tried pouring out the water, but it froze the moment it touched the ice. He seemed to brace himself. 'I'll have to read the water,' he said. For the first time, I heard anxiety in his voice. 'I've never done it...so close before.'

He told us to wait at the mouth of the tunnel and and walked a few steps onto the river. He lay down on the ice, closed his eyes and folded his arms across his chest. For a long time nothing happened. I wondered how he could stand the cold. Except for his chest steadily rising and falling, he was perfectly still.

Rioka gripped my arm. 'We should be closer,' she said.

'He told us to wait here.'

Mish's body stiffened and his back arched. His eyes opened wide, turning to globes of luminous water.

'What's happening?' said Kat. She was staring at Mish, fascinated and appalled. 'Is he having some kind of fit?'

'He's found the water,' said Rioka. 'Or the water has found him.'

Mish's body convulsed. His head and shoulders seemed welded to the ice, but the rest of him twisted as if he was made of rope. It happened so fast that it didn't look real. He started panting, his mouth opening in a silent scream.

'No. This isn't right, this isn't going right,' said Rioka. 'Something's wrong.' She lunged forward onto the river.

I pulled her back. 'Wait,' I said. 'Wait. It hasn't finished yet.'

'He's in too much pain.'

As we watched, Mish went limp. His eyes were still open but they no longer shone. They were dull, almost black, as if they were empty holes in his skull.

The river began to fracture, a thousand tiny cracks opening around his body. Two wings of ice arched over his body and folded closed, encasing him in an icy shell.

Rioka rushed forward and fell to her knees at Mish's side, but now he was sinking into the solid surface of the river. She screamed his name, her cry echoing around the vast space above us, and started clawing at the ice. Kat and I tried to pull her away, but she kept on, scrabbling desperately until the bandage on her injured hand was torn off and both her hands were bleeding. Her blood froze as it touched the river, turning a violent pink before it too was swallowed by the ice.

'We have to get off the ice,' Kat said, her voice shaking. 'Rioka, We have to get off ...please...'

At last we managed to drag her away and she collapsed in Kat's arms, shuddering.

I stared into the ice. For a moment I saw Mish sinking further down, but he no longer seemed to be made of flesh and blood. He was like a statue of himself. At the last moment the light returned to his eyes, even more brilliantly than before. He seemed to look at me, deep inside me where no one ever sees, and then he dissolved into the white depths of the river.

Mish was gone. We hardly knew each other, but I felt like I'd lost my brother. And any hope of ever getting out of this place had vanished with him. I stepped back to the others, numb with shock and disbelief.

I think we were all hoping that Mish would rise out of the ice, that the river would give him back to us. But underneath I knew that he'd never come back.

I sat there for a long time, listening to Rioka's low moaning. Kat was trying to comfort her, but she wasn't in much better shape.

'What do we do now?' said Kat.

'I don't know,' I said.

Not even Jenna could draw Mish back. Beautiful Jenna. She could draw the sickness out of Ma, but she couldn't have saved Mish. And now I would never see her again. I'd never see Dez or Ma or anyone I loved.

Why did it hurt so much just to think of Jenna? Can love happen so quickly? Is it something that seizes you helplessly, that hurts more than it comforts, that turns you inside out so completely that you don't know yourself any more?

Something I couldn't identify began to stir inside my head, as if a voice was whispering to me, just out of the range of my hearing. Mish had said that the water could feel things. Had we done something to anger it? Were we a threat somehow? Maybe if I tried to talk to it, the water might take pity on us. Maybe it might swallow me too, like Mish.

'I'm going out there,' I said. 'I'm going speak to the river.'

'What?' said Kat. 'Have you lost your mind?'

'I'm going to tell it that we don't mean it any harm.'

'You saw what happened before…'

'Can you sense the water?' said Rioka, struggling upright. 'Can you, Bo?'

'I don't know what it is, but I feel something…' I trailed off, groping for words.

'You feel what?' said Kat. 'Suicidal?'

'Maybe he can hear Mish,' said Rioka.

Kat looked as if she was going to argue, but then she just shrugged. 'I guess it might be a quicker way to die,' she said. She put her arm around Rioka's shoulder. 'It'll just be you and me, babe. We can starve together in the dark.'

I braced myself and stepped cautiously onto the river, terrified that at any moment the ice would crack and break apart.

I had the strange sensation that I was walking on air, that there was nothing beneath my feet. I stopped close to the spot where Mish had been taken, beginning to feel dizzy. It was difficult to keep my balance so I spread out my arms, like a tightrope walker I'd seen at a carnival when I was a kid. It seemed to help.

I thought of the river before it had frozen. I imagined it flowing through this cave, deep and fast. And then at last I heard it, singing inside my head.

I don't know if I believe in people's souls. I don't know what I believe about people once they're dead, if anything remains of them, if anything lingers. But something was moving under the ice, something was bleeding out from the place where Mish had been. It was the palest light, nothing more than a white shadow. It snaked away from me, twisting under the surface like a thin coil of smoke. It was Mish showing us the way, telling us what the river had told him.

I don't know how long we travelled. An hour, three hours, a day...

I followed the light under the ice. Sometimes it grew stronger, sometimes it faded until I could barely see it. The river branched several times, splitting into two, sometimes three. I followed the light. The ice flowed under me, now growing wider, now narrower, snaking between high walls of stone. I began to see visions of creatures just under the surface: monstrous black snakes, schools of yellow, eyeless creatures with mouths full of fangs and spiky wings.

And then I felt a breeze on my face. I looked up and I saw the sky, the palest of blues, streaked with pink. I turned off the engine and the quad glided out onto a broad delta, the river breaking into a dozen channels and slowly melting into the Gilla Sea.

The sun was just rising.

Dez

Morro stared at his feet. He was wearing scuffed black boots with silver flashes on the side. He looked immensely tired, as if he had aged twenty years in the past five seconds.

'Shit,' he said. 'I was hoping it wasn't me.'

'You were…you were *what*?'

'I know you won't believe me,' he said. 'But no, I didn't know it was me.'

'How the fuck is that even possible?'

There was a silence. Then he sighed and sat up. 'I told you about doubling, that there's the real me and then there's another me. Well, if you do too much of it, and I do it a lot, you can end up with two yous.'

'So which you are you now? Don't you talk to yourself? Don't you remember everything that the other you does?' I didn't get it.

'Obviously not.'

'So maybe now, right now, you are calling OpSec in to get me,' I said.

'No, I'm not. Not this me, anyway.'

'What about the other you?'

'The other me doesn't know I'm here,' he said.

'You're doing my head in, Morro.'

'Try being in my head.'

'No thanks.'

The really weird thing was that I believed him. If I hadn't believed him, I would have murdered him right there. No question. Me, who had trouble killing rats. Maybe it was how defeated he looked. I tried to imagine what it would be like to find out that, without knowing it, you had been betraying your closest friends.

I tried to focus. It was very likely that he was lying to me. Maybe I just wanted to believe him. After all, didn't I hate this guy? Did I stop hating him now I knew he was a traitor? What the hell was wrong with me?

I pulled up the Morro file. Morro Ignada, Credit ID 83456788, Security Informant code-name 'Wicked'. 3D mug shots. It was definitely Morro. Code words, meeting places, the whole romantic shebang, like on the soaps. A list of information laid.

It was a long list. It went back months.

'You really didn't know?' I said.

'I…wondered,' he said. 'There were blank times, when I didn't remember what I was doing. They were getting more frequent. But I thought maybe it was all the stress…' He was speaking without emotion now.

'But…you suspected?' I thought of the OpSec militia that had turned up in the hospital. 'Why did you even decide to be part of trying to rescue Bo, if you even suspected such a thing? Did you hit up OpSec?'

'I thought it was impossible it was me.' He wasn't meeting my eyes now. 'It would be in the records if I did tell OpSec,' he said.

I looked. Yep, there it was. I had wondered why they got there so fast. I scrolled through the reports. Morro hadn't given them the full information. He had told them a pinker cell of subversives was going to attack the hospital. No mention of fleshers at all. Enough to screw us up, but not screw us up completely.

He wanted to make things more dangerous, to dare himself. As if being an informant was a wonderful game. I thought of him walking through the front doors of the hospital, tossing the stinger up and down, the look on his face. The thrill of risking everything.

Who was this Morro, anyway? Not even he knew.

I looked in a few more reports. There was one called 'Chimeras'. I read it. The anger that had been held at bay by my astonishment surged up so suddenly that I thought I might be sick.

'So you're the one that told them about fleshers with abilities.'

'Did I?'

'You told them. You *told* them. Those experiments are because of *you*.'

Morro stared at his feet again. And then he nodded. 'I guess, if you say so. I must have.'

'Bo's dead because of you,' I said.

'Maybe he's not dead,' said Morro. 'We don't know for sure.'

'Yeah, right.'

I didn't call him any names. There weren't any bad enough. There was no point in being angry, it ebbed out of me as quickly as it had arrived. In its wake was an ashen desolation. Neither of us knew what to say next.

'You'd better tell Bel,' he said, looking up. For a moment it was like all his masks had vanished. I saw the emptiness in his eyes, and flinched. 'I guess she won't want to speak to me again.'

'Get out,' I said. My voice was shaking. 'Get out of my house.'

Morro didn't answer, he just flicked out.

I sat there for a few moments, breathing hard. I thought of telling Ma that Morro was the informant. I didn't need to guess what her reaction would be. I could hear her in the front room, talking. Voice clipped, authoritative, decisive, running things.

It was cowardly of me, but I thought I'd tell her later, after I'd looked through all the data I'd stolen from OpSec.

I had so much material it took me the whole afternoon to begin to sort out what was useful and what was not. Endless searches for keywords, filtering out the routine reports, operational files, things that didn't matter. Though everything mattered. Even though it takes me almost no time to get data, I need time to work out what it all means. You need to understand what it means in slow thinking.

The most important information was about the cull. The next in importance, the Alchems. But before I did anything else, I looked for any files to do with Ma and Bo and me. Not much more than I had found before, notes from a few skinner informants, the homebuild DNA scan that had started off the alert on me.

I also did a search for Culcullan. That struck pay dirt. A big, fat file, latest entry only two days ago.

OpSec was very worried about Culcullan. He had been presumed dead, but now they were wondering if that was correct. They weren't sure if Culcullan was one person or a group of people, but they figured that he must have been an insider, a pinker radical or radicals who had taken up arms with the fleshers. There was a list of Culcullan's crimes. They had never worked out how they were done. After a few years, when he went quiet, they had stopped investigating: now it was priority one to figure out the vulnerabilities that permitted these things to happen.

As I read through the file, I felt my breath whooshing out. At one point Culcullan downed the whole of the OpSec network and filled it with disinformation. He'd taken over the media, pumping out flesher music and political demands instead of the infonews. He had kept that going for days, they couldn't get it back, and in the end they had to shut the whole thing down and rebuild it from scratch. Most impressively, Culcullan had broken part of the Inner Veil, which was how the fleshers got into Newport City and set fire to OpSec HQ.

There was a list of the pinker radicals. I scrolled through, curious to see who the pinkers were who thought that fleshers were worth more than spitting on, wondering why they bothered. And then I jerked upright, my heart hammering.

One of them was my dad.

Flynn was a pinker. Ma had never told me that. My dad was a *pinker*.

Maybe it was another Flynn Zerkos.

There was a mug shot, a 3D vid of him turning around in a cell, the camera taking in all the angles of his head. A young, bearded guy, handsome, intense eyes. I'd never seen an image of Flynn, Ma said she didn't have any. Looking too much like Bo for comfort, like Bo would look if he had pinker skin: same mouth, same cheekbones, same eyes. Flynn was a communications researcher, whatever that means. A list of his qualifications, some of his papers. It was a long list. Suspected actions: distribution of illegal literature, membership of proscribed organisations, etc etc. Then he disappeared, suspected to be hiding in the banns.

It couldn't be him. I kept thinking that it must be some clone, they have people who are genetically identical in Newport City. It's not like the banns, where everyone is different.

I kept reading.

A report: a sighting in the banns. Meatsex violations with a flesher. Credit ID 65444326. That was Ma's ID, I knew it instantly.

'Meatsex violations'. That was me and Bo.

They finally caught up with him. Killed in combat. At least he was never arrested and tortured, which is what Ma thought had happened to him.

My god.

I could feel myself shaking. I took a deep breath and looked for any reports on Ma. There she was. Bel Inaware. Known whore and smuggler, small trader in the Ninth shijo, later the Second. On a low level watch list, known associate of Flynn Zerkos. There wasn't anything else, they had never tagged her for whatever she did, back in the day. Maybe Brian Mac had nixed any intel, but they probably thought she was just a brainless flesher. The only really long files were about pinkers. OpSec considered the rebel pinkers very dangerous, there was a lot about how the cloning and conditioning programs had to be refitted. But fleshers, who cared? Fleshers were just bodies, threatening in crowds, potentially dangerous if influenced by radical pinkers, but that was all.

Ma kept a low profile, but she liked to run things. If she had been part of this whole flesher rebellion, she would have been in charge.

Why did she tell us so little about Flynn? About everything they did?

I wanted to bawl. I would have liked to have known my dad. Who he was, what he did, why Ma had loved him. A whole hour had passed and I hadn't even looked into the cull. I was frightened of what I might find, that was why I was only looking at the data about people I knew.

I told my flesher feelings to shut up and made myself into pure logic.

Okay. The cull.

This was in a file from behind the third firewall. Only six people had the authorisation to see it, all OpSec, no city officials. The cull was being brought forward after recent events. No notice given for fear of leaks or protests. A public announcement would be made after its successful completion, signed Bremmer.

There was a long and detailed scenario of how it would happen. It went on and on, written in blank, official language. The longer I read, the sicker I felt.

The Inner Veil would be doubled in strength to prevent any damage to Newport City itself. All surviving fleshers in the inner banns to be DNA profiled, those found with mutant DNA to be eliminated after sampling for further investigation.

There was a machine called the Eradicator. A form of garbage disposal. Round up the fleshers, feed them in. Low energy usage, environmentally sound. Murder and disposal all in one neat package.

Experiments had been very promising, but they still faced challenges in scaling up for mass usage. Construction was well advanced in the Eighth and Tenth Banns.

I noted the locations, but I already knew where they were. The drilling in the Outer Banns wasn't about getting new sources of water at all. Operation planned for Ag 12.

Next week. Fuck. Next week. We had ten days to stop it.

Bo

I drove the quad to the closest shore. Kat and I laid Rioka down on the ground. Her injured hand was a bloody, swollen mess. Kat tended her wound and made her a sling for her arm, and then gave her the last of the painkillers.

It was utterly silent, the air crystal clear. I could see the broad expanse of the Gilla Sea, shrouded here and with thin patches of white mist drifting close above the surface, beginning to burn off in the sunlight. The delta's channels shone like silver. A few klicks out on the sea, the veil of Duiwel Island was visible, and beyond that the Outer Veil of Newport City was a faint glow on the horizon.

The sea made no sound at all. There were small waves, or rather there were furrows that crisscrossed on the surface, shifting back and forth. In the rising sunlight the water had an oily sheen, flecked here and there with what looked like purple filaments. How were we going to cross this diseased sea?

I walked along the shore. The sand on the water's edge was black, threaded with the long white strands of some kind of fibrous plant. From here, I could see structures, a collection of low, flat buildings.

When I returned to the others, Rioka had recovered a little. I realised I was starving. I couldn't remember when we had last eaten.

'I still can't believe what happened,' said Rioka.

'We don't even know what happened,' Kat said. 'Not really.'

'Why would the river take him? He knew the water, he could read it, it could speak to him.'

'Maybe that's why it took him,' I said.

Kat was staring across the Gilla Sea. I knew what she was thinking. We'd come so far. Home was so close. But we still had almost no chance of getting there.

I might soon be dead, I thought. All three of us might. And we'd be out here. No one would ever find us. No one would ever know what had happened to us.

We decided to head for the buildings I'd seen. As we moved away from the delta I felt a tug in the middle of my chest, as if something was pulling me back to the cave. It grew stronger the further we went, until I was so nauseous I could hardly walk. I stopped, bending over, and took a few deep breaths. And then, quite suddenly, it lifted, leaving me emptied out.

I looked back across the delta, where the water flowed out of the darkness. Mish was still there, still under the ice. He was letting me go.

The others had drawn ahead, and Kat looked back and called me up to them. We walked over hard, sharp grass that crunched under our feet. It sounded as if we were walking on glass. Nature had taken over the open ground between the buildings. Stunted, weirdly twisted trees with grey and white leaves were growing everywhere. Between them were forests of tall yellow grass, and huge-faced flowers that looked like the sunflowers I'd seen in the foodtowers. But these flowers were blood red, their stalks black. They bowed and swayed in the slight breeze that was beginning to spring up off the sea. The breeze worried me. We didn't have suits.

'The solar ferries used to run from here,' said Kat. 'In the last days of the storms they brought people evacuated from other cities to Newport City. It was one of the last places to be shut down.'

'How do you know that?' I asked.

She smiled. 'I just know,' she said. 'I like knowing stuff.'

We halted about ten metres from the closest building, a long, grey shed.

Its roof had collapsed inside, leaving a tangle of twisted steel beams. We peered through its empty windows and glimpsed a dead gau. At least, I think it was a gau. It was a long-haired, monstrous looking thing with huge paws and a weirdly elongated head. Its throat had been ripped out and the cavity was seething with green maggots. I didn't want to run into whatever had killed it.

'There were riots here,' said Kat. 'People were trying to get onto the last boats. Some of them were killed.'

'By OpSec?' said Rioka.

'No,' said Kat. 'By other people just like them.'

Kat was starting to sound like Morro. I began to wonder if she might be an Alchem. The tattoo on the back of her neck might be a clue. All Alchems seemed to be tattooed, and hers looked like some kind of symbol.

We moved around the building to its massive doors. Beneath the twisted steel were the smashed remains of a large boat. It was sitting off the ground in some kind of cradle. The floor was littered with shattered solar panels. We checked out the other sheds. Most were empty and rotting. One was like an enormous greenhouse, choked with vines and bulbous purple flowers that gave off a foul smell.

We came to a broad flight of stairs that led down to a wide pier, half submerged at the far end, and walked along as far as we dared. A large ferry lay on its side, most of it under the water. A small ship was propped against the pier, the stern half sunk, the bow pointing up into the air. Its name was written in thick red letters: MINER 3. Some strange, jelly-like creature was attached to the side. It looked like an enormous clot of blood, slowly pulsing. It seemed to sense us and slid down into the water, disappearing into the murk.

'They must have used this to get to the mines,' said Kat, studying the ship curiously. 'It doesn't look that old.'

'Maybe they had to abandon it,' I said. 'Some kind of nano attack.'

'Feral nekas. Ripperbirds. Something out of the sea. Could have been anything.'

A crane rose out of the water from the submerged end. Hanging from its arm was a steel cradle holding a large pod that sat on the water's slowly undulating surface. It was a flat-bottomed craft about six metres long with a hatch on top. Its roof was covered with solar tiles.

Our eyes met. We both had the same thought.

'Escape pod?' I said.

'Exactly,' said Kat.

The pod was maybe two metres below the pier and about as far out on the water. I measured the distance.

'It's not too far to jump,' I said.

'If you miss you'll be dead,' said Rioka. 'We don't know what's in the water...if it is water.'

We stared down at the slowly moving surface of the sea. Spirals of colour—grey, purple, green—expanded and shrank, clotting together and breaking up into threads. 'It's dead,' I said. 'It's just dead.'

I stepped back and took a deep breath. I'd done this a dozen times before, jumping for the closing doors of the mono as it left the station. Well, it was kind of the same. I knew that if I waited any longer I wouldn't do it.

I couldn't miss. I wouldn't miss. I ran. I jumped.

I didn't exactly land on my feet. I ended up sprawled at the edge of the pod, clinging to the handle of the hatch. I looked across at Kat and Rioka. Kat was pumping her fist. Rioka looked appalled.

I opened the hatch and climbed down a short ladder into the dead air inside. It looked as if everyone had left yesterday. I could see six beds that folded down from the walls, a narrow table, a wall of metal cupboards. At the far end was a control panel. All the switches were labelled. Release, power, solar, battery, heat, pump, beacon, MPS, engine. This thing had an engine?

I hit the emergency power switch. Nothing. I switched it off, then on again. The same. I did it once more. Off then on. Above my head, a single light began to glow.

I climbed up the ladder and stuck my head out of the hatch.

'We're almost home,' I said.

It took me a while to figure the panel out. It all seemed to be working, although the emergency battery was almost out of juice. I switched on the solar tiles. Thank god, they were rapid absorption, like the ones we had on the roof at home.

One set of controls, with a small visual display and a joystick, was marked 'crane'. So you could control the crane from inside the pod? Maybe things were going our way at last. That is, if the crane was still working. I pressed the power button and cautiously tested the joystick. The pod lurched upwards and I nearly fell over. I heard Kat outside, shouting my name in panic, and I climbed up to tell her nothing bad was happening.

It took a while, but in the end I managed to get the pod off the water, close and level with the pier. I'd only ever heard about boats in stories, but I know all about switches and dials. I was just a little punk again, messing about. But it was real. We were going to sail across the Gilla Sea.

Kat and Rioka climbed on and down through the hatch. Rioka was burning with fever. I pulled out one of the folding beds and made her lie down and Kat and I went through the pod. Kat found a schematic pasted inside one of the locker doors and we studied it carefully. The engine was right underneath us. On the bottom of the pod were panels that opened at the rear to expose the rudder and something called a ducted screw.

'What's that?' I said.

'It's what makes this thing move,' said Kat. She was good with tech. She reminded me a little of Dez. If everything worked out, they'd get to meet.

The pod was fully equipped. Whoever it belonged to must have high-tailed in a hurry. I wondered what had made them leave, and then began to wonder even more uneasily why they hadn't come back. It was a bit strange around here, there wasn't a lot of storm damage, not like in the ruined cities in the dasht. Maybe it was something else bad. Maybe the pod was some kind of trap… I shuddered and pushed the thought away.

Kat found packets of freeze-dried food, the kind that never spoils and, best of all, six suit belts, still in their new packaging. They were just standard issue, not the manacles they locked us in at the mines. We put them on at once and fitted another around Rioka, switching them on to low.

'Are they sending signals?' Kat asked. 'Can you check, Rioka?'

Rioka groaned and sat up with difficulty, resting her head in her good hand. 'They can,' she said at last. 'But only if you turn the signalling on.' She pointed to a switch on the belt.

Kat looked at her in concern. 'There's got to be a medical kit,' she said. 'They've got everything else.'

I found one with phials of drugs, a couple of implants and bio concentrates in a locker. Kat gave Rioka a double shot of painkiller. They took effect quickly and Rioka drifted off to sleep. We discovered blankets in a cupboard under one of the beds and covered her up.

I checked the main battery levels while Kat got the MPS running. The levels had risen a little since I'd turned on the solar tiles. I decided to keep us on emergency power until it ran out, then I'd switch to the main. Kat said that if we travelled in a straight line it was twelve klicks to Duiwel Island, forty to Newport City. This was the narrowest part of the Gilla Sea. I guess that's why the ferry station was here.

I knew I had to test the engine, but I kept putting it off. I wanted to enjoy our luck while we still had it. If it was luck, and not something else. If the engine was screwed, we would have walk back to Newport all around the Gilla Sea. Dez would have worked out our chances of survival at 0.00 recurring.

I flicked the switch, my heart in my mouth. Nothing happened at first. And then it caught, a soft vibration under my feet.

We'd leave when it was dark, once the batteries had a chance to charge.

Rioka started tossing and turning. She was mumbling in her sleep about something being switched off, the shut down, priority actions in place. I figured that she was picking up signals. It didn't sound good.

By nightfall Kat and I had sorted most things out. The emergency battery was about to hit empty, so I switched to the main. The lights went out. There was a rumble, a purr, and the whole pod trembled for a few seconds. Kat and I stood silently there in the darkness. I felt for her hand and she squeezed hard.

Then everything lit up.

I looked at Kat. 'Now, yeah?'

She nodded.

I hit the release switch and the pod dropped onto the water, rocking from side to side, water slopping against the hull. I waited until it stabilised and started the engine. There was the same long pause, the same nothing, and then we heard the outer panels open. The engine started.

Kat had set a course on the MPS that gave Duiwel Island a wide berth, approaching Newport from along the coastline. It was trip of about seventy klicks. I turned on the navigator, climbed the ladder and opened the hatch. Kat squeezed into the opening beside me.

The sky was starless, a black void. Clouds. Maybe there was a storm brewing. I didn't want to think about that.

In the distance we could see the Veil of Duiwel Island, its soft shimmer reflected on the dark surface of the water.

And then the Veil went out.

Was this the beginning? Was this how the cull started? Without its Veil, Duiwel Island was open to anything that blew across the Gilla Sea. If you were going to get rid of everyone, that's how you'd do it. Once a storm hit, everything would be over very quickly. What kind of hell would that be? There'd be no one left to tell.

Kat had gone to check on Rioka. I stayed up, staring out over the water, the engine's steady hum vibrating under my feet. We'd been travelling for a good two hours. Without the light from Duiwel Island's Veil, the night was black. It felt as if a fog was coming down.

The main power source was all we had, there was nothing left in the emergency battery. I'd switched on the pod's shield as soon as we set out. I knew that it would draw on the power supply, but it would have been reckless to leave it off: if something really toxic hit us we'd likely be finished, suits or no suits.

All the bad weather in Newport blew in from the Gilla Sea. Storms blew up quickly, rising in spirals as tall as a towerblock and blowing away into nothing. Right now it was calm. But that didn't mean it would stay that way.

I climbed back down. Kat had given Rioka another shot of painkiller and was cooling her face with a wet cloth. We managed to get her to drink a little. She was fighting to keep her eyes open.

'I picked up...signals,' she said. 'I wasn't trying to. The switch off. They were going to switch off the Veil.'

'Duiwel?'

'Yes, the island. They were going to switch off the Veil.'

Her eyes fell shut and we laid her back on the bed, covering her with the blanket. She was shivering again. We both knew she was getting sicker, but neither of us knew what to do about it.

Kat and I sat down on one of the other beds.

'They did it on purpose,' said Kat. 'They turned off the Veil and left all those poor bastards to die.'

'I knew that when I saw it happen,' I said.

'That's evil,' said Kat. 'Pure evil. What sort of person does that? What's wrong with them? They've got to be stopped.'

'Yeah, we'll stop them,' I said bitterly. 'After we get back home.'

A silence fell between us.

'Are you an Alchem?' I said at last.

She laughed. 'Do I seem that weird?'

'No, not weird. I mean...'

'What?'

'I don't know. I just thought that you might be.'

'No, I'm not anything. Just me. What are you?'

'Just me too.'

'Your ma runs a stall in the shijo in the Second, right? I've seen you around there once or twice. Seems like a good woman, your ma.'

'Yeah, she is.'

She leaned over and kissed me on the lips. I didn't move.

She sat back, studying my face. 'Sorry,' she said. 'I just had to do that.'

'No problem,' I mumbled.

'Do you have a girlfriend?'

'Yes. Well, no. I mean, I don't really know. But I think, yes, I do.'

'What's her name, this maybe girlfriend?'

'Her name's Jenna.'

'Is she lovely?'

'Yes.'

'Good.'

She climbed up the ladder and stood in the open hatch, looking out at the sky.

Brian Mac

Ag 2, 24.17 hours

Clouds all through the banns, spilling out their OpSec grunts. People are calling them ghosts. Bodies without edges. Bodies that kill. Eighteen flesh-ers dead in the Ninth last night, most of them young people.

The skinners are out big time, and there's orders to leave them alone. It almost caused a mutiny at the precinct. I'm ignoring the orders. Found one three nights ago ripping apart some young punk who'd been blasted by the ghosts and left on the street. The skinner was on the spot before the kid's body was cold. They can salvage a lot from a corpse. Not as much as a living body but enough to make some black money. I took an executive decision to delete his account.

There's no logic to where the ghosts are hitting. There's always some kind of cover, some crap about unrest, unlawful gathering, illegal activity. They'll use anything, doesn't matter what it is. There are spotter drones in the sky day and night, dozens of them. They're small, they fly low, they can look through the windows. Nightmare insects. They guide the clouds.

A kid hacked up some kind of remote and had six spotters playing chicken in the sky above Rue Balu. It was carnage. People down below were cheering as the drones flew into each other head on, exploding in flames. The game didn't last long. Four clouds rolled into the rue. Everyone ran. The ghosts blasted as many as they could, dragged the corpses into a pile and set them alight.

The new guys want in on the killing. They can taste the blood. They all want to be ghosts. The Aps have to clean up the mess. My job.

I disposed of one of the new lot last night. He was bragging in the precinct about how he'd wasted two fleshers, homeless types who were around the bins behind the shijo. He was laughing. 'I took their freaking heads off.'

My sensibilities were offended, so I followed him out of the precinct at the end of his shift. I left him where he fell. Cooked up a report, made him a skinner kill. They won't give a shit.

Yeah, it's open season on fleshers. Get 'em while you can.

Imagine if anyone found this diary. Imagining that almost makes it worth it. They think that the cloning and conditioning are foolproof. A few casualties here and there, a few 'mistakes', a few rogues. I'm a discontinued line, but they didn't eliminate us. The obedience is supposed to be unbreakable. Back to the drawing board if they look at me. I can feel it breaking all the time, those old chains rusting. I've been in the banns too long.

Bel's staying close to home, organizing. Don't know how Dez is doing. She's gone quiet. Losing her brother hit her like a sledgehammer, all the fight went out of her.

Bel loves that girl. It's fierce, the way Bel can love.

She's got the Second as tight as a drum, cloud watchers posted on every rue, a dark intel line that links the edges of the bann to the centre. Nothing comes in or goes out of the Second that she doesn't know about. She's running rings around the Aps. A gang of traders from the shijo are her skinner mob. When they find a skinner, they're ruthless. They've disposed of two in the last two days. Not a pretty sight.

Jenna got knocked by the ghosts in a raid on that rat heap she's living in. Lucky to be alive. She caught the edge of a blast, shrapnel in her hip, a bit of internal bleeding. I've put her in a safe place until she's on her feet. I called a contact in the meat trade. Malco, a doctor of sorts. He deals with screwed up pinkers who've gone deviant in a bad way.

Pinkers turn on themselves. The whole guilt thing is inbuilt. For those that can't deal with it, there are ways of shutting it all down chemically. When that doesn't work they get sick, really sick. Malco suspends them in a time warp, clears out the filth in their clockwork brains, fits them with a penitence implant, sends them home with a clear conscience.

He hates every pinker he deals with. A bitter, twisted old coot. I like him a lot.

Mayor Osborne has been all over the tubes. He looks pinker than usual these days. Bremmer is always at his side, mouth like a steel trap. He has a new uniform, all black with silver braids. He looks like a cheap toy.

But they're good, those two. They know how to feed the pinkers' paranoia, without uttering one word of truth. You have to admire them. It's a class act. Create an enemy, real or imagined, it makes no difference, and then protect your grateful people from it. Works a charm. Always has done.

The pinkers don't see the corpses lining the rues of the banns. They don't count them. They don't see the grief. They don't notice the absences. Pinkers only know one thing: that Mr Smooth and his soldier boy have made them safe.

I've got a bottle of the raw stuff and an implant that will make me feel like a young punk with a hard on who doesn't give a shit about anything. Happy days.

Reality can fucking wait.

Bo

I was dreaming of ripperbirds nesting in my bedroom at home, hundreds of them filling every available space, dozens more at the window, their sharp feathers scratching on the glass. Kat called me, and I woke up. I shook the image from my head and climbed into the hatch, squeezing in beside her.

It was almost dawn and the eastern sky was lightening to a pale yellow. The dome of Newport City was visible directly ahead of us. We were only half a dozen klicks away from the shore. An enormous bank of black cloud hung low above us. It looked almost solid, as if it was made of stone.

'Something's happening up there,' Kat said.

A small area near the centre of the cloud was swelling rapidly. A huge tumourous growth blossomed on its underside, hanging down above the sea in front of us. We both turned our suits to high.

'Is it a nanostorm?' asked Kat. I could see that she was trying not to panic.

'I've never seen one like that before.'

As we watched, the swelling in the cloud started to blister and split, flashes of light bursting from the cracks in its surface. The waves beneath began churning violently until a whirlpool opened about hundred metres in front of us, rapidly growing deeper.

We were heading straight for it.

'We have to get away from whatever the hell this is,' said Kat. She dived down the ladder.

I heard the engine kick up, but it made no difference. We were being drawn towards the whirlpool, spiralling around its edges now, closer and closer to its unseen depth.

This can't be happening, I thought. We're almost home.

Then it was as if somebody flicked a giant switch, reversing the currents. The pod was flung outwards, and almost capsized in a huge backwash that poured down the hatch. The engine stopped and I clung desperately to the ladder, praying that my suit would protect me from the water. I could hear Kat shouting, but I couldn't make out what she was saying, and then the engine powered up again. We started gaining distance.

The whirlpool was gone. Where it had been, huge sheets of spray were being sucked up into the cloud, as if was raining upwards. And something was slowly lifting out of the sea, something massive.

At first it looked like a monstrous animal, but as it rose higher I recognised in disbelief the long curve of a ship's hull. An upside down ship. Water cascaded down its sides and into the sea, to be drawn skywards again in the impossible rain. Beneath the surface of the water I saw portholes, blurry circles of yellow, and realised that the lights inside were all turned on. As the deck appeared the ship began to right itself, slowly turning on its axis as it rose with the upwards rain towards the cloud.

It was a ferry. It was so close that I could see through the windows of the upper deck. The interior was crowded with hundreds of people rushing back and forth in a panic, pulling on life jackets, falling over one another in the crush, pressing against the windows. Even through the noise of the water, I could hear their screams and cries for help.

The ferry stopped rising and continued to rotate in mid-air, suspended just below the cloud. Whether it was upside down or rightside up made no difference: it was as if the ferry had its own gravity. After a while, I realised everything was repeating itself, and then I understood what I was watching. I went cold. It was a loop, twenty seconds of suspended time happening over and over again. I was seeing all these people in the moments when they knew they were going to die.

I don't know how long I watched it. Not very long. It felt like forever. I was too frightened to move.

A sudden heavy shower broke my trance: the rain was falling down instead of up. Then it stopped altogether and the ferry began to sink back into the sea.

Kat climbed up beside me. 'Bo, why aren't you…' Then she saw the ferry. 'What the hell is that?'

'I don't know,' I said. 'A ferry sinking.'

We watched in silence as waves rushed back over the ferry and it vanished completely. We rocked in the backwash and when I looked again we were in a perfectly calm stretch of water. It was as if nothing had happened.

'There aren't any ferries out here any more,' said Kat.

'It was from a long time ago, I think.'

'What do you mean?'

'I don't know what I mean.' I couldn't shake the nightmare of what I'd seen. All those people, endlessly reliving their final seconds. 'It was… trapped in time or something.'

We climbed down and shut the hatch. Rioka's fever had eased a little and she sat up on her bed as Kat adjusted our course. We'd land within the hour.

'I've been thinking about the Outer Veil,' said Kat. 'We don't have any disruptors.'

I'd been so focused on getting home, I hadn't even thought about the Veil. I'd just assumed we'd find a tear. Everyone knew it was weakest in the Twelfth.

'Tears shift all the time,' said Kat, as if she'd read my mind. 'And they're hard to find. We could still die out here. But I think there is a way to get through.' She looked at Rioka. 'Rioka can do that thing. She can hide us. Maybe she can hide us from the Veil.'

'I don't know if I can do that,' said Rioka. 'But I can try.'

'It's our only chance.'

Kat was holding two auto-injectors. 'These were in the medical kit.

Neurotransmitters. Adrenalin shots. You know, for anaphylaxis, cardiac arrest. We give you one. You'd be totally wired. We have two, just in case.'

'What happens then?' I said.

'We get as close as we can to the Veil. We give you a shot. You hide us. We turn our suits to emergency. We go through the veil.'

'It might work,' said Rioka. 'Maybe I could fold us out. I've never done anything like that before, that big. I'd have to be really hyped.'

'Hopefully the suits are strong enough to do the rest,' said Kat.

'First we have to get to the Veil,' I said.

When we reached the shore, I shut off the power. We'd landed. We were so close now.

We helped Rioka up the ladder and out of the hatch. We carried her through the shallow water, which clung to our legs like syrup. Kat asked her if she wanted another shot of painkiller.

'No,' she said. 'I need to be awake.'

The horizon was growing brighter. Our elongated shadows stretched in front of us as the sun rose over the edge of the planet. It took us about fifteen minutes to reach the Outer Veil, walking across some low sand dunes. At our backs, the Gilla Sea rolled soundlessly back and forth.

In the daylight, the Veil looked like nothing more than a misty curtain. It almost seemed like a trick of the light, an illusion. We could feel it as we drew closer, as if it was pushing against us. It wasn't as strong as I'd feared it would be: it was patchy, erratic, fizzing like a light tube about to go out.

'There's no point waiting,' said Rioka. You could see that she was struggling against the pain in her hand, the fever that was burning her up.

'Okay,' I said, turning up my suit. 'Let's do it.'

Kat injected Rioka. The effect was instant: she convulsed violently. At first I was afraid that we had killed her and I struggled to hold her upright until she went still, her eyes wide open, sightlessly staring into the Veil. She was deep inside her mind, folding us away.

She lifted her head. 'Now! *Now!*'

We ran straight into the Veil, dragging Rioka between us.

It was like passing through a wall of fire. I thought my skin was being ripped off. I couldn't hear anything except the sound of my blood thumping in my head. I couldn't breathe. It lasted an eternity.

We fell over the other side. My nose was bleeding and my eyes felt like they'd been sprayed with acid. Rioka collapsed and went out cold.

We were in. We were home.

Dez

I didn't know how to cope with all the things I knew. Morro's betrayal. The cull. Most of all, Flynn being a pinker. Seeing my Da's face clearly for the first time I could remember.

I was two when he vanished. Two years old. He left a name, Ma's sadness, a silence we stepped around. I couldn't help feeling betrayed that Ma hadn't told us. I knew why she didn't, but that didn't stop it hurting. Bo and I had talked about Flynn sometimes, speculating who he was, what had happened. Not in our wildest dreams had we imagined he was a pinker. And now I knew, and Bo wasn't there to tell, and everything was gone to shit.

I could feel me breaking. The flesher me, the me that I'd always counted on. All those feelings that mattered so much to me, that I had defended so fiercely, going into me like knives. I couldn't bear it.

I decided to put the knowledge about Flynn aside. I could think about it later. If there was a later. The way things were going now, there wasn't going to be one. Not for me, not for anyone like me. I'd be scanned and they'd strip my body just like the skinners did and then I'd be dead.

It was mid-afternoon, already getting dark. Ma had gone out, I didn't know where. I tried to open a line, but she just pinged back. Busy. I wondered if I should send an urgent signal and then thought better of it. She would think I was under attack.

There wasn't much to eat in the house, I guess supplies had been interrupted these past days. I thought of going to get some soup at Café Boite, and then I remembered that Flora was fighting with Kojo and he probably wouldn't want to see me. I dunked some spinos into broth and ate them with a few stale mealworms I found in the cupboard.

I waited. Ma didn't come home. But Flora did.

She looked tired, too thin. Her hair was scraped back from her face in braids, and the tattoo on her cheek stood out starkly. She paused in the doorway when she saw me, and then came into the room. She had a bag over her shoulder, a taser in her belt, primed for action. Her knuckles were bleeding. Where had she been?

Not for the first time, I realised what a bad girlfriend I am. What a bad friend. Morro was right to yell at me.

I put my arms around her. She slumped against me and started crying. I didn't know what to say, so I didn't say anything.

'I'm sorry, Dez,' she said at last. 'It's just too much.'

'Yeah,' I said. I wiped the tears off her cheek with my thumb and kissed her. 'Way too much. And it's going to get worse.'

She tried to grin. 'Then let me get some food into me first. I'm starving.'

I took her hand in mine and stroked the wound. 'What happened?'

'A skinner,' she said. 'She didn't get me, but.' She lifted the taser. I saw it was set on kill. 'Bel says the skinners are in cahoots with OpSec, they're all over the Second these days. Brian Mac says the Aps have been told not to interfere.'

I knew that already. OpSec wanted more flesher samples, and how better to get them than from the experts? It made me sick.

'Let me cook,' I said. I took the bag from her. It was full of food. I hustled up a quick stir fry. Flora sat in my chair and watched me.

'You okay, Dez?'

'As much as I can be, given everything.'

'Me too. Just.' Flora stared down at the floor. 'It's so scary. If I think about what might happen, I'm so frightened. So I try not to think about it. Bel's been organising everybody, even with all the shit going down the Second's safer than most places. And it's a relief, to be able to do something.'

'How's things with Kojo?'

'Bad.' Flora grimaced. 'I didn't know things could get so bad between us. Why does he have to do this now? He said either I did what I was told or never darken his doorstep again. So, no more darkening of doorsteps...'

This shocked me. 'He threw you out? Kojo?'

'I don't think he thought that I'd actually leave. And he's too proud to go back on his word.'

Like father, like daughter, I thought. I served up the food and sat down. 'I can't believe it,' I said. 'His whole life has been about you.'

'It's about his idea of me, Dez. I'm not so sure it's been about me. I mean, me as I am. It's always been kind of suffocating with Kojo. Sometimes when he's really angry he says I'm too much like my mother. Like he's trying to save me from what happened to her. Not that I know what happened to her.'

More secrets. Us fleshers are so full of secrets. 'But Kojo loves you,' I said awkwardly. 'I don't have any doubt about that. As much as Ma loves me and Bo.' I stumbled over that. 'I mean, loved Bo.'

Flora met my eyes. 'Your ma will never stop loving your brother,' she said. 'That's not in the past.'

'Same with Kojo,' I said.

I saw she didn't want to talk about it any more, so I left it. I sat back and looked at her. I wanted to look at her forever. I wished there was time for us.

Maybe we had no time left.

'I love you, Flora,' I said. I felt shy, saying it. 'All my heart loves you.'

She grinned. 'I know,' she said. 'I wouldn't put up with you otherwise.'

Flora took out some sweet sticky cakes she'd got in the shijo and brought me up to speed as we ate them. If she hadn't been telling me such horrors, it might have been like old times. Old times being like three months ago.

She listed off those we knew who had died or disappeared. Sammy, Irul, Besty, Val, Maya, taken by the ghosts. Jenna, hurt in a raid. Brian Mac had stepped in personally there, whisked her off somewhere safe. Flora's band mate Shul, her keyboardist, shot in Rue Strugatsky in the Sixth by a skinner. No one had seen Redborg or Diyan or Hu for days. 'They're going for the avants in a big way,' she said. 'Everyone's in hiding, but the avants are getting it worst of all.'

'Why did no one tell me?' I said.

She looked at me. 'Dez, I did tell you. It didn't go in. You weren't there.'

I felt my face grow hot. 'I'm sorry,' I said. I knew as I said it that it was no use being sorry. I was so ashamed of myself.

Flora gave me her look, the patient one when she thought I was being irrational. 'Dez, there's no point in beating yourself up. You're back, and that's all that matters.'

Me again, back thinking about me. I cleared my throat. 'I did one thing today,' I said. 'I went into OpSec.'

'Yeah, Morro said,' she said.

'You've seen Morro?'

She paused, probably expecting me to go toxic, and nodded slowly.

'Did he tell you what I found out about him?'

She nodded again. 'I punched him in the face,' she said. 'And then I yelled at him.'

'I'm glad someone did,' I said.

'I think he was glad too. It was weird. He just let me do it, and when he got up off the floor he just looked…relieved.'

We were quiet for a while. I took another of the cakes. I wondered how many more cakes I would eat in my life. Maybe these would be the last.

'I found out about the cull, too,' I said.

I told her what I had read. I saw all the breath go out of her, as if I had kicked her in the stomach, and then I watched her breathe herself back in, straighten herself, brace herself, sit tall. So brave. I know so many brave people.

'So we've got to stop it.'

I didn't say anything at first. Us, a band of fleshers, against the whole apparatus of OpSec. Like we had a chance. 'How?'

'I don't know. But if we don't even try, how far will we get?' Flora picked up the last of the cakes and nibbled off the crystallised berry on top. 'Anyway, it will give us something to do before they kill us all.'

I laughed. If I didn't laugh, I might have cried. Oh Flora.

Things got a bit wild after that.

We were deep in our world, a world that was just Flora and me, gentle, golden, beautiful, and real, so real. Together we could pretend there was nothing else, we could shut out the darkness and death. I don't know how much time had passed when there was a hammering on the back door.

Stone cold fear is the biggest passion-killer there is. It was like a shock of icy water dumped right on top of us.

For a moment we just stared at each other. Then we scrambled for our clothes, grabbed our suit belts and tasers. I checked the shield. All good. Ma had set sensors up all around the house, but they registered nothing in the yard. A blur, some kind of interference, enough to show that somebody was there, but not to show who it was.

The banging on the door started again.

'Would it be ghosts?' I whispered.

'They'd just blast the door wide open,' said Flora. 'Maybe someone needs help.'

We crept through the corridor to the back door and hesitated behind it, listening. Whoever was there had gone quiet.

We readied our tasers and pressed the seal. The door slowly opened. I was ready to hit emergency, if whatever was out there was dangerous the door would slam shut. Me and Flora could make it to the cellar, get behind my deadwall. Maybe.

There were three people outside.

I blinked. In that moment so many thoughts went through my head. I thought that maybe I had died without realising it, or maybe I had stepped into a parallel universe, or that I was hallucinating. I had been so sure.

I heard the taser drop to the floor from my hand.

'Dez,' said Bo, trying to get past me. 'Dez, can you let us in?'

I pinged Ma the emergency code to get her home. She must have been around the corner at the shijo because she barrelled through the door in about two minutes flat, taser raised, suit switched up so high you could see the electric buzz around her body. When she saw Bo standing in the front room she stopped dead in her tracks.

'Hi Ma,' said Bo.

'Where the hell have you been?'

'Out in the dasht,' he said. 'Sorry I'm late.' He grinned tiredly, and went up to her and wrapped his arms around her.

'My god,' she said. 'I thought you were dead. I really thought you were dead.'

'Not yet,' said Bo.

She put her head on his shoulder and started crying. It was the first time I had seen her cry since Bo had disappeared. I looked away. This was private, this was between Bo and Ma. Even I knew that.

The other two were standing behind, looking awkward. I asked them if they wanted a brew and sat them down at the table.

'So,' said Ma, when she had got herself under control again. 'Who are these two?'

'Some friends I picked up outside the Veil,' said Bo. 'Rioka, Kat, meet my mother, Bel.'

Rioka and Kat were sipping tea, not wanting to intrude. They looked burned out, the three of them, like they'd been to hell and back, and blood was seeping through the bandages on Rioka's left hand. Kat and Bo weren't obviously injured, but Bo had lost a lot of weight in the past eight days. His bones stood out on his face and there were purple shadows under his eyes that looked like bruises.

'There were more of us, but…' For the first time Bo's voice broke, and he sat down heavily on the couch. 'It's been rough, Ma. I can't believe we made it.'

Ma was looking at Rioka. 'Can I see your hand?' she said. Rioka nodded, and Ma gently unwound the bandages. 'This is bad,' she said. 'I've got some meds, but nothing like what you need. I think you might lose it.'

'Maybe Jenna could help,' said Bo. I could tell that was his way of asking where Jenna was.

'Jenna's not well,' said Ma. 'She got hurt during a cloud raid in the

Eighth. They had intel about an Alchem base there and fried everybody.'

I saw the look on Bo's face, and my heart dropped to the floor. It was serious for Bo, then. I'd never seen him in love before, and it hurt. Not because I was jealous. I realised I wasn't jealous any more. Because I didn't want him to be in pain.

Ma must have realised the same thing, because she said hurriedly that Jenna was okay, that she was somewhere safe. But she wouldn't tell Bo where Jenna was.

'You're not lying to me Ma?' said Bo. His voice was shaking. 'Because I swear I won't forgive you. If she's dead, you have to tell me.'

'I swear I'm not,' she said. 'She's safer than any of us at the moment, and she's not going to die. And I'm not having you rushing out into the banns before you have something to eat and a proper rest.' She looked at the other two. 'That goes for all of you. Rioka, come with me, I've got something that'll help with the infection. And then we'll work out what to do with that hand.'

Bo and I exchanged looks and smiled. Ma was back in charge.

Bo

Brian Mac turned up just after midnight. He was fizzing with some kind of upper. He looked leaner than usual, his eyes alight. He'd changed since I last saw him. Ma had told us he'd been part of their mission to rescue me from the hospital in Newport City. Why wasn't I surprised? It didn't seem to reassure Kat, who was totally thrown by having an Ap in the room.

'Good to see you, bug,' said Brian Mac, ignoring Kat's filthy look. 'I knew you'd make it.'

'I didn't think I would,' I said. 'But it's good to see you too.' I meant it. That surprised me. I asked him if he could do anything about the others who'd been rounded up with us and had been left behind.

'I'll try,' he said. 'But I can't promise anything.'

Dez came out of her cellar, where she'd been most of the evening. She looked strained, exhausted. She flopped down into her chair and stared straight ahead, like she wasn't seeing us.

'Okay, genius,' said Brian Mac. 'Tell us what you know.'

Dez seemed to return to earth. She sat up, organising her thoughts, and studied us thoughtfully. Our little band of rebels. Me, Flora, Brian Mac, Ma, Kat. Rioka was in bed, fast asleep.

'All right, in brief. OpSec has built these things they call Eradicators.

They don't threaten the Veil, and they leave very little waste. They're huge machines. One in the Tenth, one in the Eighth, where they said they were drilling for water. They run on nuclear fusion, so they're tapping into aquifers to fuel them. They're not using the Newport City water supply. They've found a deeper source.'

A chill ran through me. 'It's the water,' I said. 'They're waking it up.'

Dez looked at me, opened her mouth to ask a question and then clearly decided not to ask it. Earlier that evening, I'd told everyone what had happened to us over the past eight days. I think Dez thought I was hallucinating half of it.

'Whatever you say, Bo. Anyway, they're fracking the ice to melt it and then bringing it up to fuel the Eradicators. They'll be running the Eradicators twenty five hours a day. Capacity is four thousand an hour.'

'Four thousand what?' I said.

'People. Four thousand people,' said Dez.

I heard Kat gasp. Ma looked as if she'd turned to stone.

'These things are massive incinerators,' Dez said. 'They're up and running already. Apparently they're planning to test a small prototype on Duiwel Island. Feed the entire prison population through the machine. They reckon they can empty the Middle and Outer Banns in seven weeks, seventy days. They'll do it bann by bann. The Eighth and the Tenth first. Then they do DNA scans on anyone left in the Inner Banns. Steal our DNA. Exterminate the mutants.'

So that's why they turned off the Veil on Duiwel Island. They didn't need it any more. My skin crawled with horror.

It's a lot of work to get rid of four million people. A lot of planning. A lot of tech. It takes smarts to do something on that scale, to gather all those resources, to solve all the problems. It's breathtaking.

'How do you think like that?' I said. 'What kind of brain do you have to have to work it all out?'

'You decide that the people you're going to kill aren't people at all,' said Brian Mac. 'You think of them as an infection, an infestation, a threat. It's just a problem to be solved.'

'All that terror, all that death,' said Kat. She had turned white, as if there was no blood left in her face. 'What does doing that do to a person?'

'Do we fucking care?' said Flora. I noticed that she was wearing her hair pulled back from her face. She wasn't hiding any more.

There was a silence. Then Ma spoke.

'So we disable the Eradicators.'

'I like the way you say these things, Bel,' said Brian Mac. 'Problem solved.'

'It doesn't have to be anything spectacular,' said Ma. 'We just have to hit them in a crucial place.'

Another silence.

'What if it doesn't work?' said Kat. 'What'll we do?'

Nobody answered her. We all looked at Dez.

'The weakness is where the water enters the Eradicator, before it's pressurized and heated,' Dez said. She pulled up a screen, expanding it so we all could see, and pointed. 'We hit the machines right there, in those pipes. If we put explosives in the right place, they'll blow the whole thing sky high.'

'Until they build another one,' said Kat, under her breath.

Ma was frowning. 'What does it mean, blowing the whole thing sky high?'

'It would start a chain reaction and turn the whole Eradicator into a bomb.'

'But that could wipe out the whole bann. It could wreck the Outer Veil.'

Dez nodded. 'I know. But it would also destroy the Eradicators.'

'You couldn't make a…more contained explosion?'

Dez shook her head. 'I looked and looked. Anything else, we just buy a stay of execution. They'd just repair it and start again.'

Ma got up without looking at us and started putting dishes in the steamer. We all stared at her. Somehow we knew that she would make the decision.

She came to back to the table. 'Brian can get explosives.'

'I can?'

'Don't tell me you don't have a way, Brian.'

'What would you need?' He was looking at Dez.

'Something small, that we can carry, that packs a punch. Timers and remotes. It doesn't have to be huge.'

'Let me know when you have exact specifications. I'll leave the details of the rest up to you, unless there's anything else you want me to do. Some of us have jobs in the morning.' He got out of his chair.

'No,' I said. 'No, you can't do it this way.'

'There's no other way,' said Dez. 'Seriously Bo, I've looked at every possibility. I couldn't have looked harder.'

'But you're talking about the whole thing blowing up. You could kill thousands of people.'

'Thousands rather than millions,' said Brian, pausing by the door. 'Maybe.'

'At least they'd have a chance,' said Dez. 'It will be like a bad storm. If we don't do this, nobody's got a chance.'

'You're as bad as the pinkers. You can't make that kind of...deal with people's lives.'

Ma was very quiet. I turned to her, as if I was begging. 'The water can help us,' I said.

Dez's voice was sharp. She doesn't like it when people question her. 'What are you talking about?'

'I don't know, I don't know...but I can feel it. The water is in pain.'

'Did you lose your mind out in the dasht?' said Dez.

Her mockery stung me. 'Dez, you don't know everything. Yes, something did happen out there. The water can help us. We don't need explosives or weapons.'

'You're talking about a damn river, Bo. Water. It turns into rain, it turns into clouds, it's all over the place. It's just water, it's not a...discrete entity, or anything. It turns into other water. Maybe the Gilla Sea will come and save us, huh?'

'You don't know, Dez,' I said. 'It's alive, it's like a...person. Sort of. I mean...'

I didn't really know what I was saying. All I knew was that the water was singing in my blood. It was telling me something that I couldn't quite hear, not yet, not quite.

'The water brought us home.' I looked at Kat and Rioka. 'It's part of us, it knows us. We're bound to it, whether we like it or not, whether or not we know how to speak to it. I'm sure that the water can help us. We just have to know how to ask.'

Everyone was just staring at me. I tried again. 'Maybe there's a better way than blowing up two banns. If we can work out how.'

I thought Dez was going to argue some more, but she held her tongue. She didn't understand a word I was saying, or if she did understand, she wouldn't accept it. It was just romantic Bo nonsense to her.

She turned to Brian Mac. 'Get those bombs.'

He nodded, and slid out the door.

Brian Mac

I don't think anyone is tracking me, but I'm taking extra precautions. This double life is exhausting. I'm keeping my head down, doing the minimal. Not working in a happy precinct at present. Mal's still keeping the militia off my back, a small blessing in a rain of curses. None of the old hands are pleased with what's going down. They want us there 25/10, extra shifts, the whole caboodle. People are getting frayed. The militia are aggressive, borderline insubordinate, even the Levels 5s, though they still don't know how not to obey. I just give orders. They hate me but they do what they're told. That's what we're made for. Doing what we're told.

I've had it with all that. Had it years ago, when I first invented Culcullan, when I first pushed through the threshold. They do this thing to your brain in OpSec school. You disobey, your body hurts you. Every time Culcullan fucked things up, it was molten iron going through my bones. It was like a penance for everything that was wrong in Newport City, everything we did to the fleshers. A punishment that made everything better somehow. I told myself the pain wasn't actual damage, and bit by bit it began to lessen. These days I don't get anything worse than a dull ache. Didn't mean

I wasn't glad when I killed off Culcullan and went back to being a bent Ap. I could tell myself I had helped make everything a little bit better.

Can't tell myself that any more, of course. There's no official order yet but everyone knows that a cull is coming. The fleshers, the pinkers. The militia are getting excited. Sick fuckers.

And yeah, face it. Culcullan wasn't dead. He was there all the time, every time I did an implant, every time I made an entry in this journal. He was there in every secret wall in this apartment, every feral coding, every secret line, every time I looked at Bel and remembered the man I wanted to be and failed to become. Every time I remembered that I wasn't Flynn. I loved that man. Maybe I loved him more than I loved Bel and never worked it out.

Hard to remember now. It's all so long ago.

Surprising visit tonight. Morro contacts me just after I get home on the line we'd set up before the hospital fiasco. I almost tell him to fuck off, the last thing I want to do is to go out again. Think a moment, say I'll meet him in the Underground. Take some more nosleep. I've been hitting it too hard lately, it'll catch up with me soon. Payday will be grim.

I guess I'm curious. Maybe there's so much to lose there's nothing to lose. Maybe I'm tired of hiding and I want this bastard to betray me.

He looks like shit, hollowed out. I order a bottle of raw. He knocks back a glass before he says anything. Then he tells me he's got a plan.

You poor bastard, I think. Nobody's filling you in on their plans any more, they don't dare, so now you have to make your own. He looks lonelier than I feel. A plan for what? I say.

We can't stop OpSec, he says. They'll have to stop themselves.

And why would they do that?

Morro's plan is completely reckless. He wants to frame Brenner as an Alchem. Not just any Alchem, but the head honcho. The idea is to make Osborne think that Brenner's planning a coup.

I sit back, crossing my arms. There's a lot of what ifs in this plan of yours, I say.

Osborne would get the info from a very reliable source, says Morro. Me. Why would he believe you? I say.

Because of you, says this kid. You've been keeping me under close surveillance.

Seems I've got more lives than I realised.

You've kept it to yourself, says Morro. He sees that I think it's ridiculous. It's too important, he says, you don't trust anyone in OpSec. You've collared me, caught me red-handed, got hold of secret intel between me and Bremmer.

He's so earnest I almost laugh out loud. Morro, the star of his own show. He probably watches as many soaps as Dez. There isn't any secret intel, I tell him.

He says Dez will take care of that. Forge some documents, using Bremmer's personal codes.

You think Dez will want to help you? I say. After what you did?

Morro doesn't even hear what I say. He goes on, his eyes alight with his plan. You bring me in personally, through the Inner Veil, to Osborne himself, he says. That's when I confess. I spill the beans on Bremmer.

I tell him I don't have that kind of pull, but he doesn't buy it. He reminds me that he's a high value informer and pours himself another glass of raw, as if that settles the question.

Then what?

Osborne moves on Bremmer, he says. Shit hits the fan. Plenty of it.

And maybe it's a sting, I say, and I spend the rest of my suddenly very short life at the wrong end of an AI pain technician.

He meets my eyes. I don't blame you for thinking that, he says. I can't make you trust me.

No, I say. You can't.

He sits back, swirling his drink in the glass. Then he looks up and smiles at me. I know who you are, B Man, he says.

Who's the B Man? I ask him, though I know already.

That's you, that's what I call you.

I don't like it, but I say nothing. He rambles on. He says he knows what Culcullan did. He knows what I had to do to myself to do those things. He knows that I'm two people.

I've had a rough time with myself, says Morro, but I'm thinking I've worked myself out. I'm one person now, even if there's two of me. And so are you. We can do this.

I ask him why the hell I would want to and he lifts his glass. You like blowing shit up, B Man, he tells me. And so do I. So let's blow shit up.

I hate that he's right about me. And I hate that, despite everything, I don't think he's setting me up.

Maybe the shit I want to blow up is me.

I call Bel on the way home. She's short with me, she doesn't like using lines, even lines as dark as mine. I sketch out what Morro had said, and she goes quiet.

Finally she asks me if I trust him. I tell her that I don't.

It's probably a setup, she says. When you're talking to Morro you can't be sure who you're talking to.

It's always Morro, I say. Whatever he tells himself. And I think it's an interesting idea. Worth thinking about.

She says that if I deal with Morro, I'm on my own. She doesn't want to know anything more about it. And I can't let Morro know anything that we're doing.

Taken as read.

Then I tell her I need to speak to Dez. Bel says she's asleep. I tell her to wake her. I can hear Bel tapping something with her fingernails, the way she does when she's thinking hard. And then the line goes silent.

A minute or so later Dez is on the line, her voice thick with sleep. She's patched herself into her mother's line, which according to me is impossible. I should know, too, since I invented this tech.

I ask her to forge some data, but she's speaking over me. Ma said what you want to do, she says. She thinks it's ludicrous. If they get you, they get everything you know about us. It would all be over.

I tell her they can't get anything out of a dead brain, and feel her absorb that.

You'd do that? she says slowly.

I could and I would, I say. Could I? Would I? Yes. I would.

She must believe me, because she says she'll help. I tell her what I need her to do. She doesn't ask any questions. Just laughs, once, and tells me Bremmer's code is high fidelity, it'll be tricky. I think she's intrigued by the challenge.

Then I ask if she knows whether Osborne knows about the cull, whether Bremmer is keeping it secret. She says that he was in on the early plans but he wasn't keen, and pauses. I don't think he signed the order for next week, she says. Probably not.

I ask her to double check. Less than a breath, then she's reading from inside her head. She says the plans for the cull next week were all behind the third firewall. There's a note from Osborne saying that a cull is, uh, 'inadvisable in present conditions'. Worried about damage to Inner Veil, protests, interruptions to food supplies, poisoning aquifers even with the new disposal methods, whatever. Says any major cull needs to be delayed until ground is properly prepared.

I grin sourly. Maybe Morro's fake conspiracy isn't so far from the truth. It sounds like Bremmer is planning some kind of coup.

I tell her she's a miracle. She says she'll get onto it now, since I've broken her beauty sleep, and ping me when it's done. Then she signs off.

I realise then that I'm committed to Morro's plan. Why not?

He's right. I like blowing shit up.

Bo

I was with Mish, lying under the frozen river. We were on our backs, side by side. Through the ice above me I could see sunlight. I wasn't cold, I could feel the warmth of my blood coursing through my veins. I turned my head. Streams of water ran from Mish's eyes and lips. The colour returned to his face and he turned to look at me. He opened his mouth. There were no words, there was no sound. But I heard the water speak.

It filled my body, rising inside me like a long suppressed howl. It filled me with a kind of pain, a kind of pleasure. My body opened like a flower as the silent voice of the water spilled out of me. I rose as the voice rose around me, floating on its soundless howling. It filled the whole world.

I rose up through the ice, passing through it easily, and stood up in the sunlight. The frozen river snaked over an open plain front of me, vast, white, silent. I heard someone say my name and I turned. Mish was behind me, Jenna beside him. They floated above the ice. Water flowed from their bodies, crystal clear, silver in the sunlight. Jenna said my name again. It was no more than a whisper, but I felt the sound of my name flow through me like a gust of wind. I was lifted into the air.

I looked down. The river was no longer frozen. The air around us began to vibrate. Jenna took my hand. We didn't need to speak, we couldn't speak, it was as if words no longer existed. Together the three of us fell out of the air and plunged into the water. Our bodies instantly dissolved.

We were the river.

When I woke up, it was still dark. For one long moment I felt the water receding inside me, releasing me. I knew then that Jenna and I could read the water. I knew it as sure as I knew I was breathing. We were like Mish, only Mish knew what he was. Jenna had some understanding, but I had none.

I slipped out of bed and got dressed, pulling on my leather jacket. It felt like an old friend who had waited for me while I was away.

I stared out of my window at the dark sky. I was buzzing inside. A thousand thoughts were running through my head but I couldn't hold on to any of them. Except one. The water would help us.

I had to talk to Jenna.

Ma wasn't pleased. 'I need to see Jenna,' I said, shaking her shoulder. 'I need to see her now.'

She sat up in bed, blinking. 'Bo, darling…' she said.

'Please, Ma. I can't explain, not properly. I need to talk to Jenna. There's a way to break these killing machines. I'm not exactly sure how, but everything I feel tells me that I'm right. And I need Jenna's help.'

I didn't know if she believed me or not, but she got out of bed.

'There's something more powerful than those machines,' I said. 'It's more powerful than anything we can imagine. I can feel it. Jenna feels it. I know that there's a way to use it.'

Ma didn't say anything, she just nodded.

'I'll make a brew,' I said. As I went to the kitchen. I heard her open her line to Brian Mac. I knew I shouldn't listen, but I did.

'I know, Brian, I know that,' she said. 'But this is an exception. Because I'm saying it is.'

She listened to whatever Brian was saying and sighed.

'I can't tell you. Because I don't know. He doesn't know. But he says he needs to see her and I believe him.'

They talked for another minute or so. I waited until she closed the line then brought her the tea.

'It's arranged,' she said. 'Brian will meet you. He doesn't usually receive visitors.'

I felt dizzy. I was going to see Jenna.

'You have to go easy,' she said. 'The girl's not recovered yet.'

I kissed her cheek. 'Where am I going?' She told me where Brian Mac would be waiting. And she told me to be careful.

'I'm always careful,' I said, halfway out the door.

'I've only just got you home again.'

I went back and hugged her. She put her arms around me, held me tight. And then she let me go.

I met him at the edge of the Second near the mono station, in a tiny all-night café called Lazy's. There was a bar and six stools. The place was so narrow and low-ceilinged that Brian Mac seemed enormous sitting at the bar with a drink in his hand. He looked tired.

'We haven't far to go,' he said. 'Want a drink?'

'Not really,' I said. 'Can we go?'

'Okay, bug.'

He sculled the rest of his drink and we left. He had to lower his head to fit under the doorway. We walked a few blocks, not talking. At this time of night the rues were deserted. Brian Mac had obviously had more than one drink, but he was steady enough. I felt odd, walking side-by-side with an Ap.

'Shouldn't we, you know, go there separately or something?' I said.

'Nobody's tracking us, bug,' he said. 'I'd know.'

I wished he would stop calling me bug, like he thought I was ten years old.

His place was in a lane off a small rue of tumble-down houses. It was a part of the bann that was flattened in the riots before I was born, and people had built homes out of the rubble that was left over. Brian Mac's place was behind a high wall. He opened the gate with a gene key and we crossed a small yard to a locked steel door.

He told me the building had once been an artisan's workshop. 'She made blades,' he said. 'Double forged, folded, hammered. They could slice silk or cut through stone. She forged nanocarbons into the steel. They could slice a molecule in half.'

His voice lit up with enthusiasm. I nodded, giving him a curious glance. This was a glimpse of a Brian Mac I didn't know.

'I found one when I moved in. It was hidden under the floor, like she'd put it there as some kind of offering.' he said, unlocking the door. 'Blood-red sheath with some kind of sharpening mechanism, black handle. Beautiful thing. Months of work.'

He ushered me into a kitchen and scruffy bedsit, bottles scattered on the floor, empty implants, an unspeakable couch. What you'd expect Brian Mac's place to be. I looked around, but there was no sign of Jenna.

Brian Mac went to the far wall and opened what looked like a big cupboard full of pre-packaged foodstuffs. I couldn't see how he did it, but as I watched the whole back wall of the cupboard, shelves and all, swung open. Behind was another room. You'd never guess, not in a million years. As we went through the hidden door I felt a hot, stinging blast on my face.

'That's my own little Veil,' he said. 'If it was on alert, you'd be a little pile of ash right now.'

We entered a single vast room with a loft at one end. No windows, stone floor, only the one door. The place was full of oldtech in various states of assembly, other stuff I couldn't identify. Unlike the bedsit, it was immaculately tidy. The secret Brian Mac.

I couldn't help it. I was impressed. Really impressed.

'She's up in the loft,' he said.

Upstairs was a mattress, a lamp, a blade in a red sheath hanging on the wall. Jenna was asleep, curled up under a blanket. I sat on the edge of the mattress and looked at her.

I heard steps and glanced down. Brian Mac was gone. It was just me and Jenna. I watched the rise and fall of her breath. The sweetness of it was too much. I sat there a long time, trying to bring myself to wake her up.

I wanted to know what had happened to her, how she had been hurt. I wanted to tell her about where I'd been, about Mish, about Kat and Rioka,

I wanted to tell her about crossing the Gilla Sea. I wanted to be there with her without any stories to tell or any tomorrows to worry about. I wanted just this moment, this warmth. It seemed like such an ordinary thing, and it was so miraculous.

I said her name as softly as I could. Maybe she could hear me in her dream, maybe I could enter her sleep and it would just be the two of us, far away from the world around us, this world full of fire and pain.

She stirred and sighed and I sensed the strength of her, the weight of her body shifting on the mattress. I stroked her spiky hair, and she turned her face to me. And then her eyes opened and she saw me.

'Hello,' she said.

'Hello.'

Dez

On the big day, Ag the Seventh, we were up before dawn. Ma made us all a huge breakfast, she'd got deliveries despite all the shit going down in the banns. Me, Bo, Kat, Jenna, Flora, Rioka crowded around our little table. We were all sleeping here. Everybody looked weirdly relaxed. Maybe we knew how little chance we had, and had just accepted the risk. Not trying meant we were dead anyway.

Ma was flicking through the dark tubes as we ate. 'They've started already,' she said.

'They what?' Bo's head jerked up.

'They're rounding people up already. There's hundreds of militia all over the Eighth.' She flicked further, frowning. 'Yes, the Tenth as well. They're going through the rues closest to the Eradicators, emptying out the tower-blocks.'

She showed us the snaps. Blurry images, taken from high up. Clouds heading down the rues. Dozens of people, hundreds, spilling out into the street. People running, a building on fire, a chaos of bodies, gunshots. A drone getting hit and exploding in a blossom of fire and spiralling down into the rues.

My mouth was dry. 'It's supposed to start seven days from now. Not today.'

'Maybe they decided to bring it forward after you broke into OpSec,' said Ma.

We all went quiet. I felt terror go through me, cold and deadly. The unimaginable was already happening. People would already be dying. And Ma was right, it probably was because of my break in. It was my fault.

'Finish your breakfasts,' Ma snapped. 'You need to eat.'

It was going to take all day to get to the machines. Me, Flora and Jenna were heading for the Eighth. Bo and Kat were doing the Tenth. Bo wasn't happy about splitting up with Jenna, but if his plan was going to work we needed a dowser in each team.

We were travelling undergound, because all the main rues were blocked by the militia. Ma was going to be at home with Rioka, coordinating us all. Rioka's hand was still a mess, we hadn't got her to a medic yet, but the infection had died down and she was buzzed with painkillers. Ma needed someone to keep an eye on the OpSec comms, and I would be busy.

Ever since we'd worked out the plan, I'd been down in the cellar making tech. I'd roped in Kat and Bo as my minions, to do all the easy jobs, because there was so much to do.

Now we were all hooked up via Brian Mac's sneaky secret lines. He was a bit upset that I'd worked out how he made them. He'd got away with it for twenty years. He'd used this tech to bring down the Inner Veil, to hijack the Newport City media, to run his double life, and nobody had clocked how he'd done it until me.

Brian Mac's comms used gravitational waves. It's pretty primitive compared to what I do, but it works, and it's as good as totally undetectable. He's figured out how to use it so he only needs the tech for the receptors, which is how he does his secret lines. That method pretty well scrambles any signal, making it register like background noise. But if it's gravitational comms both ends, they can't get any kind of fix. It's not just a hidden part of the spectrum, it's off the spectrum altogether.

The other thing about gravitational comms is that they can get through the Wall. Or so Brian Mac claims. We hadn't had a chance to test this hypothesis. If he was right, it solved a major problem. If he was wrong, Bo couldn't talk to the rest of us once he was past the Wall. He'd be on his own, working on the schedule we'd figured out, with no way of knowing what was happening at the other end of the banns. Not ideal. So I hoped to hell Brian Mac was right.

When I complimented Brian Mac on his cunning, he actually blushed. 'It was your dad,' he said. 'I just carried on where he left off.'

It's so simple, once you know. OpSec don't have detectors for gravitational comms. Everybody decided that it was impractical aeons ago so nobody thought of looking. Well, not everybody, obviously.

Flynn. Communications researcher. There wasn't anything about gravitational comms in his papers. He had a double life too, until it all blew up. If they'd arrested him, they would have thrown everything at him to find out what he knew. I remembered what Brian Mac said, that they can't get anything out of a dead brain. It's true, they can't. Brains aren't like computers. Maybe Flynn made sure that he was dead before they got him.

All the same, I'm beginning to wonder how much of what I can do is about the splice. Maybe some of it is from Flynn. He could have been another of those 'accidents' that aren't supposed to happen in the cloning factories, like Gloria. Maybe there are more 'accidents' than anyone suspects. I guess the pinkers aren't as pure as the authorities like to think. Maybe that's why they're so paranoid about fleshers, it's more about what they're afraid of inside themselves than anything to do with us.

The unknown. The unpredictable.

I was still really dubious about this whole water thing. Bo was shining with it, and Ma and Jenna backed him up. Kat told me that she'd seen what the water could do and we didn't have anything to lose by trying it.

I liked Kat, she had a practical air, so in the end I just shut up. After all, none of us wanted to blow up the banns. I insisted that we had the bombs, in case this damn water thing turned out to be as doolally as it sounded.

Me and Flora had to look after Jenna as well as ourselves. She wasn't in top shape: she'd caught some shrapnel in her hip, and there was some internal damage. She'd used her healing powers on herself, and she claimed she was mostly okay, but she was limping and you could tell she was in pain.

The Eighth wasn't as far as the Tenth, but we were all leaving at the same time because we'd be moving more slowly with Jenna. Plus you never know what trouble you might run into.

Ma knew all the old sewers and other tunnels that had been bored for now forgotten reasons back when the city had been built. OpSec hadn't managed to find half of them. She told us it was how they got around in the banns in the bad old days. It was always possible they had become impassable, because of rock falls and so on, so we had planned several alternative routes.

I had every muffling device I knew built into our suits. Portable shields, a field, delocation signals, the lot. We couldn't count on getting any juice to power up after we left home, so I'd bumped up the batteries. Twenty six hours power on normal, twelve or less if the suit was switched up high with all the tech lit up. If things went toxic it mightn't be enough, but it was the best I could do.

We took tasers, because they're lighter than guns. My best model, turned to deadly. Two each. Just in case.

We checked all our gear, double checked. Switched on the fields. We'd already said our goodbyes.

Maybe we'd never see each other again. It was more probable than not.

Ma opened the door, put up her hand in farewell. 'Good luck,' she said.

We walked into the dark. At the end of the rue, we split up.

'See you later,' said Bo. He was looking at Jenna. Her face lit up with that incredible smile.

'You sure will,' she said.

I hate tunnels. After a while the dead air and the dead light and the sense of weight above just gets to me. And some of these tunnels were small. The further we went, the more I felt like I wanted to scream. I kept that to myself.

We went in single file, Flora first, Jenna in the middle, me behind. We had our suit lights on low, and mostly things scuttled away from the light. Once a rat as long as my arm jumped at us out of nowhere and scared the life out of us, and a couple of times the ceiling had collapsed and we had to crawl through a tiny gap, wondering if this time we'd have to go back and try another way. It was boring and cold and exhausting. It was only a few klicks, but our route wasn't straight. We had to go south under the Seventh before turning back north west into the Eighth. We went on for hours and hours, checking the MPS against the maps in our suits.

You could tell it was tiring Jenna out, but she didn't complain. She'd had a big whack of painkiller before we left, and she had more with her in case she needed it. She was probably doing herself damage. But she's a flesher. We're tough because we have to be. She just pushed on.

We came out three streets from the Eradicator, in the basement of a tower-block. We had to climb a rickety steel ladder that was barely clinging to the walls. We only dared go up one by one. The tunnel was sealed by a steel cap, so badly rusted on that for a while it seemed that Flora wasn't going to be able to open it. In the end she blasted it with the taser until it loosened and punched it out. We crawled out and lay on the concrete in the dark, panting.

'First step.' Flora checked the time. 'We're a bit ahead of schedule.'

'Do you think anyone would have heard the taser?' said Jenna.

'I think we're deep enough underground that no one would have picked it up,' I said.

I listened. The whole place sounded empty. Then I looked around for a light. No point in wasting our own energy. There was a fluorescent just above us. I hacked into the house network and it flickered on. The basement was empty, a concrete bunker with a garbage disposal in the corner. I checked the comms in the building. Completely silent. We knew from the tubes that the building had already been emptied, that's why we'd chosen this route.

I pinged Ma to let us know we had made it and her signal came back almost at once. Well, that was something. I opened our common line, just to check in and see if it worked. Now was the test. Would Bo pick us up through the Wall?

'Hi Ma,' I said. 'We're in Rue Desbordes, in the basement. All good.'

Her voice crackled down the line. 'Haven't heard from Bo yet,' she said. 'All going well, he should be another hour or so. Use your time well.'

'How about OpSec?'

The line faded and then Rioka came in. 'I'm not getting any orders about special operations through OpSec. Just routine stuff.'

'That's strange,' I said. 'I mean, it's not like it's a small thing.'

'I know.' Even through the bad connection I could hear her puzzlement. 'I'll keep trying. They're probably using a line I haven't accessed yet.'

Bo's voice cut in. Faint and a bit distorted, but I could hear him.

'Moving well here,' he said. 'We should exit in around forty five minutes.'

'Ping me,' said Ma. She snapped the line closed. She never liked staying on lines.

'Well, the comms work,' I said. 'Thank you, Brian Mac.'

'Brian Mac,' said Flora. 'Who would have guessed? I've hated him my entire life.'

'He's…surprising,' said Jenna. 'You should see his place.'

Bo hadn't talked about it, but I could imagine. 'A mess, huh?'

'That's his cover. You walk in and it's a dump. But he's got a hidden room, which is where he put me. It's something else, full of beautiful oldtech, wild things he's made. I think even you'd be impressed, Dez.'

'I wonder how he hid it, all these years?'

'By looking like a screw up.' Jenna tapped her temple. 'Smart. For a pinker.'

'I expect that's something he learned from us,' Flora said, contempt in her voice. 'Pinkers know nothing.'

I was about to say that maybe all pinkers weren't the same, but thought better of it. I hadn't told Flora that my dad was a pinker. I hadn't even told Bo. I felt sorry about that now, maybe he would never know, but somehow there hadn't been any time. And something like that needs time. I hoped there would be time.

'I'm going to see if I can find out what's going on out there,' I said.

There was a surveillance cam on the corner of the towerblock, so I checked there first. It overlooked a narrow laneway. It was empty both ways, emptier than any street in the Eighth bann should ever be. It gave me a spooky feeling, so I started feeling around the cloud comms. They were heavily coded, which surprised me. It was like OpSec didn't want OpSec to know what it was getting up to.

I remembered what Brian Mac had asked about Osborne and Bremmer. Maybe this cull really was being kept secret. If so, it was one hell of a big secret. Bremmer had literally hundreds of his ghosts out on the streets doing his dirty work. Clouds. The Eradicators themselves, which would have chewed up huge resources. Osborne would have to be in on it, unless he was completely dense. He didn't strike me as dense. I began to feel a bit curious.

We were early, so I had a little time. Before I hooked into the cloud network, I did a search of the OpSec downloads. The Eradicators weren't mentioned anywhere except in the data I'd taken from behind the third firewall. I searched construction and came up with a bunch of stuff, plans for new offices in Newport City, luxury apartments, an experimental mining base out in the dasht. Nothing that looked like an Eradicator. Searched drilling, and bingo. It was all under 'water resources'.

What water resources had to do with OpSec beat me. I guess water security is a thing. The Eradicators had been built under cover of a huge water resource program. Well, that's what the infonews had told us about the drilling.

Maybe Osborne really didn't know about the Eradicators. He must have known about what happened on Duiwel Island, you couldn't hide that. I looked. That came under 'savings'. No resources expended on keeping up the Veil or housing prisoners, win win. No mention of how they'd disposed of all those people.

I was beginning to feel dizzy thinking about it all, so I stopped searching and checked the time. Flora and Jenna were sitting against the wall, eating some energy bars. Flora looked up. 'Found anything?'

'Not yet,' I said.

She knew I was prevaricating, that I should have mapped out what was happening already. So I plugged into the cloud network.

I got some visuals, which were so distressing I didn't look for long. There were five clouds on the other side of the Eradicator, four blocks away. They were methodically emptying every apartment, using heat sensors. They'd blocked off the banns so no one could get out. The street was packed with people being pushed towards the Eradicator. They weren't going quietly.

For a moment I felt almost crushed by despair and rage and helplessness. No matter what we did, even if everything worked out to plan, people would die. They'd been going for almost six hours already. Six hours. Four thousand an hour. You do the maths.

Every minute we waited, more people died.

I put my feelings aside. Right now, they were no use to me.

'Okay,' I said. 'Time to get dressed.'

Ma had been doing some fancy dealing. She must have had credits stashed away that we didn't know about. She'd bought smartwear for all of us, and IMR badges like that ones we'd used in the hospital, only more powerful. I'd given them a bit more oomph in my workshop, just in case.

We were going in as ghosts.

We took the uniforms out of our packs and zipped them up over our clothes. Grey, blank. Pinned the IMR badges inside our lapels, switched on our suits. Then I got to work.

I had become good at this. In a couple of minutes we were featureless militia. Flora tried some combat moves and it was uncanny, the way you couldn't quite see how she moved, the way she pixillated into the background when you looked straight at her.

We turned off the IMR badges and sat down to wait. It was too weird having them on.

'How long now?' said Flora. Not that she needed to ask. She knew as well as I did.

'Ten minutes, if Bo's on time.'

I was still figuring that we would have to bomb the thing. Get in through the security, up five floors, through a maintenance hatch into the double walls where the pipes were. Plant the bombs. Get out. Run like hell. Detonate. I went over the engineering plans for the hundredth time, trying to get it down pat. I rechecked our fake IDs. We couldn't afford to make any wrong turns.

But I'd promised we'd try this water plan first.

'Could you do your thing from here, Jenna?'

She shook her head. 'No,' she said. 'I have to be close.'

We sat and waited for a while. None of us felt like speaking. I was trying to be hard, to be ice, trying not to think of everything that was at stake.

'Jenna,' I said, after a while. 'How close do we have to get for this to work?'

I had to repeat my question. Jenna was zoning out. My heart sank. She answered me the second time. It was like she was swimming up from a great depth.

'Much closer,' she said. 'The water's in pain.'

Brian Mac

Mayor Osborne's chambers are in the high tower district of Newport City Central. The fast, noiseless elevator, the wide corridors, the cream coloured walls, the dark grey carpets…once inside the place, you feel dirty. Everything is so clean.

There are no windows, not until we reach Osborne's office. It's on a corner of the building, thirty floors up. The north and east walls are ceiling-high sheets of tinted, soundproofed glass. Everything is plush, expensive, softly lit.

We wait in the anteroom to his office for about half an hour. The young woman who ushers us in has lustrous blue skin and is flawlessly beautiful. I've never actually seen one of these, they're high class AI. Some of the bigger fashion houses use them as models.

Osborne is sitting behind his desk, facing one of the windows. He doesn't turn around when we come in. There's nothing else in the room except a couch and two armchairs, all the same soft, grey colour as the carpet. Osborne turns and gestures for us to sit down. We sit side by side on the couch. He strolls towards us, his hands folded behind his back.

Brigadier Mackintosh. I know you only by reputation, he says. Five citations for skinner hunting. Most admirable. We've never met, have we?

No, sir, I say, although we have. He just doesn't remember. He smiles then, that smug, confident smile, and tells me we needn't be so formal. I can call him Mr Osborne. Thank you very much. He sits down opposite us and looks at Morro.

I make as if to check my data. Morro Ignada, Mr Osborne. Credit ID 83456788, Security Informant 'Wicked'.

Ah, yes, he says, clasping his hands together. I look at Osborne's nails. Perfectly manicured, they don't look real. A rather dangerous character I hear. He's smiling again, the special smile of one authority to another. I tell him Morro's been neutralised, as if he needs some reassurance on this point.

Morro and I had almost come to blows over the neutralisation. It's an implant. When I switch it on, he can't talk or walk or do anything without my say-so. He didn't like it, but there was no way I'd be able to take him through the Inner Veil or into the Mayor's chambers without it. He asked if he could pretend, and I said no dice, not with all the scans.

A straightjacket, said Morro, glaring at me.

Yeah. Pretty much. Standard procedure.

I'd deviated quite a bit from standard procedure to get an appointment to see Osborne. I'd leant on Mal, saying I had urgent material for Osborne's ears alone. He hummed and hawed, but in the end he put through the official request. He was looking worse than usual. I wondered how much longer he'd last. He was like a man who knew he was finished, out of time and out of luck. He was being superseded and he knew it.

He received permission for a meeting with some low-level schmuck in the Council office, so I used some leverage I had with one of the corrupt bureaucrats higher in the Mayoral office to get my request bumped up. This man was a big fan of meatsex of a particular kind. I'd made arrangements for him over a few years and he wanted them kept quiet.

Morro asked me how he would know that I'd let him out of the neutraliser, and I said the same way I would know that he's not setting me up. It's kind of like holding guns to each other's heads. Morro relented. I could tell it was a new experience for him.

In less than an hour we're through the Inner Veil and heading for Newport City Central in an HQ moped. Morro is at my side. I've added a bit of theatre by tethering his wrist to mine with a carbon manacle. He doesn't like that either. I can feel his anger warring with his curiosity as we get closer to Newport City Central. The wide boulevards lined with green, water-thirsty trees, the shops, the crowded cafes, the fountains, the well-dressed people.

In Osborne's office he's sitting quietly, his face blank. We'd talked about what we were going to do, but there's an air about him that makes me uneasy.

Osborne leans back in his armchair, studying him. So Mr Morro has something…confidential to tell me, he says. He seems mildly amused by the whole thing. His face has that expression of superior indifference.

I snap Morro out of his straightjacket, leaving the manacle on. I've been watching this guy for a while, I say. I couldn't say anything about it. I was worried about OpSec.

Worried about OpSec?

You'll understand why when we tell you, I say.

Maybe Mr Morro can give me his revelations, says Osborne. In his own words, of course.

Morro looks straight at Osborne. It's Morro, he says.

Osborne looks surprised, a little taken aback. The prisoner is being impertinent.

Not Mr Morro, says Morro, pushing it.

Osborne shifts a little uncomfortably in his chair and asks me to get on with it. Morro swings into his act.

I've been your major informant on the Alchems, he says. That's information that's led to successful raids and arrests. All those recent high-profile kills? That's me. I risked my life for that. The Alchems are a violent mob. I betrayed them. I've been loyal to the City. But now the City's being betrayed. By Bremmer.

Part of me wants to laugh at how portentous he sounds, but I keep a poker face. Osborne's colour changes slightly, there are pink spots high on his cheeks. That's a serious accusation, he says. Why would I believe you?

I pull my portable from inside my coat and bring up a screen. These are transcripts of comms between Morro and Bremmer, I tell him. You can see Morro's involvement in the current crackdown.

Operation Pressure Point, says Osborne. I know all about it.

But there's something else going on, says Morro. I know because Bremmer thinks that I'm his right hand man. He's planning a coup.

Osborne is beginning to look unsettled. I expand the screen so that he can read it more easily. It's a beautiful fake, filled with all the details Dez had pilfered from OpSec. Bremmer instructing Morro on the cull, cautioning him on who he trusts, promising him a high position once Osborne is out of the way and the coup is complete.

This is your man, says Morro. This is what he's doing. The cull is the first step.

There isn't going to be a cull, says Osborne. His voice is a little hoarse, a little dry. The pink in his cheeks has faded. Not yet, he says.

Bingo, I think.

Morro tells him the cull is happening now. Right this second. A huge operation in the Middle and Outer banns. You should check what's going on under your nose some time, he says, the scorn open in his voice. Maybe get your people to check the flesher tubes. They're full of it. Or do you really trust the reports from OpSec? Did Bremmer bribe all your informants? How come you don't know?

Then Morro unlocks the manacle. I've no idea how. Before I can do anything, he's on his feet. Have you heard about the Chimera program? Morro asks him.

Osborne is hypnotised. He just shakes his head.

So Bremmer hasn't told you about the experimental research he's conducting? Has he told you about his trade with the skinners, the harvesting of freak genes from spliced fleshers? Has he told you about the monsters he's building, his clone Alchem army? They can turn you into ash with a look, cover you with filth that eats your skin. There are thousands of them. There are even Alchems here, in this building. Bremmer controls the lot.

I'm speechless with admiration now. Morro, I think. The star of his own show.

Osborne snaps out of his fascination and collects himself. He glances at me, his face cold. The man's mad, he says. Get him out of here.

He retreats behind his desk, reaching forward, maybe to push a button, and then freezes. Without knowing how I know, I understand that Morro has stopped him. He's paralysed Osborne where he stands.

For the first time, Osborne looks afraid.

Don't believe me, Mayor? says Morro softly. He walks up to Osborne and pushes his face close. Osborne shrinks back, repulsed. You can't stop me, can you? Do you like feeling this powerless? Maybe you'd better get used to it.

He turns on his heel and winks at me, so Osborne can't see. He's enjoying himself. Fucking hell. I just sit there, appalled and admiring at the same time. Morro starts strolling up and down the room. The Mayor's eyes follow him.

What you don't realise, Mr Mayor, is that Bremmer is an Alchem. Morro pauses, fixes him with a look. He's *the* Alchem. The cull was always a cover for something else. You were right to be cautious about it. But Bremmer brought it forward. The cull is happening *now*. And after the cull, you're next.

He pauses again, to make sure his point is being driven home. All through the banns the Alchems are waiting, he says. They'll escape the cull, Bremmer's made sure they will. And once the cull is done, Bremmer will step in. Bremmer and his Alchem monsters, his deviants, his perverted splices and monstrous clones. The Inner Veil will come down. It will dissolve into nothing, nothing will protect you. You'll be the last one into the Eradicator. Your corpse will evaporate with all the others.

Osborne is almost gagging, staring at Morro through bulging eyes. Everything he fears, everything loathes, is being stamped into his brain. Osborne is pure pinker. I can see his conditioning throttling him.

The Brigadier is one of them too, Morro says. He's been undercover for twenty years.

What the hell? But Morro keeps going. You ever heard of an operative called Culcullan, Mr Mayor?

I go cold. What the fuck is Morro doing? Osborne's eyes roll towards me. Yes, god damn it, he has heard of Culcullan. And he saw my face when Morro mentioned it.

This here is Culcullan, Morro tells him, pointing at me. You never found out who caused you so much grief, did you? You thought it was an inside job, but you never worked out who it was. But now Brig Mackintosh is running scared, Bremmer is too much even for him. He's trying to get in with you before the shit hits the fan. I'm an offering, a sacrifice. But I know the truth about him, too.

Then Morro leans in slowly, closer and closer. I can see the panic in Osborne's eyes. Morro is going to touch him. Touch his face. Pinkers can't bear being touched.

You'd better deal with it, boss, says Morro. And slowly, maliciously, he takes Osborne's face between his hands and kisses him on the lips.

I feel Morro release his control. Osborne stumbles backwards and almost falls and throws up on the carpet.

I come out of my shock and try to snap on the straightjacket, but nothing happens. Morro turns to me, smiling. You're not so clever as you think, B Man, he whispers. You didn't get both of us.

I pull out my taser and aim it at Morro. He's still looking at me, but he's talking to Osborne.

Deal with it, boss, he says again. It's a big mess out there. Bigger than you know.

I don't know where the play acting begins or ends, where anything begins or ends. Osborne hits an alarm. Morro lets him do it. What's his game?

Now Morro is glaring at me. I don't know if I'm seeing double, or if there are two of him in front of me.

Do it, B Man, he hisses at me. Set that thing to kill. Do it, you coward copper. Kill me.

There are two Morros now. One in sharp focus, one blurred. I stare at both of them. I don't pull the trigger.

I hear feet, a door whoosh open, a sudden, agonising blast of heat and static. It sends both Morros crashing into me. They've taken the full force of the blast. I can smell my clothes burning. I feel blood on my face. I don't know if it's mine or Morro's. Then everything goes black.

Bo

Kat and I came up under one of the old sports stadiums. It had been gutted years ago. It was a long time since anything like sport was played in the Tenth, but this was where it all used to happen. Kickball, Jai alai, Kabaddi, they're all still big in the inner banns. I used to love those games when I was a kid.

We'd already put on our ghost uniforms, but hadn't activated the IMR. We switched everything else on, double-checked the shields, the delocators, everything. Dez had built so much gear into our suits that I felt like a walking display.

My stomach flipped when I thought about what I was going to do. I was going to call the water, and the water was going to destroy the Eradicators. I was certain that I could do it, but I didn't have a clue how. It kept nagging at me that I was just deluded, like Dez thought.

My sensors didn't pick up any threats. We'd come out of a sewer pipe under what was left of the main grandstand, five blocks from the Eradicator. This whole area had already been emptied.

Kat and I stayed shoulder to shoulder. She was carrying the explosives. It was hard to imagine the damage they could do. If we had to use them they'd level a couple of blocks, there'd be nothing left standing. Including us, probably.

'You okay?' Kat said.

'Yeah, I'm good. You?' I said, my voice shaking.

She just nodded.

We switched on our IMRs, checked our tasers again, made sure they were on kill. I looked Kat up and down. The smartwear was convincing. If I lost Kat in a crowd of real ghosts I'd never be able to find her. Our cover story was that we were a mop-up team, flushing out any fleshers who had avoided the first big sweep.

We stepped out into the rue. It was empty, but it was clear that the fleshers weren't going quietly. In front of a small café was a pile of dead bodies heaped on top of each other. Weapons were scattered around them, where they had dropped. We passed a neka that had been shot through the head and then more dead bodies. The ghosts were leaving nothing alive behind them, nothing at all.

We went two blocks before we heard the voices. It was like nothing I'd ever heard before. I never want to hear it again. It was a continuous ululation, rising and falling, drifting towards us and then dying away. It was as if the air were weeping.

My throat tightened. Kat pressed closer to me. We kept moving. Some distance ahead, we could see a massive curtain of heat rippling against the Veil. And then we smelt it: a sharp, crisp odour. It wasn't a strong smell. You couldn't even say it was unpleasant. It was human vapour, filtered and sanitized. The Eradicator was running efficiently, it was clean. Even the stench of humans being reduced to ash was eliminated.

Then I heard something else. It was hardly more than a breath, whispering to me. It was the water. I stopped in my tracks. I could hear the pounding of my heart, the flow of my blood. Maybe the water could hear it too.

There was a towerblock across the rue. From the top we would be able to see where the ghosts were stationed. We didn't have Dez with us to hack into the militia comms, so we'd have to work it out ourselves. We crossed and climbed to the roof.

Below us, half a klick away, was the Eradicator. It was massive. People were being pushed towards it between long lines of ghosts. Their voices rose up to us with a horrible clarity, a continuous wave of broken sobs.

As we watched, a bunch of people stopped dead, forcing others to make their way past, like water swirling around a rock. They slowly moved to one side, towards the line of ghosts, who raised their weapons. We saw twenty or thirty men and women hurling themselves at the militia, who opened fire. Three ghosts fell down. The others kept firing until the ground in front of them was covered with bodies. There was silence for a moment, and then the wave of sound began again, as people were forced to climb over the corpses in front of them. The stream heading towards the Eradicators had barely paused.

I wanted the water to hear this sound, to hear this wave of tears. This wave would soon fall through the banns, it would flood the rues, it would flow in the gutters and drain into the earth.

Water will find water.

I called up the engineering plans Dez had loaded into my suit. The place I needed to get to was on the far corner of the structure. Up five floors. There was a hatch, where the water was fed in.

Kat pointed to a narrow lane that led to the rear of the Eradicator, where we knew there was a service entrance. The lane was empty, apart from a small patrol of three ghosts.

I checked the time and I pinged Dez, once, then once again. That meant that Kat and I were close and on schedule. Dez responded straight away. All good. I opened the line to Ma.

'We're almost there,' I said. 'It's time to test those fake IDs.'

'Just stay calm.'

Ma snapped the line closed.

'Very businesslike, your Ma,' said Kat.

I nodded, my mouth dry, as we headed downstairs. At the bottom, Kat clutched my sleeve. 'Bo…' she said. 'Do you think you can do it?'

'I don't know.'

'I'm going to have to use these bombs if you can't. You're going to have to tell me if it's not working.'

'I know.'

'We only have so much time.'

'I know.'

'As long as we're clear.'

'We're clear.'

We stepped back into the rue. I caught a glimpse of my reflection in a window. That was me, that ghost. A ghost in a dead street.

We'd almost reached the lane when a skinner stepped out of a doorway in front of us. Long, black hair, thin cheeks, patent leather shoes. He was wearing a smartwear suit tricked out to look like shining red sequins and his bandolier had fancy patterns. He had clearly come into some money recently.

He wasn't fazed at seeing us. 'Didn't leave much, did you?' he said. 'I thought there was an agreement.'

I hoped that the jazzed-up voice modulator Dez had jacked into my suit would do the job. 'I don't know of any agreement, sir,' I said. I sounded like one of those cheap talking dolls they sell at the shijo.

The skinner tilted his head and took a few steps towards us. 'But everybody knows. Fair dues and all that. There's plenty of flesh around for both our needs.'

I tried to lower my voice. 'You shouldn't really be here, sir,' I said. 'This is a restricted area.'

'Not for me it isn't,' he said.

Kat raised her taser and blasted him before I could answer. He fell down face first. Kat stepped over him and gave him another blast in the back of the head. His sequins went out.

'Just doing my job, sir,' she said. 'Come on, we have to move fast.'

She strode ahead and I caught up with her as she turned into the lane. 'I hate skinners,' she said. 'One of them got my sister when she was twelve. There wasn't much left of her.'

I looked down the lane. The ghost patrol was maybe fifty metres away, moving towards us. Kat must have sensed my nerves. 'No matter what happens, just keep moving,' she said.

We had our IDs ready, but we didn't know what the protocol was. Was there a sign, a salute? Twenty metres, ten, five. Kat was slightly in front of me. She flashed her ID. The patrol walked straight past us. I didn't make any kind of sign, I didn't even flash my ID.

It was cool. We were in control. We were the masters.

We stopped at the end of the lane, staring at the Eradicator. It towered over us, thrusting obscenely above the shabby surrounding buildings as if it had been dropped from the sky.

'Kat, stop,' I said.

She spun around.

'What is it?'

I looked into the blank space where her face should have been. 'Not this way, not here.'

'What? We're almost there.'

'No, no, not there, not in the machine.'

I turned back down the lane, trying to follow a sudden, insistent command. There was a rushing in my ears, a tugging in my body, that was telling me where I should go. Kat grabbed my arm and shouted, trying to pull me back the other way, but it was just noise. I dragged her along behind me.

The lane was lined with a dozen grim-faced, two-storey houses pressed up against each other, scarred by neglect, weather and time. I hadn't even looked at them when we passed a moment ago. There was a door I had to get to, a door like all the others. Third one along, painted blue. I pressed the seal and fell into the narrow hallway. Kat, still trying to drag me back, fell on top of me.

I switched off the IMR because I wanted to have a face, my face. Kat switched off as well. She was furious.

'What the hell are you doing?' she said.

'I don't know. But it's here.'

'What's here?'

'Everything I need. It's up there.' I pointed to the steep flight of stairs at the end of the hallway.

Kat followed me up to the landing. 'You're screwing up the schedule.'

'We won't need the bombs.'

'It's going to be too late...'

I opened a door on my left. It was a low-ceilinged, narrow room, tiny. A bed was under the window that overlooked the lane. A pale blue blanket, a ragged pillow. There was a table and a chair, a small cupboard. A few worn toys scattered across the floor. On a shelf fixed to the wall was a framed screenshot of an old woman in a picker's apron, standing in one of the food-towers. Next to that was a line of small glass bottles with rubber stoppers and labels marked with big, awkward lettering. The glass was misty with age and the objects inside looked as if they were lying in a cloud.

Some child had kept these things, some child who might now already have been incinerated.

On the first label was written the word *tree*. Inside was a withered leaf. On the second bottle, the word *rock*. Inside was a stone, an ordinary stone that you could pick up from the gutter in any street in the banns. The third said *fire*. It was a small lump of blackened wood. The next bottle said *dragon*. The dried, transparent carcass of a dragonfly. The final bottle was labelled *rain*. That bottle was empty. Empty now. Maybe one day long ago it had held a few drops of water.

I was standing beside Jenna. I didn't have to open a line to her. I didn't have to use any tech. She was where I was, I was where she was.

The bedroom door slammed, and Jenna vanished. I spun around to find that Kat was gone. I rushed out of the room.

'Kat!' I shouted from the top of the stairs. 'Stop. Please wait!'

She reached the front door before she turned back and looked up at me.

'I can't. There's no time,' she said. She switched on her IMR and her face disappeared under the grey, blank mask. She headed out into the lane.

I had to do it now and I had to do it here.

I went back to the bedroom and looked at the empty bottle that had once held rain. I called the water.

My whole body started shaking. The sound of my heartbeat filled the room. And then I heard the fleshers, thousands of them, being led to their deaths. I heard their voices as one voice, and I heard every single voice, children and grown men and women, young girls, brothers, sisters and mothers. It was the sound of the old and sick being carried in the arms of their families, friends and strangers, people who were afraid, people trying to be brave.

I felt their rage and their helplessness.

I called the water. And the water answered.

For a moment all I felt was terror. It was so much bigger than me, bigger than anything I had ever encountered. And it was so cold, a huge wave rising inside me that threatened to obliterate everything I knew. I couldn't stop it now, it was too late.

And then it hit me and my whole body sang with cold fire. I wasn't afraid any more. I'd never be afraid again.

The glass in the window shook. The floor heaved beneath me. My skin burned, turning to ice. I pulled off the ghost's uniform. I shut off my suit.

The bottle filled with rain.

The leaf became smooth and turned green again. The stone changed into a shining jewel. The wood cracked open and revealed its yellow grain. The dragonfly's wings began to tremble.

'Help us,' I said, my voice shaking. 'Help us be free.'

Jenna was beside me again, reaching out her arms. Tiny ice crystals bloomed on our skin and covered our eyes and mouths. A long, thin ribbon of vapour spiralled around us, wrapping us together.

I felt another presence. I struggled to open my eyes beneath the icy membrane that was growing over them. There he was, looking as he did the first day I saw him, his face a hand's span from mine, his arms around me and Jenna.

It was Mish.

We were the water.

Kat shook my shoulder. I was still in the bedroom, lying on the floor. She was kneeling beside me, her face close to mine. Behind her was a young girl, maybe five years old.

'Wake up, Bo,' said Kat. 'Wake up.'

The little girl bent over me, her face stern. 'What are you doing in my room?'

'This is Zoe,' said Kat. 'It seems we're in her house.'

I struggled to my feet to find that Zoe had lost interest in us. She was staring at the glass bottles, her eyes shining.

'Everything's alive,' she whispered. 'Look!'

She took down the bottle with the dragonfly and pulled out the stopper. The insect climbed to the lip, its wings trembling, and launched itself into the air. Zoe laughed and ran to the window and opened it. And then the dragonfly was gone.

'You can go away too now,' said Zoe, turning to us.

'You'll be all right?'

'This is my home,' she said. 'Auntie will be back soon, with the others.'

'I hope so. We have to go home too.' Kat looked at me. 'Let's go, water man. Come and see what you've done.'

We walked down to the main rue. It was crowded with people running through ankle-deep water. Some were laughing, others crying. Many were panicking, not knowing what was happening. The Eradicator towered above them, locked inside a solid block of ice.

'It started to rain as soon as I left the house,' said Kat. 'But there wasn't a cloud in the sky. And then it stopped and ice began to spread up the walls of the Eradicator. I never even got near.'

'Where are the ghosts?'

'I don't know what happened. Their tech began to malfunction when it started raining, and then the fleshers turned on them. They can't do anything without their tech.'

The Eradicator began to tremble, the ice that encased it cracking and groaning.

'Let's get out of here,' said Kat. 'It's not finished yet.'

'No, I want to see,' I said. 'The water won't hurt us.'

'Let's go.' She grabbed my arm.

I pulled away. I couldn't stop staring at what the water had done.

It had answered our need. It had listened to our tears and risen out of the deep caves where it slept, calling to the rain in the sky. It was still rising up, a fountain forcing itself through the cracking surface of the ground, turning to ice where it touched the Eradicator.

You could see the building coming apart at the seams, the machinery inside bursting as the ice expanded inside every cavity in its walls, every pipe and tunnel. Brilliant trees of fire flickered up the sides, dying as quickly as they were born. Then the whole construction began to sink into the ground, as if it were melting.

The earth started shaking violently. Kat dragged me away, ignoring my protests. The few people left in the rue were struggling against the water: it was knee-deep now and running fast towards the Eradicator. An old woman lost her footing and was swept away. She disappeared without a sound.

'Bo!' Kat screamed in my face. 'We've got to go! It's going to kill us...'

I snapped out of my daze and realised we were in real danger. The current was getting stronger every moment. I stopped fighting Kat and together we struggled towards safety. At last we reached some stairs with steel railings and climbed out of the flood. Kat was panting, holding me so hard I thought she'd break my arm.

There was a deafening boom and the Eradicator collapsed into the ground. The water roared into the gaping hole it left behind, cascading down, deep into the darkness.

Brian Mac

I wake up on a metal gurney. The walls of the room are covered with shiny white tiles. The light is dim. It looks like a morgue, but I'm not dead. Yet.

There are two Morros on the gurney next to mine. One of them is still only half-formed, his skin blurred, blood oozing from his misshapen mouth. The whole Morro has his face turned towards me.

B Man, he says. I saved your life.

Sure, I say. Like hell you did, I think. And what do I care, anyway.

I muted all our life signs. They think you're dead.

I guess that's one way of saving a life.

You should get out of here.

So your effort isn't wasted? I say. But Morro has closed his eyes. I can see he's in bad pain. He opens them again.

You're one of us now, he says. You don't have any choice any more. No way you can be an Ap after what I told them. That life is over, B Man.

Thanks a lot.

You can begin again. Whole. His eyes are blazing. They're the only part of him that seem alive.

Fucking hell. He thinks he did me a favour. But now he's whispering. I crane my neck so I can hear.

We did it, he says.

Did what?

He doesn't answer.

Did what?

He's still looking at me, but he's gone.

I manage to get off the gurney. I hurt all over. My clothes are singed, but wearable. I look like I just stepped out of a furnace.

I limp out of the room and run into a orderly wearing white coveralls. He almost passes out when he sees me. I deck him. He falls flat, rolls over. I leave him there.

They don't have much security around the dead. The allegedly dead. The left for dead. The soon to be disposed of. I have to crunch one militia guard. Break his neck. I'm ready to kill anything.

It's night. I'm disorientated. My best chance is Ava at the FeelGood Salon. Luckily the morgue's in a bad part of town.

My suit isn't completely busted. Just mostly busted. I switch on the field. It's dodgy, but at least it'll hide me from any surveillance bots. It takes me an hour to get to Ava's. I stagger most of the way, I think I crawl part of it. People think I'm I some wasted pinker tramp. I find one familiar rue, then another, start to smell the waste, feel the wretchedness, like an ache in the air. The few people I run into give me a wide berth.

I buzz the door of the Salon. Gloria opens up. I fall into their arms. Surprised clients in the lobby recoil as I fall on the floor.

I come to in the back office. Ava is there, looking all kinds of pissed off. She thought she had a dead Ap on her hands for a while. Not to mention the fact that she lost a bit of business when the clients took off, thinking there was going to be trouble.

She fills me in while Gloria makes me a brew and finds some meds. There's been something going down in the banns. Nobody knows quite what yet. Some reports of floods, others of riots.

Osborne is in Central Hospital. Official story, nervous collapse. Bremmer has been arrested. On suspicion of nobody knows what, says Ava. They're being very tight-lipped, down in Newport City Central. She looks me up and down. I'm figuring that maybe you know something about all this, she says.

I tell her I don't really know what happened. She purses her lips, but she doesn't ask any further.

It's the truth. Morro did what he'd planned to do. I was just along for the ride, not knowing where the ride ended. I guess I was supposed to kill him, that's what he'd wanted. Going out in a blaze of glory, in the top office in town. Very Morro. He was a vain bastard.

Maybe I'd wanted the same thing, for the same reasons. But hero Morro had to save me. Thanks very fucking much.

Ava, I've got to get out, I say.

Back to the banns?

I don't know. Maybe not.

Where else is there, Brian?

That's an interesting question.

As soon as I make it back to the Second, I duck into an empty warehouse to check if it's safe to go home. I think of using Mal's code, and then think better of it. They've probably already figured out that I'd been doing some illegitimate spying under that moniker. I wonder if they think Mal was in on it. Even if they don't, it's a black mark on his record, premature retirement the least of it.

Funny, the only thing that really bothers me is the blowback on Mal. Straight pinker copper through and through, disobedience is unthinkable to him. Right now he'd be feeling totally betrayed. But Mal was never a prick, and there's a lot of pricks in OpSec. All those years in the precinct, he gave me space. Sure, he knew I was good at my job. Or at least, I was good at it when my job was about keeping the Second quiet and hunting skinners. For a while there he was running the top Brig in the banns. But his decency is more than that, and I know it. I wish him a peaceful retirement with all the VR trimmings he can find time for. A little apartment in a good part of town, a nice hobby. A few friends to drink with.

I try a couple of other passcodes I keep up my sleeve for emergencies. The third one lets me in.

All hell has broken loose. The entire top brass of OpSec has been detained. Some guy I've never heard of is acting CEO. An order's come down from the Mayoral department. Activity in the Eighth and Tenth is to cease at once. They don't mention the cull, it's going to be erased, as if it never happened. Nobody knows what the fuck has happened in the banns, they reckon it was some kind of equipment malfunction. A 'drilling accident'. There are reports of riots, the militia being driven out. I wonder what went down. No talk of explosions damaging the Veil. Maybe Bo's wild idea worked.

Those kids. They've done it. Whatever it is they've done.

Me, I'm top of the Wanted list. Murder and treason. Capture alive if possible. There's no record of me passing through the Veil so they think I'm hiding out in Newport City.

Sheen is Acting Brig at the Second. Could be worse, they could have brought in Kellway. They've already done a deep search of my place under OpSec supervision. They found some hot bioware, a few records I shouldn't have taken home, took DNA samples for analysis. Probably looking for any mutant powers they now think I have, thanks to Morro. More fool them.

I rigged my lab so it didn't show as empty space on the MPS, which took quite a bit of dimensional fiddling. Nobody even suspected it was there. I feel a momentary flicker of pride.

What now?

There'll be nowhere in the banns where I can hide. To most fleshers I'm just an Ap, the enemy. OpSec will put all their resources into hunting me down. A traitor Ap is their worst nightmare. One of their own turning bad. They'll hate that worse than poison. Worse than Alchems. Worse than rebel fleshers. They'll want revenge, they'll want to make an example of me. People like me aren't supposed to happen.

But I did.

The precinct has left an AI on surveillance outside in case I come back. I use the underground entrance to the lab. Never used it before, but I made sure it was there. I guess part of me always thought that one day it would come to this. I put enough resources into giving myself escape routes, that's for sure. That's why I bought this place to begin with. And here I am. Looking around for the last time. Checking my gear, making sure I've got everything I need, done everything I need to.

I take the blade off the wall, and check its edge. Still as sharp as the day it was finished. It'll work even after I run out of ammo. I glide it back into the sheath and sling it across my back.

The last thing I do is to send an order to the Mines Department, under signature of OpSec HQ, saying that in the light of recent events all unverified flesher workers must be sent back to the banns immediately, on pain of severe administrative displeasure. Might work. Might not.

I'll make a stop at Bel's. I think I can risk that. That's going to hurt, Bel is the only reason I'd stay in this city. Doubt she'll feel the same, but hey, everything else aside, we've known each other a long time. We've got history. That leaves absences.

I'll drop off the gene key to the lab. Dez might be able to use some of this tech once everything calms down. Maybe she'll find this journal. If she does, she'll decode it in less than no time at all.

Hello Dez! It's all in here, everything you want to know, everything you don't want to know. I think you and Bo were the closest thing I had to kids. Sorry if that sounds creepy. Think of me as your weird uncle.

I loved your parents. You should have seen them when they were young. When we were all young. We were the best.

It was my fault Flynn was busted. I made the call. It was him or me, and I wasn't big enough to let it be me. I did my best to limit the damage, made sure Bel's record was clean, but I've lived with that all these years. I understand if you hate me for it. You couldn't hate me more than I do.

Flynn was incredible. Almost as incredible as your mother. All you fleshers are incredible. Living in the shadows, working it out, surviving despite everything, doing more than surviving. I've watched you all for years and you still surprise me.

Maybe I'm a flesher now. No, I'll never be a flesher. Just a little more myself. Fleshers, pinkers, we're not much different when it comes down to it. It's what we choose, what we love, what we fight, what we make of ourselves, that's what counts.

They'll never think to look for me out in the dasht. So that's where I'm heading. Maybe I'll just die out there. I don't know. I don't even know if I care.

I'm out of here. Out of this city. Out of the whole sorry mess.

For the first time in my life, I feel free.

Bo

I barely remember getting home. There are snatches. Kids whooping it up with home-mades in the Sixth, as if there were no such things as Aps. An old man dancing down Rue Armon in the First, and everyone laughing and clapping. Everything seemed supernaturally bright, as if it had been washed clean. I walked beside Kat thinking, so this is what freedom feels like.

I was scared of nothing, delirious with the surging exhilaration of the water, singing with the power of it. We had done the impossible. We had beaten OpSec. We'd stopped the cull.

We arrived home to find that Ma had broken open a bottle of Kojo's special baju and was pouring out shots. Dez's team was already there. The whole street seemed to be in our front room celebrating. Everyone knew that the Eradicators had blown and that the militia were gone, even if they didn't know how it happened.

But I only had eyes for Jenna.

She was so pale with tiredness that her skin was luminous, and there were huge shadows under her eyes. Ma had fixed her up with some temporary meds, but you could see she was still in pain. She was curled up on the couch, her arms around her knees. When Kat and I walked in she looked up expectantly, and met my eyes and smiled. My heart turned over.

She was alive, and so was I, after everything we'd been through. That seemed like the real miracle.

Later that evening, Dez beckoned me down to her cellar. I was still buzzing with exhilaration and exhaustion. She looked unusually stern, and I began to wonder what I had done wrong. I waited while she messed around with things on her work table, and I was just beginning to get impatient when she took a deep breath and told me what she'd found out about Da.

Dez was really spun out that Flynn was a pinker. Of course I was shocked, but it didn't affect me nearly as much. For Dez, it was as if her whole idea of herself had been turned upside down. Mostly, I was impressed by what Flynn and Ma did together. They must have been a wild pair, back in the day.

But it's not as if knowing that he was a pinker changes anything. He's still dead. I'll still never know what it might have been like to have him there when I was a kid, or who Ma might have been without that sadness inside her. I didn't say that to Dez, though.

'Why does it matter so much?' I asked. 'I mean, it's kind of cool. Our Da was a rebel pinker.'

'It changes everything,' Dez said. 'We're half clones, Bo. We're *pinkers*.'

'We'll never be pinkers,' I said. 'Come on, Dez. Try walking into Newport City and telling them about your new pinker heritage and see how far you get...'

She almost smiled at that. '"Meatsex violations". That's what they call us.'

'Screw them. We're fleshers. Da must have thought being a flesher was the best, hey.'

Dez went quiet for a while. 'They must have really been in love,' she said at last. 'Nobody would have liked it. Imagine if anyone we knew was with a pinker...'

'Maybe some bad shit went down. I guess we'll never find out, Ma's pretty close about that. Have you told her that you know?'

'Not yet,' she said. 'I don't know how to. I don't want it to sound like... like an accusation. Maybe later.' She was frowning. 'Mainly I wanted you to know. I was so scared that I'd never get the chance to tell you.'

I punched her arm gently. It unsettled me, seeing Dez so uncertain. She's usually a pain because she's so sure of herself, even when she's wrong.

'But here you are, telling me. We won, remember?'

She looked up and met my eyes. She still looked deadly serious.

'We didn't win, Bo. A lot of people died before we got to the Eradicators. I haven't dared to work out how many.'

I began to feel like Dez was deliberately spoiling things. We deserved a little joy, didn't we? 'We saved a lot more who would have died,' I said stubbornly. 'Plus we got the militia out of the banns. We won.'

'They'll be scared of us now,' she said. 'Before, they just thought they could do what they liked to us. Now they think we're dangerous.'

'We are dangerous,' I said.

'They might have stepped back for now, but don't think they won't punish us for this,' said Dez. 'All of us. We're nowhere near winning.'

'They don't know about the water,' I said. 'They won't have a chance against us now.'

Dez sighed. 'I don't trust it, Bo. I saw what it could do, it tore those things apart. It could do the same to us.'

I saw Mish sinking down into the ice river and pushed the image away. The power of the water was still singing in my blood, the sheer elation of it. 'The water's on our side,' I said heatedly. 'You don't know everything, Dez.'

I could see her deciding not to argue with me.

'Sure, Bo,' she said. 'I'm only saying that none of this is over. It's only just begun.'

Dez

So we threw a party. Right in the middle of the Second, in a warehouse near the shijo. We never hold gigs in the Second, too close to the Inner Veil, but for once we thought, screw them all.

For a little while, the rules had been suspended. There were only Aps around now. They'd taken the militia out of the banns toot sweet, that's for sure. Bremmer's men, I guess. Brian Mac had told Ma that OpSec was in meltdown. Morro had really put the wind up them.

Bo was gutted to hear that Morro was dead. So was I. The feeling took me by surprise. So many people had died because Morro never worked out who he was, because he was so wrapped up in the romance of himself. But he was also kind of amazing. I remembered him walking into Newport Western Hospital, tossing the stinger up and down, smiling, reckless. That moment when he told me about himself, and I realised that I wasn't the only one, that I wasn't as big a freak as I thought.

And everything he knew had died with him. With his gifts, Morro should have done amazing things. It was such a waste.

I guess it's the story of too many of us.

Flora was devastated. For once I didn't feel any jealousy. Not even the tiniest sting. Maybe I'm growing up or something.

The biggest news on the street was that Brian Mac was wanted as a leading member of the Alchems. An Alchem! We all fell about laughing. Ma just looked sad. Then she said, 'Well, he was, you know. In effect.'

I guess he was. In effect.

He'd left me a present. The key to his secret lab, with instructions on how to bypass his security. 'He said it might interest you,' Ma said. 'Once things calm down. He said it's all yours now.'

'He's disappearing himself?'

She nodded. 'I don't think he's coming back,' she said. She wouldn't say anything more about that meeting. I think she knew where he was going, but she wouldn't say. I didn't push. Whatever he had been, she had lost a friend. An old friend.

We stopped the cull. We really did. But we've all lost people.

According to Brian Mac, the new Brig in the Second is one of his men. An old style Ap who'd just be aiming to keep a lid on things. He'd have more to worry about than a bunch of kids who wanted to dance. Just to make sure we didn't get raided, and against our objections, Ma went to the precinct to get permission for a gathering. 'A concert,' she'd told them. 'For the young people. For community cohesion.'

She got it, too.

We put the word out on the tubes. Everybody came, and brought their friends. It was wild.

Flora was the headline act, but we let anyone who wanted to play have their moment. Rioka said she'd fix the sound if it got too hairy. She insisted on coming although it was only a few days since she'd lost her hand. It was healing well but it was still hurting her. I was going to make her a prosthetic but we were still fighting about it, because she wanted to pay me. Rioka said she didn't need her hand to fold the music, and anyway she wouldn't miss a party for the world. Even Ma gave up arguing with her.

Ma put some of her people on the door to make sure we didn't have any trouble, and sorted out the catering. I think she has a future in event organisation: everything went without a hitch. Bo and Flora rigged the lighting and sound. It was spectacular, lasers, IMR effects, tonnes of smoke, the lot.

Kat and me and Jenna just came and danced and danced.

We were all so happy just to be alive. People I hadn't seen for months came up and embraced me. Complete strangers. Even Kojo was coming. This was big news, he'd never seen Flora perform before. Flora and him had made up, she'd gone over a couple of days before and had a long talk. She didn't say much about it afterwards, I think it was hard, but I think maybe they understand each other better now.

Bo's concession to the occasion was to polish his leather jacket. He had barely taken that damn jacket off since he got home.

He and I were by the door when his face lit up and he ran towards some people I didn't know and dragged them over to introduce them. Tilly, Cherian, Ziyin, and Maxim. He'd met them in the mines.

'How the hell did you get out?' he asked.

'A few days ago,' said Ziyin. 'They just put us on a train and dumped us in the Tenth. No explanation. Then we saw this was happening.'

He looked around at their faces. 'Rouge?' he said. 'Didi?'

'They made it back. Most of us made it back.'

'Will?'

'Will didn't make it,' said Cherian.

My heart dropped, but I didn't ask what happened. I didn't want to know.

Jules came with her kids, all of them smiling. She gave me a bear hug, tears in her eyes. I hadn't seen her since we left her in Ava's place, wrapped up in that yellow blanket.

I thought of all the kids we'd left behind in those drawers and didn't know what to feel. Jules thinks I'm a hero. I don't.

Too many people hadn't made it. There were too many faces missing. Bo was playing keyboard for Flora because Shul was gone. Redborg should be there, they and Flora had a famous double act, but there'd been no word of them since a big raid on the Seventh.

Well past midnight, the crowd was juiced, the beats were wild. The whole place was heaving. Flora and I had been sitting to the side of the dance floor with Bo and Jenna. They weren't talking much, just holding hands, their heads close together. I think they don't need to talk, they've got some other kind of communication happening. I've never seen Bo look so happy.

Flora stood up. 'Time, Bo,' she said. 'Let's get it on.'

They disappeared backstage to get ready for their act. Jenna glanced at me and smiled. 'I'm looking forward to this,' she said. 'I've never heard Flora play.'

'Me too,' I said. 'And I've been at almost every gig she's done.'

A few minutes later Flora was on the stage. She had the static thing going with her hair and had threaded it with glitter, so her face was surrounded by a huge silver-blue halo that shone in the light. She stood there in her long silver dress, shimmering like a goddess. My god. Flora. I couldn't believe that of all the people in the world she wanted to be with me.

She held up her hands, and the crowd went silent.

'Friends,' she said. 'Welcome to our party!'

Everyone cheered and whooped and yelled.

'A lot of us didn't make it. A lot of us died. A lot of us are missing. Our hearts are broken. But we survived. We always survive. And we will go on surviving!'

This time I had to put my fingers in my ears. The walls shook with the noise. Flora waited for silence, her arms up high.

'Let's remember everyone who didn't get there. Everyone who should be here and isn't. Mish, who called the water. Morro and Shul. Redborg and Diyan and Hu. Giro, Simpa, Serim, Gaunt, Ifant, Ruby, Katsu, Little Nino. Sammy, Irul, Besty, Val and Maya. All the people I knew, all the people I didn't know. If I knew all the names, I'd say them all.'

She paused, and I saw tears glistening on her cheeks. The crowd was utterly silent now, all those hundreds of people. Still as stone, staring up at Flora, remembering.

'I'd say all the names. Every single one. No matter how many hours it took. This is for all of them. For all of us. For all of you.'

She brought down her arms and Bo was playing the hook for The Loved and the Unloved.

I knew that she'd begin with this song. We all did. We sang along with Flora, feeling every word. I don't think there was single person in that house who wasn't crying. Her voice rang pure and true, vibrating through our very bones.

The young and the old
The broken, the whole
The loved and the unloved
Remember them

I don't know how Flora got through that song, but she did. The final chords died away into silence. She held the moment, her head flung back, a warrior, a goddess, a voice for us all. My Flora.

And then she swung back to face us, started tapping her feet. Another rhythm was building up now, a new beat, getting into our legs, making them itchy.

'And what do fleshers do better than anyone else?'

Somebody in the crowd yelled back. 'We party!'

Flora laughed through her tears. 'Yes! That's what we do!'

The chords crashed in.

And we partied like there was no tomorrow.

To be continued in **Pinkers**
Read on for an exclusive extract

PINKERS

Book 2 of Newport City

The revolution has begun. But where does it end?

After the destruction of the Eradicators, OpSec is hitting back. And that's bad news for everybody.

The banns are in lockdown, making it all but impossible for Dez, Bo and their friends to resist the authoritarianism of Newport City. Bo believes that the mysterious power of the water is the key to winning their struggle, but Dez is deeply troubled about his increasing obsession.

Meanwhile in Newport City, up-and-coming soap star Erin is in trouble. In Newport City, there's nowhere to hide...

Especially if you're Erin Saba.

Erin

That day at the hospital was the first time I ever saw a real flesher.

It had been a shitty day all around. The night before, there'd been a party for the launch of the first season of *Ebolastic*, the big new soap starring Mr Mega-idol John Mecha. It's billed as an ultra-real crime show, and it's a special commission from the top. Ultra-real is going to be the new Big Thing.

Mecha plays a cop investigating flesher crime gangs who are smuggling bad DNA through the Inner Veil to destroy the population of Newport City. Before the launch, there was a lot of publicity about how it was being filmed in the rundown suburbs of Newport City, the closest thing we have to the banns, instead of in an IMR studio, with real weapons borrowed from OpSec and sometimes real ammo. I had to do a lot of posing in front of store-fronts roughed up to look like they were about to collapse any minute.

I play John Mecha's love interest, a blonde with a heart of gold and a brain of lead. I have no idea why the cop fell in love with her and, the way John Mecha treats me, neither does he. When we aren't in scenes together, he acts like I'm invisible and inaudible. But that's because, as everyone in the celebrity industry knows, John Mecha is a prick.

Did I say I hate working on it? I *hate* working on it. Dervin says it's going to be my breakthrough role, but I think the only thing that's going to break is me.

The last thing I wanted to do was party, but all the top brass was going, including Mayor Osborne and Bremmer, the chief of OpSec, and so there was no way, bar actual death, of getting out of it. My AI maid Ami had her excitement synapses turned up to the max. They must have sent out a general order.

'Tonight's going to be great!' she trilled, as she slipped my new dress over my head. It was made of some new smart fabric, feathers that changed colour as I moved and exposed most of me. 'And this dress, ooh la la! Ilati has outdone himself! You look super plus! Everyone will be in love with you!'

I stared at the dress. The pinks didn't suit me, they made my skin look lifeless. But Ami kept wittering on.

In the end I turned her off and got myself ready instead. I was doing my makeup when Dervin came in. He saw Ami standing motionless in the corner and frowned. 'They'll pick it up, you idiot,' he said.

I studied him in my mirror. He looked angry. These days Dervin was often angry, and he took it out on me.

'So?'

'So switch her on.'

'She won't shut up,' I said. 'And I've got a massive headache.'

'Fuck your headache. I don't want any trouble.'

Dervin left, not bothering to check that I obeyed him. He knew I would.

I rolled my eyes at his back and clicked my fingers. Ami returned to life, blinking as she rebooted, and took over my makeup as if nothing had happened. I turned down her voice to minimum and stared in the mirror.

Me, Erin Saba. The face of your next IMR dreamscape. Bored, although I didn't know it then. Lonely. I knew that.

The party was as dull as I had expected. Lots of speeches. I smiled like I was supposed to and posed for the vids with Osborne smirking creepily like he was planning to touch me or something and then Dervin sent me home because the next day was busy with the second series of the soap.

I was too jittery to sleep. I hate those events, they leave me feeling like my skin has a thin film of slime all over it. I told Ami to make me a martini, double strength, and when she brought it I switched her off, I didn't care what Dervin said, and I drank it sitting on my balcony, looking over the lights of Newport City Central. And then I made myself another.

I guess it wasn't surprising that I had an accident the next day. Nothing dramatic, just a stupid thing. I tripped over some cables and fell on one of the lights, and the skin on my left knee was sliced open so deep that I could see the bone. It didn't even hurt to begin with. When I looked at it, I felt sick. So that's how I ended up at Newport City Western Hospital.

The biotech had just sealed up my knee and given me a shot to kill the pain when all the lights went out. We were in a booth without any windows, so it was completely dark. The biotech, a blonde girl with the long, clever fingers of her kind of clone, let out a shriek. I didn't want to have any more accidents, so I stayed put on the table.

'Must be the generators,' said the medic. He was just there to look at me, there had been a bit of fuss when I turned up. 'But it's strange, all of them going off at once...'

We waited in the dark for what seemed like ages, but the lights didn't come back on. I began to wonder if it was terrorist fleshers, like in the episode we had just been filming, but I didn't say anything.

'Doesn't anyone have a torch?' said the medic at last, and I heard some-one fumbling in the dark. A couple of things fell on the floor with a clatter, and then there was a click and the room was lit with a cold white glow from some tiny object that looked like the instruments they use to check inside people's mouths. It was very bright after the darkness.

I sat up. 'Now what?' I said.

'All the comms are down,' said the medic, fiddling with his wristband. I could hear the tension in his voice. Maybe he was thinking about terror-ists too.

'I want to get out of here. I've got work to do,' I said.

'Best to wait until we know what the situation is...'

I didn't want to wait. 'Do you know the way to the entrance?' I said, putting on my cop voice. Like I was in charge.

The medic looked dubious. 'Yes,' he said.

'Let's go then.' I swung my legs off the table and stood up. At that point, the lights flickered and came back on.

The biotech let out a big breath and I realised that we had all been frightened, sitting there in the dark wondering if anything awful was going to happen.

The medic smiled at me in relief, and reached out to take my hand. He saw the shock on my face and blushed to the roots of his hair. He must have been more thrown than he let on. Medics have to touch people sometimes, even with all the meditech, so inhibitors aren't programmed so strongly in them, but touching me – *me!* – was about as big a faux pas as you could imagine.

He cleared his throat, not looking at me. 'This way.'

We'd just reached Dervin and Ami, who were waiting in the hallway, when suddenly the place was swarming with OpSec, the ones who stand outside Council buildings with big weapons and scanner helmets. They ordered everybody in line against the wall. An alarm went off and I began to panic. I hadn't seriously thought that there could be a terrorist attack, not in the middle of Newport City. I turned around and saw a flesher strolling casually in through the front door. Everyone started screaming and running.

I knew he was a flesher straight away. Black hair, black skin, silver jacket, silver boots, black discs over his eyes. He looked impossibly glamorous. It was the way he strode in, loose and unafraid, lawless. Nobody in Newport City walks like that. He was tossing something up and down, a baton of some sort. It'd turn three times in the air and then he'd catch it by the handle. Even in the confusion, I wondered if he was some kind of actor: I'd learned that trick at celebrity school.

I didn't run, like everyone else. I just stared.

He wasn't anything like the fleshers in our soap, who are all kinds of thick and brutish. He moved like quicksilver. Like some kind of god.

He looked me right in the eye and I saw something light up in his face. His smile switched up to dazzling. At first I thought he must have seen me in some soap, but then I felt the pull of him. It's hard to describe: in that couple of seconds I felt that he could read my mind. It was like he knew me already, like he saw something in me that was just like him. My heart hammered inside my chest like it was going to jump out.

He lifted up his hand, as if he was waving hello. And then, right in front of me, he vanished.

Of course, me being in the hospital in the middle of a flesher attack – the first since the bad old days – was all over the infonews. Dervin played it for all it was worth, and I had to do vids on all the channels and photo ops with the OpSec guys who had been there and rescued me from danger.

I knew it was shit. I knew that flesher wasn't planning to hurt me and that I hadn't been in any danger and that nobody had rescued me from anything. But everybody knows that you don't question the official story.

There was an event where Osborne gave the cops a medal each for bravery. At the reception afterwards, I asked one of the officers why the hospital had been attacked and whether anybody had been hurt and he turned his eyes on me, ice-blue and expressionless. 'That's confidential information, ma'am,' he said.

I smiled as winningly as I could, but it seemed to have no effect on him at all. 'Did they really want to blow up the hospital?'

'These are dangerous people, ma'am.'

Usually I can get people to tell me stuff, but not this guy. He didn't have a brand on him, but I began to wonder if he was an AI. Sometimes it's hard to tell the difference between a full-on conditioned duty clone and an AI. The only way to tell is if they feel pain. If you set fire to an AI, they just carry on as if nothing is happening. I saw it once, when a downtown department store caught fire. Nobody remembered to tell the retail AIs to get out, so they just stayed behind the counters, smiling as they burned.

I could see Osborne staring at me talking to the cop and something in his gaze made me feel uneasy. I thanked the cop and moved away.

In all the interviews I talked about how I had been frozen with terror and what heroes the OpSec men were and how grateful I was. That's what Dervin told me to say, and I said it. But I knew it wasn't true. The only thing I had been afraid of was OpSec running around with their weapons. The flesher hadn't frightened me at all: when I saw him, I just wanted to laugh because of the audacity of it, the cheek. The style.

When I saw Osborne looking at me, I remembered how the flesher had lifted his hand and smiled, as if he knew me. They played the footage over and over again on the tubes, and that's what it looked like. The camera was behind me so you couldn't see my face. But there are cameras everywhere. Maybe I smiled back. I couldn't remember.

Perhaps Osborne suspected that I really did know him.

I didn't know that flesher, I only wished I did. I couldn't stop thinking about him, about how he walked into that hospital. Fearless.

Shining.

Acknowledgements

It takes a village to raise a book, and this is never more true than in self-publishing. Many people helped to make *Fleshers* possible, and we are grateful to everyone who encouraged us. In particular, we want to thank Omar Sakr, Jeff Sparrow and Mey Valdivia Rude, whose insightful feedback on the first draft was invaluable. Special shiny thanks to Ellie Marney, whose support along the self-publishing road has been a joy.

Part of this book was written while Daniel Keene was in residence at The Writer's Sanctuary, Bermagui, New South Wales, with the generous assistance of the Malcolm Robertson Foundation.

And most of all, thank you to all our awesome Pozible supporters, without whom this would never have happened.

Gilded Patron
Andrea van der Wilt
Silver Patrons
Gillian Rubinstein, Brett Sheehy, Anonymous
Muses
Our four anonymous donors, Jennifer Kremmer, Jeremy Croggon, Paul Kiel, NEFFie, Stephanie Convery, Patricia Cornelius, Sandra Proksa, Veryan Croggon, Alex Kelly, Thomas Bull, Beng Oh, Jacinda Woodhead, Louise Corney, Kate Elliott, Marcus Westbury. Stephanie Cranford, Ian Andrew Porter, Mariah Wambsganss, Richard Croggon, Amanda Rasmussen-Huang, Lefa Singleton Norton, Kate Foy, Nicole Gosling, Julie Campbell, Rjurik Davidson, Talia Raso, Darcy Conroy, Kelly Gardiner, Ailsa Wild, James Williams, Kate Veitch, Kathy Sinclair, Mary-Helen Ward, Claire Rowlands, Majid Shokor, Pamela Freeman, Keith Agius, Melissa Ansell, Lisa Fleetwood, Daniel Thode, Damon Young, David Ryding, Joshua Croggon, Sophie Mayer, Lisa Dempster, Peter Wilson, Dan Spielman, Marcus Liddle, Jeff Sparrow, Robert Reid, Leah Newton and Abe Pogos.

MORE BOOKS BY ALISON CROGGON

The Books of Pellinor

The Gift (UK)/The Naming (US), The Riddle, The Crow, The Singing, The Bone Queen

Alison Croggon's beloved epic fantasy quintet is a glittering saga steeped in the rich and complex landscape of Annar, a legendary world ripe for discovery. It has been continously in print since it was first published in 1992 and has sold more than 500,000 copies worldwide.

"Rich and passionate...Supremely satisfying."
Starred review, Kirkus Reviews

"An epic fantasy in the Tolkien tradition - I couldn't put it down!"
Tamora Pierce

"Unbelievably fine, represents fantasy storytelling at its best."
VOYA, US

The Threads of Magic

An atmospheric and riveting fantasy adventure, perfect for fans of Frances Hardinge and Cornelia Funke. Alison Croggon conjures a rich, immersive world with brilliant and memorable characters in this captivating story of loyalty, courage and friendship.

"A lyrical, poetic writer *and* a compelling storyteller"
Garth Nix

"Vivid, compelling, utterly, utterly magical."
Read and Reviewed

Black Spring

In a savage land sustained by wizardry and ruled by vendetta, Lina is the enchanting but wilful daughter of a village lord. She and her childhood companion, Damek, are devoted to each other to the point of obsession. Whether drawn by the romantic, the magical, or the gothic, readers will be irresistibly compelled by the passion of this tragic tale.

"Black Spring is a lyrical masterpiece; a beautiful piece of literature that evokes as many emotions as the flawed, incredibly human characters it pays homage to throughout."
ArtsHub

"Bronte devotees will swoon. For those who take their romance tumultuous and doomed."
Kirkus Reviews

The River and the Book

In Simbala's village they have two treasures: the River, which is their road and their god; and the Book, which is their history, their oracle and their soul. When The Book predicts change, Simbala is impelled on a jourey that changes not only her life, but the lives of everyone she knows.

"A resonant, haunting story… a simply told and dreamlike tale that tackles huge questions about conservation, capitalism, colonialism and cultural appropriation."
The Age

"The River and the Book is one of those beautiful stories that will take your breath away."
The Bookkat

Find out more at alisoncroggon.com

Alison Croggon is an Australian novelist, poet, librettist and critic. She is the author of the popular and critically acclaimed fantasy quintet *The Books of Pellinor*, published in Australia, the UK, the US and across Europe. *The Books of Pellinor* was re-released worldwide in 2017 with the publication of a fifth book, *The Bone Queen*, a finalist in for the Aurealis Awards YA Novel of the Year. Other internationally published novels include *Black Spring* (shortlisted for the 2014 NSW Premier's Award) and *The River and the Book* (shortlisted for the 2016 WA Premier's Award and winner of the Wilderness Society's Environmental Writing for Children Award). Her opera libretti have been performed on major stages across Australia. The libretto for *Mayakovsky* (score Michael Smetanin) was shortlisted for the 2015 Victorian Premiers Prize for Drama, and *The Riders* (score Iain Grandage) was awarded the Vocal/Choral Work of the Year in the 2015 Australian Arts Music Awards. Other awards include the 2009 Geraldine Pascal Critic of the Year for her performance criticism, and the Dame Mary Gilmore and Anne Elder Prizes for poetry. alisoncroggon.com

Daniel Keene has written for the theatre since 1979. His plays have been performed on main stages around Australia and in China, America and Europe. He has won numerous awards, including six Premier's Literary Awards for drama, the Sydney Myer Performing Arts Award and the Kenneth Myer Medallion for the Performing Arts for his contribution to Australian theatre with the Keene/Taylor Theatre Project. Since 2000, over 80 main stage productions of his work have been presented in Europe, predominately in France. He is the only Australian playwright to have been produced in the main program at the Festival d'Avignon. In 2009 his work for young audiences was awarded the Prix Théâtre en Pages by Scéne Nationale de Toulouse. Seven volumes of his plays (French translations by Severine Magois) have been published by éditions Theatrales, Paris. In 2016 Daniel was appointed to the rank of Chevalier de l'Ordre des Arts et des Lettres by the French Ministry of Culture for his contribution to French culture. danielkeene.com.au

www.ingramcontent.com/pod-product-compliance
Lightning Source LLC
Chambersburg PA
CBHW030045130726
47901CB00007BA/1978